# TERROR BAY

First Publication November 2023
Indies United Publishing House, LLC

ISBN: 978-1-64456-607-7 [Hardcover]
ISBN: 978-1-64456-608-4 [paperback]
ISBN: 978-1-64456-609-1 [Mobi]
ISBN: 978-1-64456-610-7 [ePub]
ISBN: 978-1-64456-611-4 [Audiobook]

Library of Congress Control Number: 2023936090

INDIES UNITED PUBLISHING HOUSE, LLC
P.O. BOX 3071
QUINCY, IL 62305-3071
indiesunited.net

From birth, man carries the weight of gravity on his shoulders. He is bolted to earth. But man has only to sink beneath the surface and he is free.

Jacques Yves Cousteau

In 2006 I published an article in a surfing magazine. A lifelong surfer read it, emailed me about how much he enjoyed it, and I married him two years later. To Lee - thank you for sending the email that changed my life forever. None of this would be possible without you.

# Other books by Lisa Towles

*Salt Island (E&A Series)*
*The Ridders*
*Hot House (E&A Series)*
*Ninety-Five*
*The Unseen*
*Choke*

# And published under the name Lisa Polisar:

*Escape: Dark Mystery Tales*
*The Ghost of Mary Prairie*
*Blackwater Tango*
*Knee Deep*

# Terror Bay

## A Psychological Thriller

# Lisa Towles

INDIES UNITED PUBLISHING HOUSE, LLC

# Prologue

## *Early October*

**She knew. In her bones she knew** they shouldn't be there, and not just for legal reasons, but for all the tangled, convoluted nuances of maritime law that would undeniably stand in the way of ownership, should they find it. According to the United Nations Convention of the Law of the Sea, Canada shared maritime boundaries with Greenland and Alaska. That meant Admiralty Law regulations, plus anything involving old ships could be subject to the Abandoned Shipwreck Act. None of that mattered, though, did it? She'd already found it but hadn't followed the rules. Did she ever?

The captain had warned them of the storm, so she knew the risks and the timeline. Her gut told her she was too far in now to ensure enough air to reach the surface. But how could they possibly turn back knowing what they now knew, seeing what they'd seen? The unmistakable shape of a ship's hull still shockingly intact, a spectral hand and wrist outstretched and frozen, pointing to a door, now corroded in rust and thick barnacles, barely attached to its hinge. Around the front, a shocking face glared, jaw open, of maybe an original sailor or more recently a salvage diver, knowing what fate would become him, recognizing his killer and certain of no escape.

The eyes, laughing almost in the hollowed skull, had found it - the artifact no one in over two hundred years had thought of. She pictured the skeleton fragment as a living being, diving with antiquated equipment, slithering through the tight opening without his tank so he could grab it quickly and return in time to breathe. How many divers had perished from these temptations before? If he'd found it, that meant he'd done his research, knew exactly where to look, and had a cool enough head to hold the weighty secret in his heart. But how could he have known that one random British sailor had earlier in his life been a privateer on board a pirate ship and kept a king's ransom worth of valuables hidden in the hull  for twenty years? How could the man have known this... without being the man himself? Or maybe an ancestor.

Just one more moment, a few more feet and finagling her way through the narrow hole in the rusted hull. This had to be the place; it even looked like all her years of research foretold. In the flash of a moment, she felt the pulse of that threshold, knowing this was the line, the same line the dead diver before her had stood.

Now or never.

The storm on the surface made it the wrong day to dive. For her, it was the right day to die.

# Chapter 1

*Late February*

**I can see things in here, things** the human *living* mind wasn't ever intended to see. I know how it sounds, how it makes me sound. I'm just reporting from this strange place.

I don't know exactly where here is right now, but I also don't think I'm dead. I seem to be waiting for something, but I don't know what. I feel it, my body preparing me. Making plans – shoving things in corners, finishing less significant tasks before the insistent takeover. I can't move forward until I find it, or it finds me. I can't move at all for that matter, or breathe, or remember the *before*. This thing in my future, an intangible presence, will clutch onto my spine, feast on my innards till it's eaten the whole of my vitality. And when it clicks into place, God help me. It's happened before, I can't see it yet but I feel its warm breath on the crown of my skull, descending like a promise of its inexorable coup.

Inside the deepest me there is this knowing, a knowing of another knowing. It could be music, or a name, even a person.

*Genevieve Lucas.* Yes, my bones vibrate inside as I say those five syllables in my head. Somehow, I know that Genevieve Lucas is my nemesis and my destiny.


Water has this smell deep beneath the surface. I recognize it from my scuba exploits so many years ago. A scent that's simultaneously fresh and rank, laden with hope and death. More than that, though, the inky-blue unlit terrain is a secret cosmos unto its own. The lack of light brings about a different kind of perception down here, the way sensory deprivation in one way boosts awareness - and capabilities - in others.

My arms are floating, and my body's anchored to something soft, but with more form than a mound of sea vegetation or sand. More like a bed. But if I'm under water, how could that be? The brain in this state is capable of mysterious magic, though I can't say exactly what state I'm in. I have pure awareness without the burdens of physicality. No, please, I can't be dead. Can I? But then what is this watery grave? I say the name again to myself because it feels good and real and home to say it. Genevieve... Genevieve Lucas. It echoes, distorted by the water. I am submerged. Separate, but close.

All the Zombie apocalypse movies I've watched aren't helping. I try opening my eyes wider but only see the same bubbly nothing all around me. What's odd is that my arms and legs can move. I try kicking and punching, but my torso and pelvis are anchored. I feel anger moving through me. What the fuck is going on? I'm a detective, dammit. So detect.

Okay, what's the last thing I remember? A case, a young girl at a club shot at close range on the dance floor and nobody heard a thing. We found our suspect, Jimmy Breslin, who'd been drinking at the same club every night since, as if paying vigil to his victim. We followed him, cornered him, we had him. And now I'm here in this floating nightmare, a house without windows. Something must have happened after that, happened to me, and that's the reason for this transcendent in-between. Coma? It must be, because nothing else makes sense. I admit it's not completely unpleasant, either. Peaceful, serene almost, but with no way out. It's a quiet jail that comes with a dull ache in my heart. I'm getting used to the pain now, the pain of knowing.

Wait, now I'm diving again, maybe part of this same dream, if that's what this place is. The frigid water seeps into tiny holes in my wetsuit. My body's shivering and I'm eyeing the surface, or at least the direction I think is the surface. Then I look down and see something. A dark outline of some structure. On one side there's seaweed, brown and fine. No, it's... hair. Brownish red, the color of seaweed half flowing with the water's current, the other half held down under its head. I use my fins to move toward it.

Something yanks against my waist. Dammit, my partner pulling my cord, a sign that we're heading back up. *I see you*, I say to the figure down there. You're not dead, I can save you. I see her. Please, one more minute. She's just—

Two tugs this time, harder, more insistent, a reminder of life and death. Turn back now or else.

A hand pushes outward from the body, a woman. Oh my God, she's alive. She's... there's no... how could she be down here without any breathing apparatus, how could she possibly be...? But she's moving. She sees me. I can feel her presence *inside me*.

One final tug and the cord's pulling me backwards now against my will.

Genevieve Lucas.

The name feels right. I see her head and shoulders now, buried under the two-hundred-year-old ship. Of course she's dead. She'd have to be, right? Who are you and why are you haunting me? What do you want? Did you bring me here to this liquid jail?

The cord pulls me away from her and I feel myself sobbing. I see light from the surface. I'm rising with the pull from the cord, my partner three feet ahead looking back to make sure I don't escape, knowing full well that is my intention.

Terror.

Terror.

I've seen it. It's coming.

# Chapter 2

**First metal, scraping sounds, like a soft** roar. Then something clinking against another surface.

I returned to the dark, watery cosmos because it had become a respite. Floating, cool, buoyant, graceful, like being rocked by an invisible mother in a chair made out of heaven. Could I stay here forever? Memories were mashed up in this place, a kaleidoscope of the past – a smelly boathouse, an old man with a strange accent.

Then that scraping sound again. Oh. My. God. What was that fucking noise? Rage now, born from a low spot in my belly, rose in a red fire up to my chest. Everything irritated me, and every body part hurt. The back of my head, left side. Something happened there. Trauma.

"Okay, are we ready?" someone said. "Are you all asleep over there or what?" A man's voice.

"Sorry, Doctor. Yes, ready."

"Just going from one bed to the other now, very gently. Lift him now. On three. One… two…"

Wait, no. That was… I felt something. Pressure. Fingers under my sides and butt. Where was I?

"Did his eyes just flutter?"

"I saw it too. Go ahead, get him settled onto the other bed. Yep, you got it, that's good."

"Repositioning, one second, okay."

"Good. Gently move away now. Nurse…"

"I got him. Vitals are… still fine. I'm seeing—"

"There, again! I saw it."

"Detective?" the first voice said. "Detective Farin, can you hear me?"

Yes, I heard you. Why can't you hear—

"Blink your eyes if—"

Why couldn't I answer him? I hear you, for God's sake. Can't you hear me? I was talking, moving my mouth, feeling the sensation of the movement but there was no sound. It was like glass separating me from the world, this bright, awful world I don't want to be in.

Metal scaping again and this time I knew it was a door. Please just kill me if I have to endure that sound again. My legs were throbbing, this was new. Okay, let's start on an inventory of pain: head pain, check. My neck and shoulders were fine. My forearms ached, like deep in the bones, same with my hands. Oh, my head. I'd seriously die if I heard that screech again. Where did my blue cosmos go? I was no longer floating and could feel my heart beating irregularly. My skin seemed hot instead of cool. Why was everything so loud and pointy? I want to go back. Someone listen to me. I don't belong here. Take me back, please. Somebody! Take me back to my liquid under.

◦ ◦◈◦ ◈▪◈ ◈◦ ◦

A warm presence slithered in from a prick in my right elbow, I'd felt it climbing up my shoulder into my neck a few hours ago before I slept. They must have sedated me. And I now knew what happened to me and understood the effect it's had on my brain. Oh my God. The fingers that pressed into my body when they moved me from one bed to another gave me a glimpse of something, though not a glimpse from my own head… *but theirs.*

Whoever it was, they'd been thinking about TBI. I knew that acronym from my medical training: traumatic brain injury. Was I seeing or hearing *their* thoughts? There must be a name for this freakish new skill.

"Eyes open, here we go. Mr. Farin. Kurt, blink if you can hear me."

I blinked and nodded my head, eyes squinted but anxiously glancing up at the fluorescent lights. I tried to tell her, the bulb-nosed woman leaning over me, with my eyes that the lights were killing me, that they literally hurt. Eyes, lights, back and forth. Come on, are you getting it?

"Nothing," she said.

"Mr. Farin, blink back if you can hear me."

I fucking hear you! I'm blinking my eyelashes off. I tried to talk but something wasn't working. Something wasn't connected yet.

"He's disoriented," the woman explained to someone behind her.

Do you think I'm gonna bite you? I can't even move my arms. Wait, I wriggled the fingers on my right hard. Okay, progress. Toes next, left foot, right. I drew in a breath, careful not to pull it in too deeply because the tubes in my nose and mouth could cause me to cough.

I imagined sitting up and swinging my legs off the side of the hospital bed, placing my feet on the floor, and sinking down into the blue cosmos. But all I could do now was wiggle my toes. The staff didn't seem to notice my success, because they were just staring at my eyes. What the fuck's the matter with these people?

Some measure of time had passed, because the light in here was different and everyone was gone. Thank God. The air smelled like antiseptic, a hospital smell, but I loved the fact that there was a smell and I could detect it. I raised my eyes up to the ceiling, then down to my chest, side to side, my body remembering how to move outside of the blue sphere. This was earth. Corporeal existence. California, a hospital somewhere.

I'd coordinated a sting operation at a grungy, punk dive in Oakland called The Stork Club. A nightmare of a crowd, sweaty bodies jammed together like sardines and a wall of music that sounded like two Mac trucks crashing headfirst over a heavy bass and cymbals. Two weeks earlier, Jimmy Breslin, fresh out of prison, had shot and killed a nineteen-year-old girl right there. I still needed to talk to her parents. I was sure my partner Vaughn had done that, but I needed to do it myself, to let them see what happened to me. Then again, would it matter and why would they care? They'd lost a daughter.

My head was pounding but only on the left side. I moved my fingers like simulated piano playing, and they all moved correctly and according to the wishes of my brain. Good, one uncertainty resolved. I raised my left arm now, slowly, cautiously. The air in the room was cool, but this was not ICU, I could tell. I reached high and bent my left elbow to touch the left side of my heeeaaaa--- God what's wrong with me? Eyes squinted, chest heaving up and down. Was this crying? My head hurt but not just out of physical pain. My fingers had barely even touched my left temple, then I literally couldn't stop my sobs. I was still intubated, and I was going to choke if I didn't control myself.

Could I extubate my endotracheal tube myself? That would undoubtedly result in a loud beeping sound and cause a nurse to tear down the hall in their tennis shoes to check what had happened. No. I could wait. I pulled a slow breath in, then out. And again. I needed rest right now as much as I needed oxygen. Because if my suspicions were correct and I'd been unconscious, the next phase of my life was gonna be hell.

# Chapter 3

**I returned to the blue cosmos in** my head for a spell, a few hours maybe, and it felt different now. If I was indeed in a coma when I first discovered being there, of course it would seem different if I had now emerged from that pre-conscious state. I could move my eyes, fingers, toes, and could feel the sensation of air coming into my body through my nose. So I'd emerged. And now it seemed the blue cosmos was gone forever. Hot new tears slid down my cheeks.

Some new realizations:

1 - Everything made me feel like crying now. Too much water in my cup, not enough, and literally any kind of lights felt like death.

2 - I determined that I'd been unconscious for several days, according to the date I heard on someone's TV, which led me to number three.

3 - I can hear things. Not voices inside my head or anything, but things I shouldn't be able to hear. For instance, all the rooms in this hospital had to be about

200 square feet with 1-2 foot wall thickness separating one room from the next. If the room beside mine didn't have their TV on, whose TV was I hearing? Also, I could hear someone from the nurse's station answering the phone with, "Zuckerberg San Francisco General." How could I or anyone possibly make out sounds from that far away? My hearing had always been normal – not better than average, just average.

"Why's it so dark in here?"

A woman's voice, one of my nurses, followed by a raspy, smoker's cough. I could smell it on her uniform. I watched her enter my room and flip on the overhead light while staring at my face, like she assumed I'd cry out in pain. I pointed to my tube and made a motion with my fingers, then pointed to my nose and took a few breaths in and out.

She made some notation on her tablet, mumbled to a man in the hallway, then the two of them approached my bed for the extubation. How did I know this? Because I was awake enough and it was time. Even so – how did I know it was time?

They used a suction tool to remove any debris, then quickly deflated the cuff built into the ETT, the endotracheal tube that held it in place. I could have narrated the whole procedure. New realization – I was a doctor, or I had been once… before my biggest failure.

"Take a deep breath now," the woman said as the tube was pulled out of my throat.

I coughed gently, which I knew was a good sign considering all the potential pitfalls of that procedure. Vocal cord dysfunction, airway trauma, or spasm of the larynx were common enough.

I looked at the water cup on my bedside table and knew they'd need to wait at least an hour before starting to rehydrate me. A mask was fitted to my face for extra oxygen, with a directive to cough every so often to keep things loose. Amazing how quickly the body forgets something as primal as breathing and swallowing.

Alone in the room for thirty minutes, I pulled off the mask and grabbed the greenish yellow sippy cup, the kind they give to toddlers. The cool water went down fine but the color of the cup bothered me. This was realization #4: along with my severe light sensitivity came a sudden color sensitivity, neither of which I'd ever had before.

I'd read about traumatic brain injury in medical school and knew all of these things could be considered common for TBI patients, especially just days after coming off sedation. NDEs they called them, near death experiences. Though most of my medical training had been in pediatrics, the first four years were general medical training. The specializations didn't come till my internship and residency. I recalled that children had a much easier time recovering from TBI than adults. So the likelihood of extreme sensitivity was high, and hopefully temporary. Time would tell.

And time was the fifth realization of this new, deteriorated Kurt Farin, the defective detective. Ha! My belly rumbled in lieu of a laugh. Was I ever defective right now. Time, since my emergence from the blue void, had a presence. I could almost see it. Remember those scenes in the Predator movies from the eighties, where you could see something clear and translucent moving past the camera – a texture different from the world itself? I could see time passing slower than usual, people moving in slo-mo through something more viscous than just air and light. And sometimes it skipped forward, too. Not fast-forwarding but actually skipping to a different time marker in my near future. After the raspy-voiced nurse left my bedside, time skipped again, or maybe I just dozed. Apparently I could talk now, though I didn't remember my first words after waking. I'd heard the staff saying that I'd repeated the word *terror* while I was asleep.

I widened my eyes to see a figure darkening the doorway. My daughter, Brooke Farin, twenty-four years old who on her worst day looks like a supermodel. I felt my mouth twitch on the edges seeing her there, shoulders hunched, head low, gazing down at me as if to say, "Is it really you?"

I reached for her. She approached easily, proving this was not our first meeting since I've been here. She was crying in her subtle way of swiping tears with the back of one finger, followed by a sniff. A new dread arrived in my head – what had I told her in my stupor? Did I mention Genevieve Lucas, or some of the other things my new brain had revealed? It frightened me because no one could know yet what I knew. I needed time to process it all and validate what was real and what was artificially manufactured by my altered consciousness. The brain unplugged from itself for several days was like an unmanned lawnmower. And I was just beginning to discover where it's been.

# Chapter 4

**At some point in the past day** or so, my speech improved and I began to eat. But the buzz of the overhead lights still unglued me to the point of concern. I had a vague taste of lemon in my mouth from some kind of yogurt. There were no words for how vile the inside of your mouth felt after being unconscious for three days. And yogurt just made it worse, though I understood the logic of its cocktail of nutrients.

Brooke was at my bedside feeding me, wearing the same wrinkled t-shirt she had on last time I saw her.

"Drink this," she said.

I sipped from the toddler cup, reminding my body of how quickly I'd regain strength from basic eating and drinking. She squeezed my arm and I knew how she felt - not because of my defective-detective special powers but because she was my flesh and blood.

"I'm glad you're here," I managed, shocked by the clamor of my spoken voice. I sounded worse than Nurse Raspy. Brooke was avoiding my eyes but kept her hand on me, holding on to something she didn't wholly trust.

"I'm okay," I said.

Her head dropped to my chest, caving into the pain she'd been probably holding for weeks. I held the back of her neck, embracing her, caring for my daughter in a way that was involuntary and primal.

"I'm okay," I said again. "Better every minute."

She looked up, the shame of her tears like a pox on her soul. Lifting up, she used the back of her hand to wipe every trace of them off her still-luminous face. "There's a lot to say," she started. "And nothing to say."

I considered the comment.

"Do you remember anything?" she asked.

A Cheshire cat grin spread across my face.

"What?"

"Just marveling at the irony. Yes of course I remember everything. It's just probably not what you remember of the past week."

"I have no idea what that means."

I shrugged in response.

"Where did you go?" she asked, her face full of wonder. "Was it terrible?"

She was right - so much to say. To report, to relay details about my blue cosmos. I couldn't tell her about Genevieve Lucas, not yet. I might tell someone, but not her.

"Your nurse will be back in a few minutes," she said when I didn't answer. I could see in her face that she knew I was holding something back.

"I'll give you a million dollars if you can help me brush my teeth."

"You're set up for that in the bathroom." She pointed. "The nurse is gonna help you get up, and she and a physical therapist will be here soon. No million dollars needed. Not that you have a million dollars."

"Wait, I have a million-dollar life insurance policy. Are you sorry I didn't –" Lucky I caught myself before saying something she might never forgive me for. How could I be so crass when lines of pain and fear had woven into her young face? "I'm so sorr—"

"I don't want your million dollars," she clapped back. "Just need you to stick around for, say, another thirty years."

"Let's get me through the next week, then we'll see."

I felt another squeeze from her hands. "How do you feel right now? Are you in any pain?"

"Yes."

"Where?"

"Everywhere. Name a place."

"They have pain meds but they're being very careful," she said. "There's a specialist who's been talking to me, a TBI specialist. And also... Alena and Vaughn." She watched my face and braced for a reaction.

"They've been here with you the whole time?" I asked.

She nodded.

"Are you feeling rebellious right now?"

"What - breaking you out of here or something?"

I waited.

"Don't be ridiculous. If you could see how you look right now, you'd never ask that."

Watching emotion move through her face, I knew what they did, suddenly, why they'd sedated me. Jimmy Breslin's bullet must have flown past my head and grazed my skull. The impact of its speed, inertia, and trajectory likely caused me to fall and hit my head on the hard floor, probably causing a concussion, after which they intubated me, sedated me, and put me on a ventilator. It was the smart thing to do, and the right timing.

"Break out? No of course not. I just want to go to the bathroom and splash some water on my face and brush my teeth. Please, I beg you. Who knows when they'll get here. I'd go myself but I might end up in a heap on the floor."

She pulled away to scope out the hallway. That's my girl.

"Well, you've still got a catheter in. Hopefully I don't have to help you pee."

"Water on my face and brush my teeth, that's it, promise. Nothing gross. Don't get too close though, I'm sure I smell terrible."

"They bathed you, like sponge baths, when you were... you know." She lowered her eyes. "The under place."

"Good word for it. Let's go, before they get here."

Walking was easier than I expected, though I was paying more attention to foot placement than the sensation of balancing my body weight because Brooke was my crutch. The tiny bathroom was no more than ten steps from my bedside, five of which I did myself without Brooke's attendance. Relatively certain I could stand in one place and brush my teeth on my own, she stood guard at the door.

"Hurry up, I see her," she said.

But I wasn't hurrying. I was savoring every blessed second of the minty, gritty mush in my mouth cleaning all the bacteria that I'd no doubt built up in my vacuum. God knows what kind of dental chaos was going on in there right now. My skin showed the wrinkles of someone twice my age, and my dirty blond hair looked brown. It didn't matter what the mirror showed me, because I felt like a million dollars, comparatively speaking. I leaned over to splash a few palmfuls of water on my eyes and cheeks.

Water. The blue cosmos. But this didn't feel at all like that water. It wasn't cool or thick or reassuring. It didn't feel like an invisibility cloak and it had no smell. It just felt... wet. I put some of the pump-soap in my hands and lathered it, then went a little bit crazy with it – forehead, scalp, eyes, cheeks, chin, neck and throat, now ears, a literal soap-gasm. I might wet my pants. I was breathing heavily and got a little lightheaded as I splashed and rinsed off all the soap. With her eyes in the hall, Brooke passed a mound of paper towels to me. I opened them up, held them in my hands and tossed them in the trash. The air would dry my skin.

"She's coming." Brooke collected me from the sink, shuffling me back to the bed. "Here," she said and used her sleeve to wipe water from the tip of my nose and a speck of soap from my ear. "Better?"

I took a long breath. "You have no idea."

"You did pretty good there."

"I'll be jogging around the building this weekend."

"Better not."

"Good morning," Nurse Scary said, a young man and an older woman in tow behind her. "We're gonna get you up for a short walk just around your room. Okay?"

"I don't know, I feel pretty weak." I winked at Brooke, who was perched on the edge of the only chair in the room, my partner in crime.

"Hey," someone said from the doorway. I knew that voice. Vaughn, my partner, and the first time I'd seen him since I woke up. His dark brown hair looked shorter, mouth formed in his signature wry smile, but his glassy eyes told a different story. Maybe I meant something to him after all.

# Chapter 5

**I feigned weakness, shuffling at first, wobbling** and holding onto the wall, to make the hospital staff feel useful when I took twenty-five steps around the room on my own. They all had smiles on their faces. Hopefully they'd leave me alone for a while. Kurt: 1, Hospital: 0.

"Quit showing off," Vaughn said and leaned on the side of my bed after I was settled back under the covers. He reached his hand up and took mine in his typical bone-crusher grip. "How was your... nap?"

I watched him, remembering his face.

"There's so much I want to ask you," I said. Understatement.

"Well, all I've got are questions. Not sure I can help you there."

A nurse shouldered past Vaughn out the door, then jerked her head back with a glare. "Visitors can stay for fifteen minutes at a time right now. Mr. Farin desperately needs to rest."

"Yes ma'am."

In those fifteen minutes, I mostly listened to him talk – about the case, the club, watching his patterns of behavior and remembering he was one of the best investigators I'd ever worked with. My mind drifted to when I was first hired by the San Francisco Police Department and they assigned me to him, and how that went over at first.

"What?" he asked.

"Funny," I mumbled.

"They told me you'd need to relearn everything including how to concentrate on one thing at a time."

How could I explain to him that I was living in two realms at once? No, I wasn't really capable of paying attention and following a line of verbal discourse. It's true - I was too distracted to concentrate – but there was something else. This new me was so easily bored.

"Okay. I'm gonna let you rest, and I'll be back tomorrow. You —"

"Wait." I death-gripped my partner's arm.

He stopped and stared. "What is it?"

"We have to find her." I whispered the words but knew he heard me.

Vaughn lowered his eyes to the floor. "We did find her, buddy. Don't you remember?"

He was talking about the girl in the Stork Club, Leticia Ames. I was talking about someone else. Genevieve Lucas. Was I ready to share, and could he be trusted?

I must have looked like I was about to cry, because Vaughn sat on the edge of the bed and leaned close to my face.

"I saw something down there," I said, nervously eyeing the door behind him.

"Down… where?" he asked.

I blinked back. "Not something. Someone."

"Okay, wait. You mean—"

I cleared my throat, preparing for my pitch. "I need you to bring me a police composite artist."

"Um," he said, and released an anxious laugh.

"I saw someone, under water," I whispered slowly. "And I have to find her."

Vaughn got up and walked around the bed, fumbling through the odd assortment of objects the hospital staff put on the rolly-cart in the corner. "You said *her*. Was she alive, this woman, wherever it was that you saw her?"

I didn't know if he was just playing along or if he bought into my nonsense. "I honestly don't know."

Long sigh, then he crossed his arms at his chest.

"What?" I asked.

He shook his head. "Just surprised, sort of. There's nothing wrong with your brain obviously, or your ability to communicate, or manipulate."

"Manipulate?"

"Never mind. You said she was under water, this woman. Was she diving? Were you dreaming about diving?"

I watched his eyes, still deciding. "No, and it wasn't a dream. But yes I think she's alive, or it seemed so. I need to capture the image of her, and I need a sketch artist to do that so I can analyze the image and run it through facial recognition software." I reached out my hand and he was already shaking his head. "Please," I pressed. "You have the power to do this, and you're the only one who can help me."

"I can see there's nothing residually wrong with your brain. You're back to your crafty self. I'm sorry but no. I can't assemble a team to-"

"Not a team, one person! The sketch artist we always use. What's his—"

"Kurt, come on," he stopped me. "I can't mobilize even a one-person team for a lead based on what an injured detective saw in a coma." He paused for effect. "You know that's the equivalent of a tarot card reader. Not gonna happen."

Of course it was out of the question. I was awake and alert enough to know how it must have sounded. But I could tell from his eyes that he at least believed that I believed what I was asking. That was something.

I'd mismanaged that request, and I watched him leave obviously thinking I was out of my mind. I knew what the TBI specialist was telling him and Brooke. Alena Broderick was another story. She'd been my lover once, for a few months, but had been my friend and fellow diver since we were teenagers. I dreaded seeing her most of all, maybe because I could never hide anything from her. And now I had so much to hide. They left me here, in this room with no windows, watching annoying images blink back on the wall-mounted

TV screen of my treatment plan and upcoming appointments. At some point, two nurses came in and removed my catheter. As if having a catheter wasn't bad enough, having two women remove it was enough to induce suicide. Time to get out of here.

I tried balancing my own body weight, but the floor was too slippery in whatever socks they'd put on my feet. The cool tiles felt sublime on my bare skin when I pulled them off. Now I could grip the floor and stand up straight without feeling like I was about to collapse. I started with laps around the room, back and forth, first holding onto things, assessing how air felt coming in and out of my lungs, the rush of blood through my veins. So far I could see, breathe, drink, swallow, eat, pee, and speak with very little impairment. Good. Let's take it up a notch.

I pulled open my door and glanced down the empty hallway. When I didn't see anyone for two full minutes, I took a left out of the room, hugged the walls so I could grip the railing if I felt faint, and then took a right down a long corridor toward music. It sounded like chill instrumentals. My gait normalized quickly as I rediscovered a sense of balance, and the halls were empty, save for two men comforting a crying older woman.

Signs took up all the available wall space. Exit, No Exit, Out of Order, Proceed to Nurse's Station. I noted that Zuckerberg San Francisco General Hospital also had the words Trauma Center in its title. Made sense that they'd brought me here.

The room with the music was a large, two-person setup, empty with a window that showed a short stretch of dark orange from the last remnants of dusk. The color splash lit the tips of evergreen trees and part of the path around the back of the hospital grounds. Pretty. I moved toward it into the empty room, gliding almost, creeping quietly in bare feet, enjoying the power of independent movement, still curious if I could even live in this place anymore. I plopped into a chair by the window, gasping from exertion. Now just a scant triangle of orange lit the corner of my view.

When I squinted, I was transported somewhere else, now in a chair far from the window, looking out at grimy glass with cobwebs on the screen. In this other place it was also dusk. I could see the edge of a house, half of a catalpa tree, and in front of the dirty window a rocking chair. A thin, brown-haired, middle-aged woman gripping the wooden arms, teeth gnashing, eyes wild, death taking her over. Who was this poor soul and why was I able to see her? I took a moment to reassess my surroundings and ground myself in the angry buzz of fluorescent lights overhead.

* ~◈~ ◈▩◈ ┼ ◈▩◈ ~◈~ *

I knew I'd have to deal with Alena Broderick at some point. While I was still mentally rehearsing my words, she showed up the next morning with two cups of Philz coffee. I didn't have the heart to tell her I'd somehow lost my passion for it in the blue wild. I pointed to the light switch and made a down motion with my finger. She flipped it off. I allowed her to kiss my cheek, having just washed my face again in the sink. I sipped the dark, hot brew and closed my eyes, letting her think the taste of it was heaven but really just grateful for the idea of caffeine again. I could feel the stimulating effect after the first swallow, bringing me to attention, ready for action. Was I, though, ready? Not for her.

We did the typical hospital deal – her sitting cautiously on the edge of the bed, talking softly, trying not to tell me what I inevitably wouldn't want to hear. Her experience as a medical case worker, specifically for TBI patients, was too much of a coincidence. Then again, her work wasn't generally with this hospital system. I knew she'd have a vested interest in my release and recovery. She had an apology in her eyes, I could see it.

"Just tell me. Did you get yourself assigned to me?" I asked.

She shook her head and a piece of her strawberry blonde hair slid down from her ponytail in front of her eye.

"No?"

"Yes. I was just wondering how you—"

"How I knew? Gonna be a lot of that so get used to it," I said. "What does this mean, exactly, right now?"

"For us, you mean?" she asked.

"I mean can you get me the fuck out of here?"

"Well, not immediately, no. There's a lot we - they - need to find out first."

I shrugged. "Like what? I'm in the 11%, right? I can walk, go to the bathroom. I can eat, drink, and swallow. I can speak, and my mental capacity appears normal, or for me anyway."

She drew in a long breath. "The 89% mortality rate is for typical coma patients. Your condition, where we sedated you, has a much higher recovery rate. Yes you're doing fine. We need an MRI and an EEG, and if those are also fine, you're probably out of here in the next couple of days."

My chest loosened when she said it. "Couple of days, that's fantastic. Why the look of gloom then?"

Alena got up and paced, hands in the pockets of her long, brown jacket, which looked good with her tall, leather boots. Always stylish and trying to be so, which somehow diminished the effect.

"Has anyone explained to you what you've gone through?" she asked. "Gunshot wounds to the head come in many different flavors."

They hadn't told me anything yet, but I remembered them from my training. "Penetrating, perforating, neither of which applies here. I thought the bullet just grazed my skull."

She shook her head. "They intubated and sedated you for airway protection because of a concussion and blood loss from when you fell. You have a tangential wound from where the bullet grazed your head. It didn't lodge itself into your skull or dermis, but there are still lots of complications here."

I knew what they were, and how most of them were rare. Still, I needed to let her talk. "What are you concerned about?"

"Brain hemorrhaging, intracranial lesions are all possible, not to mention the lodging of bone fragments into the brain cavity, which can cause severe complications to a normal recovery and all of these were ruled out already. Going forward, we'll need to watch for neuropsychiatric changes, problems with concentration or coordination. You'll need to be very closely monitored, to say the least. But some of the symptoms you've been manifesting are, well, unusual for your type of injury. I've talked to your medical team about it and no one really knows what to make of it."

"The light sensitivity you mean?"

"Photophobia yes, extreme sensitivity to daylight. We'll monitor you and hopefully it will subside over the next few weeks." She stood at the foot of the bed. "You used to complain about the light after some of our dives," she said. "Do you remember?"

Even now, I can remember every moment of them. How bright the sun was in our eyes after the darkness of being underwater, and how Alena's eyes were a shade of dark blue I'd never seen on anybody else.

"Also some things you were saying."

"I know, terror. Brooke told me."

She nodded. "Some other things too, but you said that over and over. Do you know what it means?"

"Brooke thought maybe it was 'terra' referring to a place or a venue, or a geographical location. I have no idea," I said. "Why is that important enough to keep me from going home if I'm otherwise recovering better than most coma patients?"

"We'll proceed with the tests that have been ordered, then we can talk more." She moved back to the edge of the bed and placed her palm on my chest.

"Would you have missed me that much?" I asked.

She stared at her hand without answering.

"Hey, did you hear what my new nickname is now? The defective detective."

"You're defective all right. Just not in that way."

# Chapter 6

**The next morning I could barely keep** my eyes open. Blood draws, multiple tests, and medical interrogations still didn't explain my lethargy. Had they sedated me again? The 'normal, typical, customary for traumatic brain injuries' answer was getting old.

I napped my way through the MRI, just saying the word fine whenever they asked me something. Yes, fine. No problem, fine. Same for the EEG, where they taped tiny wires to my head and gave me directions like *breathe, open your eyes*. Forty minutes later I was back in my room. I flipped off the overhead light, wrestled with the most uncomfortable bed I'd ever been in and eventually passed out after they brought in a lunch tray. I didn't eat. Nurse Ratched would be in to harass me about that on her rounds. I was too tired to fight.

Where are you, Genevieve Lucas? She'd contacted me once, so logically it could happen again. Couldn't it? I sank low in the bed, in my mind, down to the floor, the core of the earth, eyes wide and searching for the outline of the wrecked ship and her chestnut hair, this ghostly specter of a woman whose name my soul knew. I said the words out loud, but they came out distorted because I was talking under water, like tiny echoes trailing each syllable. Where-where-

where are-are-are you-you-you? I know you've got something to tell me because you chose me. I need to know why, not only because I think you need my help but because our fates are inextricably linked.

Terror. Brooke told me I'd said this in my sleep. I saw her now, the woman - the edge of her hair sticking out from under the buried hull of an old ship. Terror. There it was again. That word. *I'm not afraid, I see you.* I called to her, gliding through the thick, blue water. I had no breathing apparatus and didn't need one here. This was home, I knew this place, this ship, and the woman trapped there. *Can you hear me?*

*Come*, the voice echoed. The body trapped below hadn't moved, but I heard it.

My forehead felt strangely warm in the cool water. I willed myself forward, faster, but it wasn't working because I wasn't propelled by anything other than gravity and the natural pulse of the current. I drifted forward, inch by inch, blinking in the water to get a better look at the structure surrounding her covered body. I saw a wooden hull, and the curve of a bell on deck.

*Don't be afraid*, the voice said to me.

I felt myself sinking but didn't seem to be getting any closer to her. *I'm coming, I'm not afraid. I can't seem to get to you. Help me. What do you need to tell me? What's your secret?*

*You are the secret*, the voice said. I heard it more clearly this time, a deep, sultry voice.

*What does that mean?*

*You're hiding from the missing pieces of your past. Are you ready to know the truth now?*


"Dad. Dad…"

Brooke, her voice strained with panic. Did they think I was dead? How long had I been under? How deep had I gone? I touched my chin – my new gauge of time. By the stubble I'd probably been asleep for several hours.

"I'm fine, I'm awake. See?" I brought Brooke's hand to my mouth and kissed it. Her eyes looked wild. I made an effort to sit up and look alert, for her sake. "See, I'm okay. What did I miss?"

"I couldn't wake you."

I smiled. "Did you have your hand on my forehead at one point?"

She nodded. "You felt it?"

"Yeah." I nodded. "I was dreaming and I noticed my forehead felt warm. That was you."

"What were you dreaming? Diving again?"

I didn't remember telling her anything about the blue cosmos or what I'd seen there. I hadn't told any of them. No one. I reminded myself to be cool and not get defensive, especially around Brooke. Of course I adored her, but a deeper agenda, a sort of sinister guile set into my face when I realized, in that moment, that I might need an ally.

"How do you know that?" I asked, making sure my voice was casual and easy.

"What?"

"What I'd dreamt about. Did I tell you? I honestly can't remember."

She pinched her lips. "It's all you ever dream about. Mom used to say that."

"Say what?" I hadn't thought about Caitlin in a long time. A comfortable, lovely long time.

"About you and diving. She used to say there was a part of you that never left the bottom of the ocean."

# Chapter 7

**It was official. In the time I** was under, I'd become a tea drinker and was no longer interested in the black coffee I'd loved my entire adult life so far. They said changes like this were common, in taste and preferences, clothing styles, food choices. Brooke brought me a strong-brewed English breakfast tea from the cafeteria downstairs, with milk and sugar, no less. I slurped it down, using my scant remnants of ab muscles to prop myself up in the bed. More caffeine, thank God – there was a lot to do today.

One of the nurses told me they would be evaluating me for possible discharge tomorrow or the next day. Hallelujah. I knew what that meant, of course – invasive questions and more tests. Likely physical coordination tests, agility, neurology, speech pathology, memory, psych, and the standard discussion about post-discharge care.

I passed physical therapy with flying colors. I had about five minutes of stamina but in those five minutes I could almost run down the hall. They used words like delighted. Check. I wished the psych test came before all the others, because I aced the agility, neurological, speaking and memory tests. By the time we got to the psych eval, which they said was optional, I was horrified to see Alena Broderick sitting in one of the two chairs opposite me.

They brought me to a hospital admin office done up in wood paneling with a handsome walnut desk. A bureaucrat's desk used by a man with incredibly long sideburns. What else did I need to know about him but that? Alena had a legal pad in front of her, her colleague with a laptop, no doubt ready to document my mental breakdown. I glared at Alena.

"Is this some kind of trick?" I asked her, knowing she'd likely orchestrated this.

"Come on," she shrugged. "I already told you this evaluation is optional, and your discharge is not contingent upon any particular answers." She sighed. "You've come through quite an ordeal and it's just another way that we can provide support for TBI patients. Anyway, after today you'll have some follow-ups post-discharge. You're a doctor so you know the drill."

"He was a doctor," the man beside her corrected. "Once."

Alena shot him a look. "You know these meetings are simply to put a check in the box and make sure you're emotionally fit to be out on your own after—"

"After the ordeal you've just come through," the man finished her sentence. He had some kind of drawl, I couldn't place it. "After you were shot, you apparently fell and hit your head pretty hard, sustaining a serious concussion. You were unconscious and sedated for several days. A lot can happen."

I wasn't sure if he meant physiologically or psychologically, probably both. I had my hands on my lap, chair positioned directly in front of Alena across from them in front of the desk. As a detective, Vaughn and I had conducted interrogations using behavior-influencing techniques like this. Sometimes only chairs with no table, other times too many chairs in a room. I wondered whose idea this had been. "Sure. Fine. I'm happy to answer any questions or concerns."

They were deciding, I could tell, which of them would start their plan to erode my composure. It sounded paranoid, I know. Why would they try to prevent me from being discharged? Just a feeling. I intended to pass this test just like all the others, fuckers. I was dying to get out of this place and I'd do anything at this point. I was a trained medical doctor, pediatrician, though I hadn't worked as such in over seven years. Since then, I'd been working as a detective, partnered with Vaughn, for the San Francisco PD. So at least before this ordeal, my skillset for getting what I needed from people was well honed. Show time.

Dr. Sideburns flipped through my medical chart, pretending to read notes, findings, and test results. I knew what he was doing. I reminded myself that I had a new skill in my toolbox now – the ability to summon the blue cosmos. I imagined floating through the cool blue now, imagined how the cold water felt against my arms and legs, the yellow glint of sun bleeding down into the expanse. I breathed slowly and closed my eyes. After that display, I made sure there was a tiny glimmer of a smile on my lips, to show Alena that she was in for an Oscar-winning performance.

"Something funny, Detective?" The man looked annoyed. I now had even more reason to live.

"Not funny, no. I was just thinking how well I feel." I paused to let them look at each other and plan their next move. It would go nowhere. "Just thinking about the care I've gotten at this hospital. Though it feels like it's been much longer, I'm barely three days post-sedation and other than low stamina, I feel amazing."

Alena eye rolled. "How's your head?" she asked, challenging me to make light of it in front of the other doctor.

I squinted and rubbed the tender spot with my fingers. "Sore." I winced for effect but it didn't hurt. "The pain's getting better every day."

"What's the deal with the lights?" Sideburns asked with a smirk, thinking he had me. Unfortunately for him, I'd already planned for that.

I turned my head up toward the overhead light fixture and stared. "Not as bad, today. The overhead lights in my room were making me nauseous that first day I was coming out of it. I think that sensitivity is decreasing."

He stared back, knowing, it seemed, the game I was playing but unsure how to regain control.

*Blue cosmos. Blue cosmos*, I said to myself. Now he closed the file and sat back, hands gripping the arm rests. Hilarious.

"Give it a rest, detective. Alright? I've reviewed your

background and you're recovering well so far. We'll be sending out a neuropsychologist for follow-ups to assess your attention, memory, and any cognitive impairment."

"Do I appear to have any impairment?"

The man sniffed. "Not so far but we'll test repeatedly over time to compare results. Nothing to worry about. We'll also be testing any mood disorders and psychological changes." He stared at me when he said the words. "What are you planning to do now?" he asked. "No job, no work, how will you spend your time? How will you sustain yourself economically?"

I watched the eyes, the raised hands, heard the tightness in his throat when he spoke. I made him nervous.

I pretended to give meaningful reflection to what he'd launched as a clear offensive. I sighed, tipped my head and looked at the ceiling. I knew Alena must be laughing inside right now. Or maybe crying.

"Take it slow." I shrugged. "I think my body will tell me what it needs, and what it's been telling me is mainly rest. In between physical therapy, I suspect I'll do a lot of laying around and napping, then eventually when my savings runs low, I'll cross that bridge." I didn't move a muscle. It was a brilliant answer, as was its execution. I made sure not to ruin it by too many extraneous movements. I stared but my face was relaxed and mild, gently waiting for a retort.

Alena closed my case file in front of her. "We're ordering skilled nursing to go in twice a week for PT, and counseling once a week. You okay with that?"

"Probably need it," I said, looking directly at her, waiting for Dr. Sideburns to pipe in with some jibe or insult. Alena rose, glaring down at the doctor who was still seated.

"We're done here, yeah?" she asked him, irritated.

The man rose. "Good luck, Detective."

# Chapter 8

**The next morning, my gatekeepers released me** and I was home by 11am. Alena drove me instead of Brooke, and there would be hell to pay for that one. Brooke and Alena, well, that was a long story. Alena had been my lover once, a long time ago and only for a short time. But Brooke would likely always see her as some sort of interloper. Caitlin left me a year after our son died, proving that textbooks were right - a marriage can rarely recover from the loss of a child.

By 11:20, I was free of Alena and emancipated from the flood of texts from Brooke. Yes, I was home. Yes, I was on my own here. Couldn't the world just leave me alone? Lucky for me, tomorrow was a federal holiday, Washington's birthday, and that meant no one would be showing up here to poke or prod me, bend and contort me, and invade the privacy of my mental space until next Tuesday. Whew, jailbreak for the next six days. What was I going to do with my time? It was an interesting quandary, because I felt the pull to retreat into my secret lair but an even stronger imperative to at least try to reassimilate.

Contrary to what I'd told Dr. Sideburns, I was still truly unglued by the energy and vibration of light, and not just artificial lighting either. Daylight was even worse. The brightness and imagery of light itself seemed to break something inside, something hard that was now tender and vulnerable. I could go on suffering, or I could come up with some temporary adaptation to get me through the next month or two. Maybe I'd become nocturnal.

The house on 29th Street was in San Francisco's Noe Valley southeast of Golden Gate Park, west of Potrero Hill, north of Glen Park and Bernal Heights. I used to love the views from the open space at 29th and Diamond a half a block away. We moved here seven years ago for that very view, renting just the upper floor unit from Max Sheldon, an old man who used to babysit our seven-year-old son. Amazing the acid that still pooled in my stomach when I thought of him. Ryan, oh my heart. My wife Caitlin, not surprisingly, went crazy after that. Two years later, my old diving partner and friend from childhood, Alena and I hooked up for a few months, knowing I was as unready for physical intimacy as I was anything deeper. It didn't fizzle out; it just scared me. I'm still not ready for prime time, still not completely at ease around her the way we used to be long ago. I might never be.

Max Sheldon had no children of his own, so when Ryan died, he also took a piece of Max's heart. Max willed me his house before he passed three years ago. Here I was now, with a house far nicer than I deserved, three bedrooms, two baths, a fully renovated condo with a separate sulking-studio, as I called it, downstairs, which I could rent if I wanted to. Plus some green grass in the back, which was unheard of, and no mortgage payment. With so many homeless in this city it didn't seem fair.

It took just a few hours to realize I had to move downstairs to that studio. It was lower and darker, and right now I was out of my head and couldn't bear being in the space where we'd lived with Ryan. Maybe I'd give the condo to Brooke. Honestly I couldn't bear being anywhere permanent right now. I no longer fit in this world above water. I knew I needed to be home and showered and perky by next Tuesday morning for my slew of torture sessions. Until then, everything was up to me.

I started walking as soon as the streetlights flicked on. Some nights with a travel mug of tea to keep me awake. Other nights a jacket over my shoulders. One night I walked outside in bare feet because it had rained as dusk darkened the sky and I wanted that cool wetness on my skin. It's different when it's manufactured in the shower or a cool bath. When nature dishes up a cocktail of bruise-colored clouds and cool water falling, that was a gift worth celebrating.

I knew, of course, that I was not in my right mind. I had these strange bouts of restlessness. I drove across the bridge to Oakland and gravitated to the streets near Telegraph Avenue, passing the Stork Club - where Vaughn and I had cornered Jimmy Breslin, where his victim, nineteen-year-old Leticia Ames went down, and where I went down two weeks later. We'd pulled video from the club and saw her working the crowd that night, dancing with everyone, a constant smile, alive in her surging beauty and zest for life, dressed in the typical accoutrements of a young woman coming of age – dark lipstick, low-cut blouse, trying hard to be visible, memorable.

Two weeks ago now, I'd woken from the undead. And as a result, nobody messed with me here on these dark streets. Gangs, dealers, addicts, I saw their eyes glass me up and down and quickly move on as if to say Nah, nothing there. No signs of life. They were right.

I'd stay out late and come back to the studio at dawn, pull down all the shades and try to sleep. By Monday, I'd exhausted Oakland's neighborhoods and Berkeley Hills and returned to San Francisco. Fisherman's Wharf, sometimes the Kelly's part of Ocean Beach, and I'd walk on the gritty sand with my pants rolled up to feel the cold pulse of water and remember the one place I ever felt whole.

Tonight I sat on the water's edge, submerged up to my neck every time the tide rolled in. I called out to her. There was a couple kissing and laughing somewhere behind me, no doubt mocking the crazy guy in the water, or else worried I was drowning myself. *No*, I told them with my mind. *I'm searching. Genevieve Lucas sent me a message. I saw her with my own eyes. Now I must find her or die trying.*

# Chapter 9

**I needed an ally, someone to talk** to about Genevieve. Alena? Hell no. She was on my medical team. Brooke? Also no, though if ever needed her to keep something from Alena, their long rivalry would make that opportunity irresistible. I needed someone who cared about me but was also corrupt enough to break a few rules. Maybe more than a few.

I remembered Vaughn always loved this dive bar in the Haight. Molotov's was where we used to meet on Sunday nights to play chess and plan our investigation strategy for the week. I didn't mind the too-loud punk rock or billiards games because a) there were always cats and dogs milling around the floor and b) it had low lighting. I was becoming a vampire, researching dimly lit venues in San Francisco and the East Bay, planning my future as a nocturnal human displaced by his previous life. Vaughn replied with an *OK* to my text about meeting me, nothing more. This response told me an interrogation was imminent and he might not be the ally I'd hoped for.

I got to Molotov's before him, annihilated by the wall of sound coming from huge speakers on tables in the back. I ordered drinks and walked to the last booth in the row closest to the restrooms. Didn't smell nice but good for privacy.

Ten minutes later, Vaughn stood at the table looking down, appraising me.

"You look nice," I said. "Why is that?"

"What does that mean?"

"It's eleven o'clock on a Sunday night. Why would you be, ah..." I smiled. "You had a date."

"Bingo." Vaughn sat and wrapped his hands around the bottle of Anchor Steam I'd ordered. We both used to drink that, loyal to the fact that it was brewed here. He looked at my brandy glass full of Bailey's Irish Cream and snickered. "No beer?" he asked.

"No coffee lately either." I shrugged. "Who knows?"

"I heard that—"

I waved my hand. "I've heard it all too. Sometimes they're temporary, other times not." We sipped our drinks, looking around the room, avoiding the obvious subject.

"So..."

"So!" I jumped in. "How are you?"

"Come on." Eyeroll.

"What?"

"Do you think I don't know what's going on with you?"

I couldn't help but laugh. "Yes. I do think you don't know what's going on with me. That's why I'm here." I paused for a sip of fortification. "I need to talk to you."

"Okay."

"Wait, first tell me what it is you think is going on."

He sighed and sat back. "Brooke told me you moved out of your condo and into the studio downstairs. She said you got rid of your landline, you never return her calls, you keep the blinds permanently closed and you only go out at night. I honestly wanted to come by but I thought you might need some space, you know, to process."

I was processing alright. Just not what he thought. "How would she know about the landline?"

He shook his head.

"Fine, okay, yes I'm very light-sensitive, also noise-sensitive, crowd-sensitive, I can't really eat normal food." I thought it might feel good to share all this with him, my partner of five years. It didn't. "It's like I'm undergoing this DNA-reconstruction, but while I'm awake. Everything's changed and still changing."

Vaughn rubbed his eyes but he wasn't tired. It was a nervous habit to hide uncomfortable emotions. "Well, I've gotta say I'm delighted you're not in fact dead."

"Here's to that," I said. We touched glasses and the vibe magically changed.

He took off what looked like a new leather jacket, rolled up his sleeves, and leaned forward. I made him bring me another Bailey's and then told him what I'd seen, what I heard, what I felt in that place, trying hard to put the unspeakable into words someone else could understand because if I didn't talk about it I was going to explode. He kept shaking his head, peering at me with narrowed eyes. I couldn't tell if that was empathy or disbelief.

"I need…" I said this word like my life depended on it, "to find her."

"How do you know she even exists?" he asked and sipped his drink.

And that was the essential magic of Vaughn – his undaunted adherence to truth, natural distrust of assumptions, constantly asking what no one else was willing to ask. During homicide investigations, I'd be focused on an incriminating fingerprint, and Vaughn would be standing outside in the street waving his arms asking how we knew conclusively that the killer even lived in this state. By and large, the world needed more Vaughns than Kurt Farins.

"I just know," I said as a server deposited another round at our table. "I saw her."

"The woman?" His head tipped down. "On the bottom of the ocean, buried under a shipwreck? Sorry, but that's not a reliable report."

I leaned forward. "Who sent us over those drinks? We didn't order them."

"No idea," he said.

The huddle in the corner of the room got louder, first with yelling then laughter. I heard someone say, "You can't pick a lock with a paperclip. It's a myth!"

"I have," Vaughn said in his booming bar voice.

"Ahh, see?" the guy replied from the huddle.

"You clearly have magical powers when it comes to picking locks," I said, remembering many of our cases. "You probably don't even need a paperclip. You just use your mind, right?"

"Exactly." A look of pride flushed his face.

"I think you were a burglar in another life."

"Or another country."

"Well, anyway," I said, "she spoke to me. I heard her voice."

I could sense the eyeroll before it happened. "And said what?"

"Something about hiding from secrets."

"Why are you so—"

"She's been summoning me," I blurted. "She's asking me for something. I need to find her, but I can't do it alone."

Vaughn drained his glass and used his fingers to rotate the new one on the edge of the table, around and around. "Alright. What do you need?"

I felt like excusing myself and going to the men's room to rehearse my pitch, but there was never time to do prep like that real-time in the field, was there?

"What I need… is to come back to work." I said it in my don't-fuck-with-me voice. Standoff, staring contest, me with my forearms on the table looking calm, him sitting back against the booth thinking of different ways to say no.

"That's not up to me," he said, taking the easy way out.

"Seriously? That's your response?"

"Kurt, we were told you weren't gonna recover."

"You signed the LEOKA paperwork?" I asked, referring to the Law Enforcement Officers Killed and Assaulted program. "I was only out of commission for like a week."

He shook his head slowly, painful subject. For both of us. "Donnelly signed it," he mumbled. "He asked me about it. At the time, I was at the hospital with Brooke. They told us your concussion was very serious and they honestly didn't know what to expect of your recovery."

"Look. Donnelly's not answering my calls. I'm sure you've told him that I've recovered, and—"

"Kurt, stop. Please. First of all, you haven't recovered. Get real. You're recovering. And not even doing a very good job of it, in my opinion."

"What does that mean?" I asked.

Vaughn grabbed the untouched beer and downed half of it at once. Now I was in for it.

"You want to come back to work, to the work we were doing together before this happened? Getting up every day, in the morning I mean, dressed, driving downtown? Who do you think you're talking to?"

The room started spinning. Maybe it was the Bailey's. I needed a time out. This wasn't working. Dammit. "Okay."

"Okay, what? You want to come back to work as much as you want to go on a cruise. You hate cruises. You just want the department's resources to find your mermaid ghost." Vaughn stood and leaned down to grab his jacket. "I'm not helping you with that."

"Wait, please. There's more to explain here."

"You have thirty seconds." He was standing, leaning toward the door.

"Genevieve Lucas is not only telling me something. She's leading me somewhere, leading us somewhere."

"You already told me."

"There's more to it than that. There's something we need to find. I don't know what."

He stood near the table but not too close, guzzling the rest of his beer while he worked things out in his mind. The empty glass came down on the table with a thunk. "If you use any department resources right now, it has to be on the up and up, and don't try to tell me you're ready to come back to work. Because you're not."

"I could—"

"Dude, you're so off-grid right now. Do you think I don't know that you're only awake at night and sleeping all day? If you can't stand daylight, how is that gonna work for you career-wise? You'll end up addicted to pills. You need help, that's for sure, but not from me. Psychological would be more like it."

"I know," I said, and hated him for making me say that. "They're coming, all of them, starting tomorrow."

"I'll do what I can to help you, but offline. Don't ask me to hack into any databases or run any plates or shit like that. But if you're going through normal channels, tell me what you need. I'll see what I can do."

"Day after tomorrow. Will you work with me?"
"Let's see how you do with your appointments tomorrow."

# Chapter 10

*March*

**As a test, I made myself go** out to CVS to buy Tylenol, remember how to navigate city streets and, most importantly, deal with people. It was raining when I got to my car, which made San Francisco traffic even more fun. Fifty minutes to get 1.9 miles. That was another byproduct of my recovery – claustrophobia. The wall of cars made fear pulse in my hands.

I returned home frazzled, gazing up at the house, fury in a world that had displaced me. The cold, wet rain on my nose and forehead was what I most craved. Could I sleep out here on the curb? I went upstairs to grab my laptop and fell asleep on the living room sofa under the wet breeze from an open window, dreaming of Puget Sound and totem poles. Just before waking I heard her voice again, Genevieve.

*Terror.*

What does that mean? I asked her, imagining I was down there again, floating below the surface.

*Not what*, she replied in my head. *Where.*

A little after 3am something woke me, a thud outside like someone had dropped a duffel bag from the roof. Maybe I'd watched too many heist movies. I took a cursory look outside from the picture window but didn't see anything. Probably a raccoon scavenging for snacks.

I grabbed my laptop out of the back bedroom I'd been using as an office and took it back downstairs to the studio, locked the doors and went to bed, giving my overworked brain time to rest. It wasn't working. I moved carefully through the house in boxer shorts to the spare bedroom and turned on the laptop. *Terror.* There was something about that word implanted in my head during my coma. It had to mean something.

I started with a regular Google search – "where is Terror" making sure to use a capital T. That brought back a global terrorism database, a Halloween store called Terror Town, FBI's Terrorism unit, and something called Terror on the Fox, a haunted house in Green Bay, Wisconsin. I clicked to see the second page of search results and found more Halloween stuff, the Terrorism page on FEMA's website, and a New York Times article on terrorism.

I started over, this time with just the word Terror. Movies, TV series, an online game, then there was one entry for something called Terror Bay somewhere near Kodiak Island, Alaska. That was interesting. I'd never been to Alaska and felt no connection to it one way or another. Something pointed me toward Puget Sound, but I had no logical reason for this. I'd dreamt something about it tonight but I'd never been there either. Then again, it was getting harder to trust what my mind was telling me. I half expected the opposite to be true as I recovered. Maybe Vaughn was right and a day job would put some structure back in my days. Maybe.

* -◇- -◇▩◈- -+- -◈▩◇- -◇- *

Alena convinced my doctors that I needed eight weeks of physical therapy, speech pathology and neurolinguistic assessments, which were apparently standard protocol. Oh yes, and counseling. Today was the first PT session and for some reason I was comforted by the sight of my therapist at the door. The tall, lanky fellow identified himself as Matt, first-name only, a Board-Certified

Physical Therapist. With almost no chit chat, he started by ordering me to walk around the house and he'd trail behind me observing my gait. First slowly, then faster with him assessing my posture, balance, arm swing, and agility. Then on a mat he'd brought with him, he guided me through some painful stretches that I had to hold for thirty seconds. He said he'd be back on Wednesday. The speech assessments wouldn't start till next week, though he thought I'd be fine there. One down.

The moment the door closed behind him, I made a pot of tea and camped out at the kitchen table with my laptop. Something about Kodiak Island just didn't feel right. Did anyone even live there? One minute of research revealed a moderately diverse population of roughly thirteen thousand people. I added those details to my notes file, which I'd started compiling for my meeting with Vaughn tonight. We'd agreed on 7pm, and I knew he'd show up early to spy on me and get a read on my mental state.

One thing I was getting better at now was listening to my gut. It told me to keep looking. So now that I'd identified the origin of the word terror, *she* was next on my list. Though it seemed like a very retro name, I found twenty-three Genevieve Lucas entries on social media – Facebook, Instagram, Snapchat, and three on TikTok all with inscrutable usernames. I read through them one by one with no expectations, surveying pictures, reading profiles, my radar heightened to anything that might ping my intuition. Nothing. These women were too young, mostly early twenties. I tried using a Dr. prefix, a P.E. suffix for professional engineer, then I wondered about scholars. I tried using Professor and then with the word university after her name. There, I saw it. My heart beat a little faster, and a slight sweat in my palms. Ping.

Genevieve Lucas, Marine Biologist

And she was a professional diver, attached to University of Washington Seattle, with an address on Bainbridge Island on Puget Sound. Jesus. Another ping.

I got up from the table and walked around the kitchen, pulling air into my lungs to quell the pounding in my chest. On the Google search results page, it listed her as graduating from college in 1994, which would make her about forty-nine, a few years older than me. Interesting. Now at least I had something of substance to report to

Vaughn. I purposely left out an important part of my research - I hadn't gone to Google for an image-search. Seeing the face of a woman who'd haunted me in a coma terrified me, like it would be verifiable, visual proof that I'd in fact gone completely mad. And that was more than my psyche could bear right now.

# Chapter 11

**I made sure to raise the blinds** in the studio before Vaughn's visit. Having spent the night upstairs, I forced myself up by 9am with two cups of English Breakfast Tea that had enough punch to wake the dead. After a shower, shave and two pieces of toast, I was ready and typing notes at the kitchen table when he arrived. Blinds up, lights on, he knew all my tricks so there was no use pretending.

"Morning," he said walking right in without knocking, like old times. He regarded me behind shrewd eyes and joined me at the table. I'd already set out a cup of French press coffee with cream and no sugar, a saucer on top to keep it warm.

His eyes narrowed. "What are you gonna do next? Give me a foot rub?"

"Eww. Drink your coffee. I'll do the talking today."

"Fine. What's the word?"

I took another sip for fortification. "Bainbridge Island," I said.

"Okay. What about it?"

"I'm going there and you're coming with me."

"Um –"

"There's no um about it. Bainbridge Island feels right and I recognize I need some, how should I put it—"

"Supervision?"

"Exactly." I snapped my fingers, eyes wide engaged in the energy of my pitch.

He yawned, rubbed his face and took a few sips. "You haven't forgotten how to make coffee." It was quiet on my street, no cars, birds or sounds. Just the tension across the table. He swiveled the mug in his hands. "I'm guessing you found something?"

"Marine Biologist, though I'm not certain it's the right Genevieve Lucas."

Vaughn raised his eyes to the ceiling, which he did when he was deliberating. "Well, thinking objectively here, water, diving and marine biology fit the profile of your--"

"Imagery, let's say," I cut in. "I don't want to say dream because it wasn't a dream. I found myself diving deep below the surface, and I saw her long dark hair and she was trapped under the hull of a –"

"I know," he cut me off. "It's like an old pirate legend or Oak Island folklore, not a story your best friend tells you."

He'd never called me that before. I made no mention of it and tucked it away somewhere safe. "It just feels right to me."

"I'm actually having a hard time hearing you say things like something *feels right*. That doesn't sound like you, not the old you."

"Yeah, well, the old me is dead."

He set the mug down. "I see you opened the window blinds in the whole house."

I knew I couldn't fool him.

"Good plan for your physical therapists. For me, don't bother next time."

"Fine, I won't. Are you coming with me or not?"

He nodded. "I'll come, but not because I believe your bullshit story."

◦ ◈ ▣ ✛ ▣ ◈ ◦

So he didn't believe me. But I knew I'd successfully piqued his curiosity, or maybe he was just afraid I'd walk out into traffic. Didn't matter; he was coming and that meant I had the ally I needed. Now I could properly investigate, with an impartial observer, what my soul was guiding me toward.

I arranged for the speech and language evaluation to be done tomorrow morning instead of next week because I needed to orchestrate another long weekend to give us enough travel time. Assuming that went well, in combination with a glowing report from physical therapist Matt, I was sure I could concoct some excuse to cancel a week's worth of post-discharge therapies. The only wildcard was Alena.

Vaughn refused to drive to Washington because it would take too long. I admittedly wasn't keen on flying right now and never loved it to begin with. I'd have to deal with the discomfort. I was getting used to that. So I scheduled, booked, and paid for us to fly from SFO to Seattle direct on Delta, and was surprised to get two seats together in the very front of the plane. From there, I rented us a car where we'd make the one hour and forty-five-minute drive on route 305 from Seattle to Bainbridge. We needed a car there because I had no idea where we were going. I could sort out directions later, but I'd be using my inner compass for this trip and didn't want to feel trapped by logistics. Vaughn knew I wasn't ready for this trip and he was right. But I had no choice. I prepped by making myself eat three meals a day, up by 8am and lights out by 11. If I was gonna fake it like this, I needed the strength.

Today's Cognitive Linguistic Evaluation, they told me, could take 3-4 hours and would review attention, perception, memory, and reasoning, as well as social communication abilities. My speech capabilities were fine, better in some ways. An older woman named Carla knocked on the door in a long, flowered hippie-shirt holding out her card that had too many letters after her name to fit on one line. Her voice was warm and friendly, but the eyes told a different story.

The first thirty minutes were an exercise in mental fortitude and patience, and I knew the outcome could have profound consequences on my availability to investigate my mermaid ghost. Fine, I could play along. I imagined I was meditating, breathing in and out in very calm, even, controlled breaths. To her I probably appeared thoughtful, reflective even. After the initial set of questions to gauge my awareness of my current environment, we moved to my memories of what happened before the accident, before Jimmy

Breslin's bullet ruined my life, pretty much. Carla listened to my rendition, typing notes on her laptop that I suspected had less to do with my report than my demeanor.

"Let's talk about your nightmares," she said.

"How do you know I have them?" I asked. "Do all TBI patients?"

"Not all." Slight smile, which showed deep wrinkles, as if her face wasn't asked to smile very often. "Are they the same every time you dream, and how often do you have them?"

I had a choice here, several actually. I could tell Carla, a veritable stranger and most certainly not my ally, the truth about what I'd experienced during and after, and she would very likely recommend long-term psychiatric care. Brooke had no Power of Attorney over me, so it was ultimately up to me whether I went along with it, but that could complicate my ability to go back to work with Vaughn. I'd read about coma and TBI in medical school, of course focusing my attention on children. I'd been a pediatrician unable to save my seven-year-old son from an incurable disease. And hell no, I wasn't telling Carla about that either.

I decided to revert to the same, worn-out stories I'd read in medical journals and hope that would get this woman out of my house as quickly as possible.

"Not exactly the same and not every night." I paused to give the impression that I didn't want to share it, allowing her to use her skills and expertise and feel triumphant when she came away with a page full of notes.

"How do they make you feel? Curious? Frightened?"

"More curious than frightened, but I'm in a house that I can't seem to get out of. It has no doors."

I saw the corners of her mouth twitch, recognition in her eyes. "Anything else?"

"I'm not tethered there, but I feel tethered, like I can move around but I can't go far." That part was true. My eyes were half-closed and I'd changed to present tense in my rendition of it. She was typing faster. This was good. I did a few more descriptions like that, then rubbed my face and looked up at her. "I haven't had any dreams at all this week. I mean, they're probably not over but they're less frequent and I seem to be sleeping better, like longer in a stretch."

"Good." I watched a movement of her hand and her eyes that resembled going to the top of the page and clicking File/Save. "Your speech and language seem fine to me, Mr. Farin. I'm recommending a GCT of 15, which reflects only mild impairment. I'm on vacation for the next ten days but I'll schedule something for us at the end of the month. And if you have anything you'd like to talk about in the meantime, you can contact the office and my partner will be happy to speak with you."

I felt like jumping up and down. "Thank you." I held out my hand. I considered her vacation an early Christmas present. Fifty-nine minutes and she was gone. Whew.

# Chapter 12

**With that annoyance out of the way**, I could spend most of my time researching Puget Sound, while also keeping up to date on SFPD activities and open investigations. I no longer had access to any of the databases we used to track open cases, leads, and files, but I remembered which were the most high-profile and urgent. I sure didn't miss the politics of crime investigation and law enforcement, and Vaughn had even less tolerance than I did for those hidden agendas.

That would be my opener, I think, to hopefully get Vaughn talking about bureaucratic roadblocks, because he seemed to have endless energy for that. Who knows – maybe I'd be able to help. Vaughn was a talented, big picture visionary with no tolerance for granular details or the patience to track them. That was always my department, in his eyes. We'd have just under two hours' worth of flying time and the same amount of driving time, which would be my opportunity to launch my strategic pitch.

After the car reservation was set, boarding passes printed, suitcase pulled from the upstairs closet and a few things packed, I made my third of cup of tea, then poured it down the drain remembering I couldn't have caffeine this time of day and expect to fall asleep at a decent hour. My phone buzzed just as I placed a bag of decaf Darjeeling in a cup of boiling water to steep. Decaf - now I really felt dead.

I picked up my phone and called Brooke. She picked up on the first ring, which meant she was probably waiting for my call.

"Hey, Dad."

"Hey, sweetie." She sounded tired. Even so, her voice lit up a tiny lamp in my heart. "How are you?"

Pause. Probably the wrong question. "How am I?" she repeated.

"I'm sorry," I said. "I know I've been a little hard to reach lately."

"Forget about that. How are you doing? Are you okay?"

I tried to get through the pleasantries and excuses while scheming how to tell her about our upcoming trip. Maybe I shouldn't tell her at all. I couldn't remember being so conniving before my accident. Now it seemed for every interaction I was gaming for opportunity – for solitude, resources, support, anything I didn't have. It just didn't seem like me. Like what Vaughn said about my using language like "this just feels right". That was true – I never used new-age language like that before. In fact, we'd always made fun of that sort of hippie theatre, as we called it. Now I was the one on stage.

I gave Brooke a report of all my constructive news – physical therapy, speech and language, psych eval, and my schedule-normalizing practices. I sensed she wasn't buying it, because now she'd stopped talking again. I was sitting in the living room upstairs with my back to the windows facing the street. I heard something down on the front porch. God, no. Was she here? Fuck. Would she use her own key or knock? I quick-scanned the room for incriminating evidence and what I could hide quickly. Amazing how fear inspired efficiency. In twenty seconds, after muting my phone, I'd snapped my shaving kit, jacket, extra shoes and tech into the suitcase, zipped it shut, and stood it up against the wall behind the curtain, which hung behind one of two living room armchairs. Caitlin and I had picked these out together. I'd love to just toss them out the window.

"Brooke, can you hear me? The call may have—"

"Open the door, Dad." She rang the bell. Great.

I laughed loud enough so she could hear me. "Why didn't you say you were here? You don't have to ring the bell, you know that."

"Do I?"

I jogged down the staircase, opened the door, grabbed my daughter by the shoulders and looked in her eyes before pulling her into me. "You okay?" I asked.

"Are you disappointed I didn't call first?" Her brows were raised in opposition.

"Well, you did call first. What's going on?"

She followed me up the stairs, then ran past me and tore through the front door, stomping around in loud shoes room to room, opening doors, checking behind pillows. I smiled to myself. She was an investigator looking for evidence to support a theory. I secretly loved it, and also loved the fact that nothing would make her look behind the living room curtains. I was feeling pretty slick, Brooke sulking on the other living room chair, staring blankly out the window right above where my suitcase was tucked away.

I took the sofa opposite her. "What's the matter?"

"I think you're full of shit. That's what the matter is."

"Explain." As I awaited her inevitable barrage of imposing questions, a new idea hatched in my head. I was like a cartoon villain rubbing his hands together. Shame on me. Here goes nothing.

"What, did you talk to Vaughn? I never could trust him. What did that rat bastard tell you?"

Her brows rose again. Good. "He said he thinks you're planning something, he just doesn't know what."

"What does that mean, planning something?" I feigned anger. "Yes, I'm making plans for how I'm gonna piece my life back together."

"He told me not to tell you this, but he thinks you've been out all-night walking around alone, sleeping all day, and he's gonna ask you to come and stay with him for a few days so he can keep an eye on you."

I tried to keep a stoneface, but I just loved Vaughn for that cover story. It was beyond clever. It was bloody genius, proving undeniably that I meant something to him and, more than that, he believed at least some part of my story. The ultimate triumph.

I rose and pulled the suitcase out from behind the curtain, using one of my favorite tactics of all time – sandwiching a lie between two truths.

"What's –"

"You're right," I said. "I think it's a good idea actually, just for a few days. He's gonna let me do a few ride-alongs with him just so I can see how it feels, but mostly I'll stay in his apartment and watch movies and take his dog for walks. I think it's a good next step for me." It was enough to get her off the chair and over to the door. But not enough to convince a natural skeptic.

"You're vulnerable right now, Dad, in several different ways."

"Someone's been spending too much time with Alena."

"Any time with her is too much. I've been talking to people, consulting. What you went through medically makes you emotionally impressionable for the first month or so, prone to extreme highs and lows, depression, withdrawal, not to mention physical symptoms."

"Yeah I've noticed."

"Mentally vulnerable because of course you can't coordinate tasks and remember things with the same agility you used to before —"

"Before Jimmy Breslin shot me in the head, you mean?" It felt good to say it out loud and hear the sound of his nefarious name bounce off the walls. It reminded me that I wanted to visit Leticia Ames' parents. Maybe today was that day.

# Chapter 13

**Vaughn and I had been texting to** plan our escape. I said I'd meet him at the airport, and he called me two seconds later.

"No driving," he said, another term of engagement.

"Why the hell not? I've been practicing. Okay never mind, I'll Uber."

"No way, airports are too chaotic. I'd never find you. You'll end up en route to South America."

"Vaughn," I exhaled. "I'm not an invalid."

"You kind of are, actually. Right now, at least. I'll pick you up."

"One condition."

"No conditions, I'm leaving in twenty minutes. Be ready."

Instead of answering, I counted back from ten. I pictured him drumming his fingers on his leg.

"Okay, what?" he asked.

"I want to go see Leticia Ames' parents. I was planning to do that anyway and, assuming you haven't already been there—"

Pause.

"Look, I know I no longer work for the—"

"Fine, I'll take you," he said.

"Well that was too easy."

"That case got you shot, comatose, and essentially discharged from the PD. You've earned the right. See you in twenty."

* ◇ ▧ ✦ ▧ ◇ *

By some miracle, there was a parking space right outside my house when Vaughn drove up. I took it as a sign. He climbed out of his hundred-year-old Jeep Cherokee smiling, looking for me on the front porch where I was waiting with my suitcase ready to find my destiny.

"I'm starving," he said after I closed my door. "I don't suppose —"

"Not if we're gonna stop and see Leticia's parents. We can eat at the airport. Where do they live?"

"Mission. Twenty-first and Folsom." He'd memorized the address from the case file.

"You've been there?" I asked, wondering under what circumstances he'd visited the family.

"Yep."

"With Donnelly?" I asked, our former boss.

"I went alone," he said.

"Did you tell them we were coming today?"

"I didn't want to get their hopes up about Jimmy."

He was right. "I don't suppose you're allowed to reveal any new leads in the case?"

"Not much. He's gone underground, and my informant tells me he's planning to leave the country soon, which means he'll take a train with fake ID."

I liked this part of the Mission. The sky was a deep blue and the air crisp but there was little wind. The perfect balance. 21$^{st}$ and Folsom had a huge park and playground on one corner, with the usual zoning mishmash of storefronts, residential homes, and memorable architecture. We parked a half block away and approached the door of the Ames family home. I was the one who knocked, feeling obligated since this errand had been my idea. I still wasn't even sure what we were doing here. Somehow, I felt like I needed to share my fate with the family so they'd know Jimmy took something from both of us, and maybe that might make them feel a little less alone in their grief.

Leticia's mother answered the door, her husband behind her with his hands on her shoulders. She was short and stocky with a sagging face, hunched shoulders, grief eating its way through bone and blood. I'd been there. I remembered that purgatory. The woman opened the door wide. "Yes?"

"We're from the San Francisco Police Department." I no longer had a badge to display, so the moment turned awkward while they waited for it. "I was wondering if we could have a minute to talk to you." I made sure not to mention their daughter's name and remembered from the casefile that Leticia had three sisters, she'd been the oldest.

Mr. Ames tucked his wife away in the other room. He returned to the front entry and instructed us to have a seat on a sofa, while he stood awkwardly over us.

"What can I do for you?" he asked, standing tall. Vaughn looked at me, a cue that he wanted to talk first. This had always been our play – him the volatile bad cop, me the gentler voice of reason.

"Mr. Ames, I'm Detective Vaughn. I was here a couple—"

"I remember you. What can I do for you gentlemen? Is there an update in my daughter's case? Did you find him?"

"We're still working on that," Vaughn said under his breath. "We've turned up some new information but have yet to locate him."

"And no new information about his connection with my daughter?"

Vaughn shook his head. "Not yet. I'm sorry. But rest assured it's our top priority and we're investigating every possible avenue."

I would have left out the 'rest assured' part. The old man looked on, interested, waiting to hear the reason for the interruption to their evening of pain, considering we essentially still had nothing of consequence to offer them. I glanced at photographs on the mantel of what was probably Leticia with her three sisters, four beautiful girls with the same dark hair, eyes, and refined features. I rose. My turn.

"Mr. Ames, my name is Detective Kurt Farin. I was one of the original investigators in your daughter's case. I came here tonight to let you know that I was there the night we found Jimmy at The Stork Club. We used information we uncovered and tips from one of our informants to determine he'd be there that night."

"You tried to stop him. I heard the report," the man said.

"He shot me," I added. The man looked at the floor and backed up a few paces.

"That bullet put Detective Farin in ICU, Mr. Ames," Vaughn said. "He's not fully recovered yet from a severe concussion and he's been discharged from the PD. He just wanted you to know—"

"I wanted you to know that even though I can't work on your daughter's case anymore, I-I," and my voice caught. Tears filled my eyes; I couldn't help it. "I care. I just wanted you to know that. You lost your oldest daughter, and your family will never be the same because of it. One way or another we're going to find him and bring him to justice." I came forward and reached out my hand. The man grasped it. His hands were cold, of course they were. His heart was barely beating.

"Thank you for coming, Detective. I hope you recover."

"We'll be in touch when we have more details to share," Vaughn added as we slipped out the front door. I liked how he'd said *when* instead of *if*. I was careful not to slam the door when I left last but also made sure to close it. It made a quiet click behind me. I always loved the Mission. Where else could you find a beautiful mural on every street corner?

"Detectives," Mr. Ames called from behind us. "Wait, please." He closed his front door and crept down the front stairs to meet us at the car. Interesting that he didn't ask us back inside. He had something to share that he hadn't shared with his wife.

"You learned of a connection?" Vaughn asked over the roof of the Jeep.

Mr. Ames nodded, lips tightly clamped, eyes wide.

"Before you start, how did you learn of this connection?" I asked, quickly realizing I shouldn't be asking any questions. You don't work for the PD anymore, idiot. Get used to it.

The man sighed, swallowed and wiped his mouth. "My daughter. My oldest, sorry, second oldest daughter. Leticia told her, I just learned, something about her boyfriend, Marcus Reyes."

I snapped a look at Vaughn. "Did you know Leticia had a

boyfriend?"

"No. Keep going, please," he said to the man.

"Jimmy Breslin tried to kill Marcus Reyes, Leticia's boyfriend, twice in fact. Now Marcus has vanished and left town about two months ago."

"Does he know about your daughter?" Vaughn asked this time.

"I don't know. I only just found out about him yesterday. Daughters don't speak of boyfriends to their fathers."

Vaughn and I took in this new detail.

"I think Jimmy killed…" The man paused again and looked at the ground. "I think Jimmy killed my daughter as a warning to Marcus if he testified against him."

I was on the passenger side of Vaughn's Jeep with Mr. Ames. Now Vaughn walked around the front of the car and stood opposite the man, making a circle, sensing there was a deeper story here.

"Do you want to go—" Vaughn said, looking back toward the house where four dark-haired women huddled at the front window.

"No!" the man blurted. "Sorry, no. Right here is fine."

"Alright then. What's the connection between Leticia's boyfriend Marcus and Jimmy?" Vaughn asked.

"Marcus witnessed something that would place Jimmy at a crime scene with criminal intent in an open federal case."

Vaughn scratched his neck. "A capital murder case?" he asked. It seemed unlikely that we hadn't seen that in our search.

Mr. Ames nodded. "He was going to testify. Leticia wanted him to walk away. That's what my other daughter tells me."

"Why didn't he?" Vaughn asked. "Walk away I mean."

Mr. Ames shrugged. "He's a lawyer. A prosecutor. So justice, I guess."

Jesus.

"With the District Attorney's office?" Vaughn asked.

"I don't know. I think it's a private firm."

"What firm?" Vaughn pulled out his phone to record the name.

The man looked at the ground. "I don't remember. You can find him online, I'm sure. Gransky-something."

# Chapter 14

**"So they knew each other.** Holy fuck."

Vaughn didn't respond, he didn't have to. I knew what he was thinking. Every investigator felt it when something like this came up after the fact, wondering how you missed it, what steps were left out.

"Seems like big news, don't you think?"

"How are we doing on time?" he asked, changing the subject. "Dinner?"

"No." It seemed odd, Vaughn's deep hunger and passion for food. I'd lost most of my passions, maybe temporarily, maybe not. Strong coffee, fine pinot noir, New York style pizza.

"Well, with this new information, I need to get this data added to the case file. If there's no time to stop in at work, I need to at least call---um—"

"Dude, it's okay," I stopped him with a gratuitous nod. "I know someone's taken over as your partner. I'm fine with it." I was only unconscious for a few days, in ICU for ten and out of work for a few weeks. It seemed unthinkable that they'd dismiss me so easily, unless they thought I wouldn't recover. I knew it was a painful subject and I dreaded bringing it up again, but I was the farthest thing from *fine with it.*

"Actually, no one's been officially assigned. But I'm getting all kinds of support that I never got before."

"Really?"

"Hell yeah. Admin support, evidence processing, like preferential treatment since I'm suddenly running solo."

"Do they bring you lunch too? Maybe you should've gotten me shot a long time ago."

"Ouch." His face sank.

"Sorry, inappropriate joking must be part of coma recovery." I pulled out my phone and Vaughn navigated through the city to SFO.

"How'd you get the time off?" I asked him.

"For this trip?" He winked. "I have the flu."

"You know what that means, right?"

"That's superstition. I'm not gonna get the flu."

"Just sayin'." I looked up Attorney Marcus Reyes and found the Google listing for his firm. "Got it - Gransky, Tatum, Barnard and Nguyen, with two offices. And... this is interesting. They've got offices in San Francisco and Seattle." I looked at him and smiled. "It's a sign."

"Of?"

"That we're headed in the right direction."

"Actually, we're not."

"What now?"

He pointed. "The on-ramp's closed. They're detouring us through downtown. What time's our flight?"

In sixteen minutes, Vaughn managed to navigate us to 280S and then 101 to the airport. He must have been a cab driver in his previous life.

"So... what's going on with you and Alena?" he asked, deftly weaving through traffic.

"Nothing. Why do you ask?"

Smirky grin, head shaking.

"Okay. I don't know what you heard, but she's installed herself on my medical team as my official case worker, even though she's not even part of that medical system. The whole thing's preposterous. I'm ignoring her as much as I can. She came to you?"

"Crosswords."

I laughed.

"She told me they'll help your brain recover. She gave me a stack of them to give you because she knows you want nothing to do with her right now."

"There's nothing wrong with my brain. In some ways it's better than it was before. The problem is my nervous system's shot."

"Isn't that typical right now though?"

I looked at him.

"I did some research while you were… out. Apparently all the circuitry in your brain is altered so it's not surprising that your nervous system is booting back up, so to speak." He shrugged. "Read a few medical blogs is all."

"I guess. I'm trying not to think about it."

He turned his head and glared. "Well, we're about to get on a plane, you know that right?"

"Watch the road. What about it?"

"Even a raised voice could get you arrested now. Planes are operated these days like a military compound."

I ignored his warning and had a feeling there would be more of them. It was a weird time of day to fly, departure at 4:40 arriving in Seattle at 6:47. The line of passengers to board showed the plane barely even half full. Mid-afternoon now, the sky started to darken, thank God, satisfying the vampire I was quickly becoming.

Cabin lights off, I felt the initial lift of the plane and its rise to cruising altitude. When we reached 10,000 feet and could use Wi-Fi, I opened my laptop, dimmed my screen and brought up Google. Vaughn never got the chance to call in the new lead from Mr. Ames, so he emailed his new partner, still pretending he hadn't been assigned one.

I closed my eyes, allowing my newly opened mind to decide what I should research, igniting my previously nonexistent intuition and imagination. I found myself gravitating to more esoteric things now - energy healing, astrology, dream symbology and synchronicities, like they had more relevance now. Maybe they did.

Floating in the cool liquid of my blue cosmos, something in the center of my chest eased. A constant tightness, maybe from birth, relaxed anytime I was underwater. There was something umbilical, womblike about this place, even if it was just a mental construct. I widened my eyes and blinked a few times under my imaginary goggles and drew in a slow, even breath from my regulator. There was plenty of air in the tank, but I still breathed slowly and evenly like I'd been taught early on.

In my mind, I moved forward to get a view of the expanse. It looked different from when I was last here. Brighter, maybe reflecting an earlier time of day, but there was no direct sunlight shining down. In my early diving days, I'd flown all over the globe exploring old shipwrecks like in the British Virgin Islands, cave diving in Florida and the Yucatan, Norway, and eventually ice diving under grounded icebergs in the arctic near Baffin Island. Alena joined me for those dives, so many that it was hard to picture being in the water without her. All told, our friction felt heavy on my heart. Maybe that would work itself out too, someday.

Instead of Alena, another presence hovered behind me now in the dark - an image with a secret and, I sensed, an agenda. Something caught my eye to the left, a school of small fish, probably herring and, behind them, the edges of a coral forest, light on the ends and darker in the middle with open cavities, a typical lair for eels. I had no interest in disturbing them, so I floated around the outcropping. Behind it something dark was sticking out, but not coral this time or sea vegetation. *Hair*. Her hair. Genevieve's head was pressed into the ocean floor, face down, one hand reaching out and the rest of her body covered by a large, dark structure. Before, it resembled metal with reflective flecks. Now it looked like wood. A ship's hull, or so it appeared from the familiar curve of a bow. When I'd been here before, I felt such a compulsion to reach her, to touch her with my hand as some sort of sanity confirmation. Test and verify, right? And now it looked more surreal, like this was just the imprint of her, a shadow of where she'd been - once. In my heart, I felt like she wasn't really dead, if she had even existed at all outside of my upside-down brain.

"How's it going, partner?" Vaughn leaned into my shoulder and nudged me.

"Quick flights are so pointless."

"Here we go."

"I'm serious. By the time you get nestled in and comfortable, it's over and then it's time again to haul all your luggage, stand in line."

"You'd rather spend twelve or fifteen hours driving?"

"Maybe, yes."

Vaughn was nodding. "See?"

"What?"

"This is what I told you. Traveling sucks. Traveling is stressful, super inconvenient, unpredictable, and you're not emotionally agile enough yet to roll with it."

"You're right, I'm not." I stretched my lips into a smile. "That's why you're here."

"Okay, buddy, I got you. One day at a time, right?"

"When we land it'll be time for dinner."

"Hallelujah."

# Chapter 15

*April*

**A flight attendant recommended Spencer's Steak House** just past the airport rental car hub. The Marriott, where I'd booked our room, was a mile away. No issues getting the car, other than Vaughn insisting he was the driver for the entire trip because I was still impaired. No argument there. The flight exhausted me and I had no fight left, tonight anyway. Vaughn seemed impressed by my splurging for a nice room. I was glad I'd made him feel like he was important to me. He was, of course, but even more than that, I was glad I'd made him feel needed. And not because he'd been my friend and partner for five years. There was something else, something sinister - leverage. Was I turning into a gangster? I couldn't exactly pinpoint when the change started happening. I used to be selfless and compassionate. Now, like someone else was inhabiting my body, I was all and only about personal gain. I didn't like how it felt, but I also wasn't willing to hide anymore either. Welcome to the new irreverent me.

I'd noticed the chairs in the Marriott's Aqua Terra restaurant, the next morning, were an annoying shade of bright red, another sensitivity. But the breakfast was served in an adjacent room with low lighting, gray wooden tables and dark brown chairs. What a relief. Vaughn and I seemed to be bickering a lot, and without the comedic undercurrent of fondness like we'd always had before. I knew I was short tempered and irritable now, vexed by the stress of traveling and constant daylight forced upon me. I could tell Vaughn didn't know what to make of me and my new set of quirks, unaccustomed to walking on eggshells around me or anyone else.

"You're driving, I'm talking," I said between bites of egg and sips of coffee. Hotel restaurants could almost always be counted on for good breakfasts.

"No idea what that means, but okay."

"You're insisting on doing all the driving, fine. But when we get to Bainbridge Island, I'm doing the talking. This is my investigation."

Brow raise. "Okay."

"I'm the one who—"

"I said okay. I'll take your lead and I'm here for support, wherever it's needed. But just to be clear, it's not my fault you can't drive."

"Alena?"

"Brooke. She made me promise. Not sure why you'd want to drive, anyway."

"To feel normal for God's sake," I said with an unintended whine.

He was shaking his head and it was barely 8am. At this rate he'd probably be flying home alone.


Highway 518N turned into 99N. Five miles later, that road turned into the ferry launch, where we drove our rental car onto the lower deck.

"We're on a ferry, in a car. What movie am I thinking of?" he posed. I missed the movie trivia games from our long stakeouts. This time, I knew it was a memory test, probably concocted by Alena. I tried not to blame him. He was worried about me. I could see it, a new vertical ridge in the middle of his forehead that was never there before.

"Shoot to Kill," I said.

"Good guess," he smiled. "Nope."

"Okay… got it. Double Jeopardy. Ashley Judd." I laughed. "She actually drove his car into the water. Don't worry, I'm not that crazy." Hopefully that was true.

* ─◈─ ◁◈▷ ✚ ◁◈▷ ─◈─ *

It was too cloudy to see Mount Rainier or even the Seattle skyline from the ferry, and too windy to stand on deck. Vaughn saw me huddled with my arms wrapped around myself in one of the indoor, downstairs booths and asked if I'd be more comfortable sitting in the car. It was an unkind joke and meant to be so. Aggravating him without even trying. A bad sign.

We drove off the ferry ramp and followed the curved exit road to the highway, ignoring each other, both enjoying the silence.

"Okay, navigator," he said finally. "Navigate."

I squinted to shield the view of my phone from the blinding sunlight, which stimulated a still-tender part of my brain. I felt like crying. "That's right," I managed, pointing straight ahead. "Wyatt Way Northwest, keep going. You're gonna follow that around, then turn left on Eagle Harbor and right on Taylor."

"Address?"

"5276 Taylor."

"Got it." Vaughn drummed his fingers on the steering wheel. A hard question was coming, I could feel it.

Long sigh, then, "Can I assume someone will be expecting us?"

"No," I answered quickly.

The car slowed, screeched to the edge of the road and rolled across the gravel. "What are we doing here? I mean, Jesus. Seriously?" He clicked the motor off. Cars were speeding past us. We were in a dangerous spot, barely even on the shoulder.

"Can't we—"

"Give it to me," he said.

"Give what to you?"

67

"All of it. Come on." He waved his hand. "All the details, right now or I'm leaving."

"I knew you were thinking of leaving."

"I wasn't until now!" He flattened his hands on the steering wheel. "I'm sorry," he said in a quieter tone. "Who lives at 5276 Taylor?"

I shrugged. "Genevieve Lucas."

"*The* or *a*?"

I shrugged. "That's what I read online."

A single nod. "And where did you hear that name? To begin with, I mean."

"You know where." I turned my head but didn't look in his eyes. "I just sort of knew of her when I woke up."

"Okay. And then you did a search for every Genevieve Lucas in the United States? West Coast? What?"

"I looked on social media and found a bunch of young women, early twenties with that name and none of them felt right."

"What about this one *felt right*?" he asked, mocking me.

"She's my age, for one thing. A little older. And she's a marine biologist."

Nodding. "Keep going."

"I also read something about diving." I braced myself for another outburst but instead he leaned back, hands on his thighs, thinking. "Okay, that's reasonable. I get it. And you didn't call first and tell her we were coming because—"

I laughed. "I'd sound like a fucking stalker or a mental patient."

"Right." He turned to face me. "What are you looking to find here, Kurt?"

I got lost in a moment listening to a fragment of a Maroon5 song from a passing car. It was a great question, great song too. I noticed Vaughn wasn't starting the engine until I gave him an answer that satisfied, I don't know, whatever test he was conducting. Did he even know what that test was? The constant microscope of him, Brooke, and my medical team was starting to break me.

I closed my eyes, trying hard to ignore the roar of traffic flying past us. I leaned back like a diver falls into the water from the gunwale, tumbling, deeper, turning around to get oriented, looking out at the expanse of bubbly blue, fish, and sea vegetation, basking in the immense landscape of quiet. I realized, just then, that it wasn't the lights that bothered me but noise. Noises that never bothered me before. Nothing matched the insulated silence of deep water.

I came back to Vaughn's question - what did I need from this encounter? It was a straightforward question and he was right to ask it. I was pulling a thread, following something that my heart and soul were leading me to. I guess I needed validation, to see if Genevieve Lucas looked like the woman in the blue cosmos, to see if she felt familiar and if I felt as familiar to her.

"Are you sleeping, or did you even hear me?" he asked.

"What am I looking to find? I don't know why I say this, but a piece of myself."

# Chapter 16

**"There." I pointed at what looked like** a summer cottage with natural shingles and yellow-painted window trim.

Vaughn slowed the engine, hovering at the edge of the driveway. "How do you know?"

The house number wasn't visible from this angle. I shrugged.

"You just know?"

"I guess."

I liked this house. It was two houses, really, with in-law quarters in the back. I liked the driveway paved in tiny, black pea gravel. The landscaping was mature but not manicured. Vaughn monitored me for some kind of definitive lightning bolt in lieu of a house number. I nodded, because I knew some part of my broken brain had led us here.

We parked in the front part of the property directly under the odd set of yellow windows, which meant the car wouldn't be visible. Did she even live here? Did she have renters living in the back, or her mother, or did she use it as a private office? My imagination was running wild. And wasn't there another building here somewhere, near the water? How would I even know that?

Before he'd even cut the engine, I got out and walked through the front yard of the property with my arms around my body, sniffing.

Honeysuckle, maybe from here or a neighbor's adjacent yard.

Black tar – someone must have just repaved their driveway.

And a faint odor of low tide. Most people hated it but I'd always loved that musky scent of salty sea and stale shellfish, when the ocean disrobed and showed us its bare skin.

"Okay," he said getting out to meet me, hands dug low in his pockets. "What's the pitch?" He was glassing the neighborhood with one eye toward the house, like he expected an old man to stumble out with a shotgun.

"I'll just tell her—"

"Tell her what?" someone asked. "Who are you?"

A young woman, early thirties, light hair, thin scarf coiled around her neck and cuffed pants glared at us from the corner of the house. I'd just noticed that there was no visible front door from the street. Bad curb appeal. Perhaps I shouldn't share that right now.

"Um, hello!" My voice came out too chipper. Now she'd think I was a real estate agent. I took one careful step toward her. Vaughn was closer to her and didn't move a muscle.

Her eyes were quick, darting from one to the other, performing a fast-track threat assessment. I could tell she was busy and had no patience for nonsense. Her right hand gripped a pen and her fingernails were scratching the cap as she eyed us. "You know this isn't a parking lot, right?"

The woman's small face was a perfect oval, the untrusting eyes close together, apologetic mouth, and what looked like beautiful hair jailed within dark brown clips. Just like Brooke.

"Can I help you?" Now the tone had changed.

"Sorry, we might actually have the wrong house," I said. "We're looking for someone named Genevieve Lucas, who I think is much older than you." I was fine with that pitch, actually. It was slightly apologetic, somewhat disarming without being ingratiating. She was taking too long to answer. What could that mean?

"What do you want with her?" she blurted.

Vaughn and I froze. OMG. Had we found her, found the right house but just the wrong woman? Was she old enough to have a thirty-year-old daughter? Now, suddenly, it felt real. I took in the woman's bookish visage, chiseled features, smooth complexion, and a sadness that hung from the edges of her eyes. I don't think I'd ever envisioned even getting this far, so I had no idea how to respond. My hands were shaking.

Vaughn gave me a single nod. I opened my mouth but couldn't speak. "We read about her work and wanted to ask her a few questions," he said, thankfully filling the silence.

It was working. The woman didn't move toward us but she didn't back away either. The threat assessment was taking longer but I sensed we were going to pass. It could have been a reflection of sunlight from something on the roof of the house, but there was something shiny on the woman's face, her eyes, one eye in particular. Was she crying? Oh God. What have we done?

"I'm cold," she said finally. "You'd better come in."

We followed her around the left side of the house, stepping on the gravel walkway that always felt like a foot massager under the soles of my shoes. I watched the mechanical way that the woman's thin body moved. She stepped up the stairs, revealing muscular calves when her pant legs rode up.

"In here," she instructed, holding the door to a sunporch. Vaughn went in first, since he was the one who'd made a good impression on her. We waited until she motioned us to follow her into the house. It smelled like plants or soil or something. No. Riper than that. Vegetables, or more like seaweed. That low tide smell again. Was it coming from inside? Of course, Genevieve Lucas, or the one I'd read about online, was a marine biologist attached to University of Washington at Seattle.

Vaughn and I hovered, unsure where to go or what to do once we got inside the gloomy interior. I could tell this woman didn't live here but she knew the house well. She pulled keys from her pocket and set them on a side table, then looked thoughtfully back at us, still in the threshold between the sunporch and the living room. She did not invite us to sit; I thought that was noteworthy. Instead she sinched her thin jacket around her body and stepped slowly toward us so we formed a semi-circle.

"Should we... do introductions?" I asked, terrified of the response, then wished I hadn't.

"You can tell me who you are and what you're doing here and then we'll see." She spit out the words all at once.

Vaughn did that disarming routine that always worked so well. It involved a sort of exhalation, slight smile, lowering of his head, shoulder shrug. Apologetic bordering on pathetic. "I'm Detective Vaughn, San Francisco Police, this is my partner Kurt Farin."

I liked how he said that for simplification, despite how it was no longer true. I gave her a quick nod, then my eyes moved to Vaughn, terrified of what he might say next.

"Kurt was shot in the line of duty, sustained a gunshot wound to the head which left him unconscious for a number of days. And... when he woke up, he started saying the name Genevieve Lucas." Another shrug. "That's really all I know. Kurt can add more details."

The woman stared wide-eyed at me, unblinking eyes that I thought were brown but now looked dark blue. They blinked at an uneven pace, as I watched her brain trying to process this ridiculous report. Almost a minute, an unthinkable span of time, passed before anyone spoke, letting Vaughn's words fill the room. "Is this true?" she asked me, her eyes filling up.

"Yes," I said.

"Out of nowhere, you –"

"Not nowhere, no. Out of my, well, impaired unconscious state."

"You were in a coma?" she asked, the eyes studying my face.

"I just said her name out loud when I woke up," I said.

"Please, have a seat."

She motioned toward the living room but didn't move or lead us in there.

"Do you know her, or did you know her before you were, um, injured?" she spoke slowly, like she was being careful with her words.

"No."

The woman inspected the floorboards, moving her feet slightly, nervously, still standing. "So, you're saying that you—"

"I saw her," I blurted.

"What?"

"I said I saw her. I heard her voice, too."

Vaughn closed his eyes and shook his head.

The woman came into the living room now and sat on the sofa

across from us, where we sat in armchairs. The furniture was oddly placed, each piece too far away from the others, lacking in intimacy with no discernible color scheme or décor. This had to be someone's summer home.

"We've revealed some pretty personal details here and introduced ourselves," I said. "I think it's your turn."

Now there were tears in her eyes. Oh my God. My hand covered my mouth in an involuntary move.

"Are you Genevieve Lucas?" I asked, knowing this was not the woman I'd seen in my head, underwater in the blue cosmos.

"No, but you're not in the wrong place." She wiped her eyes. "Genevieve Lucas is dead. She was my mother."

# Chapter 17

**We sat there like that, the three** of us in our respective seats in a dreary living room, musty from long-shut windows, mostly unlit, the woman negotiating her tears while appraising the unbelievable story I'd just served up. Vaughn and I, eyes wide, not breathing, took it in now that the words had been spoken to somebody else, making it more real.

"What's your condition?" she asked breaking the silence, startling me. "Are you safe, I mean, is it safe for you to be out walking around?" It was an interesting question, considering all the other possibilities.

I said "Yes" and Vaughn said "No" at the same time.

Her chest rose and fell with one final breath before speaking. "Okay. I'm Anabel, Genevieve Lucas' daughter. She lived here in this house. I live in the guest quarters in the back. For now," she added.

"I'm so sorry for your loss," Vaughn managed, and thank God he did because I was about twenty thoughts away from that one. It was the right remark at the right moment, something I could never get right. Genevieve Lucas was dead. Jesus. I rose and went to the front windows.

"Do you mind if I open these?" I asked.

"Yes," the woman said.

I opened the window, I couldn't help it, all three on that side of the house in fact. Anabel Lucas watched me, Vaughn hoping and praying, I was sure, that I didn't do anything too extreme. We'd made headway, accomplished at least two of our goals for this trip already.

- Genevieve Lucas did, in fact, exist in the world.

- We'd apparently found the right Genevieve Lucas, because when I said that I'd seen her and heard her voice, her daughter wept.

- And now we also knew the Genevieve Lucas who contacted me in the hospital… was already dead.

Had I expected otherwise? Not really. Okay, maybe I did. I was leaning down, gulping the fresh air from the open windows in through my nose, holding it deep in my lungs before blowing it out my mouth.

"You okay, buddy?" Vaughn asked.

"Yeah. Just need a minute."

"What does this mean, though?" Vaughn was asking now, addressing the question to Anabel.

"Hold on," I said. I moved back to the chair but didn't sit. "May I inquire… when she died?" I asked, like this detail might have some bearing on things. "I mean, years ago or—"

"It just happened," she clipped.

"When exactly?"

"Four months ago, almost to the day."

I sat to consider this detail.

"I hear her too," she said softly. "Driving mostly, and sometimes when I'm asleep. I don't know at the time that's who's talking, but —"

"But you know when you wake up," I interjected.

She nodded soberly, eyes still narrow and untrusting, hearing my words yet not convinced.

"Look, would you mind if I walked around outside a bit? Just in the backyard? I need some air."

"Go ahead," she said and disappeared into another room.

Vaughn grabbed my arm when I stood. "Where are you going?"

"I gotta get out of here. I'm suffocating."

"I'll go with you."

"No. Please, stay with her. I've really upset her and you're doing a great job as the stabilizer."

"Alright. Don't do anything stupid."


I felt like I might throw up. Grief roiled out of me, upward from my deep innards. My stomach and chest felt hot, vibrating with a force inside my body I'd never felt before. Equal parts nausea and sorrow, I ran, first from the steps on the gravel toward the guest cottage and then beyond that, behind it into a garden area. I sobbed as I walked, my chest heaving, my stomach still feeling strangely warm. I knelt on the ground with my hands on wet grass and just allowed it to overtake me, this force… whatever it was. I let it all drain from my eyes and nose onto the long green blades beneath me. On my hands and knees, I leaned back into yoga Child's Pose, my arms out straight in front of me, head resting on my hands, choppy sobs knifing through me.

What was happening? I think this was the first time I'd expressed any grief since waking up in the hospital, and probably long before that. Wind cut through hair on the back of my head. I heard seagulls squawking over me. I surrendered to it, this quickening. Then came a round of shaking. The scent of grass and flowers calmed my nervous system. I smelled rose and honeysuckle in the garden before me. The sun was trying to emerge from behind a dark wall of clouds, a tiny glint in the grass. Was there hope for me yet? I sat up, still with my knees pressed into the cool earth. And I heard the voice again. *Come.*

I can't say it came from anywhere in particular. When I looked up, I saw the most fantastic yard. Its shape was that of a winding road, but grass-covered, embellished with shrubs in the ground, plants in large, decorative pots, winding around the back of the property in a westerly direction leading toward the water. Loving my solitude right now, I walked the path and followed it forward, listening for another clue, that sultry, raspy, insistent voice. I remembered from medical school how memory and the olfactory system were serious business, evoking powerful and often instantaneous emotional responses from the slightest trigger.

The garden path wound around to the right, past a small but stately-looking gardener's shed. This had to be the end of the property, because the beautifully manicured yard ended in a gray, overgrown tangle behind the structure. I'd stopped walking so I could assess, not sure where I was exactly and knowing if I went too far out there'd be hell to pay, from someone. Wait. What was that?

From my position on the path, I leaned my head a few degrees left and caught the outline of an old building, originally white and now a weathered gray. The line of its left side was slanted up, away from the water. I moved my head to see the edge. *Come closer.*

She'd spoken again, my Mermaid Ghost, in the same timbre, volume, and pitch that I'd heard underwater. It didn't chill me like before. Maybe I was getting used to it, which seemed problematic in several respects. To me, this qualified as auditory hallucinations, and I had no post-discharge pharmaceuticals on which to blame this effect. Also problematic was the fact that I'd now need to outright lie to my medical team when I saw them next week, unless of course they failed to ask.

I kept going, following the path around to the left and saw the same tangle of dead brush stacked against the back of what looked like a hundred-year-old boathouse. I drew in the pungent low tide scent, my nose still blocked from my outpouring, and came around the front of the structure. There was an opening, where a door used to be attached to hinges that had also worn down from time and weather. A larger opening, the size of a garage door, led to a stack of old canoes hung on hooks on the left side and, on the right two rusted aluminum canoes, assorted life jackets, random oars and paddles.

I felt heat again rising from my belly to my chest. Oh God, not again. I covered my mouth with my fist, breathing fast into my rolled-up hand, tears again falling from my eyes. Was this what a breakdown felt like? Breathe, Kurt. Breathe. Okay, I kept breathing in, breathing out, moving step by step through the open cavern, smelling something that resembled glue. Oh my God.

"Here he is!" Vaughn's voice calling out behind him. "Hey,

we've been looking for you."

I turned and saw my friend, a man who'd called me his best friend, his outline darkening the smaller open doorway.

"You okay, buddy?" he asked.

I shook my head and stood there, my legs wobbling from the latest sequence of grief. "I think I've been here before."

# Chapter 18

**Three hours and two brandies later, I** felt a bit more composed. It was obvious that staying in the Seattle Airport Marriott would be inconvenient, considering the nearly two-hour commute. Anabel said we were welcome to stay in the main house, so Vaughn left to check us out of the hotel and bring our stuff.

"I mean, it's not clean," Anabel warned, she and I standing in the hallway that led to the bedrooms in the back of the house.

"I'm sure it's fine, more than fine," I said.

"I'm a bit of a neat freak," she added. "Kitchen and bathroom are hospital clean. Everything else, well, you'll see."

"You're okay in the guest house alone?" I asked her. "It looks huge."

"It's not really, the garage just makes it look big. There's only one floor with one bedroom, one bath, kitchen, and a small den. It's perfect for me. I've been living there for three years."

"Oh?" I wanted to hear more about her life.

"We worked together."

"So you're also a marine biologist?"

"By education yes," she explained. "But not in practice, and I'm not a diver like her. I'm more of a researcher."

"What's your area of interest?" I asked. I could tell she liked the question.

"I research industrial threats to marine ecosystems. My mother was on the exploration side of things. I've launched a number of academic studies to gather data, I do a lot of writing and, lately, a lot of lobbying, which my mother thought was my real strength but a complete waste of time."

"Lobbying for the environment?" I asked. "Not to me." Understatement.

The hard lines around her mouth softened. "She always said I'd be a wonderful litigator, that I was naturally good at negotiation. She badgered me to go to law school and get a real paycheck. Persuasive writing, too, everything she hated. Research was just never her thing. She was more hands-on."

"An adventurer," I said and smiled.

Anabel Lucas pressed her lips together, almost like she was stopping herself from talking.

"Can I ask you… I'm not sure you're ready to talk about it. I'm _"

"How she died?" she asked.

I nodded. "Was it a diving accident? And did it happen here?"

I asked carefully, dying to tell her what I saw. It had all seemed too fantastic a story to articulate to sane people. But now Genevieve had spoken to me again, and here, which meant something more. I was sure I'd been in that boathouse before, though I had no conscious memory of it. How did one relate to the other? I needed to see where she died, that would be a start. See if it resembled what I'd seen in my head.

"It was a diving accident but not in Puget Sound. She'd been diving a lot lately, in Canada, and in Alaska."

"Cold water." Another thing we had in common.

"Yeah, she loved the cold. She was into wreck diving, and there are a lot of shipwrecks off Kodiak Island."

Cold water? Shipwrecks? I tried to keep a straight face, quietly jubilant that there was now another point of alignment between Genevieve Lucas and me. I'd seen her with my own eyes in the water half pinned beneath what had looked like the hull of an old ship. Though I didn't think she was wearing a wetsuit at the time. Her left arm was reaching out and it was her bare skin.

"Did she find a ship?"

Anabel moved into the living room and sat on the far end of the sofa. "She found it alright."

"What happened?" I moved to sit beside her but she got up the minute I did, her palms up.

"I'm sorry. I can't do this now." She left, letting the door crack hard against the doorjamb. The sound echoed. Afternoon sunlight spilled long shadows from the curved back of a chair against the hardwood floor, dry and scuffed. I stood at the bay window in the dining room looking directly out at the bright sky, practicing my daylight tolerance.


My phone buzzed sometime later. It was Vaughn calling me. "Hey. Are we checked out?" I asked.

"Yeah, and I called the Gransky law firm and made an appointment for us to talk to someone tomorrow morning."

I considered this. "This ought to be good. Talk to who exactly, and about what?"

"I said we have a few questions about maritime law as it relates to salvage ownership. The woman said that was the primary area they cover and that they'd be glad to offer a free thirty-minute consult."

I nodded. "Cool. That'll get us in the door anyway, though we're interested in nothing of the sort."

"Well, so far."

"Are you on your way?" I asked.

"Yeah, I'm about an hour out. How's it going over there?"

"Ah. Well, it appears I asked the wrong question again and she left. You did leave me alone with her. This was bound to happen eventually."

"Should I book us a hotel near the ferry launch?"

"No. She invited us to stay and I think we'll be okay. Hey Brooke's calling me. Can I—"

"Yep, see you soon."

Of course I sent the call to voicemail. What in God's name would I even tell her? I wandered back to the boathouse as if pulled by some invisible cord through the winding, green channel, past a carp pond, piles of dead vines and sticks layered behind the ancient structure. In my head I was down there again, sinking lower into the dark expanse. I was still able to summon the blue cosmos and implant myself there. Sitting on the ice cold, concrete floor, I was mentally floating down through the water, a trail of bubbles around me zigzagging to the surface. But this time my eyes were open. The smells in here took me back somewhere, a long time ago. Before this trip, I'd never been to Bainbridge Island, never even been to Washington.

So how could I have been here before?

I pressed Brooke's number in my contacts, because she was the only person who could possibly help me. Voicemail. "Hey sweetie," I said. "I'm fine, honestly there's nothing to worry about. I'll be home in a few days. But there's something I need your help with, and I think you're the only one who can help me with it. Give me a call when you can."

Anabel had crept in while I was leaving the message. She glanced around the boathouse, looking bewildered that I'd be sitting in the middle of the floor. She pulled her hair into a bun and lowered herself to the cold floor and met my gaze. "Your wife?" she asked.

"Daughter."

She nodded. "Look, I'm sorry –"

"You have absolutely nothing to apologize for. I'm some strange guy who showed up and crashed your party in the worst way possible. You were nice enough to offer to let us stay here. I shouldn't be – are you still okay with that?"

"Stay as long as you want. It'll be a comfort to have someone on the property."

"You get lonely?" I asked, quickly regretting such a risky question considering our last encounter.

She shook her head. "It's nothing."

"You hear things. Just like I do. Don't you?" I asked, already knowing the answer.

You could have heard a pin drop in there. "You know, it's been four months, but I never really grieved. I kept going with my work, using its structure and rigor as a support, never really talking about it to anyone. About her." Her voice was calm and steady "And now here you are, a not-so-random stranger, opening it all up again."

"I'm sorry."

"I'm grateful," she countered. "Maybe it's time."

# Chapter 19

**"What do you hear?" I asked her.** We were still in the boathouse sitting in the dark, the smell of mold and rot hanging low in the air. She wasn't bothered by it either. The sliver moon peeked above the horizon in a gray and orange sky, dripping a reassuring white glimmer on the water.

"Nothing like creaking doors in the night or anything."

"Do you ever walk along the water down there?" I pointed out to the right side of the island.

"Not for a long time," she said. "When I was little, we used to go down there and throw rocks in the water. For some reason I loved doing that. That's what she told me. Now it's all marshy and not really walkable." Anabel stretched her legs out straight and leaned back with her hands behind her, completely fine getting her nice clothes dirty. She looked prim but she was a scrapper, probably like her mother.

"You asked me before how she died."

I put up my hands. "That was way too invasive, you don't even know me."

"Don't I, though?" She mumbled it to herself. But I heard her.

I just stared now, wondering, listening to the water hit the rocks on shore, and to the question, gauging how it felt making its way through my body. Had I actually been here before? Did I have some connection with this place? I had to, or how else would I have found my way here?

"She was on a dive," Anabel said. "Alfred sent her the details of it, the coordinates, the dive plan."

"Alfred?"

"Alfred Ligetti, an old man she knows. He lives over there." She pointed to a spot on the south part of the island. "He's not a diver himself, not like her anyway, but he's a sort of shipwreck historian. They go back a long way."

"You said shipwreck."

She stifled a laugh, like that was a long story. "She'd been obsessed with this British naval ship, well, that was her latest obsession, and she was in northern Canada diving."

"Whereabouts?" I asked.

"This one's off King William Island in a territory called Nunavut in the Canadian Arctic archipelago. Anyway, middle of nowhere, basically. Alfred got her a permit. She'd been there before too, last year."

"A dive permit? Is it a historic site?" I asked.

"The ship sank in 1846."

"I guess so."

"Yeah, not only do you need a permit, but you need literally perfect conditions because of the location, otherwise it's a deathtrap."

"What was she looking for?" I asked, feeling like we'd veered onto an important topic. I stayed quiet and waited.

"That's another story, but she sometimes took off her gear to get into a small space, and—"

"You mean removing her tank and pulling it through? That's radical. I know people do it, but it comes with extreme risk. Diving's risky enough to begin with."

"I know. She was very experienced and she'd only do it for very short periods. It made me crazy. I hated the idea of her diving at all, honestly."

"Why?"

Anabel Lucas looked at me like I'd asked her to take off her clothes, her mouth frozen in this sort of awe.

"I mean, I've been a diver all my life," I explained. "I was just curious why you hated the idea of it."

No answer. More staring.

Okay, obviously that was a bad question, or at least the wrong one for right now. "Okay, no worries. You were telling me about King William Island?"

She nodded and breathed in to compose herself. I examined the dark gray sky with its thin stripes of orangey pink above the waterline. A million-dollar view.

"She got trapped down there," she said finally, her voice still calm. I had a feeling she'd taken a tranquilizer the last time she left the room.

"Did she have a partner with her?" I asked.

"Someone Alfred sent, a young guy who'd been diving with her for the past few years, Jerome. She went off in a different direction than their dive plan specified, not unusual for her," she added. "Jerome couldn't find her and he had to return to the surface. The captain of the dive vessel went down there with a full tank and a spare, but he never found her. A few hours later, Jerome returned to the dive site with the dive plan to retrace their steps. She'd added something to the plan, a notation but he didn't know what it meant. We still don't." She gave me a hard look.

"He found her?" I asked, realizing the risk of this conversation. I watched her closely.

One quick nod. "He found her in a part of the ship's hull. It was explicitly off limits to dive inside the ship, prohibited by the terms of the permit."

*A ship. A shipwreck. Just like I'd seen.* What was Genevieve Lucas looking for inside that ship that was worth dying for?

"Where's Jerome now?" I asked. "Could we talk to him?"

"We?" she asked.

"Vaughn and I." There I go again, thinking like an investigator, like a police detective even though I was no longer part of that world. "Sorry, you've probably already done that."

"Actually, there's no sign of him, not since she died. He didn't come to the memorial service and no one can reach him."

"Do you think he blames himself?" I asked. She blinked back. "Or do you think he could be responsible?"

"Responsible? In what way? She didn't have her oxygen tank on when Jerome found her inside the hull of that ship. She'd taken it off to get inside."

"I'm sorry," I said. It was all I could think of and I knew she needed to hear it.

"Everything was a death wish to her. You know?" she looked up. "One final dive, one final trip, one more time to see if she missed something."

"Missed something. Was she looking for something specific?"
More staring.

"What was the name of the ship?" I asked.

"Terror."

"What?" I couldn't breathe.

"The HMS Terror."

That word had gotten lodged in the back of my brain while I was under, and I'd never given it any thought before that. Then when I woke up, Brooke said I'd said it in my sleep. Had she, Genevieve, put it in my head? I needed some time alone to sort this out.

"She's a treasure hunter." Vaughn's jubilant tone snapped me back to the boathouse, the outline of him glowing from the moonlight in the open doorway for the second time.

"How long have you been here?" Anabel shot back.

"Long enough to hear that her dive partner disappeared the same day he found her. Sorry, I don't know how to not be a detective. I brought food, you guys must be hungry." Vaughn balanced a pizza box in his open palm.

"I am." Anabel got up and reached her small hand out to me in the dark, symbolic in a way, though it should have been the other way around.

◦ ◦◦◦◦◦◦ ✦ ◦◦◦◦◦◦ ◦

"I think we've all got a lot to think about. Why don't I go heat this up for us." Anabel took the pizza and disappeared into the dark, giving us a few minutes alone.

"She's right," I said.

"What are you two doing in here? You have two houses out there and this whole beautiful property and you're holed up in this… it's nasty in here."

"Telling stories," I said. Understatement.

"I'm starting to think you're a part of those stories, yeah?"

I stretched my legs and turned 360 degrees to gauge the space, small boats piled against the back wall, which obviously hadn't been used in fifty years. "I know I've been in this boathouse before."

"I thought you said you'd never been to Washington."

"I did say that, yes."

"What makes you think otherwise?"

"The cold, salty, moldy smell that has a faint scent of tar and glue. Do you smell it?"

"I smell mold, and it's gross frankly, not to mention a health hazard. I'm outta here. Come on."

Vaughn walked ahead and I followed. There were no lights out here now, other than some solar lights shining in the carp pond, and yet my feet and gait seemed to automatically know the bends of the path toward the house. So creepy.

"I liked what you said in there," I said.

"Which part?"

"You said 'she's' a treasure hunter. Present tense. A nuance, I know."

"I think you're interested in what she was looking for. I'm more curious about the dive partner."

"There were two," I said. "The young guy, who dove with her and seemed to vanish right after Genevieve's body was found—"

"Interesting timing, don't you think?"

"And an old man," I said, ignoring the question and approaching the back of the house. I turned around to face him. "Alfred Ligetti, she said he lives on the south part of the island. We need to find him."

"Why is he significant?" he asked.

I smiled, secretly delighted to acquire this clue. "He's some kind of shipwreck expert."

Vaughn studied my face. "And?"

"Because that's what she was doing down there."

"Wreck diving."

I nodded. "I know she was a marine biologist, but I think her secret passion was salvage diving."

# Chapter 20

**"Looking for what?"** Vaughn leaned in closer.

Anabel opened the sunporch window. "Pizza in about fifteen minutes."

"We'll be right in," Vaughn said, then grabbed my arm to move us away from the window. "Are you thinking—"

"I don't really know anything. But based on what Anabel said, I think Genevieve found something, like something of value."

"And you think someone killed her, someone who knew she'd found something and wanted to stop her from retrieving it?"

"Possibly. Anabel said she was an experienced diver. But she also said she routinely took off her gear if it got in the way of something she wanted to see," I added.

Vaughn nodded because he was cut from the same cloth. "Risk taker."

"Right. So I guess I've got a lot more questions to ask her."

"I can look into the dive partner who disappeared. What's his name?"

"Jerome, that's as far as I've gotten." I considered this as we moved toward the back steps. I could smell the pizza from outside and hadn't realized how hungry I was. I wondered how my stomach would handle food after this afternoon.

"Isn't that why you brought me up here?" he pressed.

"Sure, go ahead. I'll find out his last name." I stopped walking. "I need to go down there."

"Down where?" He looked bewildered.

I stared, answering with telepathy.

"You want to go - on a dive? I don't know if that's a good idea in your present state, and I'm sure Alena and Brooke would kill me if I allowed it."

"Allowed?"

"You can't be serious."

"I need to see what she was looking for."

He pointed up to the windows. "Just ask her daughter. She's twenty steps away from us."

"I don't think she's gonna tell us much, honestly."

"Why not?"

I sighed and turned away from the open window. "Not to state the obvious but we're like complete strangers, she's riddled with grief, completely depressed, and why would she trust us?"

He looked at the sky. "She trusts you. Already." Vaughn stepped back two paces. "I think this is why you brought me here. To help you arrange a dive. And if you did, that's pretty sly, bro."

"I didn't even realize this until today, so there was no premeditation. Even still, I need to do this."

"Where? Where's the site?"

"Northern Canada. Nunavut."

"Lord."

<hr/>

Vaughn brought in the overnight bags and I went inside. Splashing cold water on my face always felt like instant renewal. Right now I needed it, but my little ritual was interrupted by buzzing and beeping on my phone. I toweled off and peered without touching it with wet hands. I could see the missed calls in the notifications banner. Brooke, Brooke, Brooke, Alena, Alena, Brooke. Great.

"Hey," Vaughn knocked on the bathroom door. "Where am I

staying?"

"She said we could take any room, and there are sheets in the closet. Pick whatever one you want. The bags are across the hall." I opened the door. My phone beeped again in my palm.

"Popular guy," he said. "They're gonna call the police, you know, if you don't fill them in."

"Don't tell them anything! Please, promise me."

"No deal. I said I'd come up here to help you and that's all. My discretion was never discussed. And furthermore," he whispered now, "I still think you lied to me about your real agenda. You'd better be nice and I'll think about it."

I brought my bag to the room across from the bathroom and Vaughn took the one at the end of the hall. I was plugging in my phone charger when I heard his footsteps behind me.

"All kidding aside, you'd better tell them something. Tonight."

"Okay, okay, I will. Let me eat first. I'll think of something." I'd already thought of something. But he wasn't going to like it. Neither would Brooke.


We ate on paper plates, Anabel standing against the back wall in the kitchen rattling on about her aquatic ecology research and her paper on the protection of reef building coral species. Vaughn had asked her about her work. That was genius, because it took the intensity of our hapless situation down a few clicks.

I didn't dare ask anything else about Genevieve, though I'd come away from the conversations of the day with a trove of unanswered questions that were making my head pound. I excused myself after two slices and locked myself in the bathroom with my phone.

Earlier, I'd left Brooke a voicemail to call me, which she may have heard and ignored. New text tactic: *Hi sweetie, sorry I missed your calls, I'm fine. I'm hoping you can help me with something. LMK when you see this, it's important.*

Vaughn had left his phone on the bedside table in the back bedroom. I had that with me too so I could monitor whether Brooke texted him when she got my message. She hadn't yet. Maybe she'd help me with what I was about to ask her. And maybe it was snowing in hell.

"Have another piece," Anabel coaxed when I returned to the table. "I'm full and I don't think you've eaten anything all day, have you?"

"I don't eat as much now, since..." The vibe in the room instantly changed. "Sorry, didn't mean to be a downer."

Vaughn looked at her. "I think he's entitled."

"Absolutely. It's hard to believe how fast you've recovered," Anabel said, and I could tell she meant it. We ate and drank beers that she'd brought over from the guest house and did the chitchat thing and tried to feel comfortable there. But it all felt so forced. I just wasn't ready for any of this yet.

Vaughn had set up a meeting for us tomorrow morning at the Gransky law firm, where Leticia Ames' boyfriend, Marcus Reyes, worked before he disappeared. I used that as an excuse to get to bed early and rest. Vaughn was talking to someone on his phone in the other bedroom and Anabel had me lock the back door after watching her enter the guest house. I liked how she waved to me from the door, like a little girl waving to a long-lost friend. Had I really been here before? How could that be true if I had no conscious memory of it? Project Brooke was conceived to help me with that very thing. Maybe tomorrow she'd get back to me.

I slept without really resting. I was laying down, head mashed into a mushy pillow mismatched with the firm mattress, staring out into yet another world of unfamiliar darkness. First it was the darkness of my own head, then the darkness of the undersea world to which I'd traveled. This room had the hardest bed, I'd checked, purposely giving Vaughn the better mattress because I needed him right now. It also had a cheap clock radio on the bedside table. That's how I knew I'd been sleeping in bits and pieces. 1:45am. Then 2:40. I'd take what I could get.

I wondered about Anabel, everything about her. In some ways she reminded me of Brooke, similar in age and personality too. With Genevieve gone, who did Anabel have in her life to help stabilize her during that loss? Boyfriends, lovers, research partners? Did she work out at a gym, how did she spend her weekends? My paternal feelings surprised me, not because I felt the need to take care of her but more like protection. She seemed vulnerable here on this forgotten island. Or maybe some part of me felt like Genevieve had been murdered, and Anabel could be next.

On my second trip to the bathroom, I wandered into the kitchen remembering that this house had been vacant for four months. Naturally I looked in the fridge – the invasive equivalent of snooping through someone's medicine cabinet during a party. It smelled like lemons, the shelves sparkled, condiments lined up in neat rows. Hospital-clean, she wasn't kidding. A jar of mayonnaise on the bottom shelf had to have been designed by someone colorblind - blue label, brown cap. I opened the freezer and found two mostly empty containers of pistachio ice cream. My heart softened. It was Ryan's favorite flavor.

Vaughn was snoring loud enough to wake Anabel in the guest house, I could hear him from here. I went back down the hall to my room and, when I closed the door, I saw a light on outside that I hadn't noticed before. A glimmer from the street that showed a face that couldn't actually be real - a face at the window staring back.

I recoiled, nearly losing my balance, and heard a faint tapping on the glass. Wasn't this room on the second floor? Someone had to have climbed the large sycamore tree against the house. I stood frozen on the carpet wondering what to do. I could flip on the light, but startling the intruder could make things worse. Any normal person would have been terrified. I crouched down six inches and squinted to make out the face. Now the man waved his hand and knocked four times. The window was behind the headboard. Why not? I wasn't sleeping anyway.

I kneeled on the bed and reached up to unlock the window. It was the kind I had in the condo, with a lock at the top that you pulled forward to lift. I raised it up and saw the man's breath as he exhaled the cold, night air. It smelled like cigar smoke. Round, weathered face, early sixties, long hair that was silver and wavy, close-cropped mustache and beard with intense dark eyes. A perfect movie villain.

"Um…" I said through the screen. "Hello?"

"Hello!" The man snapped his head forward when he spoke, man on a mission. Wait, I knew that voice. I'd heard it somewhere. My stomach rolled just like it had in the boathouse earlier. God, not again.

# Chapter 21

**"Bit of an odd place to meet."**

The face was steel. "You are here about Genevieve Lucas, yes?"

Eastern European accent. "Seeing as I'm sleeping in her guest room, you could say that." I craned my neck to see out the window behind the man. "How did you—" I waved my finger. "The tree?"

"My bones might be old, Mr. Farin, but my heart is nimble."

"You have me at a disadvantage, then. How do you know me?"

He formed his face into a half-smirk and widened his eyes. I took them in, the round face, the way his hair grew only on the lower part of his head. Broad shoulders. In the same way that the mind feeds you fleeting fragments of dreams upon waking, it conjured an image of me as a little boy walking by the hand of a tall block of a man on a pebbled beach at the water's edge, him pointing into the water, distracting me, it seemed, from something going on behind us, from someone the grownups were talking about. Shouting, arguing, voices tense, women sobbing, uniformed men running. Nausea flooded my stomach and chest and my head ached suddenly. Somehow, it was this man's face in my head.

"Would you like to come in? It's freezing out."

He shook his head. "I'm not allowed. Meet me in the street in front of the house," he said and wrapped one arm around an upper limb, preparing his descent. Was he going to jump? I suspected the accent was Serbian or Croatian.

"It's three in the morning and thirty degrees out," I called after him but he didn't answer. I redressed and put on my jacket. I thought about waking Vaughn, but the momentum of curiosity pulled me out the front door before I had the chance.

I saw the man's shape under a dim light, no one else outside on the quiet street. I paused there, no crickets, but I heard some night birds tweeting to each other, and the hoo-hoo of an owl overhead. Looking up at the black sky, I could feel a door in front of me, a door I hadn't yet opened. I approached the man slowly, eyes peeled for any movement in my periphery, expecting to be jumped by a team of thugs who would dump me in the trunk of some old car. Too many crime scenes. Too many movies.

Here we were, opposite each other in the middle of Taylor Avenue, sixty feet from the house, our hands thrust low in our pockets, each of us waiting for something. The moon was high and bright. I could see his face clearly now and could tell he'd been formidable once, handsome even, before age and sadness wore him down.

"So, are you like some kind of retired spy or something?" I asked, instantly regretting my use of the word retired. This man had easily scaled a large tree.

"No."

"Why are you not allowed inside?"

The man gestured at the house with his head. "Her."

"Who?"

"The wicked witch of the west."

"Anabel?" I chuckled.

"You don't know her."

"True. And you do?"

Another knowing glance.

"Okay, enough. I followed you out here. Who are you and what do you want?"

"A friend of the family. A friend of Genevieve. Old friend." He looked at the ground and wrapped his arms around his body. "I know you're here to get answers, Mr. Farin. I can give you those answers."

"How could you possibly know what I'm looking for when I don't even know myself?

"I know all about you, Mr. Farin."

"What are you talking about? I've never met you." I rubbed my eyes, shocked by the cold air.

"You are here," he outstretched his arms, "on this beautiful island to find a missing piece of your soul."

"Wow." I shrugged. "Imagine that."

"Go ahead and mock me if you wish. You'll get there."

"Where, exactly? And at what price would those answers come —answers you say you have to my unasked questions?"

"My price." He nodded. "A fair question. My price is your trust, to believe what I tell you."

He looked sincere, and what benefit would there be to deceiving me? "I'll try."

"Good. Let's walk then," he said and headed down Taylor away from the house.

"Where are we going?"

"I think you know."

"The boathouse." I nodded. "It's the other way."

◦ ◦ ⬥⬥⬥ ✛ ⬥⬥⬥ ◦ ◦ ◦

There were no streetlights overhead on this part of the road, but the moon lit our path. The man's dark green jacket had a coating on it that made it slightly iridescent. I followed that with my eyes, along with the sound of his footsteps to keep up. There were more owls here, nearly every ten steps. Or was it the same owl?

Whatever old part of me had woken as a result of my head injury loved being out here. Cold, dark, and silent. If I stopped walking and closed my eyes, I might be able to imagine being underwater. I breathed deep, the freezing air prickly in my lungs. I smelled low tide. We were heading to the water. This must be another path to the waterfront, one that didn't need to walk past the guest house where Anabel had been living. The wicked witch of the west, seriously? She was a ninety-pound, thirty-year-old researcher. Was he talking about the same person? He was right, I didn't know her. But I'd spent the entire day with her and I understood a few things already:

- Anabel Lucas didn't feel loved by her mother.

- She resented her mother's interest in diving and knew she had a secret obsession, which I still hadn't identified.

- She had a secret of her own she kept hidden from the world.

Taylor Avenue was shaped like a backwards J and we'd just wound around the curved part, ending on the other side of the rocky beach near Bainbridge Marina.

"You're not turning back, are you?" the man asked.

"I'm three steps behind you," I snapped. It sounded grumpy and was meant to. He stopped a little before the boathouse and turned to look out, facing the water. Half the sky was covered in ghostly clouds, the other half clear enough to see an assortment of stars, with the sheen of dark water flowing below.

"Beautiful."

"We were standing right here," he mumbled absently.

"You and Genevieve?"

He shook his head. "You and me. You don't remember?"

"I'm sorry, um—"

"Don't worry. It will come."

"Why have you brought me out here?"

"You really don't know?" he asked.

I suddenly felt vulnerable, realizing I no longer carried a gun since the department had declared me dead. My backup, Vaughn, lay snoring in the larger bedroom with the nicer bed, oblivious to my adventure. Brooke was right, though I only acknowledged it now. I really wasn't well enough to be traveling alone, working or responsible enough for important tasks. By some miracle, I awoke able to speak and move correctly, but I also knew some integral re-wiring had happened.

I considered the question and nodded. "I think you're gonna tell me that Genevieve Lucas's death wasn't accidental."

"That's a start. Keep going."

And the next epiphany only came when he turned his head toward the water, showing the right side of his face under the dim light of the moon. That profile, his bone structure. My God, I know this face. "*You're* Alfred Ligetti? The old man Anabel mentioned. Genevieve's dive partner."

"Am I that old?"

I meant to laugh but instead my chest caved in with emotion. I covered my cold face with my palms, ashamed for the second time today of my tears. Could it be true that one part of me recognized this man and other parts didn't? Could the brain compartmentalize like that? Some part of me remembered his face when he turned his head. I felt like I was losing my mind.

"How old was I?" I wiped my eyes with my sleeve.

"The last time you were here? Six or seven I guess."

"I have no conscious memory of being here. Only from you just now and from the smell of the boathouse." I left out the part about his face.

"The brain, Mr. Farin, is a mysterious place."

"Where's her other dive partner? Jerome."

The man moved his head left and right. "You're asking the wrong question."

"Did you kill her, then?" I blurted. I really don't know why I said it.

"He would never do that." It was Anabel's voice this time, but I couldn't see her. I turned and bent low to peer into the darkness behind us. I saw the edge of a white jacket come out from behind a tree.

"Anabel? What are you doing out here? I hope I didn't –"

"She's spying on me like she always does," Alfred said.

"I told you to stay away from the house!" It started as her normal voice and escalated.

"Okay, look," I said backing away. "There's obviously something going on here that's none of my business."

"This is absolutely your business," the man said.

"He was in love with her," Anabel said, this time to me but glaring at the man who towered over both of us.

"I loved your mother, yes," he said. "She was like a daughter to me. I wasn't in love with her. You were just jealous of anyone who took her away from you!"

"You're right. I was." Her voice was an ice pick.

100

The noise from their shouting echoed off something inside the boathouse and the water beside us. I wanted time alone with Alfred to ask him what in God's name I'd been doing on Bainbridge Island forty years ago, but I felt like something was about to erupt here between him and Anabel and I wanted to try to stop it.

"What happened to your mother?" I asked Anabel, hoping the redirect would calm her down.

"Alfred, please, do the honors," she said. "After all—"

"Okay, this again? I made the dive plan and that means I should be held responsible for her death. Why don't you have me arrested?"

"She drowned."

All three heads whipped around to the left. It was Vaughn's voice now. Jesus Christ. Who else was out here?

"It was in the police report," he added, then moved toward me under the spill of moonlight. "You didn't think I was gonna let you go out into the night with a stranger, did you? I promised Brooke I'd look after you."

"And this must be your partner," Alfred said.

"Former partner, yes, and how exactly do you know that? Or maybe what I should be asking is what don't you know about me? I feel sick."

"I should think so, Mr. Farin. When locked doors in the brain suddenly unhinge themselves, people have gone crazy for far less."

"So, you're a psychologist, I'm guessing?"

Anabel stepped away from me and snickered. "He's a treasure hunter. They both were."

# Chapter 22

**Cold air slithered up my pant legs** and sleeves, seeping into my bones. I announced I was leaving. Alfred Ligetti said he would find me tomorrow so we could continue talking. I asked Vaughn to make sure Anabel got inside okay and I took off ahead of them, running under the canopy of trees to get my blood moving again. I felt my new avian friend following me, the reassuring blanket-flap of wings over my head.

After I got back inside, I flipped on the hall light to see the wall thermostat outside the bathroom. Miraculously it worked. I turned it to seventy, returned to what was temporarily my room, and closed the door, pretending to sleep in case Vaughn wanted to talk. How could I possibly sleep now though? I made sure the window was locked and sat cross-legged on the floor next to the bed by the heat vent, a quilt double-wrapped around my body. I breathed into that stillness and imagined being pulled down into a deep expanse. In my head, I tried to summon whatever had been waiting behind the door that Alfred Ligetti mentioned. The door that had been locked all this time. In my head I could see the rocky beach we'd just been on, the boathouse, and a long-haired man towering over me, holding my hand as we stood still at the water's edge. Alfred Ligetti, what a trip.

* —❖- ⟨❦⟩- ✛ ⟨❦⟩ -❖— *

We left at seven the next morning to get to the Gransky law firm, not because it would take us two hours to get to downtown Seattle but because Vaughn was a gifted planner. Some people had the ability to get across town in thirty minutes. Other people, the planners of the world, left themselves fifty because they planned for unforeseen contingencies like traffic jams, construction delays, and lack of available parking.

"How'd you sleep?" he asked me, pulling the car out of Anabel's driveway.

"I'll tell you where I slept. On the floor. And I feel more rested than I would have on that hard mattress. How are you even driving without coffee?"

"There's a coffee bar on the ferry, and another walk-up one at the launch in the parking lot."

"Planned for everything, as usual."

Vaughn turned his head. "Not everything, apparently." He meant my visitor. "How did all that go down? Did he have your phone number or something?"

I laughed.

"What?"

"He's seventy-something. He climbed the tree in front and knocked on the bedroom window in the middle of the night."

"If he knew we were here, why didn't he knock on the front door or ring the bell?"

"Anabel blames him for her mother's death."

Vaughn parked in the Bainbridge Island Ferry Terminal launch parking lot and got two coffees from the walk-up counter. "No tea, sorry."

"Coffee's better in the morning anyway. Actually, tea upsets my stomach."

Vaughn eye-rolled me.

I knew we were both sleep deprived. "Gunshot wound,

concussion, perhaps you recall…"

"I know. I'm sorry," he said. "Your idiosyncrasies are just exhausting."

"Fuck off."

"Fine."

After five years, I was well used to his early morning distemper. No more talking, I decided, until he'd drank at least half the coffee in his cup.

He bought our tickets and drove the rental car onto the ferry. I couldn't help thinking of the old movie "Shoot To Kill", imagining Sydney Poitier chasing Clancy Brown and Kirsti Alley around the lower deck. Two flights up to the main deck, we grabbed surprisingly comfortable seats, each looking out opposing sides, braced by the cold wind and sea water spitting up into our faces. He hated that, I could tell. And God I loved it.

"What's our game plan?" he asked, breaking the thick silence.

I glanced at what was left in his cup. "How should I know? You made it clear this was your investigation and I was no longer a part of it. Remember?"

He clicked his cup down and formed his hands into a T shape, taking a moment to strategize. "Time out, buddy. I'm sorry, okay? I didn't mean to be unkind."

"Did you mean what you said?" I asked.

"Hell yeah, I meant it. You're literally exhausting to be around right now. You were never high maintenance before, not like this. Now you're like Adrian Monk walking around triggered by literally everything. I'm trying to be compassionate but it's agonizing."

It hurt to hear but I liked the fact that he'd said it. Besides being an insightful investigator and a gifted planner, he had a capacity for honesty that most people didn't. This alone might be his most admirable trait.

"Thanks for pulling off the cork. I always know where I stand with you. It's a rare gift, believe me."

He looked sheepish.

"I am trying, I've been trying. But you're right, I'm not really fit to be around anyone right now. Not even you."

"Let's talk about Leticia and Marcus Reyes."

We agreed Vaughn would do the talking at the Gransky firm, with us posing as potential clients looking to hire Marcus Reyes because we'd been referred to him – knowing all the while he'd been missing for two months. The firm was a five-minute drive from the ferry launch with a free parking lot on the north side of the building. Bonus. We pulled open two large, tall, walnut doors reading Gransky, Tatum, Barnard, Nguyen Law Offices and were told to wait. By the time we settled into two seats in the lobby, the same woman looked over the desk at us.

"Someone will see you now."

We followed a short, smartly dressed older woman from the lobby to a glassed-in conference room.

"Bob Brady," a man said, shaking our hands. "No one from HR is available right now but I'm an attorney here and would be happy to chat with you."

Thirties, overweight, wrinkled jacket, no tie. I'd always liked the no-tie look. I listened to Vaughn launch our phony pitch about Reyes, research we were pretending to do, and how we were consulting with a number of maritime law firms to educate ourselves. It was a great pitch. Complete bullshit but well executed.

"Who referred you?" the man asked, to which Vaughn turned toward me for obviously some form of theater. Sure, I was game for anything.

"I'm not completely sure of his name, but I think it came from Trudy," I said to Vaughn. To my knowledge, neither of us knew anyone named Trudy.

"Trudy met with the guy?" Vaughn asked, brows contracted.

"From what I understand yes and based on our research and our aggressive timelines, he recommended Marcus Reyes and said he'd worked with him previously before."

We both looked at Bob Brady, as his face decided on the validity of our story. I was guessing no. Even so, I kept my face poised for battle, arms on the table, hands clasped, ready to be cooperative and provide false information when needed.

The man sighed and sat back. "Okay. I'm not buying how you came to be referred to Marcus, but you went through the trouble of coming here so you must have a legitimate maritime law concern.

So. Here's what I can tell you: Marcus hasn't been here in two months. Actually, it's more like three now."

Interesting how the man didn't ask who we really were.

"Did he quit?" Vaughn asked.

"He said some kind of family emergency," the man added.

"And sorry," I interjected. "Is he a law clerk or a partner or—"

"Neither. He's an Associate, which means a lawyer who has passed the bar but isn't yet a partner."

"Are you a friend of his?" Vaughn asked. Risky question.

"Marcus is young but he's excellent," the man volunteered. "And no, we're not really friends. He's new and no one knows him that well yet." He sat back, symbolic of a door closing. "So, what type of business are you both in and what type of help are you looking for? I'm sure I could find someone else you could consult with about whatever questions you might have."

Vaughn looked at me again, and we sat there in a silent conversation, acting like we were deciding something, when actually we were just letting the clock run out. We'd gotten what we needed. Marcus had been missing for almost three months. That was long after his girlfriend Leticia Ames was shot and killed, and after I was shot by the same man, Jimmy Breslin. The question, then, was whether Marcus Reyes knew what happened to Leticia and was in hiding, or had Jimmy gotten to him too?

# Chapter 23

**We stayed in Seattle for the afternoon**, eating an early lunch, then to the Central Waterfront on Elliott Bay Shore, then Pier 57, all way too crowded for my low tolerance. The Washington Park Arboretum seemed like a more genteel option, for me anyway. We stayed for two hours walking slowly among the shaped garden beds and gravel pathways, offset by flowering shrubs and vibrant color. I drank in this perfect respite while Vaughn disappeared into his phone. On the way back to Bainbridge, I texted Anabel to ask if it was okay if we stayed another night and, if so, we could bring back dinner and eat together.

The thirty-minute delay followed by her unenthusiastic *Sure, be home by six* let me know we'd already worn down our welcome. Plus, the story changed an hour later to *I have to work late tonight, make yourselves at home and use the key I left under the mat.* Vaughn and I got Italian takeout and ate it on the sunporch under the chirp of crickets, cold air pouring in. With everything to think about, I barely noticed.

As I left the beach late last night, Alfred said he'd message me today. It came in at 9pm:

## *4990 Eagle Harbor Drive, 10:00*

I wanted to go alone, just like I wanted to do everything alone these days. Solitude was always within reach, but with someone checking on me, observing me, unraveling my composure.

Alfred Ligetti, my new gold mine of a contact, invited me, not Vaughn and I, to his home to talk. Apparently, he liked the dark and the nighttime as much as I did. Vaughn's argument was that I'd brought him up here to help me and so he needed to be in on the ground floor for any research. It's not that his rationale was unreasonable. I just wanted Alfred all to myself. If what he said was true, and he wasn't in fact gaslighting me, then he was an important part of my past and history, not to mention baggage I wasn't yet ready to face. I didn't necessarily want to share all that with Vaughn yet either.

Anabel hadn't yet returned home and I don't know why that made me uneasy. I distracted myself by the tall, billowy trees on the five-minute drive to Alfred's place on the south side of the island. On the flight here, I'd read about Winslow, the town center, and seen images of the scenic vistas of dense forest. If I really was losing my mind, there were worse places.

Vaughn knew I was upset that he'd pushed in on the meeting, so we didn't talk en route. Probably better that way. Alfred was waiting in the open doorway as we walked up the slate pavers. It was a nicely manicured front yard with solar lighting.

"Well, this is much more civilized than last night," Vaughn said and shook the man's hand, re-engaging his personality. "I'm Kurt's former partner at the San Francisco-"

"I know who you are." Alfred said, but looking at me, obviously wondering why Vaughn was here. He motioned us to a small study on the left side of the house. He closed the door to the room, though I wasn't sure anyone else lived here.

"Would you like a drink?" he asked me with his back turned toward the windows.

I put my hand up. "I think I'll wait till after."

"After?" he asked.

"Truth is, alcohol doesn't agree with me anymore, same with coffee. Since…"

The man turned to face me, respectful in his old-world way of properly listening to people. So much about his generation has been lost.

"Now," I shrugged, "I'm relegated to drinking tea."

The round face spread into a wide grin. "Tea is the beverage of kings, Mr. Farin. It is the elixir of vitality, sustenance. Energy and clarity."

"Okay fine, I'd love some tea if you're making some."

"And for you as well, Detective?" he asked.

"Hell, no. Whisky if you have it."

That lightened the mood.

Alfred nodded. "You're not fussy."

"Kurt makes up for that very well."

"Geez," I said but secretly liked the reprieve. Vaughn and I hunkered close to the fire, where two crackling logs struggled with a flame.

"What's the matter with you?" Vaughn asked under his breath when Alfred disappeared into the kitchen.

"Me?"

"You don't want me here right now. Do you?"

"No," I said like it was obvious.

"Why the hell not?"

"I don't know. It's painful for me."

"What specifically?"

"According to you, everything."

"Well why did you make me come up here with you then?"

I leaned in. "Because you're the only one I trust."

"Not even Brooke?"

Like a butler, Alfred Ligetti returned to his cozy, wood paneled study carrying a small, black tray holding two glasses and what looked like tea in bone china. My wife, Caitlin, was into tea and, even more than that, teaware. She had collections of fine English bone china and, her favorite, Russian Lomonosov porcelain - beautiful cobalt and gold patterns used by Russian royalty. I took the cup from the tray and dipped my nose close to the brownish liquid.

"Darjeeling?" I asked.

"It's my own mix of Darjeeling and Earl Grey. Sacrilege, I know. And whiskey for you." He passed a glass to Vaughn.

"Thank you." Vaughn sipped. "So, what are we doing here?"

"I'd like to know more about the backstory between you and Anabel," I added.

"Be that as it may, I've invited you here to tell you a story. Anabel is her own worst enemy and all the things she refuses to deal with in her life eventually come crashing down. As you both saw last night."

Alfred sipped from his whisky glass, stared into the fire for a moment, then lowered the glass to the tray with a clink. He leaned to the edge of his chair, forearms on his knees. Storytelling on a cold night on a secluded island by a fire. What could be better?

"You came here looking for answers, Mr. Farin. I'm going to tell you everything Anabel didn't about her mother."

"Because she doesn't know?" I asked. "Or because she didn't want to?"

"Both, I'm afraid."

"I suspect her death was not accidental," Vaughn said.

"Anabel already said, well almost said that she'd taken off her tank and ran out of air," I said and watched Alfred's face for reaction. Lips pursed, sunk deep in one of the leather club chairs, hands gripping the arms, blinking through what looked like a storm of thoughts.

"The problem wasn't that she took off her tank," he added. Vaughn and I were at attention. "It's what was in it."

The energy in the room changed. Vaughn put up his palm. "Jerome was the only one diving with her that day?"

Alfred nodded.

"And who was in charge of managing the oxygen gas mixture in their tanks?"

Alfred looked at his shoes and sighed. "I was."

# Chapter 24

**Finally, I was starting to understand the** Anabel-Alfred connection. She blamed him. Both Vaughn and I seemed to understand the need for delicacy here in these next few questions. I leaned closer to the fire to gather my thoughts.

"What happened, Alfred?" Vaughn asked.

"Jerome found her on the bottom and she was unresponsive. There were no indications of anything, just that she… appeared to be dead."

"With her regulator, BC and tank off?"

Alfred gave a slow nod.

"What kind of area was she found in?" I asked, still remembering the image clearly in my head.

Alfred leaned back and crossed his legs. "She'd been investigating the hull of a ship. A part of her was, sort of, trapped under it, or that's what Jerome reported anyway."

*Trapped under the hull of a ship.* Unbelievable.

"Could you repeat that?" I asked. Vaughn turned his head.

"She was trapped," Alfred obliged. "Jerome came back to the surface to let me know. I was in the boat monitoring them, and we called in emergency services."

"What was Jerome's condition when he reached the surface?" Vaughn asked, zeroing in on the boy.

"Condition?" Alfred laughed slightly at the question. "He was terrified, of course. Frantic."

"How old is he? I asked.

"Twenty. Twenty-one. I don't know for sure. He's in the process of getting some kind of PADI certification, he has one already. Genevieve had been working with him as a sort of mentor, and he became very interested in salvage diving."

Vaughn smiled. "Bit by the bug, eh?"

"You could say that."

We all paused, sipping and reflecting.

"It's been four months and you still don't know what really happened?" I asked.

"I have a theory with no conclusive evidence. Not yet."

"The police report lists her death as accidental," Vaughn said, watching Alfred. "You don't think it was. Do you?"

I could almost see a glass ball in the center of Alfred's chest breaking into bits.

He clasped his hands, as if in prayer. "I—would never hurt her. Never! But you asked me a question and I will answer it. I don't know if you were asking in an official capacity, detective, or unofficial, but no I don't believe in my heart that Genevieve's death was accidental. What I can assure you of is that I prepared the tanks with Jerome the night before the dive, and they were exactly right the last time I touched them."

"Do you think Jerome could have—manipulated the mix sometime after that?" Vaughn asked.

Alfred shrugged. "Possible. Not likely."

"Would he have had access to the tanks after you filled them?"

He nodded. "He could have accessed them, yes. They were not locked up. But he wouldn't have known where to go to manipulate the gas mix. That would take special equipment, someone willing to help him do this and, don't forget, this took place in northern Canada so we were in an unfamiliar environment."

I sighed and let that information sit. "Does Jerome know enough about diving to know how to do that?" I asked. "That's a very tricky process with a lot of math involved, depending on the depth of the dive."

"I don't think so."

"I'm gonna let Kurt take over," Vaughn said. "He's been a diver all his life."

"Well the obvious question is motive," I said. "Why would Jerome have done something like this? But we've also got some logistical questions that need to be answered first."

"Like?" Vaughn asked.

"How deep was the dive?" I asked Alfred.

"Fifty to seventy-five feet."

"Okay, anything less than 180 feet means that you've got normal air in your tank, rather than a mix of air, nitrogen and small amounts of helium, which you use at greater depths. So, for the air mixture, that's typically twenty-percent oxygen and roughly eighty-percent nitrogen."

Alfred nodded, blinking.

"So if someone sabotaged their gear by changing the oxygen to nitrogen ratio," Vaughn asked, "could that have killed her?"

Alfred gave me a sideways glance. "Certainly it could. Especially if they didn't add any nitrogen and had her breathing pure oxygen. Jesus."

"Getting back to motive, you said Genevieve was Jerome's diving mentor. Was there any tension between them?" I asked.

Alfred swirled the last speck of booze around the bottom of his glass. "Jerome wanted the experience, and Genevieve got a puppy dog following her around, helping her with her work."

"Work?" I asked.

"She was a marine biologist studying the effects of climate on marine ecosystems, especially deep-water ecosystems."

Vaughn raised his brows. "Come on now, Alfred. You've invited us into your home, shared your whiskey with us."

"And tea," I added.

"Marine biology was not what Genevieve cared about. Was it?" Vaughn asked. "I think that was her cover, a legitimate reason to be diving in those locations, and a valid excuse to be digging around the remains of famous shipwrecks. Her legit credentials were probably how she got her permits."

I blinked at Vaughn, not having had time to debrief him on the conversation I'd had with Anabel about her mother and the final dive.

"What was she looking for on the HMS Terror?" he asked.

Alfred popped out of his chair. "Refills, anyone?"

Odd timing. I rose and stretched my legs, roaming around the back part of Alfred's house while Vaughn went with him to the kitchen. Tidy, unused rooms with thoughtful décor. This man had a lot of secrets.

"The HMS Terror was a British warship," Alfred said when we returned to the study. "Called a bomb vessel, it and another vessel, the Erebus, got stuck in the ice in the early 1800's in Baffin Bay on their way to the Bering Strait. The tragedy left 129 men stranded, and about two dozen perished."

I looked at the floor, giving the expected moment of silence to the gravity of so many dead sailors.

"There was no treasure there, though," Vaughn said. "Am I right? When it was discovered, they found historical artifacts, some of great significance, but not what you'd call treasure. So, what was she looking for?"

"Trouble," he said, the word interrupted by the sound of my phone. I never kept the ringer up but something must have jostled the volume button and it startled all of us. 206 area code was Washington.

"Hello?"

"It's Anabel. Sorry to disturb you." I put her on speaker and held out the phone.

"No worries," I said. "Vaughn and I are down the street with Alfred."

No response.

"Everything okay over there?"

"You have a visitor," she said in a harder voice.

I looked at my watch. 10:40pm. "At your house? Who?"

"He says his name is Marcus Reyes."

# Chapter 25

**"Did you leave Anabel's address with the** Gransky firm this morning?" I asked Vaughn.

He shook his head. "Hell no. I left my mobile number and said we were staying at a hotel downtown."

"You didn't specify Bainbridge Island?"

"Nope."

We stared, wide-eyed for a few seconds, realizing the implications. Someone had tracked us here.

"Do you think it's Marcus at Anabel's house?" I asked, nodding to a sudden realization. "Or more likely Jimmy?"

"Shit. Alfred, we've gotta go. Now."

"I'll go with you," he said.

"No, please. This is –"

"I've got a gun and I know how to use it. And if Anabel is in any danger, you cannot keep me away."

Well, everyone needed an Alfred Ligetti, in that case. "We should text Anabel and ask her what the guy looks like," I suggested.

"Do you know what this man Marcus looks like?" Alfred asked us both.

"I don't," I said.

"I saw his picture on the Gransky website," Vaughn said. "Young guy, clean shaven, dark hair combed straight back."

"Interesting," I said. "Description remind you of anyone?"

Vaughn made a clicking sound, thinking it through. "Jimmy's tall though, at least six three. How do we find out how tall Marcus Reyes is?"

I thought of Brooke. "How tall was Leticia Ames?" I asked Vaughn, Alfred beside me watching our process.

"I think, from the police report, I recall five foot three or so."

I picked up my phone. "Let me try and find her Instagram account and see if there's a picture of her and Marcus."

"When did you get so social media savvy?"

"Brooke," I shrugged, bringing up the app. I was already connected to Leticia's Instagram account from our previous investigation of her. I searched through her profile images, food, modeling, clothing, new makeup recommendations. "They were engaged," I mumbled, thumbing through her grid. "I don't think I knew that."

"Her father didn't mention that either," Vaughn replied. "Is there a picture of them?"

"Yeah, but it just shows him kissing her cheek and her smiling, not a full-length shot. Inconclusive for our purposes right now. Damn it."

"Good try. We gotta go."


Bringing Alfred was against our better judgment. We didn't know him well, we didn't know who was waiting for us at Anabel's house and he knew nothing of the background. Plus, the fact that he was comfortable using deadly force just presented another variable of uncertainty. Truth be told, though, if that was Jimmy Breslin waiting for us down the street, I'd be glad to have extra reinforcement. What concerned me was how he found us. It meant he had to have been tracking us from San Francisco. And if he had, that also meant he knew Marcus was on the run and he wouldn't be satisfied with him merely not testifying. Marcus Reyes was Jimmy's next target. And if we got in the way we could be too.

At Alfred's suggestion, we headed down Eagle Harbor to Taylor because Marcus or Jimmy would be expecting a car to drive up this late at night in the cold. My leather jacket was zipped to the quick and we jogged, the three of us, like covert soldiers in the middle of the empty street, glad for the moonless sky, trying to get a read on what was going on at the house. We approached from the south side. I could see the empty driveway.

"No car," I whispered, catching up with Vaughn.

"Unless it's further down the driveway." Vaughn motioned us past the house but still out in the street so the motion detector lights wouldn't pick up our movements. "Confirming, no cars in the driveway except for Anabel's Toyota."

"How did he get here?" Alfred asked.

Vaughn took two steps toward the house. "We need to get closer, to see in the window. I know what Jimmy looks like. I'll do it, you two stay here. Okay?"

"Roger that," I said.

Alfred and I sank back into the shadows beneath an overhang of evergreen limbs that smelled like spruce. I knew what Vaughn was doing. I'd noticed the berm outside the guest room window. He was crouched now on top of that incline, hoping to see who was in the house with Anabel. He resembled a cat from this distance, crawling on his knees and elbows closer to the house. An overturned wine barrel was under the window covered by an empty planter. He pulled off the planter and peered into the room from the right edge. I saw his arm lift, his head facing up. He was pointing into the room. What did that mean? The man? Anabel? I had a terrible feeling that we never should have come here on this ghostly errand to find a dead treasure hunter. God forgive me if I'd put this young woman in any danger. Now he disappeared heading toward the back of the house.

"Has he seen something?" Alfred asked.

"He gestured toward that guest bedroom and then went around to the back. I don't know what that means." I watched Alfred's face contort in frustration. We still knew so little about him. Under more normal circumstances, Vaughn and I would have found a way to check him out. Now we were flying blind on nothing but trust.

"Well, we wait. Meanwhile, what is happening to the precious Anabel?"

"Not the wicked witch today?" I countered.

"She is still the wicked witch. But she is also very important to me. Relationships are not so black and white, are they? Tell me about this Jimmy fellow," he said. "Is he likely to hurt her?"

"He might," I blurted, whereas the old me, pre-injury me, would have certainly softened it for his benefit.

Alfred flinched. "Who is he and what does he want?"

"He's an assassin. Mostly what he cares about is money. But he's not the biggest fish in the pond. He was hired, I don't know by whom, to hit a bank president. What he didn't know was that the guy was involved in something much bigger. Jimmy showing up with intent to kill in an open Interpol case put him in the wrong place at the wrong time, and someone saw him. Marcus Reyes is a lawyer who was on site with the feds because he had relevant intel about Jimmy's target, and Marcus witnessed Jimmy shooting at the bank president. He missed, but that shot compromised the federal case and ruined a year's worth of research - in an instant blowing a singular opportunity. That also wasted a lot of money, time, resources. You know how it goes."

"No. I do not."

"Well now Interpol's looking for Jimmy to uncover his connection to the bank president and who hired him. The feds had Marcus lined up to testify against Jimmy, naming him in open court. The day before that happened, Jimmy shot and killed Marcus' girlfriend, Leticia Ames, we think as a symbol to influence his silence. Marcus took off and has been on the run since. That was a few months ago."

"And what's your connection, Mr. Farin?"

"I was Vaughn's partner, San Francisco Police Department detectives, for the past five years. We were investigating the murder of the girlfriend, and we tracked Jimmy to a club in northern California and cornered him. He fired a shot in my direction, it hit my head, I fell and got knocked out, then he got away."

"Hence your coma. I'm sorry."

I heard the snap of a branch, probably Vaughn coming back through the brush. I hoped, prayed it wasn't Jimmy.

# Chapter 26

"Hey." It was Vaughn whispering from the dark, out of breath.

"Did you see Anabel?" Alfred asked.

Vaughn came into view and nodded once.

"Is she—"

"She was lying on the bed on her side, eyes closed. That's all I could see."

Alfred leaned down and put his hands on his knees. "Did you see any blood on her?"

"No. And I didn't see anyone else in the house."

"Great. That means—"

"Yeah, I know," Vaughn said, completing my thought. "Jimmy's probably out here somewhere looking for us."

Alfred slipped behind me and took off running toward the house.

"Go," Vaughn said to me, and we took off behind Alfred. "Head toward the front of the house, I'll take the back."

"Got it," I said, reminding myself that neither of us was armed. I ran around the front under the yellow windows facing the street to the side and up the short set of steps. It was dark enough so I could peer in the window easily, aided by the glow of a streetlight. From here I could see all the way through the house to the door of that back bedroom. I gently gripped the knob on the entry door, unlocked. Before going in, I decided to retreat and check the back of the house to coordinate with Vaughn and Al—"

A loud bang and the sound of shattering glass broke the silence. It came from the back of the house. Had to be Alfred. He'd kicked in the back door and broken the window. Jesus.

"Hey," Vaughn said, motioning me inside. "No one's in here."

"Is she okay?" I asked, tearing through the dark house after him.

Alfred was already in the back bedroom, kneeling in front of Anabel, his palm on her forehead, then his ear beside her mouth. "She's alive," he managed through a cracked voice gurgled with fear.

Vaughn reached up toward the light switch.

"Don't touch the light," Alfred said, calmly. Of course, he was right. "He'll be expecting this. Your friend. The assassin."

I heard the blame in his voice. "Ana, wake up. Can you hear me?" He gently tapped her cheek.

Anabel moaned and reached her arms up to her forehead.

"My head. He hit me in the head and the belly."

"I need to get her to the hospital."

"No, I'm okay," she mumbled. "No internal injuries, I can tell. I'll heal. Too much commotion right now will jeopardize your operation. You need to find this guy. I need some water, please."

"I'll get it," Vaughn said.

"Anabel, how tall was he?" I asked her. "The man who hit you."

"Very tall."

"Any accent?" I pressed.

"No."

"Wearing a suit?"

"No."

I turned to Vaughn. "Marcus is a lawyer and probably would have been wearing a suit."

"Yeah, the height sort of gave him away. Did he have a gun?" he asked Anabel.

"That's what he hit me with," Anabel said, her fingers returning to her head.

"She might have a concussion," I said to Vaughn when he delivered the glass of water.

He kneeled low and pressed the glass to her lips with his hand on the back of her head. Alfred was on the bed behind her now cradling her, his eyes wet with tears. Whatever complexities there were between these two people, this man loved her.

"We need to get her to my house. Can you run back there to get your car?" he asked Vaughn, who looked thoughtfully at me. He didn't want to leave me here alone.

"Go," I said to Vaughn. "I'll stay with her. Alfred, can you monitor the property?" I asked. "You've got the only weapon."

Alfred leaned down to see Anabel's eyes. "I'll be right outside," he whispered.

"Thank you."

Having this ten-minute hiatus alone with her, my job seemed clear. First, I searched the house. With the lights off, it was impossible to see anything other than vague shapes. But nothing looked out of place. Anabel was holding her head and molded into a fetal position when I returned to the back bedroom. Alfred was right. She probably did need a hospital or at least an urgent care facility.

"Anabel," I whispered. I touched her head and felt around gently with my fingers for anything wet. She jerked when I pressed her back. "Tell me what happened."

"Mmm." She tried to sit up. She nodded, like she'd been expecting the question. "I need some water."

Vaughn had already brought her water. She hadn't touched it. I handed her the glass but she shook her head. Was she delirious? I made her take two sips.

"I was looking for my keys," she said. "Sometimes I forget to put them on the rack and leave them in my purse, and then I'm frantic looking for them the next morning."

I had trouble imagining her frantic.

"I was fumbling through the other keys on the rack when I heard a knock at the back door. Scared the hell out of me. No one ever comes here at night."

"You didn't recognize the man?" I asked.

"No, and I didn't open the door right away either."

I couldn't imagine why she opened the door for him at all, a woman living alone on a secluded island.

"I asked who it was. The guy said Vaughn told him to come here and he apologized for being late. He said he got detained at the office."

Office, good one. Jimmy was no dummy. Bastard.

"I let him in, thinking of course you guys told him to meet you here. I realized I shouldn't have done that but by then it was too late. He was already in at that point, walking around the house, touching things, opening doors. I asked him his name so I could let you guys know he was here. He said Marcus Reyes." She wrinkled her eyes and nose.

"You didn't believe him?"

"He said he was a lawyer, but he wasn't dressed like he had a professional job." She paused, blinking. "His hands. They looked like... all of him did, like he worked outdoors. He looked more like a hitman than a lawyer. By the time I realized that, it was too late. He pushed me into the back bedroom and started rummaging through drawers and cabinets and things. I couldn't figure out why."

Anabel glanced up at my eyes like she was checking my expression. She was lying. She knew what he was looking for. The tangled webs we weave.

"Did he say anything else?" I asked.

Her face hardened. "Who the hell is this guy and—"

"His name is Jimmy Breslin and he's –" I paused to find a word that might soften the effect of the ugly truth. "He's a police informant. Vaughn and I have worked with him before."

"What is he—why is he here, though? He knew me."

"What do you mean he knew you?"

She didn't answer, pounding me with a hard stare, accusing me, it seemed, of some kind of conspiracy, looking for an explanation. I couldn't give her one, because the room started spinning. My fingers gripped a handful of the blanket on the bed under her for stabilization. Jimmy Breslin knew Anabel Lucas? Did that mean Jimmy had some connection to Genevieve Lucas? If so, that meant something larger was going on here.

"Excuse me," I said and ran to the bathroom, nausea rising up my chest. Genevieve, where are you? I feel like I've never needed you more. I ran tap water into a dusty glass on the sink and swallowed slowly, then returned to the bedroom.

Anabel was gone.

# Chapter 27

"Here," she said, behind me holding a damp kitchen towel, I guess intended to cool my face. She returned to the bed and collapsed on the same pillow that held an indent of her wounded head. I knew all about head wounds, though mine seems to have been more internal.

"The man, whoever he was—"

"Jimmy Breslin," I said.

"Fine, Jimmy Breslin posing as Marcus whatever his name is. He badgered me with one question while he backed me down the hall and, in between blows from his clenched fist, he said 'Where is it, where is it?'"

"Where is what?" I mumbled, mostly to myself.

"Then at one point he asked, this time shouting, 'You know you have it. She gave it to you. She must have.'"

She? Okay, I was more certain now. Jimmy knew about Genevieve Lucas and what she was searching for all her life. One step ahead of us as usual. That was about to change.

"Quickly now," I said, getting Anabel into the living room so we could file out once Vaughn arrived with the car. "I need to know what your mother was chasing down there."

Blinking. "Down where?"

"Don't play dumb, Anabel. Your life was spared tonight but Jimmy Breslin's not just an informant. He's a skilled assassin and he is not playing around. We can help you because we know Jimmy. We've been chasing him for months. He's the one who shot me. Jimmy put me in ICU for two weeks. I've got some payback ready for him, to say the least."

"I didn't know that."

"Contrary to what I originally thought, he's not here tonight for me or for Vaughn. I think he's here for you. As unbelievable as it feels to say that, because it was so random that I decided to come here--"

"Mr. Farin, in my heart I don't think there's anything random about you being up here." Anabel pushed hair out of her face and blinked. "You were meant to be here right now, and I think you're a part of this place. Of everything going on here."

"Look," I sort of laughed, gasped, and cried in the same gesture. "You need to tell me right now. What was your mother looking for?"

She lowered her brown eyes, showing two rows of long eyelashes. She was beautiful in a way that everyone knew but her. One nod, as if she was deciding just now to finally trust me. "Trouble."

That was what Alfred said, too. "In what way?" I asked. "What was she hunting for all this time? It was one thing. Wasn't it?"

She nodded.

"Whatever it was," I said, "it got her killed."

"Pearls."


Anabel took off toward the back door. "Where do you think you're going?" I bellowed.

"If we're leaving tonight, I need to bring a few things with me. I need to go to work tomorrow."

I followed her into the guest house, shocked by the beautifully appointed, luminous space, tiny LED lights decorating bookshelves with books neatly arranged by color and shape, Tiffany floor lamps, what looked like hand-knotted Persian rugs covering a hand-scraped wood floor. Every pillow on the sofa was perfectly placed. Orderly, to say the least. She didn't turn on any overhead lights; she didn't need to. You could see everything in here. It felt like a meditation room and smelled faintly of vanilla. Did I really have to leave here? I watched her move around quickly, pulling items down from closets, drawers, grabbing things from the bathroom counter, and then to the kitchen, where she tossed a box of granola bars from the cupboard into a small gym bag. I watched her swallow a few pills out of my periphery while I called Vaughn. What was she taking?

"Sorry, I'm coming," he said. "Couldn't find my keys. Don't go outside until you see the car. Where's Alfred?"

I looked out the living room window and, right on cue, I caught sight of Alfred's long hair moving into view. "We're all here," I said.

"Then where the fuck is Jimmy?"

"He's not here for us, bro." My God, he'd come for Anabel.

<hr />

Headlights lit up the dark driveway. "Let's go," I said to Anabel behind me, eyeing Alfred as I came down the steps. I pointed at the driveway. Alfred took the front seat and I helped Anabel into the back.

"Where are we going?" Vaughn asked.

"Go back to my house," Alfred said. "We can talk there. I need to think and plan, and we need to look at Ana's head wound. If I don't like what I see," he said to her, "you will go to the hospital and don't try to—"

"Fine, whatever." She shrugged.

Vaughn drove slowly down the deserted street, under a ceiling of brooding clouds and scant moonlight, my eyes peeled for sudden movement knowing Jimmy was out there somewhere. Alfred had him park behind his house and we entered through the back door.

While Alfred attended to Anabel, I dragged Vaughn into the kitchen. We huddled around the sink.

"What? You're the color of chalk," he said.

"Jimmy came for her, not us."

"I thought I heard you say that but then thought I must have misunderstood. How do you know this?"

I shook my head. "He was asking about her mother, said things like 'Where is it, you know you have it, she gave it to you.'" I rubbed my face with my open palms. "God almighty. Do you realize —"

"Wow, um—" he said and let his voice trail as this new reality sunk in.

"While I was unconscious, I literally saw Genevieve Lucas in my head and she spoke to me, almost summoning me up here. I've heard her speaking to me several times since I've been at this house, too, beckoning me to the boathouse. I looked online and found this particular Genevieve Lucas, but it just as easily could have been another Genevieve I decided to track down. It was totally random and—"

"Quiet. Keep your voice down," Vaughn said.

I nodded. "It was so accidental coming here, so random. And… what the fuck? Now I find out Jimmy, of all people, knows about Genevieve?" I stepped back to take a breath. "I asked her what her mother was looking for all this time."

"Did she tell you?"

I leaned toward him a few inches. "Pearls," I whispered and felt a slight tremor in my body as I said it aloud.

Vaughn leaned against the counter and crossed his arms, a grin sliding into his mouth. "Then she really was a salvage diver. Did you get any details? Like what pearls in particular?"

"I don't know yet. But I'm sure Alfred knows everything; he was her dive partner." My phone buzzed with a text.

"What time is it?"

Vaughn glanced at the clock on Alfred's stove. "Ten after one."

"It's Brooke. Give me a minute." I looked down to check the text. *I'm here, and I'm up and can't sleep. Call me if you want.*

Didn't sound too inviting. I walked around Alfred's house, deciding a number of things. Vaughn stayed in the kitchen, Alfred in the hall wringing his hands, Anabel attending to her wound in the bathroom. Might as well be now. I pressed the number to Brooke's cell.

"Hey sweetie," I said when she picked up on the first ring.

"Wow. You never call me right back. Do we both have insomnia tonight? What are you up to?"

"Just talking with Vaughn about a previous case we worked on,"

I said, trying to sound as casual as possible.

"Tell him hi for me," she said.

"How's work lately? I've been meaning to ask you." It was a hot topic and, therefore, a risk. "How long have you been there now?" After getting her marketing degree, Brooke had reluctantly taken a job at a friend's company as an Event Planner and started job searching again after the first week.

"It's bearable for the moment."

"Are you awake enough to hear a request?" I asked.

"Sure. What's up?"

"Do you remember those big, clunky trunks Pappy kept in his attic?"

She laughed. "I remember we used to climb on them when I was little and then get yelled at for being up there. Like bodies were buried inside or something."

"I did too when I was little," I said, only barely able to remember my father now. "I think he died when you were three or four. So, there's something I need from one of those trunks and I'm wondering if you might be willing to go over there and see if you can find it."

Silence.

"Do you remember how to get there?" I knew she remembered. We had gone three or four years ago.

More silence. "What are you doing, Dad?"

"What do you mean? Look, I—"

"Where are you right now? Answer my question honestly or I'm hanging up."

"Geez."

"I mean it."

I sighed. She'd stated her terms. "Washington."

"The state? Are you serious?"

"Yep."

"What are you doing? Not what are you doing up there but what are you doing with your life right now? Are you escaping? Are you having a breakdown? Does Alena know you left California?"

"That was about four questions. Let me see - yes, yes, and no."

"What about your treatments? You're not well, or even close to being recovered and you know it." She was whining. I was gonna lose it if she started crying.

"There's nothing scheduled till next week," I said of my appointments. "I came up here with Vaughn to help him work on a case. And no, I'm not working for the PD again because I know that's what you're thinking. I just have some history about a case and he needed my help." Okay, some of that was true at least. She wasn't responding.

"What do you need at Pappy's?" she asked with a long sigh.

I closed my eyes, leaning my elbows on the cold, granite island in Alfred's magazine-worthy kitchen, thinking about Genevieve and who would have wanted her dead.

"I want an old magazine. A Life Magazine if I'm not mistaken," I said. "It's all faded and has a picture of a barn on the cover. There's a small news clipping tucked into it, on the page of an article about a ship. That's what I need."

"Why?"

It was a fair question intended to gauge the justification for what would inevitably be a huge inconvenience. And I had no answer. "Will you just look for me and let me know if you find it?"

"When are you coming back?" she asked like her answer was dependent on mine.

"No more than a day or two. Three at the most."

"Fine. You'll be home this weekend then. We can look for it together."

# Chapter 28

**Vaughn had made a pot of coffee** while I was talking to Brooke. He set out four mugs, cream, sugar, spoons, and set the pot on a coaster on the coffee table in Alfred's main living room. What a beautiful home. So, this was how grownups lived. High end furniture, equally beautiful furnishings, like rugs, pillows, curtains, textiles. I had a feeling he'd done it all himself, too. There was a large marble statue in the corner, an abstract female nude on a four-foot pedestal. This was a man who lived well, had artistic taste and surrounded himself with beauty. It made me wonder where he got his money.

We gathered everyone to hear the story I insisted Alfred and Anabel told us. Not a minute after we sat, my phone rang again.

"Hey," I said to Brooke.

"Didn't mean to ruin your day but check your texts."

I hung up and opened my text messages. Shit.

"What?" Vaughn asked.

I showed him the text exchange Brooke had forwarded between she and Alena Broderick:

*Hey Brooke, how are you?* Alena had written. *I'm looking to check in on your Dad. I stopped by and rang the bell a few times but there was no answer. Do you know if he's okay?*

*Have you called or texted him to check? Or are you just driving to the house like a freaking stalker?*

*You know he won't answer my calls.*

*That's your problem.*

"You're lucky," Vaughn said, looking at Alfred and Anabel. "Everyone needs a Brooke."

"Who is this Brooke?" Alfred asked.

"My daughter." I picked up the coffee Vaughn had poured for me, grateful for the caffeine and hoping it might quell the pounding in my forehead. I took two quick sips. "I think you two have a story you need to tell us."

"Yeah," Vaughn said. "And who's Ben?"

Two panicked faces stared back at us, at each other, then to us again.

Vaughn rose and brought back a picture from the fireplace mantel with a framed newspaper clipping of an image headlined "Ben and Margarita".

"Maybe this'll jog your memory." He displayed it to them then passed it to me. The image showed Alfred smiling between a dark-haired woman and a man. It was captioned as *Treasure Hunter Ben Lucas with wife, Genevieve Lucas and Alfred Ligetti.*

Now that I could see how she'd really looked, alive anyway, I stared at the woman. She and Ben were wearing wetsuits, Alfred in plain clothes. Genevieve had a chiseled, somber face, slender body with long dark hair slicked back. Her face seemed so familiar but I was sure I'd never seen her in real life. Time slowed again for me, no one moving while I lost myself in that photo, that face. She was real, she'd actually existed, which meant I was neither crazy nor delusional. Something had drawn me here to this woman's life. I didn't dare move.

"This is your father?" I asked Anabel. She looked like she was about to cry. I remembered hearing a story in the mid-eighties about a shipwreck off Florida, a bounty of riches with years of legal battles.

"I'm gonna lie down," Anabel announced, still clutching the couch pillow in her arms as she left down a dark hallway.

"I remember that story," Vaughn said. "The Santa Margarita and the Atocha sank in the 1600s."

"So do I," I said in agreement. "Was Ben part of Mel Fisher's original expedition?" Fisher, I remembered, was a treasure hunter from California best known for his finding the 1622 Atocha off the coast of Florida.

"No," Alfred said. "He would have been too young. But he was part of another salvage team in the early 2000s." He stopped and wiped his forehead with the heel of his hand. "That team discovered a sealed, lead box that contained a number of gold chains." He cleared his throat and looked into the hallway leading to the bedroom. "And a huge cache of natural pearls."

"Okay, wait," Vaughn stopped him. "Ben Lucas is Genevieve's husband? And Anabel's father?"

"Yes. He died seven years ago."

Something fluttered in my chest. Seven years ago was the year our son Ryan died. Another weird synchronicity.

"I'm sorry to hear that," I said. "How did he die?"

Alfred leaned back and took a breath. "Up until recently, I thought—we all did, that it was medically related. He had Type 1 diabetes. I wasn't with him, but he was diving, hadn't taken his insulin and slipped into a diabetic coma. He died a few days later." Alfred looked back toward the bedrooms again.

Vaughn sipped the last of his coffee and refilled his mug. He wrapped his palms around the cup and nodded through these new details.

"How well did you know Ben?" I asked Alfred.

"Way back."

"Okay, so you've provided some good background for us," I said. "What's the rest of the story?"

Alfred raised a brow but didn't move or speak.

"Look, we're sitting here right now because of this story," I went on. "I thought our coming here was random, a sort of esoteric wild goose chase based on something I saw, or thought I saw, and a name I found on the internet that felt like it matched up with some loose threads. I begged, actually threatened Vaughn if he didn't come with me because, frankly, I'm still compromised after my medical ordeal. And come to find out, a fugitive that we'd been tracking in San Francisco is now looking for us up here. Or at least I thought he was up here pursuing us."

"He's not. He's chasing Anabel," Vaughn interjected. "Why do you think that is?"

We both looked at Alfred, now, who had his arms crossed in defiance.

"I'd bet my life it's got something to do with the Santa Margarita."

* -◈- ⬧- ✛ -⬧- -◈- *

There was another short break, where we all sort of dispersed within the house, working through it all. The story itself seemed to have a sort of mind of its own – a shipwreck and the mythology of treasure and peril, influencing the vibe between us. Vaughn stood at the front door, Alfred vanished into the kitchen, and I sat in a chair by the window looking out into the dark night. The curtains were drawn but I could see the shape of Alfred's yard and property through the window sheers. The branches on the trees were moving. The wind must have come up.

"I have a question," Vaughn announced when we assembled together again. "Does Anabel know her father was a thief?"

"Jesus, Vaughn. What the fuck is wrong with you?"

"Keep your voice down," Alfred stood up. "That's Anabel's father. Do you understand?"

"No, Alfred. I don't understand," Vaughn replied.

"The day Ben Lucas died was the day a part of me died too. For God's sake I introduced them."

"Did he or didn't he take some of the Margarita pearls from that second salvage expedition?"

Alfred nodded, eyes closed.

"Was Genevieve involved in this heist?" I asked.

"She hated the idea of it. She left him because of it."

"But I bet she knew where he stashed them," Vaughn said in a singing voice.

A long time passed before Alfred replied. I heard the hoo of my owl high on a tall branch outside. I listened for the wind but heard only silence. A truth slid up my spine. There was no wind. What had moved the tree branches out the window?

"I think someone might be outside," I said. "I saw something."

"When?" Vaughn asked.

"A minute ago. I thought it was the wind."

In an instant, Alfred was behind the curtains holding his gun in one hand.

"See anything?" I asked.

"No, but if your assailant came from that way, he'd be making his way around the front about now."

"I'll go," Vaughn said and got up. "Alfred, keep watch out the window. Kurt, check on Anabel. She's who Jimmy's ultimately interested in."

Anabel was in bed sitting up at attention, no doubt hearing everything we'd said.

"Did he follow us here?" she asked in a meek whisper.

"Maybe. But you've got three bodyguards."

"What does he want?"

"I suspect he's hunting the Margarita pearls, like everybody else."

# Chapter 29

**The question of Jimmy's motivation nagged me.** Of course, Anabel was right – anyone who heard about the pearls wanted them. But hunting them, taking steps to find them and investigating their path of destruction brought exposure. To Jimmy, his motivating reason was apparently worth that exposure. Why? Money, credit, his name in the newspaper? There had to be more to it than that.

Vaughn and Alfred spent an hour on patrol outside and saw nothing. I reported Jimmy's intrusion to the Seattle Police Department. They sent an officer to take Anabel's statement and said they'd patrol the neighborhood for the next couple of nights.

At 5am, Anabel asked me to drive her back to her house and she would make us breakfast. Vaughn said he wanted to check out Marcus Reyes' apartment and talk to his neighbors to see if there were signs he'd been back there. What I needed to know was if Jimmy's interest in the Margarita pearls was for himself or if he was acting on behalf of another player. My assignment, of course, was to get as much out of Anabel as I could about what her father found and what he'd done with his stash. The plan was to meet back here at lunchtime. What I hadn't told Vaughn yet was that I intended to go there myself – to the location of Genevieve's last dive.


"Did you sleep at all?" I asked Anabel back to her house.

She was stirring eggs in a pan. I was tasked with making coffee. Seemed like it was all I'd had to drink lately so I poured myself some water.

"A little. A heard a sort of thump in the back of the house outside."

"You didn't mention it last night."

"I just remembered," she said.

I nodded. "Sometimes that happens. What kind of thump?"

"I was half asleep and wasn't even sure I'd heard it. But it seemed like someone dropped something heavy. I don't think that guy's actually here for me. I think he's here for Alfred."

"Why do you say that?" I put two cups on the table and grabbed napkins and forks.

"Alfred was her diving partner. Her best friend, really. He was there on all the dives. He knew everything she knew. Not only that, he and my dad knew each other forever. I think if anyone knew where Dad stashed those pearls, it was much more likely Alfred than me."

"What about your mother?"

"Of course she knew. I'm just saying from that guy's point of view, Jimmy, if he's as close to the situation as he seems, he'd probably think Alfred would know more than I would. I'm Ben's daughter, so of course he'd want to insulate me from any blame or harm that could come from what he took. If he even took them."

Smart thinking. "Maybe you're right. I'd like to stay here tonight if you don't mind. Vaughn can stay with Alfred, so both of you are covered."

She nodded, taking the first forkful of eggs. She chewed slowly, holding her jaw.

"Did he hit you there?" I asked gently. It hurt to even think about Jimmy's brute force on her delicate face.

"No. Everything's just sore today. Good coffee, by the way," she said with half a smile. That made my day.

# TERROR BAY

Anabel went to work at her office at the University of Washington's School of Marine and Environmental Affairs. I had her guest house and the main house to myself for a while. I ate the rest of the eggs out of the pan, rehydrated, took a shower, changed clothes for the first time in two days, then walked the path from the guest house to the rocky waterfront, no longer bothered by daylight. I could even drink coffee again. I had time and space now and a lot to think about - like what Jimmy's next move might be, where Ben Lucas could have hidden his stash, when Brooke might get back to me about Pappy's attic trunks. More than that, though, I wondered if now was the right time for me, medically speaking, to dive again.

Brooke's text message last night was a worthwhile warning that Alena was looking for me. I probably had a day's grace, or not much more than that, before I'd need to call her with some story.

I was wearing two sweaters and a pair of worn work gloves I scraped off the floor of the front porch. It was freezing out and the sky scared me today, full of dirty secrets. I could almost see them tangled up in complex clumps of blue and black, with long streaks of gray in between. A harsh wind bit at my cheeks and forehead. Funny taking refuge in that boathouse – the décor-equivalent of a turnpike men's room. From inside, I could see the shape of the island stretching down to the left. And lights. Blue police lights. What now?

I moved to the water's edge, where wind created a current of tiny ripples. Some gusts spit water up onto my pants. Squinting, I could see the outline of a craft and recognized the deep V-hull shape, flared bows, wide side deck roughly twenty-five feet long. Probably a Commander 28 made by US Watercraft. I'd seen that model patrolling the San Francisco Bay harbor. But this vessel wasn't on any routine patrol. I was aware of the Blue Light law and I could see the lights rotating, without any sound or siren. This boat may have recovered a body in the water and was taking it in. Jimmy? I had to think quickly. The vessel was headed toward me and, if I stood in the water and waved my hands, they might see me. Could be an opportunity in disguise. Then again, it could be an opportunity to get in trouble and end up as a witness in a murder case.

Without taking the requisite time to consider the ramifications, I waved them in. They saw me and came in fast, then slowed. I stood on a rubber tire that someone had rolled onto shore, to make me more visible. An officer stepped onto the deck, walked out to the bow and grabbed the rail with one hand, waving with the other. A second officer stood on the opposite side of the rail with binoculars, watching me more closely. Note to self: don't do anything stupid.

"Need some help here, sir?" the first officer asked.

"Just wondering what you guys are doing here."

"Routine patrol of the island. Why do you ask?"

"Well, because we had an intruder here in the middle of the night, an armed gunman who barged into the house. Then we were followed to my neighbor's house later in the night."

"Did you call this in and make a report?"

"Yes, we did. My friend gave a statement," I said. "But then when I saw your blue lights just now, I thought that seemed like sort of a coincidence, for a sleepy island like this. I wondered if you'd maybe found our intruder."

"What's your name and house number?" he asked.

"5276 Taylor. My name's Kurt. I don't own the house but—"

"That's fine, an officer will come by there shortly."

"Thank you," I said. "Did you find him?"

"We'll be in touch."


They didn't answer me, and now I'd made a spectacle of myself at nine o'clock in the morning. But I'd also just brought more visibility to the presence of Jimmy Breslin on Bainbridge Island in the same twenty-four-hour period as his assault last night. So, all the better, right? Time would tell.

The vessel motored back out to open water and docked in a cove halfway down the island. I sat on the tire outside the boathouse watching them through binoculars I found hanging on a rusty nail. While watching sea gulls hovering over the waterline, the officers disembarked carrying something heavy onshore. Thirty minutes later, the vessel returned to its patrol, first heading south and then circling round the east side to come across. But the boat never docked, and no one rang the doorbell to hear my story and discuss my concerns. I watched for them, listening for sounds in the front, now second-guessing my decision to engage them.

When I turned back toward the house for the third time, I caught sight of two uniformed, capped men running alongside the west perimeter of Anabel's property, hiding behind trees along the way. Like snipers. Wait. What were they doing? Were they here for... me?

# Chapter 30

**I managed to creep inside through the** side door and quickly moved down the hall to Genevieve's bathroom, crouched low and crept under the open window hoping to hear conversation between them. Instead, I heard their heavy footsteps and the squeaky sound vinyl makes when it rubs against itself, then a short whistle one of them used to communicate directions to the other. They were preparing for a take-down. What the fuck was going on, here? Did they think Jimmy was in the house?

Now I heard a creaking sound on the wooden stairs leading to the side door where we'd been entering the house. Next, the screen door closed against the old, wooden frame. They were in the house. I'd noticed both officers were armed, and I was the only one home. Reality check - I had one choice if I didn't want to end up leaving here in a body bag.

"Is somebody here?" I shouted from behind the bathroom door. I sounded paranoid, probably because I was. "Hello? Who's there?"

"Come on out slowly now, sir, and nobody's gonna get hurt."

It was the officer who spoke to me from the patrol vessel.

"Just open the door and we'll all do this very calmly," he said.

"Do what? You said you'd be here shortly. Why are you walking in my house with guns? Wouldn't you normally ring the doorbell and take a statement?"

I heard whispering behind the door. They were in the hall about ten feet away. I turned to get a look at the bathroom window, but it wasn't large enough for me to crawl out of easily. It also looked like it might be too old to jack up the glass sufficiently for me to fit. I desperately needed to text Vaughn, but my phone was charging in the kitchen. Fuck! I closed my eyes and sent him a telepathic message. Sure, this wasn't anything I'd ever done before, but now that my injury had rendered me new attributes, it was worth a try. The message I thought in my head was *At house, in trouble, need backup.*

"Sir, if you don't come out of there voluntarily, we will come in and retrieve you. And that will result in us making an arrest and taking you down to the station."

I was certain they would do that anyway. "I'm sorry but on what grounds would you be arresting me? It was us calling you late last night when an intruder entered this house and attacked our friend Anabel Lucas."

"Is Ms. Lucas in there with you now, sir?" The officer was closer to the door.

"You mean is she here in the bathroom with me?" I laughed. "I don't think there's room for more than one average-sized person in here at a time. You should have the police report from last night. My partner, Detective Vaughn, called it in a little before 1am last night. Do you have a copy of that report?"

Another pause. "Nothing was called in, sir. Now please, come on out of there so we can talk calmly and we'll take your statement."

Nothing was called in? What the actual fuck? I was standing there when Vaughn called him. Was he faking the call and calling someone else instead? Why would he do that? The shiny, metal door handle rotated slowly to the left. My head felt hot with the odd sensation of smoke coming out of my ears. I felt faint so I held onto the edge of the sink for support, still crouched near the floor.

"Where's Ms. Lucas now, sir? If you just tell us where she is, this will all go a lot easier."

"She said she had to go to work. She left about an hour ago, shortly before I saw you guys out back. I watched you hoist a body out of the vessel and onto the dock. Whose body was that?" I asked, knowing I was taunting them, knowing I was putting my own life in danger by this line of questioning but, somehow, I couldn't help it. It's like I was outside of myself and someone else was talking, having taken over half of my consciousness.

"Open the door Mr. Breslin or we're coming in."

* -◇- -◈- ✛ -◈- -◇- *

Mr. Breslin?? Did they—how could they think I was Jimmy? I opened the door and put my palms up in front of me. One of the officers grabbed my wrist and, with his other hand, holstered his firearm. With the same hand, he grabbed his cuffs and clasped them around my wrists in front of me and pulled me to the living room sofa. My mouth remained open, still stunned.

"What did you say?"

"I'm sorry sir? What did we say when?"

"You called me Mr. Breslin."

"That's your name," the officer said like it was obvious.

The room turned dark and everything grew cloudy. I thought I could hear bubbling water in my head, like my blue cosmos rising up to save me from whatever Twilight Zone I'd haplessly entered. "My name is Kurt Farin and I live in San Francisco. I'm here with my partner, Detective Vaughn. We're with the San Francisco Police Department."

"Get his ID," one officer said. "Check it."

I felt hands on my waist, my hips, butt, fumbling through pockets. They pulled out my wallet. "No badge, sir."

"Mr. Breslin, I don't know who Kurt Farin is, or why you're trying to use his identity. What's your business up here, on the island and with Anabel Lucas?"

I was having trouble processing anything past Mr. Breslin. Did they actually think I was Jimmy, that I'd infiltrated Anabel's house, and I was the one who'd assaulted her? Nausea folded into my stomach. "I-am-not-Mr.-Breslin. I'm Kurt Farin, I told you. Look at my driver's license. Call my partner and ask him. Mr. Breslin is a police informant and organized crime operative from San Francisco. He was involved in a hit a few months ago, and Vaughn and I were up here investigating that case because he's still at large. We have reason to believe he was here last night, hence the report that you say you don't have."

"We'll get to all that when you give us your statement."

I laughed. "That was my statement."

"Just one more question before we go. Can you do that?"

I stared back at the man's face, his gold aviators framing a square bone structure, punctuated by the salt and pepper edged crew cut. These guys just didn't seem like cops to me. Fucked. So royally fucked.

"What have you done with Ms. Lucas?"

# Chapter 31

**I don't know how I didn't pass** out right there and hit my head on the coffee table. Probably because I was getting man-handled off the couch and pulled to my feet. We were heading toward the door, one officer in front of me, one behind, both of them with a hand on me... as if I could run at this point. My phone rang – not buzzed with a text but an actual ring.

"I think that's my daughter. May I please answer and let her know you're bringing me in?"

The two men paused and looked at one another.

"You haven't arrested me yet so I should be allowed to answer a call. Even if I had, I'm allowed one pho—"

"Get it," one officer said to the other.

"Where's the –"

"For God's sake pull it out of his pocket," the front officer said. The other wrestled his hand in and pulled out the phone, pressed the green button and held it out to me. I should've left it on the charger.

"Talk," the man said.

"Dad? Dad! Thank God. Are you alright?" Brooke sounded out of breath.

"I'm – um—why do you ask? Are you okay?" I asked.

"Um… are you with anyone right now? What I mean is, were you picked up a –"

"There are two police officers here," I confirmed, calmly.

"Dad—"

"And I'm pretty sure they're in the process of arresting me, but there's been a huge mistake. Can you take me off speaker phone?"

I looked up to find two shaking heads.

"Dad! Listen to me very carefully. They're not cops," she said in a quieter voice.

"Okay." Like that wasn't obvious.

"They're with you now, like at this moment?"

"Yes," I said staring at them.

"Then it's too late." I heard her sobbing. I hated when she cried. "Oh my God."

"What is it? How did you know that—"

"I can't say, I'm sorry. They said they'll kill me if I talk to anyone."

"Who said that? Listen, try to get in touch with Vaughn and tell him to meet me at the –" I turned to one of the officers. "Are you taking me to the Bainbridge Island Police Department or-?"

"That's about enough," the officer in front of me said. "Hang up," he said to the other, who snatched the phone out of my hands and disconnected the call. They marched me down the side entrance steps and closed the door behind them.


Everything was sideways. My mind was frantic with wild scenarios of Brooke being abducted, beaten. I'd failed Ryan as a father and now I was failing again. It was too much.

Now early morning, the sky lightened, traffic filling in the empty spaces on the freeway. So far, I wasn't taken to the Bainbridge Island Police Department, but they removed my handcuffs once they got me into the backseat of the squad car. That right there made no sense, if I was as much of a threat as they led me to believe. Of course, the first thing I did was text Vaughn with a request to put a squad car on Brooke's apartment, maybe even assigning an officer to shadow her. He didn't reply and, besides, Brooke would never tolerate that breach of privacy. I even tried to text Brooke back and she wasn't answering. Alfred Ligetti had texted me his number but, somehow, I felt like he had been behind this ruse, whatever it was.

We'd left the island and now were driving in Seattle at an oddly slow tick, with the driver nervously glancing left and right every time we stopped at a traffic light. So, they'd left me here in the backseat with my phone and didn't seem at all concerned with what I might be doing. I could literally call 911 right now and claim that they'd beaten me and that I had injuries and needed to go to a hospital. Curiosity well intact, I needed to let this play out.

We swooped into a large, two-story parking garage, using a key card. Then we headed to the lower level, parking in one of the choice spots up front labeled SPD. The door opened. One of them dragged me out by the elbow and handcuffed me, this time with my hands behind my back. I'd put my phone in my pocket with a seventy-five-percent charge. That might be important later tonight. That is, if I was still breathing by then. Maybe it was just because the sun was especially bright today, but the garage seemed extraordinarily dark, even for a dingy parking garage. I blinked a few times hoping my eyes would auto-adjust like they should. We walked, both of them holding one of my elbows, away from the sunny street entrance toward the elevators. About fifty feet away, they slowed their pace, stopped, gave each other panicked looks then glanced left and right.

We were waiting for someone. The wind had been picking up all day. The gusts from out on the street made a howling noise that echoed down here, making it even creepier.

"What's going on?" I asked my captors.

"Be quiet," Alpha Dog said.

Certain they weren't police officers, I now wished I'd paid more attention to their faces. Alpha Dog seemed more like special forces than a garden variety street cop and cop #2 had shoulder length hair and seemed more like an informant. There was so much I didn't understand about the world right now, the identities of my captors and who hired them was just simply lower on the priority list than other things, like Brooke. My hands trembled at the thought.

Brooke was right and my captors weren't cops, but how had she known this? That also meant they'd somehow hijacked the patrol vessel in the harbor.

So, whose body had they picked up?

Cop 2 looked at his phone.

"Don't," Alpha Dog said. "We'll wait."

Our position in the garage was sheltered by the heavy overhang but still exposed to the elements by the open sides. Sand and debris blew up past the door from the heavy wind.

I caught sight of something to my left beside a huge, concrete pillar. Turning my head would be too overt, so I pretended to sneeze, lowered my head, and looked left as I rose back up. Vaughn, thank God! The sight of his tall forehead and bushy eyebrows relaxed the anxiety in my chest. Even if I couldn't talk to him, knowing he knew where they'd taken me was the best possible news. With both captors huddled over Cop 2's phone, I looked left again and saw Vaughn's head and torso beside the pillar, eyes wide, index finger over his mouth.

The elevator chimed and the doors opened to a tall, suited man with a stern face and bald head. "Gentlemen," he said with a crass smile, then raised his brows at the fake officers.

"Yes sir, we got him."

"Mr. Breslin, I presume," he said, looking at me.

I couldn't help but shake my head. "Why do you guys think I'm Breslin? My name is Kurt Farin, I keep telling you. Look at my license, for God's sake. How many times do I have to say it?"

The new guy looked amused by my claim but shrugged and motioned to the officers. He pressed the elevator button and, while we waited, I half expected Vaughn to fire a shot toward the street as a diversion. He was smart, much smarter than me, and he had a lot of self-control. Who knows what you could accomplish in life with a weapon and those credentials. Why was he here right now? But the bigger question was, why wasn't he helping me?

A loud boom sounded from over our heads. Instinct pulled me to the ground. My two captors scattered somewhere. Had someone read my mind and actually fired a shot? People yelling. Running. A woman crying. Something heavy had fallen onto the floor in the commotion. My captors were close but no longer attached to me.

"Hey."

Vaughn, behind me still at the concrete pillars. I was facing the street with my back to him.

"Nod if you can hear me," he said.

I gave one exaggerated nod.

"I can't tell you anything but go along with them calling you Breslin for now. Nod if you just heard that."

"Why the fuck would I do that?" I asked.

"Because being Jimmy Breslin right now is safer than being Kurt Farin."

With no idea what he meant, I trained my eyes on the phony cops, huddled twenty feet away with the man from the elevator looking back to check on me every few seconds. I heard Vaughn's footsteps coming a few feet closer. Luckily a car was exiting the garage, so my captors didn't see him.

"The story that's being shaped," Vaughn continued, "is that you were the one who assaulted Anabel, and that you're Genevieve's killer."

# Chapter 32

**The last thing I heard from Vaughn** before they took me up the elevator was that he'd stay down there a while and, if I could get away, to meet him here at the same pillar. Right.

The police precinct headquarters on the second floor was done up in dark grays and white, dimly lit with under-cabinet illumination as opposed to overhead lights. It didn't look like any police precinct I'd ever seen. Maybe it wasn't. The vibe was slow and steady, hushed voices, and stacked boxes everywhere. Where did my captors fit into this chain of command, if at all? We were walking between two rows of cubicles toward a dark-haired woman, uniformed, eyes glued to me. There was something about her face. And though I didn't specifically recognize her, my new divisional system of scary vs. non-scary people indicated she was the latter. Officer Feliz, her nametag read.

They sat me in a chair in a cubicle, hands still awkwardly cuffed behind me, which made my neck ache. In hushed voices, I caught *here, there, island, Breslin, coming*, and *girl*. Girl probably meant Anabel.

As they moved off toward the corner of the room, I relished the momentary solitude to process Vaughn's alarming report. How did he know all this? Was I really supposed to pass myself off as Jimmy Breslin, the gangster who'd killed Leticia Ames and shot me? It was preposterous and probably too impossible to pull off.

Next, a large woman in a flowered dress with no nametag arranged herself behind the desk in my cubicle. By the size of her bun, her auburn hair had to be down to her waist.

"Okay Mr. Breslin, you're gonna answer a few questions for me and then we'll get you processed in."

"What does that mean?" I asked. "Am I being arrested for something? And I'm not Mr. Breslin. I've told the officers who brought me here three times already that my name is Kurt Farin. My license is in my wallet if you'd like to verify that. Just for the record, Farin sounds nothing like Breslin."

She lowered her eyes to the desk.

"I haven't been Mirandized either."

She shot a *what the fuck* glance at the officers. More mumbling behind me. I realized I also hadn't seen the front of the building, the marquee, the identifying brand of the Seattle Police Department.

"But sure," I said, going along with it, whatever it was. "Happy to answer any questions."

"That's more like it."

I took another look around the space. The walls, lighting, floors, even the furniture looked wrong. "How long has this precinct been open?" I asked.

The woman's fingers froze on her keyboard. "I don't know, two maybe three months. It's temporary while they're renovating our official precinct downtown." She looked up at me with raised eyes. "Now. Name and address?" she asked.

I wriggled in my chair, trying to stretch my shoulders and—

"Name and address," she repeated.

I hadn't answered her because I was thinking about what Vaughn told me. Another reason was when I moved my shoulders, the handcuffs separated a half inch. They hadn't clasped them all the way. Seriously? These guys weren't cops. Unless they'd done that on purpose.

"Could I bother you for some water?" I asked her in my most genteel tone.

She looked up, waiting.

"Kurt Farin, 344 29ᵗʰ Street, San Francisco, California."

Deflated sigh. "So, you deny that your name is James Breslin?" she asked.

"I emphatically deny it. I know Jimmy Breslin; my partner and I at the SFPD have been tailing him for the past two months."

"Gabrielle," the woman shouted. "Bring Mr. Breslin a cup of water please."

"Sure," someone said behind me.

The handcuffs weren't clasped. I could get out of here. I didn't dare move and I pretended this wasn't true. Besides, it was probably a trap.

The woman stopped typing, got up, and went down the hall. I decided I wouldn't fumble with the cuffs unless they'd left me completely alone for five minutes. Thirty seconds later, a woman approached from behind me and set a cup on the desk.

"They said I could take these off of you while you drank your water."

She avoided my eyes. The cup was empty.

"Thank you very much," I said.

The woman had a cuff key in her right hand and reached behind me. Interesting. She inserted the key as if they'd been locked and then opened them, pulling the rings from my wrists. She knew. She knew they weren't locked and she pretended. Why?

"There you go. Go ahead and drink up. I'll wait."

"Sure, thank you again."

The woman watched me stare into the empty cup. What was I supposed to do, drink a cup of air? After gazing down into it for a moment, I lifted it to confirm it was empty, and then turned it over. Someone had written a phone number on the bottom of the cup in blue pen, a 206 number and, above that, a note that said *Memorize this: 206-455-6549.*

Whoa.

I set the cup back on the desk and nodded to Gabrielle, my co-conspirator.

"Thank you again." I pulled my arms behind me. Would she put the cuffs on for real this time? No. Again, the cuffs were on but not locked. My mind raced with possibilities. Gabrielle stood over me with a knowing expression, waiting. For what?

"Is there a men's room I might be able to use?" I asked.

She smiled and nodded. I'd gotten it right. Now, obviously, I was able to communicate telepathically. Another post-coma talent? "Right down that hall." She pointed toward a door twenty feet ahead.

"Thank you. Of course," I said, "I sort of need, um—"

"Oh yes, of course, your hands." She laughed. "Let me get those for you."

For the second time, the woman pretended to unlock my handcuffs. It was like being in a play, a really bad play. She stood, eyeing me and gesturing toward the door ahead. Fine, I'm going.

I took off in slow, even steps, arms at my sides, and touched the steel handle. As I pushed the door open, I noticed a red arrow pointing right had been taped to the door. I paused and looked back at Gabrielle. She watched me, nodding, then jerked her head in the direction the arrow was pointing. Had she put it there? I opened the door slowly, reminding myself to look nonchalant in case a camera was recording my movements. The stairwell was dark, had a staircase going down and then a hallway straight ahead. At the bottom of the stairs, I took the hallway, eyes peeled, ready for anything. I pulled out my phone and turned on the flashlight, looking for another red arrow. Nothing. What was that number again? 206-455-6549.

I backed up to the door again and started over. Ah, now I saw it, an arrow on the wall over the staircase pointing down. Okay. The stairs were well lit, which was both good and bad. Easy to see arrows taped to the wall but also easy to be seen. I had to believe someone wanted me to get out of here and was taking great risks to help me right now. Who and why, though? Vaughn? Just keep going. Stairs. One flight down, no arrows. I used my flashlight, still no arrows. I came around the corner toward the next flight down and saw the red color on the wall again, this time a message written in red ink:

*Go down to Garage. Wait till someone knocks before you exit.*

I think I was one flight up from the basement. I followed the steps, listening for footsteps above me or any other sounds. The bottom of the staircase was a landing no bigger than three feet square. I sat on the second stair and rested my head on my knees, catching my breath, wondering if I could even remember my life before my accident, before waking up and being sucked down this rabbit hole. Was any of that old Kurt even left? Another thought occurred to me at the same time: maybe I've been a hollowed-out edifice since Ryan's death, and maybe this was the first time I'd felt alive since then, since I was contacted by Genevieve, since I'd started tracking her down. I was running for my life. Maybe this was how alive was supposed to feel.

Knock knock knock.

Thank God. I exhaled and stood to open the door. Please be Vaughn. Please don't be an armed gunman. I had no weapon, no defense other than my wits. I grabbed the knob, turned, and opened it quickly, a smoosh of cold air blowing my face. No one was there. Oh, come on! I entered the parking garage and walked around, listening for footsteps.

My phone buzzed with a text. I was afraid to look at it. It was Brooke. She'd sent me four photographs. Thank God, that must mean she was okay. Pictures from Pappy's house were still loading, so she'd found them. But what about her captors?

I backed up to the stairwell door and looked straight ahead. Squinting now, I could see something written in red on the concrete pillar Vaughn had been standing behind. But it wasn't his handwriting, nor was it like the red writing I'd seen on the wall two floors up. This was more like the red message on the precinct door inside their suite – a fatter marker had made this message. Were there two people leading me around now? So that meant Officer Feliz, whom I'd seen upstairs, and the water fairy, Gabrielle. My guardian angels? Good, I needed them. Checking again for onlookers, I moved close to the pillar. It read, *24-Hour Fitness, 3 blocks, Locker 500.*

There was a small arrow next to the text that was pointing to Yale. Was there even a 24-Hour Fitness there? Of course, this was downtown Seattle. The corporate crowd working here would want to work out before and after work. I took one more scan inside the parking garage for Vaughn, who'd told me to meet him here if I could escape. I texted him again but there was no response. *I've escaped. Where are you?*

# Chapter 33

**Now past 6pm, I was starving.** The 24-Hour Fitness on Yale miraculously had no one at the front desk. It would be so easy to let my mind run away from me, thinking everything that happened now was part of the same orchestration of events that helped me escape from the temporary police precinct. I slipped into the gym through the main entrance, stopped along the way to grab a vending machine granola bar and headed to the locker rooms. Heart thudding, I tried to look like I belonged there. I didn't. Wrong clothes, dripping granola crumbs on the floor as I walked, I hadn't been inside a gym in over four months.

Three towel-waisted men in the pool area, two at the lockers to the left, I hit the last row of them searching for one numbered 500. It was not only unlocked but strategically positioned on the bottom row, providing even more cover for whatever was inside. I heard laughing in the next row of lockers, someone talking on the phone, loudly no less. Social faux pas. The worst part was that I didn't have a backpack or bag of any kind to hide the contents. Act like you own the place, I kept reminding myself. I pulled open the locker door.

There was a plastic folder and, funny, a plastic gym bag folded behind it to carry it in. They'd thought of everything, hadn't they? Did they also have a getaway car waiting outside? If they did, it probably wouldn't be taking me where I wanted to go, which was to Anabel's house. I needed the familiarity of the boathouse right now to access whatever memories I'd suppressed so many years ago. I decided reviewing the contents here was too dangerous. I thought of a restroom or shower stall but even that came with some risk. I slipped the folder into the backpack and hooked it over my shoulder, heading for the next location: Bainbridge Island.


It was crazy to go back there after the events of this morning. But that was ground zero for me, and any developments in this case had to be coordinated through Anabel or I'd be working against myself. What were my choices? Rent a car and my credit card activity would be scanned. It wasn't likely that they'd had time to clone my phone, though I still wasn't clear on who they even were in this case. *They* could be Alfred Ligetti, for all I knew. If my phone wasn't cloned, I could schedule an Uber back to Bainbridge. Even better, a hotel off the freeway because they'd expect me to be flying home to San Francisco at this point.

I stood outside under the eaves of a Victorian building waiting for my Uber, which should be two minutes away. I chose a La Quinta in Yarrow Point because it was neither near the airport nor the ferry launch to Bainbridge, so they'd never look there. The driver read the address out loud. I nodded. I swear he kept watching me in the rearview, yet I knew paranoia was a slippery slope. I wondered if they'd tucked a tracker in my clothing. I checked my pockets, felt nothing, drew in a few deep breaths and resisted the urge to make idle chatter. I also resisted the next urge to open the folder I'd retrieved from the locker. Not here. Not while I could be seen. Secure a room with a bed and a lock on the door, food, and water. The rest would come later.

I checked in under the name of the first face I saw inside the police precinct - Officer Feliz. I used John Feliz. And through the same miracle that cleared my entrance into 24-Hour Fitness, the front desk concierge hadn't asked for my driver's license. When did that ever happen?

* ─◈─ ◈▓◈ ✛ ◈▓◈ ─◈─ *

Water, a hot shower, and fresh coffee made from a coffee maker intended for elves, I felt like a new man, though still starving. I ordered a cheeseburger and salad from an Appleby's down the street via Grubhub. While I was waiting and still wearing the hotel bathrobe from the back of the bathroom door, I sat on the toilet lid and paused in a moment of vigil before opening the small backpack. Inside the manila folder was a slim, rigid, ring-bound document holder labeled *Dossier* containing about twenty plastic sleeves. Inside the sleeves were sheets and reports as well as full-page sized photograph collages.

Photo 1 - Genevieve, an underwater shot showing what looked like a small pouch in her right hand, her left hand touching a large, brown object.

Photos 2 and 3 on the next page were of Genevieve and another man, labeled on the bottom as Ben Lucas, looking down at some kind of map, the details of which were too blurry to make out, and then another photo of a map of something called Terror Bay.

Photo 4 - Genevieve and Anabel, both wearing wetsuits with wet hair standing on the edge of what looked like a harbor at night, a starry skyscape behind them. Anabel's a diver? She told me she didn't dive. No, wait, she'd said she wasn't a diver *like her*, her mother, which could mean many things.

I flipped the page and there was a knock at the door. Thank God, dinner. I closed the dossier, slid it into the manila envelope, zipped it in the Ziploc bag and hung the bag on the back of the bathroom door with my wet towel over it. Through the peek hole I saw a woman carrying a tray. Why a tray?

"Can I help you?" I asked through the door.

"Food delivery." A raspy, female voice.

"Leave it outside the door please."

Pause. "I was told to deliver this to you personally."

Shit. Now what?

"Mr. Feliz, your food's getting cold. Please open the door."

Feliz? So she'd asked the front desk who was in Room 211? Wasn't that against privacy laws? "Show me some identification first."

"Sure." The woman held a gun up to the peek hole, then lowered it into her black leather jacket. She could potentially shoot the handle off the door if I refused. But her energy didn't feel threatening.

With the chain lock engaged, I opened the door two inches to get a look at her, keeping my foot against the panel in case she decided to force her way in. Officer Feliz, the woman from the precinct, stared back with beautiful brown eyes and fake eyelashes. She moved closer to the door and nodded. "Take the chain off. Now."

"Nice manners."

"Sorry, I've got an agenda."

"Do you also have my dinner by any chance?"

She held out a white, plastic bag. I took the chain off the door and opened it. She entered the room and closed and locked the door behind her, then looked out the peek hole.

"Are you expecting someone?" I asked.

Gun in her hand, she gestured toward the bathroom.

"What? You have to pee?"

"Go," she said.

"Well, I'd prefer you didn't shoot me so yes of course, officer, I'd be happy to go to the bathroom with you. By all means."

"Shut up." She followed me in and closed the door behind us.

"Move, go, shut up. Anything else?"

She looked up and raised the gun to her chest.

"Fine, I'll be shutting up now," I said. "What do you want?"

"Where is it?" she asked, looking around the bathroom. She checked the back of the door, removed the towel and chucked it in the bathtub, pulled off the duffel bag and unzipped it, handing it to me.

I took it and sat on the toilet seat cover again. "What?"

"Take it out."

"The dossier?"

Loud sigh. "Yes, the dossier. Take it out and read it. Memorize it because I'm taking it with me."

"Oh, okay, that makes perfect sense. Plant it in a gym locker so you can—" I hung my head and sighed. "What the fuck is going on here?"

Now the gun was pointed directly at my face. Amazing how silent you get when looking down a barrel.

I looked at the folder and flipped straight to the typed documents, which I hadn't gotten to yet. But my eyes were distracted by a fifth photograph on the last page, which I hadn't noticed before – same crew – Ben Lucas, Genevieve, Anabel.

"Uh-huh," the woman said, watching me closely.

There was another figure on the right edge of the photo looking down at something – I couldn't see what. I pointed.

"That's right," she said.

"My God. How—" I'd take the image of that face to my grave. It was the face of Jimmy Breslin. What in God's name was Jimmy Breslin doing in a picture with Genevieve Lucas?

# Chapter 34

**"I feel sick.** I need some water."

"Throw up later and read the goddamn pages. I'm not waiting all day."

The woman stood over me but she wasn't tall, no more than about five foot four. Something about her face seemed familiar. I took in her features to challenge this feeling but couldn't pinpoint it. Something. Feliz – I searched my memory for that name somewhere. The gun was back down at her side but I didn't dare fuck with an angry, armed woman. Plus, I wanted to stick around long enough to understand her agenda. Her bright red fingernail was pointing at the folder. I looked down wishing I had my glasses with me, which I usually didn't need except for reading very small print. I squinted.

"Will and Testament? What is this? Whose?"

"Read it."

"Jesus, it's Ben Lucas' will." I looked up, searching her face for an answer. "Where did you get this?"

"Need to know basis. Read it out loud, the circled part. Now."

There was a dark, red Sharpie circle around one clause on page three of the document. "I devise and bequeath my collection of Margarita pearls to Attorney Marcus Reyes of Gransky, Tatum, Barnard & Nguyen, 135 Elliott Avenue." I looked up. "Um... what the hell is this?"

She looked at me like I should know the answer.

"How and why did Ben Lucas even know Marcus Reyes?"

"Good question."

My mind spun through these new strands, working to weave a conclusion that would make sense. "First of all, he was pretty young to even have a will. Forties, right?"

"Irrelevant."

"And if he left them to Marcus... Well, wait." I shook my head. "If he left them to anyone, he had to implicitly be in possession of them."

"Keep going."

"If Ben Lucas left the Margarita pearls to Marcus, he probably did so to protect his family, Genevieve and Anabel, because Genevieve was still alive when he died. Right?"

"Right."

I stared at her face and then at a dark spot in the corner of the ceiling, my eyes wandering while my brain processed these inscrutable details. "I don't—if Marcus was the beneficiary of a cache of priceless jewels, then Leticia Ames – Leticia was—"

The woman's palm went up to stop me, then that palm reached back to cover her face. She muffled this sort of shame-cry that she accidentally let slip out, hand on her mouth, fingers quickly removing the evidence dripping from her eyes, smudging her black mascara.

"What did I say?" I asked softly. "I'm sorry."

The woman opened the bathroom door and headed toward the outer door.

"Wait a minute! You force yourself in here and hold me at

gunpoint and make me read this thing – I think you owe me a bit of an explanation young lady. Don't you think?"

She stopped walking. "Young lady," she mumbled, showing a rack of perfectly straight white teeth. Another thing that looked familiar. Where the fuck did I know her from?

"Okay." She nodded and moved back into the room and sat on the corner of the queen bed. "What were you gonna say about Leticia?"

Her voice cracked when she said that name. "Well, Leticia Ames is really why I'm here. She was shot in a nightclub by a guy named—"

"Jimmy Breslin," the woman said. "I know too well."

"Jimmy was looking for Marcus because he was about to testify against him, and we, my partner and I, believed Leticia was killed as a warning to Marcus if he testified. She was shot in—"

Her palm went up to stop me. "The Stork Club in Oakland, California."

"How would you know that?"

"She was my sister."

"Oh my God."

"Well, that's not completely true actually." She met my eyes now, blinking, tight-lipped, deciding. "She was my sister… Coretta."

"I'm not following you," I said, knowing whatever uncomfortable moment we were caught in was important.

I watched her set the gun on the bed so she could rub her face with both hands. "I'm Leticia," she said, finally. "I'm Leticia Ames."

"How…"

"When I started dating Marcus and we found out about the pearls, Coretta was afraid something would happen."

"Because of that?" I asked.

"Yeah, because of that. She told me something like a hundred people have died trying to find them. She threatened to tell my father and said whenever I went out alone, we needed to trade places. Marcus and I had a fight that night and I wanted to go out, to clear my head. Coretta wouldn't let me go. She went to the Stork Club in my place."

I closed my eyes reliving that night.

"She carried a gun and knew how to defend herself and she said I'd be safer that way."

"You let her go?" I asked, immediately wishing I hadn't.

"She was slippery. She said she was going to the bathroom and left through the window." Pause. Then, "She was my older sister. I couldn't stop her."

"So, when Jimmy shot her that night, he thought it was you." I watched her face. "And that means he doesn't know you're still alive."

"Right."

I paced the worn brown carpet, stopping at the curtains and reminding myself to keep them closed. "What's Marcus' connection to Ben Lucas? I mean, I know Ben bequeathed the pearls to him in that document, but why?"

"They worked for the same company, a large marine services conglomerate that has a legal division. That's the Gransky firm where Marcus works. Ben worked for their marine operations division as a salvage diver. He was part of the 2007 operation, and it was their crew that found the lead box containing the pearls. They were both involved in the long process of authenticating, appraising and then insuring them. Dangerous business, let me tell you. Every day was like going to war. You can imagine with a treasure that valuable."

"How valuable?" I asked.

"Billions."

"I can't even imagine."

"Well, you will," she said, "because you're a lot deeper into this than I ever was."

"How could that be? I just got here. I know virtually nothing."

"You might know more than you think. Let me ask you something. How long after you first uttered the word *pearls* on Bainbridge Island did your life start to fall apart?"

Interesting question. My life had already fallen apart, actually. "About twelve hours, I think. Now let me ask you something. What the fuck is Jimmy Breslin doing in a picture in this dossier?" I pulled the photo out of the sleeve and held it up.

"He owns the dive shop Jerome's been working out of to get all his PADI certifications," she said. "You know, Jerome, Genevieve's young dive partner?"

"Sorry, wait. Jimmy owns a... dive shop? You can't be serious."

"Yeah, not far from here."

"Under what name?"

"His own. James Breslin. Plain sight, you know."

I thought this story was unbelievable before. Now I didn't know what to think.

"Look, you'd better lay low for a while." She motioned for me to give her back the dossier. "And La Quinta doesn't constitute laying low. Do you know someone who—"

"I don't know anyone up here."

She rose and moved past me toward the door. "Well, you'd better figure it out. I'll be in touch."

"Wait. You've gone through a lot of trouble to warn me."

Now she turned full on. "You almost died trying to bring my sister's killer to justice. You didn't know the bigger picture of what was going on. In my opinion, you've earned the right to know the truth, so I'll keep you on the right track as much as I can."

I considered this. "What are you doing in Bainbridge if your sister was shot in Oakland?"

"Lookin' for you. Full circle, right? Look, they know where you are and what you're looking for. So, watch your ass."

"Who's they, and are they also looking for Vaughn?"

"Need to know, bro. Be cool. Your dinner's getting cold."


Be cool. Funny. After my guardian angel left, I took the now-cold food out of the Grubhub bag on the counter beside the TV. Officer Feliz—what a trip. I knew I'd never be able to call her Leticia. I went into the bathroom to get dressed and wash my hands, a symbolic act of cleansing away the sordid story she'd told me about two sisters, buried treasure, a dive shop, and a killer on the loose. I used extra soap.

A thunk came from behind me in the room, or more like the vibration of it on the floor. What now?

# Chapter 35

**My stomach knot wrenched even tighter.** I turned off the water and put my ear to the door but heard nothing.

"Hey, it's me," I heard a man's voice as the door opened. Vaughn.

I opened it slowly, imagining wringing my hands around his neck. "For fuck's sake, man, what are you doing?"

"Sorry," he said, with his not-sorry voice.

"What, you learned to pick a locked hotel room door too?"

"No. They gave me a key. I said I was your husband."

"Could you just kill me right now? Put me out of my misery?"

"I think there's a waiting list for that. For real."

I shoved past him into the room, letting my body fold onto the far bed, face buried in the pillow stuffing. I'd reached my limit.

"Look, you gotta get out of here, like now," he said.

"I'm about to eat dinner."

"I don't think you appreciate the gravity of –"

"Gravity?!" I jerked up and swung my legs to the floor, stood and moved two feet away from him. "What-the-fuck-am I-supposed-to do?" I was sure they heard that in the lobby.

"I just want to—"

"Dude, dude," I stopped him. "I assure you that I do, in fact, appreciate the gravity of this super fucked-up situation. But here's the thing: I am not fucking Jason Bourne! What am I supposed to do here? Hire some underworld fixer and get a fake identity, take a boat to Algiers and end up in South America or something?"

"That's actually not a bad plan."

I crouched, sliding back against the wall in the corner of the room. "I'm just a doctor."

"I thought you were a detective."

"I used to be a doctor. For most of my adult life I was a doctor. I loved that life. I loved working with kids." Sigh. "Until—"

"Sorry," he said, and I knew he meant it.

"It's okay. I stopped practicing medicine when I couldn't save my son. I didn't think I was qualified to be a doctor anymore. I still don't."

"But you miss it?"

"Tonight, I do." I took a long breath and got up to drink some water, stopping to fondle the paper bag on the desk, suddenly not hungry. "I suppose you know, or think you know who was just here."

"No."

"Wait a minute. So, you know I'm here but you don't—"

"Just tell me. Who was here?"

"Officer Feliz, from the Seattle PD precinct."

"No, I didn't know that," he said.

"Well, you obviously know a lot more about this racket than I do."

He shrugged.

"Have you seen Officer Feliz, like really seen her?"

"No, is she a looker?"

I knew he was joking, inappropriately adding humor to a tense situation because that was his trademark. I didn't appreciate it now and especially about her. Something about Coretta and Leticia felt sort of sacred. I might as well tell him. "She's Leticia Ames."

"Leticia? What do you mean?"

I brought him up to speed, at least the story I'd been delivered so eloquently. Whether it was true or not was another matter. I unfolded the cold burger from the wrapping and, oh my God, it smelled delicious. I took two bites and sipped the warm Coke, diluted from the melted ice. Vaughn waited, watching me, cooking up something with his dark, blinking eyes.

Fortified slightly, now I was ready for what I'd been preparing in my head. "Where did you go?" I asked in a high school principal's voice. "You and Alfred. Where did you guys go, and what were you doing in the parking garage of the police precinct? Did you know I was there?"

"Um…"

"If so, how? Do you know how I got out and where I went—no, where I was directed to go after that? Did you orchestrate my escape?" I paused, took two more bites and another sip.

"Anything else you'd like to know?" he asked. "My mother's maiden name, the whereabouts of Jimmy Hoffa?"

"Don't be an ass. Answer the question."

"Was there one in particular—"

"Cut the crap," I sighed, staring blankly at my partner. "You heard what Leticia reported. Ben's will indicated the pearls go to Marcus Reyes."

"I heard you."

"Jimmy operating a dive shop?"

"I don't know anything about that, but it wouldn't surprise me to learn that he'd performed brain surgery."

"I don't know what to make of any of it either, but you seem to be about ten steps ahead of me in whatever this tangled web is. I'd like to know why."

Vaughn shook his head. "I wish I could give you the details you need. But I can't."

"Need to know? That's what Leticia said, too."

"Something like that."

I leaned my hips on the desk; my head slumped forward. "It's just all so random, it's hard to—"

"Kurt, listen to me, this is important."

I was listening. I just didn't know who I was talking to anymore.

"It's not random, none of it. Do you hear me? And it goes back a lot further than you might think."

"What do you—"

"That's all I can say right now. I'm sorry."

"Who are you working for, here? Are you, like, a fucking CIA operative or something? You were my partner, for God's sake. For five years! Last I heard, you were a detective with the San Francisco Police Department. What are you now? Working for the FBI... Department of State?"

"I came here to tell you that they know where you are and you've gotta get out of here. You can't stay here tonight."

"Leticia said I can't go anywhere near Anabel. And if they're tailing me, whoever the fuck they are, I obviously can't go back home. What am I supposed to do?"

Vaughn rose, absorbing my question, nodding his head. He came close and leaned his head toward me. "Survive, bro. Find a way."

* -◈-◈▩-✛-▩◈-◈- *

I watched my partner leave. I heard the door click behind him, still unable to believe he was just leaving me here, though I did notice a wad of cash he'd dropped on the desk on his way out. I picked it up and counted it. Ten one-hundred-dollar bills. Okay, so at least I had means now, since I obviously couldn't take money out of my own bank account, or not without alerting whatever secret network was monitoring every breath I took.

I don't know why, but I turned off all the lights. The center of the room seemed the safest place. I stood there, Vaughn's cash in one hand, legs spread apart, whipping my head back and forth from door to window. Door, window, all the while thinking of that Clash song "Should I Stay Or Should I Go." But there was really no debating it. These people, according to Letitia Ames and Vaughn, knew I was here. So, wouldn't they naturally be able to track me leaving? What point was there to sneaking away somewhere if they would be on my tail anyway?

My eyes adjusted to the dark. I walked around the room to do something with all my nervous energy. Money still in my hand, I moved between the two beds, then to the far corner with the lamp, bathroom, door. Good, I'd walk laps around the three hundred square foot room and try not to bump into furniture until I figured something out. Now that the room was completely dark, it occurred to me to open the curtains. This gave me an advantage over anyone watching from the street, which I had a perfect view of from the corner by the bed. Good, my brain was in gear. Keep going. That's right, find a way.

My paranoid brain. No, it wasn't my brain. It was my heart that told me something happened to Vaughn while I was hospitalized. Had he thought I was as good as dead and inquired about moving on to work with a different agency? Or had he been tapped for a Special Ops assignment? I just got the feeling that his life was no longer his own and that now, in some way, we were no longer on the same side.

# Chapter 36

**I folded the money neatly into the** invisible compartment in my wallet, one of my Pappy's old tricks, and kept doing laps around the beds, bathroom, the door and back. My heart was thudding faster, more oxygen to my blood and brain. If I was being tracked, how were they tracking me? A camera in this room? Probably, and it would be easy enough to install. But they had no way of knowing I'd end up here. Leticia could have planted it, sure, but why? She already knew how to find me. My phone must have also been cloned. Prepaid Trac phones were available anywhere now, Target, Walmart. There might be a 24-hour Walmart nearby.

What was the thing about the phone number to memorize? Maybe it was Leticia's and she'd written it on the bottom of that cup?

A bigger question still loomed in my mind - where could I go to disappear tonight?

- Homeless encampments. I still could be seen leaving this place and, without any stuff with me, I might stick out and be memorable, even in a tent city, which would defeat the purpose.

- I could simulate drunkenness, act disorderly, and get myself arrested and taken to jail to dry out for the night. Sure, this would very likely work, but it would only buy me one night's worth of safety. I needed a longer-term solution.

- Fake ID. A site called IDGod could turn around a fake ID in twelve hours, but shipping could take as long as three days, one or two if expedited. That could be useful, that is if I had a place to hole up and survive for the next forty-eight hours. Not a bad solution. Tabled for now.

- Travel. Somewhere. Anywhere. Other than Anabel's boathouse, my desire to head north to where Genevieve had last dived buzzed in my hands. I had to get up there somehow. The HMS Terror shipwreck was in Nunavut, Canada. Did I have my passport with me? No. Did I even know where it was? Yes, but asking Brooke to overnight it to me would require explanations I wasn't ready to give. If they were monitoring me, and if they'd cloned my phone already, it would be better to avoid Uber because of the trackback to my device.

- Taxi. I'd be less visible than riding a city bus, I'd pay in cash so there was nothing to track electronically. Call it in from a pay phone and—wait. Was there any such thing as taxis and pay phones anymore? I went into the bathroom, with the light still off, looked online on my phone and found City Cab and Orange Cab. Also, you can usually find a payphone at gas stations and burger joints.

There, found it. I'd pick up a 148th Street bus two blocks away and take it to a Burger King on Pine Street. Google showed it being permanently closed, but I'd bet the pay phone was still there. I'd call for the taxi from there. But then what?

My phone buzzed five times. Odd, it never made that sound. Brooke, I'd totally forgotten about the images she'd sent, which had still been loading earlier when I looked. Or maybe I just wasn't willing to acknowledge that my obsession with finding Genevieve

Lucas had put her in harm's way. I went into the closet near the door this time, closed the door halfway and sat on the floor against the back wall to read her text.

*Hi, went to Pappy's, that attic's nasty and smells like mold. You owe me big time. Here's what I found. If you need anything else from there, you can go there yourself when you get back. When will that be exactly?*

I hated her last question because the concept of home had never felt farther away. At this point, I wasn't sure I would ever be able to go back, and how could she avoid the subject of her being attacked or abducted? The pictures told me she was okay, somehow, but failed to explain her frantic phone call earlier.

There were eight pictures. The huge, dusty, black leather oversized trunk, a picture of the interior showing its wooden compartments, dividers, and drawers, a Life Magazine cover and the front page of a feature on a missing girl, a National Geographic article on what looked like a shipwreck, and then three snapshots of old photographs that instantly caused a tightness in my chest: a vintage, rusted children's merry-go-round, a broken down school bus, and what looked like… a boathouse.

A text came in from Brooke. *LMK when you've gotten them, I know they'll take a while to load.*

I knew Brooke. This was the old 'bait me with an easy question' trick. I was in no mood for hard questions right now. But in the last few days, my life as I'd known it had very quickly distilled down to two categories: allies and adversaries. I needed Brooke to keep being my ally because right now I might not have anyone else.

*Got em, thank you so much and sorry it was so much trouble.* But what my heart wanted to write was an apology for putting her in harm's way. The idea of men barging in and manhandling her would forever be a poison in my heart.

*Np*, she wrote back. I knew what that meant, too, in the secret language between fathers and daughters. It meant that she too wanted us to be allies and, with that desire, meant the desire to control certain outcomes. She wanted to know where I was, so she could whine and manipulate me to come home and stay out of harm's way. Unfortunately, the world surprised me by letting me know that nothing is what it seems.

We'd been talking on Facebook Messenger, which showed when your recipient was active or not. I wished I'd done it on text instead. So, I downloaded the eight photos she'd sent, stored them in my iPhone Files, and viewed them one at a time from there, still hidden and nearly suffocating in the tiny hotel room closet. I hoped it was a safe place to hole up for another few minutes. I knew the clock was ticking before the next knock on my door.

I went out of order, starting first with the school bus and the rusted old playground carousel. My brain worked through the images, scraping off the residue of old fear and pain. I felt nailed to a moment I hadn't chosen, but I'd sent her there, to that cold, awful house with its chipped paint and wicked secrets. So once again, I was the cause of my own suffering.

My face was stone as my eyes bored holes into the digital images. I recognized that bus. I'd seen it, we played in it, hid giggling under its vinyl-cracked seats and tugged on the ancient windows frozen open. There was another kid who lived on the street, a blonde-haired girl with thick glasses. We saw the broken-down bus from an attic somewhere, and just past it was the children's carousel, rusted even back then. We never played on it because it felt like death down there, like it was cursed or something. Brenda, that was her name, the girl with the pigtail braids, who claimed she was the smartest one in her class.

I moved to the next picture, which my gut knew was Anabel's boathouse even though it looked nothing like it in the photograph. It looked newer, whiter, and it stood alone on a lot without any overgrown brush hiding its edges. So, Alfred was right. I had been there before after all. My God.

Pop-pop! I heard two shots fired outside in front of the hotel. I grabbed the cash, phone, food, closed the door behind me and took off down the stairwell across from my room. I felt empowered by the fact that I had a workable plan for how to get out of this building and out of town. The rest I'd have to figure out later. The street-facing door opened onto a cluster of small storefronts. I crossed slowly, behind a teen boy wearing a long gray hoodie. Lightbulb moment. I gave him a hundred-dollar bill for it and now had a better way of blending in. With this one garment, the possibilities were endless.

The 148th Street bus took me to Burger King and, though there was no pay phone, the gas station across the street had one. It smelled like it had substituted for a port-o-potty. I wished I'd brought rubber gloves and maybe a Hazmat suit to pick up the receiver. I deposited two quarters and arranged for an Orange Taxi, which they said would take twenty minutes. I killed time by shopping in the gas station convenience store, then returned to the pay phone in case the cab arrived early. I must've looked like fresh bait – man alone on the street, middle of the night. Even in the hoodie, I looked like I didn't belong there. Three pushers approached in succession, about twenty feet apart, clones of the same malnourished forty-year-old with dirty hair and red eyes. The ganja fairy first, followed by crank, and the third was peddling blow. Knowing they could probably kill me, the doctor in me felt a swell of compassion. Couldn't I help them in some way? The last guy peered at me like my face looked familiar. Stick to the script, Kurt. Pick up a cab and you'll be safe for now. Vaughn's prophetic words echoed: *Find a way.*

The cab was twenty minutes late and the drug fairies weren't going away. They'd gathered on the next corner, huddled close together and turning back every few minutes, I was sure making plans to overtake me. If they started walking toward me, and I headed in the other direction, I'd end up getting chased and God knows what else. No weapon. Unfamiliar city. Holding nine hundred dollars in cash. Fuck that.

I was not going down like this. Not tonight.

# Chapter 37

**Defiance comes from anger. Anger can be** instructive, empowering even. I felt it rush up and flush my cold cheeks, it shook and warmed my palms. Good. I would need it.

I stood facing them, my three dope-pushers, head up in a bring-it stance. Was I really worth the trouble, though? What about me made them think I had anything of value? I desperately wanted to pull Vaughn's cash out of my wallet and stick it down my pants or in my shoe or something. I'd need to wait till they were turned away and not paying attention. One of them kept looking back to check on me. Probably addicts working for cash to buy their next fix. Interesting thing was that pushers were often very competitive, yet these circled together like a team. Of course my paranoid mind went to the most conspiracy-rooted theory – that maybe they weren't drug pushers at all.

"Hey, man, call for taxi?"

I was so intent on being invisible, I hadn't heard the Orange Cab pull up. From the next block, six eyes watched me climb into the back. Fuck them. Fuck this city and whatever dark force was trying to suck my lifeblood. I would find out what happened to Genevieve

Lucas. That's why I came up here. That's why my soul sent me here. Whatever else happened was secondary.

"You are Kurt Farin?" the driver asked with the car in park. He turned around. I nodded. He smiled and reached his hand over the seat. "Omari Farah," he said and waited for a reaction. "We have similar names, no? Farin, Farah? We might be relatives." His face broke out into laughter. It was a kind face. Not a threatening one. Ally. Definitely ally.

"Nice to meet you, Omari." Young, thirties, his skin a deep brown and a squared-off afro framed the round, intrinsically friendly face.

"Call me Daniel."

I laughed. "A nickname?"

"My middle name. Daniel is a common name in Ethiopia. Many cab drivers in Seattle come from Ethiopia."

"I didn't know that, I'm new to the area."

"Have you been there?" the man asked.

"To Africa? Not yet. I hope someday," I replied, and wasn't that how all taxi conversations went? Pleasantries. Platitudes. Holidays. The weather. Then when politics reared its ugly head, that's when headphones were pulled out of pockets and purses.

"Kurt Farin," the driver repeated. It reminded me that I'd given him my real name. Not Breslin, and not some made up name. Authenticity came with risks though. I could be tracked. He could be working for 'them', for all I knew. "What are you doing in this neighborhood, man? You stick out like a sore thumb here."

"Daniel, your English is excellent. Impressive that you know phrases like sore thumb. Did you go to school in the states?"

He nodded. "Here and in Ethiopia. So, Mr. Farin. Where are we going tonight, you and me?"

I noticed my driver was quick to redirect from the topic of education. The problem was, I didn't know how to answer his question. Safe as I felt within the tinted confines of his Toyota Corolla, a car idling on this empty street in view of dealers was attracting attention.

"Do you like stories, Daniel?"

He drove us out to the waterfront, to Elliott Bay overlooking Puget Sound. My eyes took in the gleaming lights reflected off the ripples of current, the sky dark blue with a tinge of pink, remembering the dark expanse of blue cosmos, my secret shelter. Now close to 3am, I loved observing the kinds of people out of their homes and conducting business this time of night. An old man in a suit with a hat and cane on the boardwalk. Old people don't sleep much, or so I'd heard. A young woman wearing tights and a skirt up to the tops of her thighs walking fast.

"You want to tell me what you're running from?" my driver asked me.

I loved the continental mishmash of his accent. "Not what. Who," I said, thinking. "Truth is, I don't know exactly."

"Maybe you saw something you shouldn't have?"

I kept my eyes on the water as Daniel weaved the car in and out of side streets, like he was going somewhere in particular. I didn't ask because anywhere was safer than my hotel room.

"I didn't see anything, but some people think I know something, which I don't."

"What do they think you'll do with this information you don't have?"

"Use it to find something of value. Immense value," I mused.

"And that is really all there is, right?"

I looked at his eyes in the rear view.

"Other than people," he said, "there is really only one thing in the world that powers literally everything we see around us. Leverage."

A philosopher-cabbie, that's original.

"You want to draw things into your life that have value. Sentimental value, monetary value, market value, because those things make you feel like you intrinsically have more value in the world, in a competitive landscape. Know what I mean?"

"Interesting theory," I said. "Are you an economist?"

"It is more than just a theory, Mr. Farin. When you have things of value, you have means with which to exchange them for things of even greater value, and then it keeps going up and up and up like this. You are either in possession of or know about something of importance. For anyone who knows this about you, you are now what we call in economics a commodity. You have perceived access to something of great market value. And if this item is either well known or rarified, your possession of it means you, as an individual, have even more potential market value."

Daniel Farah had stopped on a side street on the outskirts of downtown, near the entrance of a narrow parking garage under a four story, brick building. I was listening.

"Think of yourself as the Hope Diamond, Mr. Farin. Objects like that need protection." He turned back at me and grinned. "As it turns out, I can help you with this."

At some point in our conversation, Daniel had turned off his meter. Presumably he worked for Orange Cab and was responsible for his vehicle and also the fares he collected during his shift.

"That's great to hear," I replied with unease. "Why'd you turn your meter off? Are you working for them?" I emphasized 'them' and could see from his eyes that I'd disappointed him.

"You think I'm going to *rub you out* as they say in American gangster movies?" he asked, then erupted in laughter. "I'm sorry. You are in a grave situation and that deserves respect. You don't trust me, and why should you after all? I turned my meter off because I own this Orange Cab franchise. I bought it." More smiling. "I am an enterprising, young business owner."

"You certainly are. What are we doing here, Daniel?"

Another laugh. "You haven't told me where you need to go. So, I thought I'd stop the car and let you think about it in this safe container on a quiet side street."

I nodded. "Very thoughtful."

"I sense you need to disappear. Is that right?"

"What I really need is to get to Canada."

His large, brown eyes blinked back. "Not a problem."

"You can get me there?" I asked, skeptical but willing to entertain any options.

"Not me," he said, then he pointed up to the building and grinned.

# Chapter 38

**"Yo, man, get up!" Daniel's bright eyes** flashed in the rear mirror while he barked into his phone. "I got a client, that's why, so get your ass down here. On the street. No, I'm not bringing him up. You need to come down here and talk to him first. That's what we agreed." Daniel drummed his fingers on the steering wheel. "Oh stop it, you know you never sleep. I'll bet you were ironing dress shirts. Go ahead, admit it. Okay, if you're not interested…" Daniel laughed, cupping his hand over the phone looking back at me. "He'll be here."

"That's your—Canada connection?" I asked.

"Just wait, he'll be down. He's even more ill-tempered when you wake him up."

I used the ticking seconds to finger-comb my hair and rub off something gritty that had been irritating my face all night. Brooke's photos were calling to me, to some old, unattended place in my heart. But the fact that I couldn't contact Anabel right now made that indulgence even more pointless.

I'd been facing the street. There was a hard knock-knock at my rear passenger window. I flinched, turned and saw a large face in the darkness. A man motioned for me to slide over on the bench seat. He opened the door and joined me.

"Hello," he said gently.

"Hello," Daniel replied from the front seat, mocking him.

The man gave a dreaded expression. "Must you always—"

"Yes, I must," Daniel said.

"Daniel, I thought we agreed no more night runs," the stranger said.

My cab driver shrugged, looked back at me in the mirror, and winked. "You see, Mr. Farin, I care about human connections. And all he cares about is money. He's the real economist here."

"Daniel, shut it, for God's sake." Then the man looked at me. "I'm sorry, Mr. —"

"Who are you?" I asked.

"A man who thinks he knows everything," Daniel interjected from up front.

"I do think I know a mite more than you do, since I'm ten years older than you."

"But you act ten years old," Daniel said.

"Um," I said, hands outstretched. "Brothers, I'm guessing?"

Daniel laughed. The other man looked down and shook his head.

"Kurt Farin." I extended my hand to the man seated awkwardly beside me. I mean, why not use old world manners if you can, right? He shook it. "Thank you for letting us interrupt your sleep."

"What brings you here to my door tonight?" the man asked. I still didn't know his name. But if he was Daniel's brother, I decided right there that he was grandfathered into the Ally Club.

"He needs to get to Canada," Daniel explained.

"Can you make things like that happen?" I asked.

The man sat back and got comfortable, bending an ankle on his knee. A glow from a streetlight far away lit up part of his face. He had a close-cropped mustache and a few days' worth of stubble on his chin, which softened his chiseled features. The two men looked nothing alike. "Let's get to know each other a bit first. Shall we?"

This man had more of a British accent but, like Daniel's, I couldn't quite place it. "Sure," I said, wary of the possibilities. It was only then that I noticed that the man was wearing a starched, white dress shirt and a handsome suit jacket, both of which looked nicer than what you find in department stores. Definitely custom made.

"My name's Yafet."

"But he goes by Victor," Daniel said, "because he thinks having an Americanized name gets people better paying jobs."

"Yes, please, call me Victor, Mr. Farin. Asking my brother to shut up, I've discovered, only makes him talk more. So, like a fly buzzing around the corner of the room, I choose to ignore him."

Daniel held up his hands, but I sensed a fondness between them.

"Mr. Farin, would you say you're a man of the world or a man of a town?"

I liked the question and tried to think two steps ahead of him to gauge what he really needed to know before agreeing to help me. "Of the world I suppose. I've been around a bit, it's true."

"And what activities have pulled you around the world?"

"Well, diving for one. It's something I did for a long time, then not for a while now. You could say it's pulling me again."

"Pulling you where?"

"Down, I guess." I laughed. "That's where the ocean is."

"Quite right. You're sort of a broken stereotype. Wouldn't you say?"

"Oh, I don't know, I've never thought of myself that way. I always thought I was sort of boring."

"What are you, Mr. Farin?"

"Okay. Self-definition type of thing?"

The man named Victor widened his eyes but didn't nod.

"I'm a doctor. I guess when you boil me down to my essential elements, that's still how I think of myself, though I haven't practiced medicine in seven years."

"Interesting."

"Why?" I asked, wondering what Daniel was doing in the front seat while we went through this pointless exercise.

"Because if it's something you love so much, I'm wondering what happened to make you change course. And it's also interesting because I too am a doctor."

"Really. What specialty?"

"Cardiology. I was the head of ER Cardiology at a hospital in Addis Ababa."

"A hiatus for you as well maybe?" I asked, knowing the balance of power in the conversation had just changed and now he was answering my questions.

"You could say that. You see, the professional licensure process and standards are most definitely not the same here as they are in Ethiopia. In this country I cannot just get a job as an ER Cardiologist, not as yet. Anyway, I'm guessing you are not from Seattle?"

"Is it that obvious?" I attempted an easy smile, but I don't think it worked. He was waiting, and I sensed two things right now – that this question wasn't optional, and that he somehow already knew the answer. I could have said *New York* to watch for ticks or reactions in his face, but it was too late, or maybe too early, for any more games. "San Francisco."

"And what part of your life in San Francisco made you want to run away?"

"Who said I was running away?" I asked, knowing it sounded defensive, but more as a stalling tactic in response to such a direct query.

"Come now, Mr. Farin. Let's agree to respect instead of disrespect one another, shall we? It's nearly four in the morning and you've just hired my brother's cab to take you to a safe place. What I need to understand, in order to help you, is whether you're running from or running to something. I ask this because I offer services in both areas. I'll let you decide while we move upstairs out of the cold, if that's agreeable to you."

Amazing how the body forgets about things like climate when fear-fueled adrenaline was pumping through your veins. Victor went first, Daniel motioned me ahead of him. It was a narrow, dark staircase that bent left after a four-foot landing. I heard an echo up ahead when Victor coughed, the sound bouncing off a high ceiling. He flipped a switch that lit up the interior with dimmed puck lighting, a nice touch. The ceilings were not only high, but they had tall beams exposed in the A-framed ceiling. It was an industrial feature you sometimes see in hip, urban eateries. This was a downtown office building, probably originally a factory that had been converted to condo units. It felt good up here. Warm, some kind of waxy candle smell, and tiny chimes clinking somewhere. That was another thing I never would have noticed before my accident. Spaces to me, back then, had no particular feel. Buildings performed a function, and those spaces provided clues about the humans who committed the crimes we investigated.

I'd been walking around Victor's house like I lived there – moving from room to room. I could hear the two brothers bickering, quietly, in the living room. On the way, I walked through what looked like a small den with a TV and, sure enough, an ironing board with about twenty freshly ironed dress shirts. Hilarious. I couldn't help but laugh.

"Do you—run a dry cleaner or something?" I said to Victor.

"You're making fun of me, Mr. Farin?"

"Uh-huh. But you're also wearing a very nice shirt, and I'm not. So really the joke's on me."

"Being an outsider in a country like this has many disadvantages," he said. "I've got a lot to prove of myself before I can earn even basic credibility – as a businessman and as a man. A clean, starched, fine dress shirt, especially a white one, can be the difference between a multi-million-dollar merger going through or not. Dress shirts are the world's best equalizer. Please, have a seat. I'll bring us something to drink."

# Chapter 39

**Daniel looked bored but kept quiet.** I was sure they'd done this routine before, maybe many times, Daniel as the hapless bait and referral partner. He needed to stick around to make sure Victor closed the deal and services were planned, scheduled, and paid for, and then he'd get some sort of cut. Theoretically, I didn't mind arrangements like this, because I understood how certain personalities were naturally suited to certain things. I don't know what kind of drink I'd been expecting at 4:30 in the morning, but Victor re-entered the living room with a tray of tea service, which I could smell from ten feet away. "What is that?" I asked, recognizing the scent of some kind of green tea variety.

Victor poured the brew into three china teacups. "Put your nose right there," he instructed, pointing just over my cup. He poured the light brown liquid. I smelled the toasted rice grains. "Gen-Mai Cha," I said.

"So, you're a tea drinker." I'd just scored an advantage on Victor's scorecard. I should introduce him to Alfred.

"Only recently, but yes." He didn't ask and I didn't volunteer anything further. I sat, drank, and listened to him tell me about all of his From and To services.

"So your From services wipe away traces of me wherever I go and track me to make sure I'm not followed."

He pinched his lips. "An oversimplification but yes."

"I think the Running To category interests me in the most immediate way right now."

"Canada?"

"Canada."

"Where exactly?"

I breathed. "Nunavut."

Victor's eyes blinked for a second too long. He knows. He knows what's up there, knows what I'm looking for. He quickly shook himself to attention, realizing that I was studying him as much as he was me. I checked Daniel to see if he too had made the connection. Head back, eyes closed, snoring.

Victor and I talked money. He said $2500 for a new Seattle driver's license and US Passport, and travel across the border by truck. I asked him about paying via credit, to which he said $3000 because the transaction gets routed through one of his other ventures, an education-based consulting firm. It all sounded very reasonable for small-time organized crime.

"Can that be traced?" I asked. "These people have been watching me since I got up here."

"Of course. Everything can be traced. The question is, can it be traced in time to find and apprehend you. I doubt it. This should buy you a week or so by the time you get up there. Is there anything else you need?"

"A burner phone."

"Sure. That'll be about—"

"I'm not paying extra for it," I said. "Throw it in or no deal."

Shoulder shrug. "As you wish. A brand-new burner phone, done. Any more… demands?"

He had a smirk on his face so I could tell he didn't mind the sting of the phone. Just business, right? Sure.

I stared back, ticking through an invisible list of the pros and cons of spilling everything in my head to him. I wanted to solicit his help getting me a dive permit, but that would be overtly admitting what I was planning to do. Plus, he knew already. He had to.

I shook my head. "When will it all be ready? I'm anxious to get out of here, as you could probably guess."

"Yes of course. I should think ten or eleven tomorrow morning. You can stay here in my guest room, shower, shave. I may even throw in a fine dress shirt for you."

"Thank you, Victor." Adversary disguised as an ally.

I laid awake a while, appreciating how the pitch blackness felt on my eyes and brain, running through the pictures from Brooke, Ben Lucas' will, Officer Feliz, forgetting for the moment that she was actually the young girl we'd thought had been savagely gunned down by Jimmy. Could she really be Leticia Ames? If so, what was she doing in Seattle? Probably laying low, considering she was supposed to be dead. And I still wasn't clear on the connection between Ben Lucas and Marcus. Sure, they worked for the same firm. Being colleagues was one thing. But leaving part of your estate to him and something that valuable? Officer Feliz had answers prepared for all my questions. I just wasn't buying them.

I knew Brooke could feel that I was in trouble right now, that father daughter thing. I just couldn't pick up that phone right now and open the pictures and see what she'd sent me. I could barely deal with my present, let alone all the parts of my past my mind had been hiding from me. I wondered where Vaughn went after he left my hotel room, and about Alfred Ligetti. It seemed obvious that they were working together.

In my dream I'm floating, more like drifting, underwater but without a wetsuit or tank. The water's freezing but I don't mind. It's dark down here, that exquisite, hollow dark blue that's only seen in deep water. I have fins on, so I can move upward, and then use my hands and fins to pull myself down. I'm about twenty feet from the surface, I can tell by the look of the reef – the brightness of the sunlight from the surface and the variation of colors. I hear something, a creaking sound not indigenous to water. It's something that doesn't fit with my surroundings. I remember this from when I was just waking up, an irritating metal sound that came from the door to my hospital room pushing open and closed. Another creak. I startle and jerk my head to the right. Yellow and black fish, two of them, leading a school of smaller, blue-colored fish toward the surface. Has someone followed me down here? Do they know what I'm doing, know I came here without a permit? I have to find her. Don't they understand? Genevieve was here in these very waters before she died. I saw her, in my mind I did, her hair, face, her bare shoulders and long, graceful arm extending out from the hull. I need to find that ship, not because I think I'll find her, but because I need to find what she was looking for down here, what she was searching for. Ben Lucas' pearls. Did he bury them at the bottom of the ocean? That made no sense. So why was she down here? I can't breathe now. Something's pressing on my nose and mouth, I feel it. But down here there's nothing but me, fish, and the water.

"Jesus!" I snapped awake wondering whose hand was on my mouth. Then a light shined in the dark room – a flashlight shining on Vaughn's face. He removed his hand and placed his index finger over his mouth. I took a breath, blinking my eyes awake, quickly transitioning from my dream back into Victor's guest room. Vaughn sat on the edge of my bed facing the door, just as he had in my hospital room when I woke up.

"Fancy meeting you here," I said.

"We've gotta go," he said and stood. He looked at his watch. "Ten minutes. Looks like your friend left you a few things." He pointed to the chair. A shirt and jacket draped over it with a folded note. "And there's a tray outside the door. Do you want it?"

"Victor likes trays," I said and smiled.

"Victor?"

"Tell you later. He's not here?"

"No one's here."

"I won't bother asking how you tracked me."

"Good, no more talking. Get dressed. I'll bring in your hospitality tray, Highness."

Victor did have a certain quality that made you feel important to him, revered almost. Old world, that's it, with his fine, tailored clothing and expertly brewed teas. He's a fixer, like I'd joked about with Vaughn. Was I becoming a fugitive? Had it already happened?

The note read, *The shirt is my gift to you, the jacket a loaner. Bring it back to me someday. Your documents are in the pocket. Good luck with whatever comes next.*

I didn't entirely trust him but I couldn't help but like Victor. And I hoped I might see Daniel again with his cosmic taxi that happened to appear at exactly the moment life fails you.

"I lied, I'm not bringing your tray in," Vaughn said from the hallway. "This is delicious." I heard him chewing something. I put on the shirt and jacket, they fit perfectly. I emerged from the guest room and saw Vaughn eating the last bite of a croissant. There was a pot of coffee and a large bowl of fresh blueberries and raspberries, almost gone now. Clearly Victor was born in the wrong century.

"What's the plan?" I asked, grabbing the cup from Vaugh and sipping the coffee.

"I believe this is called enabling a fugitive," he said.

"Much obliged."

"What's with your documents?"

"You rifled through my pockets?"

"Before you start your interrogation, you have some things to answer for first."

"Like?"

He wiped his mouth and took the cup back. "What do you need a passport for?"

"You know why," I mumbled.

"You know I can't let you do that," he said.

"Oh? How exactly do you intend to stop me?"

# Chapter 40

**I thought a lot about what Daniel** said about leverage. He was right. I knew a secret about Vaughn. I mean, it wasn't a secret from SFPD. You can't get a job anywhere hiding a secret like that. They knew about his prison history, but because he was a minor it didn't impede his succession in the law enforcement hierarchy, or not after sufficient conversation.

What they might not know was his history with an abusive father who used to lock him in the basement, sometimes for days at a time, once without food or water – hence his propensity for lock-picking and other forms of escapism. He'd shared the story with me while on a long stakeout, when we were on the trail of a serial rapist, not long after he'd learned about my son Ryan. Those two stories had bonded us together as new partners, the shared pain of family trauma. What was wrong with me that would make me even consider using that story as leverage? I blamed it on my injury. Since waking up, I seem to have left something behind in that cool blue cosmos, an ethical self-guidance system I'd previously used to ensure the care of others' feelings. Now I had no qualms about using his history to influence him to get what I wanted. I didn't know how to make him understand, though he should because we'd been partners working alone together every day. You can't hide your secrets for very long with a partnership like that.

He'd told me, when he first woke me up, that we had to leave Victor's house in ten minutes. We'd been here almost an hour and I was ready to go back to bed.

"Aside from the obvious fact that you skipped out on a—"

"A phony arrest?" I asked. "I didn't skip out. I was led out. Someone went through a lot of trouble to get me out of there, and I think it was you and Officer Feliz working together."

"So now it was a phony arrest."

"For fuck's sake, whose side are you on, anyway?" I stared, dumbfounded, studying Vaughn's expression. It was a face I used to know so well, predictable almost. We'd been seated in the same chairs as Victor and I had just a few hours ago, when we sipped tea like old world gentlemen.

"Aside from your current law enforcement issues, is it even safe for you to dive right now, so soon after your injury? What would Alena say if you—"

I tipped my head. "You wouldn't."

"Did I say I'd tell her? I'm not your mother. You can do whatever you want. If you want to go to Canada and dive one of the most controversial dive spots in the world, go ahead. You'd be traveling in disguise, using a fake passport, which is a felony by the way, using a fake driver's license, not to mention burning a hot trail that your pursuers will inevitably—"

I waved my hands in the air. I was more than just compelled to find the truth about Genevieve Lucas. That truth felt more like life or death than anything in my past. Except she was my past. I felt it even though I didn't have the details. My body knew it, and some part of my mind too, that she was my past and my future.

So I leaned forward in the chair and folded my hands in front of me, head aimed at the floor, partly in shame to avoid his eyes. "I'm so trapped here I can't breathe," I whispered, "like I'm stuck somewhere I don't want to be, an unfamiliar place. Every single cell in my body is trying to break out, like pulled by some massive, invisible force." I looked up now, orchestrated at precisely the right time. Shame on me. "I think that's something you might understand."

I watched the facial tick erupt on his face, a momentary flinch that was immediately concealed with the rubbing of his right eye. "I know what you're doing," he said. "It's not gonna work."

I stood. "Let me make it easy on you. You have two choices right now: let me go and trust that I know what I'm doing or come with me."

"Option one – you don't know what you're doing. As for option two, I don't have a current passport and I'm not willing to employ your friend Victor for an underworld alternative."

He was looking for contrition. I wasn't sorry. I stared back unblinking, waiting for his answer. But it didn't come.

"Okay," I said and moved to the door.

"That's it?" he asked, surprised.

"Life or death, man. That's what the truth is worth to me now. Catch you later."

* ⁃◈⬛✛⬛◈⁃ *

I didn't wait around for his reaction, his whining, or his inevitable manipulation of guilt disguised as logic. Of course I needed his friendship; he was one of the only ones I had left. I just about loved the guy, if I was being honest with myself. But the air outside was cold, colder than I expected. And it would get a lot colder before I found my truth. So I'd better brace up.

I kept myself from street view by standing in the parking garage under the building, which also served as a wind-shelter. I used my phone to book an Uber because, at this point, I just didn't care anymore. My ride was nine minutes away. I wished it was one minute, or else wished that Vaughn had already gone. What was he doing up there in Victor's house? I no longer had room in my head for Vaughn or Victor, because staying alive and getting myself safely to Canada was going to take all of my brain power and resourcefulness, not to mention a miracle.

My Uber driver asked me where we were heading. "North on I-5, keep going for about fifteen miles. There's a truck stop off of Exit 58."

Riding across the border in a long-haul rig had been my idea, though you still needed to pass the Customs checkpoint with proper ID. Victor, or so it had been planned, had booked me passage on a ToysRUs tractor trailer headed for their corporate headquarters in Burnaby, British Columbia, with a driver who would give me a generic (no photo) company badge on a lanyard, that I would flash to the customs agent when I passed over my license and passport, all of which would read the fake name I got from Victor.

I don't think I'd taken into account rush hour traffic. That meant crawling through the wall of cars at ten miles per hour, making me more visible than I'd like to be right now. The truck stop, according to Waze, was eight miles ahead and would take us thirty-five minutes to reach. The problem, of course, was the driver I was supposed to be meeting there to take me across the border. I had no way of reaching Victor, nor any idea of the identity of my driver. "They'll find you," Victor had said. At some point, I had to have faith that by listening to my inner voice I'd end up okay.

I checked my phone and remembered Brooke's photographs. The eerie school bus with its missing door and opened hood had left a sour taste in my mouth, which turned acidy when I saw the rusted merry-go-round. I'd sent Brooke to that house, to find me a picture I knew was in there, a picture I'd seen and memorized with some ancient part of my brain – the boathouse. Why was a picture of Genevieve's boathouse in a trunk in my father's attic? The next picture was of a magazine article spread. I remembered that too – a barn on the cover and a four-page spread about an old shipwreck. I zoomed in and saw it was National Geographic, not Life like I remembered. The article was titled "Uncovering an Arctic Mystery". The print was too small to read, or easily anyway. This meant something. I just wasn't sure what yet. And the final photo was of the last item I asked her to send. She'd found it alright, just like I remembered. A shipwreck article with an old news clipping stuck in its pages like a bookmark. I closed my eyes, bumping around in the back of the Uber, remembering the yellowed, torn edges, and a young girl's face on the top of the page with the text below it. "Missing Girl Aged 10", the headline read. The caption under the little girl's photograph read, "Genevieve Lucas, disappeared from Terror Lake near Terror Bay, Kodiak, Alaska".

# Chapter 41

**Caitlin always said I was good at** compartmentalizing, often lumping men together in this worn stereotype. So when my stomach started growling at the site of the Eat Dine truck stop, I immediately shelved the troubling images from Brooke. How it could be true and what it could mean was too much for my mind right now. So I lost myself in the slideshow of imagery out the window. *Eat Dine.* An entrepreneur somewhere decided that addressing basic human needs in caveman speak would bring in revenue. I think any word in neon lights on a lonely stretch of highway that promised food would be a sure thing.

I stayed in the back of the Uber long enough to tip the driver while glassing the area from that safe, enclosed space. The restaurant was small, not more than two rooms and a bar, with one hallway for the restrooms on the far side and a parking lot on the left large enough for about twenty tractor trailers. My heart was pounding before I opened the door, on the precipice of yet another horrific turning point in my life crossing some cosmic threshold of no return. Here goes nothing.

"Everything okay back there?" the driver asked, probably

wondering why I was still in his car.

"Yep thanks, have a good night." I pulled myself out too quickly, swaying when I stood. I closed the door to his black sedan and opened another to an unknown future containing borrowed jackets, fake passports, and felonies. What else would I be willing to do now?

The place smelled like French fries, could be worse, with a steady din of chatter as I moved through the length of the room looking for a seat. One open space at the bar sandwiched between two large men, I folded my hands on the counter and looked up to show I was ready for food. A fast moving, thin woman in a black apron flitted past and dropped a menu in front of me.

"Right with you, darlin'," she said.

I liked any woman who called me that. She looked like the only server in the whole place; no wonder she was running. On her way back, she pulled a clean cup and saucer from under the bar and poured coffee into it without asking if I wanted any. Of course I would, right? This time of the morning. Wait, what time was it, and come to think of it what day was it now? I ordered ham and eggs with toast and hash browns. Fat, salt, carbs, and protein, which should be enough to propel me to the next point on my journey, wherever that was.

Looking around, I noticed no one else was looking around. I needed to blend in with the crowd of people eating and checking their phones. My heart sank when I pulled mine from my pocket, knowing I couldn't ignore the pictures from Brooke. The newspaper caption said that Genevieve Lucas had disappeared from Terror Bay, Kodiak in Alaska when she was ten years old. Based on the year, I would have been seven years old, which would have been about how old I was when I was here on Bainbridge Island, at least according to Alfred. Interestingly enough, it was the same age Ryan was when he died.

I gulped the hot, strong coffee wondering, of course, if the child in the newspaper article was the same Genevieve Lucas, and why an article about a little girl in Alaska would have been in Pappy's attic trunk all these years. I couldn't ignore the impulse. The feeling was growing stronger – that I somehow had a personal stake in the game and my connection to Genevieve went further back than my gunshot wound.

"Here you go, sweetheart," the woman said, sticking around long enough to meet my eyes. Her forehead was sweating over green eyes framed by gentle wrinkles. She stared at me a moment too long, so now I was wondering if she was my mark. She spun on her rubber sneakers and grabbed the coffeepot, filled up my cup and pretended to bend down. "End of the bar," she said with a quick glance, then scuttled off again in the other direction.

I took another bite of eggs, not quite soft enough to my liking, and let my eyes glaze over the place, pausing momentarily on a man at the end of the bar wearing dark glasses. I'd seen him when I came in. Come to think of it, he'd turned and watched me enter.

I wasn't sure whether to avoid the man or watch him full-on. He was staring at me now, so I set down my fork and stared back waiting for a sign. Are you my driver, I asked him with just my eyes. Without seeing his face, he looked blocky, tall, in a red NY Knicks baseball cap. He reached up and raised his glasses a few inches so I could see his eyes. He smiled, then quickly brought them and the smile back down. Alfred! Thank God.

I tossed a twenty on the counter, stopped at the restroom, then stood out in the cold just past the side entrance door. I saw the red baseball cap move past the front of the diner toward the parking lot. He gave a quick whistle and turned his head to summon me, pointing to a rig parked out near the exit. I moved purposely through the lot, steering clear of moving rigs and following a trucker exiting the men's room. I kept ten feet behind him and then split off to the passenger side of Alfred's rig. I grabbed the rail and stepped on the running board, then the top step, and opened the passenger door.

"Hop in, partner, on a schedule here," someone said.

I entered and closed the door, with a quick check to make sure it was him in the driver's seat. My mind was a hurricane of questions.

"Close your door harder, it needs to click," he said.

To meet this request, I had to step down, grab the handle with both hands and yank it shut. It still didn't click. How did people ride in these things, let alone drive them?

"That's fine. Put your seat belt on," he said, businesslike.

"Are you gonna tell me what's going on here?"

"I'm taking you past the checkpoint and across the border to Vancouver. Your next driver will take you to Calgary, and from there you're on your own."

I listened, taking it in. "Thank you. That's not what I meant." He kept turning his head away from the road to gaze at me. He looked angry. "What are you doing here, Alfred? Are you gonna tell me you work for Victor Farah?"

"The way things work up here, Mr. Farin, might be a little different from your world in San Francisco."

Rage reddened my face. "Did you have me arrested? Just tell me that. And what I'd like to know is—"

"No! You did that all by yourself. What were you thinking?"

"What are you talking about?"

"By standing on the goddamn shore and flagging down the Harbor Patrol, that's how. Are you mad? What could you possibly have to gain by doing that?"

"By creating another report about Jimmy Breslin being up here, I created more justification for his arrest. I thought the SWAT team out there was for him. They about gave me a heart attack."

"Check your pocket," he mumbled, shaking his head and waving his finger.

"What pocket?"

"In your jacket. The left inside breast pocket."

Didn't know I had one. I fumbled with it as he angled the rig onto the freeway. "What about it?"

"Feel something?"

The small, plastic case felt like a box of TicTacs, or a very small surveillance receiver. "Yeah I got it."

"Find the envelope you got from Victor, the one with your new credentials."

I pulled my wallet from my pants pocket and slid out the envelope.

"Remove the bug."

"Bug."

"A listening device. A round obj—"

"I know what it is for God's sake. I just wasn't—" I'll be damned, I hadn't even noticed. While I was there, I made sure the passport and license were intact, then my fingers found a tissue in the bottom wrapped around something hard. I pulled it out. Was this from Victor, or Vaughn?

"Your next driver is supposed to be someone in Victor's network."

Network? And that implied that Alfred was also part of that network. Nothing would surprise me now.

"If you're approached by someone at the next stop who's not wearing a red baseball cap, get in the truck and let him take you to Calgary. But it's not who we were expecting. Plant the listening device in the crease of the seat and attach the receiver to your phone so you can hear if he makes any calls. Don't tell him anything about yourself but pay attention to any questions he asks you."

Of course I'd run surveillance before while working with Vaughn, legal wiretaps, phone taps. This just didn't feel right to me. Then again, nothing about my life since I left San Francisco has felt even remotely right. What was I doing en route to Canada and running from the law? Suddenly I wasn't sure if I could even do this.

# Chapter 42

**"What's my cover story?" I asked him**, assuming they'd already figured that out too. "I'll need one for customs—"

"Don't give them any extra details," Alfred said. "You're simply a businessman with a client in Calgary. Period."

I nodded, thinking of a strategy for remembering all these directives required for this sudden life of crime.

Alfred took his hand off the steering wheel, which was scary in a rig like this, and pulled two business cards out of his wallet. "Use this. Your fake name is Richard Norberg, right?"

How could he possibly know this if Victor said it was strictly between he and I? They were generic business cards for a company called Benson and Pinter, M&A Strategy Consultants.

"Don't give the customs agent too much information. You'll look nervous and that will alert their radar."

"Understood. Businessman. Client. Calgary. Got it. I guess I'm —"

"Not you guess. You are."

"Okay, right," I self-corrected. "I'm a partner at Benson and Pinter and we help companies with mergers and acquisitions."

"In what way? What do you do exactly? A good rehearsal in case someone asks you later," Alfred grinned at the mental exercise.

"Right. An established company wants to acquire a small startup because their offering will help the larger company's portfolio. But they might have very different, often opposing cultures that can't successfully mesh without intervention. That's where I come in."

"Doing what specifically?" he asked.

Role play, fine. "I'm a cross between a mediator and a psychologist."

Alfred nodded. I could tell he liked my answer. "So that's the story you'll use for your next driver. Don't try to sound too smart and keep it short. Understood?"

"Regardless of the color of his hat?"

"Are you making a joke, Mr. Farin? Because I'm trying to keep you alive."

"Actually I was serious."

"Yes, regardless of the hat and also for anyone else you meet. You'll need to get yourself from Calgary up to Nunavut. Is that still your ultimate destination?" he asked, not hiding his disapproval.

"You know what my destination is. Why else would I need to complicate my life in this way? I want to see where Genevieve was diving when she died. I need to get down there. I can't explain it any better than that."

Inside, the story I'd told myself about how I was able to see and hear a dead woman was because of the magic of my unconscious brain. Either that or I was crazy.

The freeway was empty with just a few cars scattered in each lane proceeding at their own pace with their own timeline and agenda. Everyone stuck in their own worlds, even the truckers at that stop – all churning through the conflicts of human drama.

"I know a few things about coma," Alfred said after a spell.

I could see his right eye looked large and glassy with unfelled tears. Loss. I waited.

"My brother," he said and cleared his throat.

"He passed on?" I asked.

"I wish he had. A car accident left him in a coma for two weeks. He never recovered. Can't speak." He shook his head and turned his head toward me. "You... how were you..."

"I'm sorry to hear it," I said. "I was lucky I guess. I was shot, and though the bullet grazed my skull, I fell and hit my head, bad concussion, and that left me unconscious."

He nodded. "After that, I became a sort of expert on the metaphysical aspects of consciousness, and where we go, so to speak."

That word, go. So maybe he did understand.

"The reptilian brains—" he made a swirling motion with his hand— "sort of die in a way, and the higher mind takes over. Of course they're the same, right? And also not at all the same. The brain is the physical, intellectual center, the master computer that regulates, quite beautifully most of the time, all of the systems that keep us alive. You're a doctor, I don't need to tell you. The mind, though, or higher mind as we sometimes say, is the gateway to the spiritual realm. Your physical brain recovered well from your injury. You can talk—" his voice cracked. I saw the pain he still felt, maybe even resentment for how I'd recovered and his brother hadn't. "You can move around. I assume eating and drinking are not problematic. But what of the higher mind, what happens to the spiritual or metaphysical connections your mind made while you were unconscious? In that state—"

"Blue cosmos," I blurted, surprised almost that I was willing to admit that to someone I still didn't really know, or trust. Maybe because this was the first moment of understanding of what I went through, my heart so desperately hungry for validation from someone other than my medical team. The words just came out.

"Tell me about this place, or is it even a place?" he sounded curious.

"Oh yes," I said. "It's a place alright. I remember it. I can go there still, in some strange way, when I close my eyes, when I allow myself."

"Are you afraid? Did this place scare you?" he asked.

I laughed slightly. "Everything *but* that place scares me."

"She came to you there?"

I shook my head. "It was more than that. She lured me there and then, somehow, here." I laughed but felt like crying.

"You don't need to explain it, then, your need to reach the blue cosmos. You need to be there because she wanted you to go there.

That's a good enough answer for me."

I turned toward him. "Thank you, Alfred." My gratitude sounded mechanical but I couldn't think of anything better to say.

I didn't share this with Alfred, but something had been following me ever since I emerged. I kept getting farther from myself, the realest me there ever was, down there in that cool dark place where I was in touch with my deepest essence. Something woke up while my brain was unplugged, something elemental, an ancient being who lives, no, hides in a dark place most humans don't ever get to contact. It changed me and was still changing me. This being woke up, and I was becoming more and more like it. Like somebody else.

In the Uber, the driver had a song on the radio, I didn't notice or remember it until now, a delayed response. That song, "When the Truth Hunts You Down" by Sam Tinnesz, I love that guy and his brooding anthems. I'd felt that lately too, something emerging... I thought it might be an idea, or a messenger, but now I think it's a truth, and isn't that what truths were really? Messengers trying to deliver something that you're not ready to see. It was close now, I could feel it. All the pieces there but all mixed up, pixilated almost. It's coming, this truth. It's looking for me, hunting me down like the song says. Alfred says he understands. He lost his brother so maybe he did.

He leaned forward again and pulled another document from the back pocket of his pants. "Take this," he said and passed it to me, a folded, full-sized sheet of paper. "The front has directions about where to find diving gear. You'll need to apply for your own dive permit. It takes twenty-four hours, longer for non-residents."

"Okay," I said but didn't look at the document. Instead watched his face, his wrinkled brow and narrowed eyes scrutinizing something he saw behind us.

"What is it?"

"Look at the back of the page," he said, avoiding the question and keeping his eyes on the rearview.

"What?"

"Turn the page over. The back of the sheet has something you're gonna need as well."

It was a crude, Sharpie version of a map that looked like a loose sketch of some underwater features. It was too dark in the cab to see it properly. Besides, I was more interested in the shape of the headlights that had been following us for the past twenty miles. Now they'd sped up and were directly behind us.

"Do you see them?" I asked.

"I've been watching them for the past hour."

# Chapter 43

**I slipped Alfred's folded map into my** back pocket, then pulled it out again, folded it smaller, and tucked it in my wallet. I had no faith in it yet but, even so, it seemed worth protecting.

We were approaching the Canadian border; the checkpoint signs made it feel like a military installation. I readied my Richard Norberg credentials to pass to Alfred. While he slowed the rig and fumbled with his documents, I couldn't help but wonder if his were fake too. For me, it would be a new point of no return.

Uniformed border guards with guns held crosswise over their bodies lined both sides of the throughway. It felt surreal, like one of those teen dystopic movies. We proceeded slowly, following directions, holding out our documents. One officer opened Alfred's door and made him step out, leaving me alone in the passenger seat. They asked me to climb down, ushering us to an area demarcated by painted yellow lines, asking us our names and our business. The clouds looked strange. I pretended not to notice so we could quickly get through the checkpoint. They asked almost nothing of us and let us proceed, which seemed suspiciously easy. Once back in the rig I couldn't take my eyes off the sky, the wrong type of clouds for this time of day. I wasn't dreaming again, was I?

"Where's my drop off?" I asked Alfred when we got back on the road.

"Truck stop café just over the border off Highway 99. We'll be there in ten minutes. Remember what I said about your next driver?"

I rolled my eyes. "If he's wearing a red baseball cap, he's Victor's contact. If he's not, God knows where I'll end up."

He kept his eyes on the road. "Plant the listening device in the front seat, regardless. After he lets you out in Calgary, you can monitor his calls and see what he knows."

"What are you talking about? I'll be sitting up front with him."

"The range isn't that long on those devices," he said, ignoring my question. "Anyway, Victor thought you might need it."

"Is this a drop off or are you coming in?"

"I'll come in and we'll get a booth in the back. Someone will walk past us on the way to the rest room and pick something up from the floor, suggesting we might have dropped it."

"That's our mark?" I asked, laughing. Mark. What other tradecraft terms would I start using now? Jason Bourne after all.


It's funny what guilt does to your perception of the world. We ate in silence, lost in our own thoughts, but I swear every face in the diner was looking my way, and not just one-time but turning every few minutes to monitor me. I was clearly paranoid after my overt lawlessness of crossing a country border under false identity.

Alfred tapped his index finger on the table with his eyes on the front door, waiting as we were for our "mark", who never came even after we paid the bill. Something in the planning had gone wrong. Was my next driver detained, or dead?

"I'll take off now," Alfred said, wiping his mouth with two napkins crumpled with anxiety and ketchup. "Stay here for a few minutes and then wait outside for your driver. If he comes, don't contact me. If no one approaches you in the next twenty minutes, text me and I'll come back around. We'll figure something out."

"You can take me all the way to Calgary?"

"No."

It was a moot point, because someone approached me in the lot.

I'd been waiting on the passenger side of a long-haul rig for some furniture store, Leon's, I could see now from the yellow logo on the side. I was about fifty feet from the diner's side entrance when the door opened. A kid, teenager it looked like, dressed in an oversized hoodie with the hood over his head, baggy pants, took ten steps toward me and stopped to light up what looked like a blunt. He walked purposely to me.

"Hey, man. Buy some weed?"

I didn't make eye contact. "No thanks," I said and moved a few feet closer to the front of the rig so I could see in front of it. The kid looked harmless, probably weighing no more than a hundred twenty pounds, if that. I turned to check behind me and now he was a foot away. Jesus. I turned and faced him.

"Hey," he said, again.

"What, dude? I'm waiting for someone."

"Yeah, me, asshole," he said and slid back his hood to reveal a young, clean-shaven face and dark, curly hair.

"Sorry?"

"You're waiting for me."

I must've looked confused because he shook his head and eyerolled.

"Keep up now. Jerome man, I'm Jerome?" he said as a question, waiting for me to put the pieces together.

"As in…"

"Yeah, Jenny."

"Jenny?" I repeated.

"Gen-e-vieve." He pulled a red, folded baseball cap out of his back pocket and put it on his head. Ah.

"You're my driver," I said.

"Right. Get in."

I climbed up into the cab seriously wondering if my driver was tall enough to reach the pedals. But he sat comfortably in the driver's seat and looked like he knew what he was doing. We took off on the freeway heading east toward Calgary with me trying to remember the details Alfred had shared with Vaughn and me at Genevieve's house about her diving partner. He'd said Jerome was her student, he was getting another PADI certification and Genevieve was mentoring him, and he'd been with her on her last dive. He could be a wealth of information that I needed right now, or he could stonewall me, or he could also be working on the other side, for everyone on Jimmy Breslin's payroll trying to stop me from finding the truth.

I decided to run through the basic details first. "So. You're working for Victor?"

"Yeah."

"And you've been paid for this trip?"

"Yeah."

"And you're taking me to—"

"Yeah, man, Calgary. I'm driving you to fucking Calgary. Shut it, would you?"

"Okay… anything else?"

"Yeah. Give me the bug Alfred gave you."

I didn't much like his aggressive attitude, but I had no other options. His nose, mouth, and brows contracted, temporarily changing the shape of his face. I went through it in my mind. He could be a junkie and high on meth instead of just pot and, in which case, completely unstable while operating this ginormous rig. I handed over the listening device and the tiny receiver, which I'd put in my jacket pocket. He opened his window and threw it out.

"Wonderful. What do you want next, my shoes?"

"Show me the map."

"What map?" I'd gotten that from Alfred, so how would Jerome even know about it?

"The map Alfred gave you. Let me see it."

"How would you even know about a map?"

"Because I made it, asshole. Now hand it over."

Unsure whether he was armed or not, I did as he asked, wondering if I'd be able to reconstruct the image and if I was likely to make it to Calgary in one piece.

Without taking his eyes off the road, he unfolded it, held it up to his face flashing something on the bottom, crumpled the page into the size of a golf ball and stuffed it into an open console pocket below the dash.

"Oh perfect," I sighed and squirmed in the bucket seat. "What are you doing?"

"Buckle up, because I've got some things to say and they're gonna go against everything you've probably heard over the past few weeks. Or however long you've been up here."

"Here? As in where?"

"Neverland, Narnia, wherever this whole thing is for you."

I had no idea what he was talking about, but his agitation seemed more like cocaine use than a blunt.

"As a point of interest, there was someone following us, Alfred and me, the whole way here after we crossed the border."

The guy shook his head with an exasperated exhale.

"I'm guessing that was you?"

"Listen up. First—" he pulled a folded page out of the same console he put the crumpled map— "look at this. Use your phone flashlight."

I rubbed my eyes and tried to scrutinize every detail – a white sheet of paper with another map drawn again in a black Sharpie.

"It looks like the same –"

"Keep looking."

"Wait." I paused on something on the bottom I hadn't seen before.

He smiled. "Got it?"

There was a large "IB" written in the bottom corner with an arrow pointing to the hull of whatever wrecked ship was represented here.

"Is that the only difference from the other version you gave to Alfred?" I turned and looked at him now. "And why would you give Alfred a different version? I thought the three of you—you, him, and Genevieve were—"

"I'm sure you did. I'm sure Alfred told you stories of how we were thick as thieves, right? Diving together, with that picture on his mantel of him, Jenny, and Ben. He's not what he seems." He'd lowered his voice, and his vibe when he said it. It was more than resentment. There was wounding there. Disappointment.

"Okay…" I paused a beat to let his words sink in, like I was trying them out to see if they fit. They didn't. "And I should trust you because—"

"No, dude, you shouldn't trust anybody. Now and as a general rule."

I leaned down to stretch my lower back, which ached from the thick cushioning in the bucket seat, and to rub weariness from my face. "Alright. What's IB mean?"

"First of all, is your body acclimatized to cold water diving?"

"Geiranger Fjord in Norway at six degrees Celsius," I answered somewhat in a huff, a little put out by his question, this barely adult smart ass who had somehow learned how to drive a rig.

"How long ago was that?" He had to ask that.

"Look, this is really—"

"Want me to just drop you off here on the side of the freeway and you can find your own way to fucking Nunavut? You realize that's where you're headed, right? Do you even know anything about that place? It's the middle of freaking nowhere. There's literally nothing there, and you're gonna stick out if you're dawdling around town like a clueless tourist."

"Alright I hear you, for chrissake calm down. Why are there two versions of the map? And what the hell is IB?"

# Chapter 44

**My driver ignored the question, and my** phone buzzed with an incoming call. Vaughn now. I wondered if I should even pick it up. How safe was it to talk in the presence of Jerome?

"Hey," I said.

"Don't worry, I won't ask you where you are because I know you wouldn't tell me anyway."

"Why wouldn't I?" I asked. "Maybe because you already know?" I didn't wait long enough for him to answer. "Where are you right now?"

"Seattle PD."

"Did they pick up Jimmy?"

"No, but they know where he is."

"Do me a favor and please keep an eye on Anabel."

Pause. "Okay." Another pause. "Anything else?" There was obviously something on his mind.

I was dying to know if Brooke was okay, but I didn't dare ask him for anything else. "That's it for now."

"Why are you so worried about Anabel?" he asked, with irritation in his voice.

I considered how to answer this straightforward question. Problem is, there wasn't a straightforward answer, or at least not a coherent one. "Because I'm starting to think what happened at the Stork Club was more about me than about Leticia Ames."

"What does that mean? Of course it was about you, and me. We'd been chasing Jimmy for months. He knew he was being pursued, knew he'd never get away with offing a girl in the middle of a crowded night club."

I shook my head, keenly aware of Jerome sitting next to me. He was probably recording me right now.

Vaughn sighed. "What are you thinking? That there's some—"

"What do you think Jimmy was doing there that night? We never established that, not conclusively."

"The same thing an arsonist does when returning to the scene of a fire, no?"

"No."

"And he wasn't looking for other victims—"

"Leticia Ames wasn't a random hit," I cut in. "Her murder was deliberate and intentional to send a message to Marcus Reyes, her boyfriend, about potentially testifying against him in the fed's case with the bank president."

"So you think Jimmy knew Leticia would be there because he'd been following her or something? So then what was he doing there two weeks later?"

"Waiting for us, man. What else? He knew we'd go there as a natural step in our investigation to motive. Jimmy Breslin went there that night because he knew we'd be there. He was waiting for me."

When I hung up I realized we were screaming down the freeway in this eighty-thousand-pound rig. I could see Jerome's death-grip on the steering wheel. I tightened the seat belt over my shoulders.

"It was Genevieve's idea to make two," Jerome explained of the two maps.

"But didn't Alfred dive down there with the two of you?"

"Alfred hasn't been on a dive since 1975, when the diving accident he caused left his brother in a coma."

"So that's what happened. Alfred mentioned his brother. He also said he, Ben Lucas, and Genevieve were a diving team."

"They were," Jerome said. "Alfred was the boat captain, navigated to the dive sites, managed permits when needed, filled the tanks, paid for shit, glad-handing, took care of the gear. The bank account and logistics."

Jerome grew quiet after that. I kept my eyes glued to the road to make sure he didn't drive us into a ditch. I still couldn't tell if he was naturally high energy or a tweaker.

"Am I correct to assume that this map, these maps, I should say, are maps to where the Margarita pearls are hidden?"

Jerome nodded. I kept going.

"And you made two maps because you didn't want Alfred to know where—"

He nodded more emphatically now.

"You didn't trust Alfred. Good, neither do I. Now I know I'm not crazy." I remembered what Jerome said about the pictures on Alfred's mantel, and the expression on his face had looked wounded. "You don't trust Alfred because you think he killed Ben Lucas?" I watched his face and waited.

Nothing at first, then a single nod.

Jesus. I'd said the words before really thinking through them. "Because he loved Genevieve?" I ventured.

"Yeah, that. We all loved her, Alfred loved her in a different way though. He thought Ben was dangerous and was gonna get her killed."

"What are you not telling me? I'm listening but this story has so many holes in it, it's not even a story yet."

Jerome laughed out loud, a full smile showing with his head back, like an evil cartoon character. "Those motherfucking pearls have been the scourge of everyone who's ever touched them. They're cursed. They missed them, Alfred and his brother. They were on the original dive site on the Santa Margarita. Ben Lucas was on the salvage crew that dove down there later, in 2008, so he found them when Alfred and his brother had missed them the first time. Alfred always hated Ben for that."

"Hated him enough to kill him?" I asked.

No answer.

"Alfred said Ben died in a diabetic coma when he didn't take his insulin. But you don't believe that?"

Again no answer. So Jerome thought Alfred killed Ben. "What about he and Genevieve?" I asked.

A chuckle this time. "He introduced her to Ben, and for Genevieve it was love at first sight. Both of them, actually."

"Which left Alfred outside again. What about the map?"

"Before Ben died, he told Jenny, as he called her, that he'd stolen some of the Margarita pearls and hid them in a dive site. Not the Margarita wreck but another one."

"The HMS Terror," I said. "Why would he go all the way to Nunavut, Canada though if the Margarita sank off Florida?"

Jerome turned and stared, his dark eyes blinking as if communicating in a secret language. "You don't know, man?"

"How would I know?"

"I think you know. You might not realize it, but I think you know. Anyway, Ben told me before he died to make two maps, to give one to Alfred and a second one, an altered one, to Genevieve, and he told me exactly where he'd hidden the pearls."

"So you know where they are," I said, mystified at this punk as the keeper of such a potent commodity. "TB – I assume that means Terror Bay?"

He nodded.

"And IB?"

"Right. That was the part I left off of Alfred's map."

"What is IB?" I asked, finally getting to it.

He shrugged. "I don't know. But Ben gave me the name of someone in Calgary who would know. Someone he used to dive with. Some old dude."

"He's expecting us?" I asked. "This contact?"

"No. But he'll talk to us if I show him the map Ben Lucas told me to make. That map's my wild card."

"Yeah and you're mine."

* —◈ ◈▪✛▪◈ ◈— *

I surmised that Jerome didn't actually know where the pearls were hidden but had an idea of the general vicinity. Big difference. And so far, according to Jerome's story, Alfred had both the access and motive to kill Ben Lucas, but I still wasn't buying that as truth.

We stopped once for fast food, supplies, and a bathroom break. I liked how Jerome chose a tiny place a half-mile off the freeway rather than a visible, crowded truck stop. I ate a few bites of a chicken sandwich, dozed for an hour, ate some more, and slept some more. I reviewed the images again that Brooke had sent from Pappy's attic, but my mind was in overdrive and I couldn't think clearly. I hadn't prepared myself for a twelve-hour trip, and my primary job was to make sure Jerome stayed awake and kept us on the freeway. That meant me staying awake. I wished I'd gotten coffee. We were close enough to Calgary now that traffic had thickened. I had Waze opened on my phone.

"How are you doing? Need some water or anything?"

Jerome shook his head. "I'm fine," he said.

"How are you able to stay awake on a long drive like this? Do you do this all the time?"

"Thinking about sex."

It scared me how long it had been since I'd even thought about sex, with only a vague recollection of it at this point. I didn't share that detail. "That keeps you awake on a twelve-hour drive?"

"Yeah try it sometime. It works."

"Okay, whatever. I need to ask you something," I said.

We were almost in Calgary, so there was little time left. Jerome nodded like he knew what I meant, again surprising me with an air of maturity that didn't match the rest of him.

"The last dive?" he asked.

"You were with her, right? I guess I need to know what really happened."

"During the dive, or what happened to her?"

"Both," I said but I would have taken either.

He didn't answer.

"So where's the stop?" I asked, changing the subject.

"Place called Bottlescrew Bills. See if you can find it, on Tenth Avenue. And before you ask me again, no we don't have a meetup locked in with my contact. But he's a crusty old sailor who apparently goes there every day."

"How do you know him?"

"This is where he goes, drinks, lives, whatever. We'll start here and see where it takes us."

I nodded, not minding the fact that he'd used the term us. Alfred had changed, in my mind, to adversary and, such as he was, Jerome was my only available ally at the moment.

# Chapter 45

**"What kind of a pub is open** at eight in the morning?" I asked as Jerome geared down the rig and lumbered through an empty, dirt lot across the street.

The neon lights to Bottlescrew Bills shocked my eyes, still weary from long-haul road burn. I followed Jerome across the street, a wiry beanpole with a long stride and bad attitude. He pulled the red baseball cap from his back pocket and put it on.

"What's his name?" I asked.

"Janus. Your proverbial crusty old sailor who's spent twice as much time on water than land."

Couldn't possibly be the same Janus that Alena and I worked with on our drift driving expeditions in Norway, sailing us around the Fjords. How many of those could there be with that name this far north? "How old is he?" I asked.

"No doubt younger than he looks."

From the door, I spotted his signature long, ruddy face and prominent jaw. Same guy alright. He sat alone in the window seat of a large wooden table. Jerome was wide-eyed, communicating some panicked telepathy to me.

"Janus Lind," I said in my best presenter-voice, complete with a wide smile.

The old man barely turned but held out his hand. "Farin, right? Carl, Kurt?"

"You have a good memory. That was –"

"For an old coot, you mean?"

I shook his leathery mitt. It barely felt like skin.

"Sure, when it comes to beautiful women maybe. How's your... whatever she was?"

"Alena." I nodded. "She's... a friend."

I turned to Jerome, who looked mortified that I'd spoken to the guy first. Funny.

"Excuse me," I said and went to find a restroom. It was an opportunity for me to stand aside and watch Jerome's body language from the back of the bar while I feigned a phone call.

He joined the man at his table, leaned forward, pumping himself up through the usual posturing. Meanwhile, I checked the distance from Calgary to Nunavut – 1600 miles north into the Arctic Circle, or else a four-hour flight. Using my fake identity to cross into another country was one thing, but commercial flying under those credentials was the next level up. Not sure I was ready to cross another line. Or maybe it already happened.

Jerome was seated when I returned, explaining something to Janus, who I could tell wasn't the least bit interested.

"Where is it?" I asked Jerome.

"What?" he shot back in his hood voice.

I sat at the head of the table with my body facing Janus. "Any chance you know what IB refers to in the context of an old ship?" I asked him.

"A ship or a shipwreck?" he asked with a glint in his eye.

"Let's say a ship for now." I felt Jerome glowering. "Jerome, didn't you have a question about that?" He looked as if he might have a stroke, so I kept talking. "Jerome had a map," I said, "maybe he left it in the rig, but it's a hand-drawn map of a ship and it has the letters IB in one of the corners."

Janus looked away and nodded. "What about it?"

"We're trying to find out what that means."

I was careful in my execution. Janus was smart, I remember. Not just street smart but intelligent, analytical, and educated. He'd of course know what we were after.

"Let me see the map." His command was clear. Janus and I stared at Jerome, who wasn't moving. "Hundreds of ships have wrecked off the coast up north," he went on.

"I'm looking west, actually, near the Columbia River," I said.

"Oh?"

"The SS Dix sank in the early 1900s," I said.

"1906," Janus shot back, eyes fixed on Jerome for some reason.

Of course he assumed we'd be talking about the HMS Terror, so I chose something in a different direction, maybe to make things more interesting, or to not be so predictable. Miraculous that I even remembered it.

"She sank in five minutes," Janus added. "Bet you didn't know that."

"No, I didn't."

"What's your interest in it?" Janus asked with a bit more curiosity.

"Well…" I laughed as if he'd caught me. "It's hard to find. Isn't it? That alone interests me. I like a challenge."

Janus smiled back with sinister eyes, playing along but not buying our line of bullshit. I remembered those dives, the high stress adventures of my youth.

"It's supposedly 500 feet down. Jerome's got a map so we can find it. Thing is, the notation on it doesn't make any sense."

Jerome sat frozen with his arms crossed.

Janus wriggled out of his heavy, wool peacoat and leaned forward. "Anything in particular you're looking for if you're able to find it?"

"The propeller's supposedly still completely intact. I for one would love to see that."

"And I'd love to see that map. Otherwise, I'm not sure I can really advise you. Either of you."

I glanced at Jerome, who shrugged, defiant, finding his voice again. "It's my only copy so we'll just say it's in a safe place."

"Didn't your friend Victor Farah vouch for me?" Janus clasped his gnarled hands. "Otherwise how would you have found me?"

I blinked back. Daniel and Victor. Of course Victor would have set this up as part of my running-to service package. How I would have loved a cup of Victor's excellent tea right now.

"Jerome, show him the goddamn map," I barked.

"Nah. I don't think so," he said, leaning his chair back. I so hoped that chair would tip over.

"Shit!" He grabbed the edges of the table when it did. Janus and I shared an eyeroll. I held out my open palm to Jerome, who deposited the folded page with a slap. What a jackass.

I opened it and set it in front of Janus. "What will it cost us to learn what IB might stand for in the context of a map to a wreck dive site?"

"Cost is an interesting word, Mr. Farin. I'll tell you what IB means, but that won't solve any of your other problems."

"Like what?"

"Getting there, convincing the Canadian government that you should have a permit even though there's no record of Richard Norberg ever having dived anywhere, not to mention finding someone to take you out there."

Richard Norberg. So everyone knew my fake name at this point. And here's where the real negotiating started. Janus Lind knew we had absolutely no interest in the SS Dix. He knew our interest was the HMS Terror, and he probably also knew about our other agenda.

"It's really up to you, Mr. Farin. Are we going to work together or work against each other?"

My phone buzzed again with a text from Vaughn. *Bad news about Jimmy*, he typed.

*Oh?* I typed back.

*They had him and lost him.*

*About par. What about Anabel?*

*She hasn't shown up for work in two days.*

* ⊸❖⊸ ✦ ⊸❖⊸ *

We ordered coffee and breakfast rolls. The server asked us to pay right away because of a shift change. When I pulled a twenty-dollar bill from my pocket, out popped a note written in my own handwriting, which I remembered writing in the hospital: *Find her, no matter what.* Was I closer than ever now? Or was Genevieve's fated boathouse where I would always find a part of both her and me?

While we ate, Janus explained the term inner bottom, IB – a dank, unlit lower deck in the bilge area used mostly for storage with little traffic and activity.

"You're saying you could hide anything down there because no one had access to it?"

Janus shook his head. "There was access, if you were a junior officer, maybe, assigned to inspect and familiarize yourself with all parts of the ship, or a lower-level crewman assigned to pull things out of storage for use by the officers. Just not a lot of visibility, and ultimate privacy." Janus smiled when he said it.

At this point, we were all talking about the HMS Terror and the Margarita pearls without ever mentioning either of them. It seemed Janus and I were enjoying the game a bit more than Jerome, who was still butt-hurt at having to give up his toy to a stranger.

"Interesting that you say privacy," I said. "Where would someone hide something, for instance, in the inner bottom of an old ship? You mean just in a random box or something?"

"Up until more recently, the boards of a ship's hull were held together with a gluey substance, pine tar, and there could be different preparations of it. Sometimes it was harder. For other projects it was softer, mounds of it that felt doughy almost. You could, in theory, push something in there, and from the outside it would never be visible."

"But how would you get it out?" I asked.

Again that flinty grin that reminded me of Quint from the movie "Jaws". He'd just given up his biggest secret, making me wonder if everyone in the world knew where Ben Lucas had stored his stash except me. "How do you soften hardened pine tar? Especially old pine tar?" I asked.

"The age of it doesn't matter none, you'd use the same thing. Heat."

We chewed on that for a few silent minutes, sipping coffee, chewing the stale rolls the server left on the table. Bar food.

"I gotta head back to Vancouver soon," Jerome said.

"So this is the handoff Victor set up?" I asked him.

Jerome eyed the two of us – Janus and me, and his map laid out on the table's surface. Knowing he was about to snatch it, I took out my phone and snapped a photo.

"My phone number's on there if you need anything."

I found the photo in my phone and expanded it to see the number. Jerome took his map and walked out without another word. Janus rotated his chair and put his forearms on the table, like finally the two grownups could talk.

"So," he said.

"Right. As to your earlier question, I'd like to work together."

He rubbed his fingernails through the gristle on his chin. "We're talking about the HMS Terror?"

I nodded.

"Margarita pearls?"

Another nod, after which a grin crept into the folds of his wrinkled face.

"Your lucky day I guess. I'm also a pilot."

# Chapter 46

**"It's a throwaway plane," Janus said as** we climbed into the Cessna Skyhawk 172S. "I've got more than one."

Funny how there was very little conversation about this next phase, like it had all been carefully orchestrated for me ahead of time. I followed Janus' directions as if pulled by some invisible thread, the same invisible thread I'd been following for months now.

It was too loud to talk and the ascent was bumpier than I expected. I tightened my seat belt, wondering how he came to know about my connection to the Margarita pearls. Did everybody?

"You probably spent a half a million dollars on this," I said at about five thousand feet. "Are you doing that well for yourself these days?"

He didn't answer and, instead, prepared me for our landing in Iqaluit. "Roughly four hours, depending on wind," he said. "Shouldn't be too bad today."

"Refueling?" I asked.

"We should be good. I get five hours or more of flying time from the 53-gallon fuel capacity, probably more as it's just the two of us with no cargo."

Right. Weight. "What about dive gear and permits?"

"Leave that to me. I was just trying to scare you earlier. I've got a permit and I can bring one guest at a time."

His old quirkiness was amusing but it all sounded too easy. This site required an archaeological permit, which the Canadian government stopped issuing several years ago. "Maybe we should talk about your fee," I said, knowing that conversation should have happened before I ever got in this vessel.

"Standard ten percent of anything recovered."

"And if we don't find anything?"

Shrug. "The risk I take."

So obviously he wasn't in it for the money. That's the Janus I remembered. I couldn't ever recall my eyes being this wide, drinking in the bounty of landscape below us, shapes and schemas unfolding larger and larger with our ascent. I tried to relax despite being jostled around from the tug and push of wind, letting my mind wander. There was so much to consider, details to organize, decisions to be made. This might be my last opportunity to piece it all together, and I couldn't help feeling like everything went back to Jimmy and that fateful night. Jimmy Breslin, I only now realized, was connected to everything that had gone wrong in my life. It felt like a logical separation at first - my life in San Francisco and this wild goose chase through the Pacific Northwest. But now, Vaughn and I had established a connection between Leticia's boyfriend, Marcus Reyes, and the Margarita pearls. Alfred was connected to Victor Farah, so by one degree of separation, the pearls were also connected to Victor. And now Janus. Did Janus know Victor? He mentioned him at the bar but didn't seem to recognize Jerome. How else would he make a connection between me and the pearls?

In the end, the focus of my research had all come back to Jimmy. What was his connection with the Margarita pearls, and how did the missing Marcus Reyes fit into that plan? According to Ben Lucas' will, he left his cache of pearls to Marcus. The two of them worked for the same company, but other than that I was missing some key details. Did he bequeath the pearls to Marcus because it was safer for Genevieve and Anabel that way? Maybe. Or maybe there was another reason.

Janus' Cessna sputtered. I felt the engine stall and then restart.

My hand gripped the edges of the seat as I watched Janus. Movements seemed to normalize after a few seconds. The landscape below us was whiter than thirty minutes ago. We had to be over Northwest Territories now, with a large body of water that had to be Great Slave Lake.

"Sorry about the cold, the heat exchanger's not working," Janus said, pointing to my hands, which I'd been rubbing together.

"I don't mind the cold," I said. "What's your route? Yellowknife heading east to Iqaluit?"

"Exactly," Janus said. The engine sputtered again. Please let us make it there in one piece.

"Have you had trouble with this plane before?"

"She was manufactured ten years ago. I bought her in 2019. I've done a bit of work on her lately. Planes take a lot of maintenance."

"Engine work?" I asked, when it stalled again. This time the engine sound grated, forcing itself through more revolutions to turn over. It did, but barely. I looked out the window trying to gauge our altitude, breathing deeply in and out. Please don't let me die up here.

"This one's a 172S so no carburetor. There was a fuel injection issue that's fixed now. I replaced a failed cylinder head a few months ago. The only other issue was a leaking fuel servo."

"Fixed?" I asked.

He paused. "It stopped leaking so no. I thought it was something else."

Janus' face looked tense, his eyes closely scrutinizing the gauges and dials on the flight panel. Another stall, this time longer than the others. I felt the plane free-floating for a moment, while the engine decided our fate. OMG. "What are our landing options?" I asked.

"We're about halfway between Yellowknife and Baker Lake."

I was staring down through the flight deck windshield. "What's there?"

Janus' face was stone, still staring at the gauges.

"Looks like a lot of rock."

"Wilderness, that's what's down there," he said. "The most raw, pristine wilderness you ever saw. And a lot of water. Little lakes everywhere."

Another engine stall, a recovery, then another stall. A cold terror mounted in my chest as I considered how high we were from the ground.

We were going down. Fast.

A sudden force thrust my body back against the seat and upward, causing my legs and arms to fly in the air and slam down again in a hard thunk.

"What the fuck was—" Before I got the words out, I smelled and saw smoke pouring from the rear. "Janus!"

"We're fine, it's done this before."

"We're not fine, Janus! You need to land this thing!"

He worked the magneto ignition switch while looking down, assessing potential landing locations. The vessel started shaking left and right now, a hard knocking motion like a washing machine that gets stuck with wet towels on one side. The engine was barely engaged. It felt a bit like floating while it decided how much life it had left in it. Then the nose lurched forward and we picked up speed. Oh my God. Brooke…

A sudden thrust knocked us backward as if the engine had dropped a few inches. We were falling now in altitude, quickly, floating down through layers of clouds and opposing currents of air. My stomach was in my throat; my fingers couldn't grip any tighter without snapping off.

"Janus. Janus! What's happ-"

# Chapter 47

*May*

**Cold. So cold. I pulled the air** into my lungs from my nose, cheeks and forehead, ears, hands. What was that knocking? A loud, metal clang, metal against metal, rhythmic, bang - - - bang - - - bang - - -

"Harder," someone said, a man's voice, high-pitched, stressed. Where was I? The hospital again? Please no.

Some period of time had passed since I was last awake because it felt even colder now and my feet were numb. I checked my toes; they could still move, fingers moved, I blinked my eyes a few times. I pulled a quick, deep breath into my lungs, which ended as a coughing fit. Then muffled voices somewhere close. I felt something hard and solid under me, so obviously we'd crashed because we weren't moving. Where was Janus? I called out to him. My voice was thick and raspy. "Jan-us, Janus. You there?"

I dreamt of my Pappy, an image I'd held in my mental archives of him in swim trunks near a spring in Florida from the only bona fide summer vacation of my childhood. He left us later that year and we never heard from him again, other than secondhand updates from my uncle. He wrote me a letter when I graduated from medical school and shipped it to me with signature delivery so I couldn't say I'd never gotten it. Was just like him to do that. I never read it all these years, never opened the envelope. I still wondered about it sometimes.

I heard nothing around me now but held the belief that someone was trying to extricate us from wherever we were trapped. For now, I kept my attention on myself and my body parts. I tried moving my knees and rotated my hips left and right. All still worked and, not only that, it was more confirmation that I was awake. Why was this significant? Because I'd developed a new fear lately: a fear of being unconscious.

Doctors have described consciousness as a ladder. Anesthesia was a form of gradually climbing down a ladder to different states depending on the severity of the medical procedure. When waking from my unconscious state, I'd succumbed to this nebulous nightmare of in-betweenness, which had become my blue cosmos. I knew it, I recognized it, I was sure my mind had constructed it as a survival tactic. I loved it there – the fear came from not being certain I could find my way out. Janus' engine trouble was obviously worse than he thought. His plane crashed somewhere north of Calgary and east of Yellowknife, Northern Territories. And now we were stranded in the middle of nowhere. But at least I wasn't stranded in consciousness-limbo like before. I felt strangely reassured, delighted almost, that I woke up immediately after the crash. I was alive, and no doubt about to enter a new circle of hell.


"Okay, Mr. Farin, I'm an Emergency Medical Technician. Can you hear me?" someone said, lights flashing in my face.

"I hear you," I said. How did he know my real name when I only had my fake credentials with me?

"Great. Now try not to talk, sir. We need to get you out of there and assess your injuries."

"I can feel all my limbs and I think I can move okay, though I can't take a deep breath without coughing. My chest hurts when I breathe."

"Broken sternum," someone mumbled from behind the man talking to me.

I stayed quiet, listening, letting them do their jobs. A woman crawled in on my left and positioned herself behind me. Two male voices were behind her, one said the word *stretcher*. I thought about sitting up and trying to walk, but if I indeed had a broken sternum that would be a terrible idea.

*Come...* Genevieve's voice from deep inside my head, that ethereal sound from another realm, had become so familiar I barely flinched when I heard it now. I must have dozed off again. *Come*, she repeated.

Where? I wondered, refusing to close my eyes, refusing to slide back into my inner cosmos. I was alive here in this tundra. I could feel. I could breathe. I could see my breath in front of my face. I can smell the remnants of coffee on my stale breath. I'm alive and I'm going to stay that way. I hear you, Genevieve, but I'm not going back there. The blue cosmos is my past. As of now I'm going forward.

*Come*, she said again.

*I'm coming*, I said through telepathy. *I'm going to Terror Bay to see what you saw there, to see what you buried there, or tried to unearth before somebody stopped you. You found Ben's Margarita pearls, didn't you? Who stopped you? Someone knew what you found; someone led you to them only to stop you before you could retrieve them. Someone you trusted, I know this now. You didn't die from lack of air, you didn't die from negligence by taking off your tank. Someone messed with the air mixture in your tank and timed it so precisely as to know exactly how long it would take you to get down there and find the pearls, likely in the inner bottom of the HMS Terror. Are you still there?*

*We are connected,* the voice said. *In death we are connected, but we were also connected in life. You will soon discover the truth.*

*Who did this to you, Genevieve? Who planned such an elaborate scheme for your unjust, untimely death?*

*What you ask you already know.*

"On three," someone said, a woman's voice and not the woman

who was behind me. "I got his head," she said.

They rolled me onto a soft stretcher. I could see the crumpled ceiling of the cabin no more than a few feet over my head. The woman pushed the top of the stretcher downward, as I felt myself sliding on some slippery blanket they'd positioned under me. Smart idea. "Keep the IV intact."

I felt pressure in my left elbow and my skin felt cold. It was Alena's voice. Here? Good God.

"Hey Mack, can you hear me?"

It had been her pet name for me three lifetimes ago, up in the cold, dark midnight sun, diving by moonlight, hypothermia always just inches away. Living on the edge. There were two Kurts in our group, so she invented a name for me that she felt, at the time I suppose, was more befitting to my personality. Men named Mack were undoubtedly Vietnam War pilots, Navy Seals, not nerdy medical scholars. Had I really been that to her once, to someone? I was starting to warm from the three layers of space blankets over me.

"What are you doing here?" I asked, surprised by my venomous tone.

"You called me," she said.

I opened my eyes all the way and there she was staring back, her luminous hair pinned to the back of her head. "I still love you, you know," I said. I meant it too.

"What did you say?"

I'd said it out loud, another thing that was melting away in whatever thaw was happening in my deep soul. "You heard me. I don't really care what you think about it either. But I certainly didn't call you."

"Do you want me to go?" she asked. Already we were arguing.

"What do you mean I called you?"

She reached into her jacket and pulled out her phone, fumbled with it for a second and held it in front of me. It showed an incoming call from my phone number four hours ago, which would have been when Janus and I were in the air. Had I? In a panicked moment had my fingers instinctively reached for my phone to text her? The whims of the fragile human heart.

"Did I leave a message? I honestly don't remember."

"No." She looked down. "I just sort of, I don't know, felt you were in trouble."

"And you geo-tracked me?"

Sigh, head goes back, eyeroll, her signature move. "Well considering your plane crashed in the middle of fucking nowhere, aren't you even a little bit—"

I reached up and grabbed one of her hands. "Yes." I nodded. "Thank you for being you. Now please tell me Brooke's not with you."

She shook her head as two EMTs pulled me outside and loaded me into an emergency van. Another EMT was taking my vitals, while my brain worked through the details. How could Alena have gotten to me so quickly? She was walking around the perimeter of the plane.

"Alena," I called to her. "Where's Janus?"

She looked back, mouth closed, face somber. My God.

"She was the pilot?" she asked.

"He, J-a-n-u-s," I spelled it hoping it might trigger her memories of him. I waited. She moved closer, crouching down to my eye level.

"Janus Lind?" she whispered. I watched fat tears fall from her eyes. "What the hell are you doing up here with Janus Lind?"

"Stop pretending like you don't know."

"What—"

"How long have you been following me?" I forced myself to sit up.

"Sir, you need to lay back down flat until we get your heartrate stabilized. Okay?" Large, muscular hands from an EMT slid my elbows down to my sides and pulled the blankets back up over my chest.

"Can you tell that woman I need to talk to her please? Her name's Alena."

"I'm right here," she whispered from behind the EMT.

"You've been tracking me since I left San Francisco, haven't you? Were you in Seattle the whole time I was there?"

She shook her head. "I've been in Calgary for the past three days. Waiting for you."

"How?"

"Vaughn told me what you were doing up here, or what you were planning to do. He said—" she stopped and looked around— "you'd gotten in some trouble," she added, crouched beside me now. "That you were on the run. I thought you might be in danger, you know, medically speaking." She paused to clear her throat. "I was terrified of the idea of you diving in your condition and Vaughn suspected that's what you were planning."

"So that means... you're coming with me, right?"

# Chapter 48

**I was pulled out on a stretcher** and carried into a heated tent where I remained for the next hour. Needled, prodded, and interrogated by one emergency medical worker and two RCMP officers. Overhearing them, I learned that Janus' Cessna crashed on its left side and skidded half a mile before stopping on the banks of Great Slave Lake near Yellowknife. Janus got crushed by the collapsing fuselage. What felt like a broken sternum was some serious bruising but no broken bones. A black spot was forming in the center of my heart. Janus was taking me up here. This was my mission. Had I not pursued this course, our old friend Janus Lind would still be alive.

Alena didn't answer my question about accompanying me on the Terror Bay dive. Because she was a medical worker, the RCMPs released me into her custody, but not before having me provide a lengthy statement and making Alena promise to get me to a hospital in the next forty-eight hours. I used my real name in the official documents because I was tired of pretending. And no more *running from*. Only to. We spent the rest of the day and night in a two-room suite at Chateau Nova in downtown Yellowknife, where I was delivered in a wheelchair to a large, soft bed, room service, with

Alena doing yoga in the other room.

"I need to shower," I said, standing in the doorway to the main room, watching her body move fluidly through sun salutations. She stopped, unashamed from my gaze and utterly removed from her beauty. She helped me into the bathroom and waited outside till I was in the stall with the water on. I knew I'd probably need her help, not having fully assessed my own injuries yet but sufficiently grossed out by my body odor. I let the hot water pummel the top of my head while I soaped my hands into a thick lather.

"Ohhh God."

Pain surged up from my chest into my head and I couldn't contain it anymore. My body shook under the thunder of the water and I let it, allowing shock, fear, anger and desperation to have their say. What made it worse was that Alena was seeing this vulnerable display. I moved my soapy hands slowly over my arms and face, then death-clutched the grab bar with one hand to wash the rest of me. I swear the water draining was brown, emblematic of my sordid undertakings.

She knocked on the sliding glass doors finally and handed me a tiny bottle of shampoo, cap off.

"You'd make a good concierge," I said. The shampoo was mint scented and definitely an improvement.

She opened the door wider. "Done?"

"Good enough for now."

She turned off the water, hooked her hand in my elbow, and passed me a towel. I noticed she didn't glance at my body when she had the chance. Oh how the wounded heart never forgets love. If she didn't care, she wouldn't be here right now I suppose. Still, I wondered about her true loyalties. Was she really up here for me?

I slept like the dead for nine hours and at 8am we ate a full breakfast in the restaurant downstairs. I'd slept too long and had the headache to prove it. We talked about diving logistics while I sucked down coffee number three.

"You're moving better this morning."

"I'm sore literally everywhere." My eyes bored into hers, saying the words I couldn't bear to speak.

"Janus?" she asked, only a slight comfort that she knew me so well.

"It was my errand," I whispered. "I can't get past it."

"Kurt, it just happened. Give yourself time. Anyone would feel the way you do right now. Do you even know where you're going?"

I nodded. "Yes, and I have a map of the dive site. But I need a permit, or we need to find someone to take with us that has a permit for that site."


Alena booked us a flight from Calgary to Iqaluit, the capital of Nunavut, the northernmost province in Canada just across the Labrador Sea from both the southwest tip of Greenland and Labrador on the south side. I'd read somewhere that the average temperature in Iqaluit was 0 degrees Fahrenheit, ranging from -22 to 30.

I booked us a room in a hotel called The Discovery and arranged to pick up a Budget rental car near the airport. The direct flight on Air Canada was nine agonizing hours and I nearly needed sedation just to get me on board. Alena had me doing deep breathing exercises on takeoff and, once we reached cruising altitude, I was intermittently fine. But every time the plane jostled, I had a mini panic attack. I couldn't imagine internet access so far north, but the plane was equipped with Wi-Fi, and Alena let me use her MacBook while she slept. She woke up as a flight attendant was dropping off two box lunches, which I stored on my tray table to give her more room.

"Hey," she said. "I was really out. What time is it?"

"I don't even know what day it is. You were asleep for two hours."

I watched her do all the Alena Broderick things she always did to ready herself for the next activity: three deep breaths, stretching her shoulders and neck, then pulling her hair from her ponytail to shake it out, finger-combing it back and then up it went again, this time into a combination ponytail/bun. The display came close on the awe scale to watching her take off her bra through one of her sleeves.

"So what's your report?" she asked, lowering her tray table and inspecting one of the lunches.

"Good news or bad news first?"

"Good please."

"There's tons of research publicly available about the HMS Terror. I watched several YouTube videos of the interior, found some ship schematics, learned about the overall region and got educated about what really happened there."

"They crashed into each other, right?"

"They left England the same day in the 1840s, the Terror and the Erebus. They got entangled, their masts collapsed and they got stuck in the ice for nineteen months. No survivors and no one knows conclusively what happened to the crew."

"In what way is that good news?"

I look a long breath. "You need an archaeological permit to visit the dive site, which of course we don't have, and the one person who had one... was Janus. Not only that, the Canadian government stopped issuing new permits, even archaeological ones, unless they get rights to any artifacts discovered down there. It's a big political mess right now."

"You always did have great timing," she said in between bites of ham and Swiss. She'd meant it tongue in cheek, but she was right. Nothing felt right about this, and we were wasting considerable amounts of time and resources on what looked like an unattainable quest. When she fell asleep again, I logged her out of Google and logged myself into Gmail to send an email to Brooke.

*Hey sweetie, Hope you're doing okay. Alena's up here with me,* I typed, hoping and praying Alena hadn't told her about the plane crash. *We're doing some more research and I'll get in touch when we reach our hotel in a few hours. I'd love to talk if you'll be around tonight. I need to check in with you and make sure you're okay.* And that was all true. But what I left out of the email was my request to send her on another wild goose chase to Pappy's attic. For some reason, since waking up in Janus' crushed Cessna, I now felt ready to read that letter from my father, the one he sent to me so many years ago. She agreed to go to Pappy's once. So maybe.

I rested my eyes in the sea of darkness out the windows, searching for some signs of habitation in this northern tundra. We'd occasionally pass over small clusters of dim lights. The air in the cabin had cooled in the hours we'd been aloft, but that wasn't what chilled me. My mind worked to unite the details of my unanswered questions into some sort of meaningful narrative. It still felt like a mobius strip of deceit. Jimmy Breslin had more in mind that night at the Stork Club than just killing a young girl. He was sending a macabre warning to her boyfriend that testifying against him in open court would be unwise. And he was sending a message to me as his primary pursuer – to back off.

They offered fresh coffee and I drank some. I knew I needed sleep but every time I closed my eyes, I imagined Janus and I in his plane with an engine on fire. I spent my time online researching Jimmy's original case file.

The one person who had the most interest in those pearls was Alfred Ligetti, so I failed to believe that he was just handing me off to Jerome for the rest of my journey. No way. I'd bet a thousand dollars he'd be waiting when we got to Iqaluit.

I stepped over Alena's legs while she was sleeping to stretch my own and use the restroom in the back of the craft. The cabin lights were dimmed and most of the other thirty or forty passengers were asleep.

"Look," a man said in the back, pointing out the port side windows.

I leaned down behind him and peered into the dark blanket of stars and a stripe of neon green bisecting the horizon and fanned out on one side. My God, the aurora. How could I have forgotten this from my diving years in Norway?

The man looked back at me, saw me smiling and nodded. "You've seen it before, yeah?"

"Been a long time."

"There!" He pointed and now next to the vivid green was a new stripe of light blue or more like aqua. We stood there, both of us, hunched over the seats watching a display that seemed meant just for us, the color fields and shapes carving deep lines in the sleeping night sky.

"I'm Anton," the man said. I rose tall and took a look at him. Clean shaven, wearing an impeccable royal blue suit with a double-breasted blazer, very European. He was tall, thin, with light brown hair and interesting features. "Care to sit?" he asked, summoning me to one of the seats beside the light display. He took the window and I took the aisle. "Anton Weiss," he said, really wanting me to know his name for some reason.

"Hello. Kurt," I said, for some reason pointing to my chest rather than offering my hand.

"What are you doing up here?"

"Treasure hunting," I blurted. Wow, my filter really was broken. With so many ways to answer that question, I'd chosen the most controversial one. The man raised both brows and smirked.

# Chapter 49

**We talked like that for a while** in the back of the plane, in the semi-darkness of the cabin under the staggering aurora display, me giving him generalities and him in the so-called import export business. I'd heard that one before. Since when did importing and exporting require three-thousand-dollar suits? Don't go there, I told myself. He's just a well-dressed businessman of dubious intent.

"We'll be landing soon," I said, and rose. "Nice talking." I moved back to Alena, who was awake and reading something online.

The Iqaluit International Airport was a long, red building, so much smaller and saner than most, meaning we disembarked on the tarmac, luggage already piled onto the single conveyor belt inside. A welcome respite.

Alena left before me. I found her huddled on one of the perimeter chairs scrutinizing her phone.

"I reserved us a car," I said, wondering why she'd hurried out ahead of me.

"Sorry." She looked up, deer in headlights. "It's work, just got a sort of alarming text. I'll be right with you."

My new friend, Anton, was picking his bag off the conveyor belt and motioned me to him. "Where's your luggage?" he asked, urging me, it seemed, to invent a story to explain my presence there. Had he been waiting for me? Come on Kurt, cut it out. Don't become Alex Jones.

"Don't need any this trip," I said casually. "I'm not staying long." I paused long enough after saying it to not seem like I was changing the subject too quickly, another of my newer talents. "How about you, do you live here?"

Now he laughed, head back, rack of teeth displayed. They were capped, noteworthy. "Nobody really lives here, except locals who were born here. I'm from Vienna."

Of course he was.

"I'm curious, then. What would bring an importer exporter all the way to Nunavut? Must be something worthy about this place, no?"

* ❖ ❖ ✦ ❖ ❖ *

Hotel and rental car booked, what I hadn't prepared for was ice-covered snowpack on the roads amid nearly constant darkness. I insisted on driving the SUV, Alena sulked beside me like a sullen teenager. No more than twenty mph, luckily there weren't many cars on the road. The Discovery Hotel in Iqaluit was nicer than the pictures, and every staff member looked like a magazine cover. Alena didn't like the fact that our room was on the first floor. She was in a sour mood ever since her mystery text "from work" in the airport. There would be no scantily clad yoga in this hotel room. One room and one bed, no less. She'd have to deal with that.

"Are you gonna tell me what's bothering you?"

She opened her mouth and was about to say it's nothing.

"It's something, so don't do that."

"Nothing you need to worry about, put it that way."

"I don't know why but I know it's about Brooke somehow." I stared. "Would you keep something like that from—"

"Turn off your thought-police. Save it for your coma club friends."

"I only wish I had some."

She didn't say sorry, and I knew she wasn't. She also hadn't refuted my claim about Brooke. I'd text her tonight.

"You can't go down there," Alena said. "You weren't well enough before, and you're certainly not now."

"I'm going."

"Tell me why."

"I owe you no explanation and you don't have to—"

"Do you have any idea how much time I've wasted—no, invested in your wellness?" she asked. "I've spent the past week in Canada conniving and cajoling everyone who would listen so I could find out where you were."

"Why? To stop me from diving? Or is there another reason?"

She covered her face with her hands. We were both exhausted, and neither of us wanted to be here.

"I need—no," I started again. "I feel compelled to see where Genevieve was on her last dive. I need to understand what happened to her and why," I said, assuming Vaughn had brought her up to speed.

"You're obsessed."

"Determined. There's a difference."

"And you know conclusively that's where she was?"

"Yep."

"How?"

"I'm tired, Alena. You're making me more tired."

"How do you know for sure?" she pressed.

"You know, you missed your calling as a litigator."

"I've been told that." She smiled, her eyes persisting though.

I took a long sigh, trying to summon a few more bits of stamina. "Alfred Ligetti told me."

"Okay. What else?"

"What do you mean?"

"What other evidence do you have to support the fact that—"

"Evidence? Seriously?"

"I heard you have some kind of a map."

I shook my head. "Who told you that? Vaughn, the rumor mill?"

"Do you?"

"Do I have a map? Yes, I have a map." Heavy sigh. "Before you ask me where I got it, I got one from Alfred. And then I got another one from Jerome, Genevieve's other dive partner."

"A map of what? Does it have the exact location?"

I stared at her. "Are you asking if I have the latitude and longitude coordinates? No."

"Not what I mean." She sighed and pulled her hair out of her ponytail. "Where do you think the map location refers to?"

"Nunavut, obviously. That's where we are now." I squinted at her.

"You know that, right? Did the map have Nunavut on it?"

"You mean did it have that word on there? No."

"King William Island?"

I started to see where her annoying line of inquiry was going.

"Did it mention the ship? The HMS Terror?"

"No. But it did say Terror Bay on it."

She nodded, taking this in. "Anything else?"

"Something about a permit."

"And you thought that meant the HMS Terror?" she asked, arms crossed.

"Well, yeah, because you need an archaeological permit to dive there. I heard now you even can't do that anymore because of government regulation. What are you thinking?" I asked.

She moved to the middle of the bed. I could see her holding something back.

"You're thinking the map refers to someplace else?" I asked.

"Well, it says Terror Bay on it. How many Terror Bays are there in the world?"

I stared.

"Have you checked?"

I remembered the clipping about a small child named Genevieve Lucas disappearing off Kodiak Island. If I could get Anabel to go back to Pappy's, I might be able to learn more details.

"You told me the HMS Terror sank in Nunavut, right?" she asked.

"Yes, over fifty miles from where she was abandoned and thirty miles from the wreck of the Erebus." I watched her face slowly reveal something to me, her eyes widened, face relaxed, egging me onto this new truth. "Are you saying, what, that there's another Terror Bay?"

She nodded slowly, leaned back to grab her phone off the

bedside table. She held it up. I reached to grab it from her desperately wanting to check her text messages. Instead I looked closely at the map on the screen and zoomed out with my fingers.

"Alaska?"

Alena nodded. "Off Kodiak Island."

My God, the clipping. I stayed quiet for a long time pulling it together in my mind. I nodded, blinking at the screen, blinking through my past with Alena up here in the bitter cold, my distant past playing hide and seek in a broken-down school bus. So maybe Ben Lucas, or Genevieve, hadn't buried the Margarita pearls in the HMS Terror Bay. The SS Dix sank off of Kodiak Island in 1906.

"That's possible, actually."

Alena sprawled out on the bed, propping her head up on her hand. "A fakeout?" she asked.

"Possible."

"Why though?"

I nodded through more details in my head, blinking them into formation, my heart begging for an answer to the eternal why. If Genevieve thought Alfred Ligetti killed Ben – her husband – out of either protection or jealousy, she'd likely want to keep Alfred's paws as far away from those pearls as possible.

"What do you know about how she died?" she asked me.

We both snapped to attention at the sound of a loud thump at the end of the hall.

"Ground floor rooms are a terrible security risk," she mumbled while I listened at the door for follow-up sounds. Nothing.

I took her through the details of Genevieve's last dive. "Someone messed with the mix in her tank. I'd been thinking it might be Jerome, her young dive partner."

"Does that jive with your inclinations?" she asked.

Inclinations. She would have never used that word before. Did she think I had visions or special powers? "What, do you believe me now?" I asked.

She smiled and looked down. Was that shame I saw on her face? I couldn't tell. I used to have her every expression decrypted. "I believe you believe it."

I nodded.

"The mind is capable of all kinds of inexplicable magic, under the right circumstances."

"Or the wrong ones," I added.

"Could Alfred have been the one to change her mix?" she asked.

"Possible, but another angle I hadn't considered is Jimmy."

"The guy who shot you? How is he involved in this?"

"Long story, and more than you know. He owns a dive shop on Bainbridge. He also had a motive for killing Genevieve… if he knew where the pearls had been hidden. As far as access, any of them could have done it, potentially. The question is, who had a more likely motive for getting her out of the way? Alfred, Jerome, or Jimmy?"

# Chapter 50

We ordered burgers at the Granite Room restaurant and drank cognac by a gigantic, stone fireplace in a lounge alcove. I moved the end table so Alena and I could pull the chairs closer together for privacy. Well-fed and lubricated from the alcohol, the strain of the crash seemed to melt away by the minute. I couldn't help but feel energized by the idea of the SS Dix. Was Genevieve wily enough to elude the pearl's pursuers by pretending that Ben buried them in the HMS Terror, only to protect their real location in Alaska?

Could I really let my guard down for a quiet moment by a fireplace with a pretty woman at my side? It seemed too good to be true, and probably was. We spoke in hushed voices about the Dix, access to Kodiak Island, and the HMS Terror, both of us keeping watch in all directions.

"Kodiak Island's a lot closer to Bainbridge than Iqaluit," she said, tilting her head, trying like me to make this new line of inquiry stick.

"Probably a three-hour flight," I said. "Are you sure you're not promoting this new idea just to prevent me from diving again?"

"Brooke made me promise I wouldn't let you do it, but you

already know you shouldn't dive right now, even aside from the plane crash."

I knew it was risky. Everything was right now. But if we were going to hash out a possible plan, Alena needed the benefit of all related details. "Genevieve Lucas may have had a connection to Kodiak Island," I said.

"Did her work take her there? Wasn't she a marine biologist? I would think the intercoastal area would present all kinds of opportunities for studying marine ecosystems."

"There's something else. She may have grown up there."

I filled her in on the newspaper article, and on where I'd found it. She listened, draining her glass. We made our way back to the HMS Terror topic and Janus' dive permit. I drained the rest of my cognac at the mention of his name. Ryan, now Janus—guilt begets guilt.

"Another?" I pointed to her glass.

She formed her mouth into a charitable smile and nodded, but I knew she didn't want one. I took both glasses to the bar and sat on one of the high, padded stools while a twenty-something bartender poured Courvoisier into fresh glasses.

"Here, let me get those for you." The aurora borealis guy, Anton Weiss, was now dressed in a dark gray version of the same suit. How many did he have?

"Oh please no, but–"

"I insist," he said, and ceremoniously removed a gold credit card out of an eel skin wallet. His hands looked suitable for a jewelry commercial.

I felt Alena's eyes on me without looking. "Thank you," I said, fresh out of fight. I knew I'd just bought him leverage and us trouble. Of course I had to invite him back to our alcove. Thank goodness there were no chairs.

"My friend Alena Broderick," I said walking us back there. "This is Mr. Weiss. We met on the plane when you were sleeping."

Anton touched her glass and flashed his toothy grin. "Lucky man," he said to me.

"Salud," she barely managed, with no tolerance for players.

"Um, sorry. Let's see if we can find another chair somewhere."

"No please, take mine." Alena popped up, handbag already on

her shoulder. "I've had enough to drink and had enough of this day, honestly." She leaned into me and kissed my cheek, for his benefit I was sure. "Lovely dinner, thank you."

"Well, problem solved then." Anton Weiss settled into Alena's seat and I remained standing and watched her head down the first hallway.

It felt like another moment of truth, hard decision-making and high stakes negotiations, none of which I felt ready for. But it amazed me how something like Victor's pressed shirt and jacket equalized the playing field, like he'd known about this encounter before it happened. Maybe Anton Weiss was on Victor's payroll as well.

I set both our glasses on the small, square table beside my chair and crossed my legs, simulating comfort and relaxation. This was an opportunity in disguise, an opportunity to learn. Sure. Use it, I told myself.

"So what types of things does your enterprise import and export?" I asked, diving right in. I chose the word enterprise with great care, knowing his elevated opinion of himself would likely overpower any other urges.

Legs and arms crossed, he leaned in with a conspiratorial whisper. "Antiques," he said.

"Oh? How interesting, and such a wide playing field because there are so many types of antiquities." Especially in remote northern Canada. Right.

He shook his head with a scowl. "No, not antiquities, nothing so exotic. My company works with more pedestrian varieties, mid-range furniture and so forth."

"Even better. I have a fondness for certain types of antique furniture."

"Do tell," he said, exaggerating his interest with raised brows.

"Well, I don't have an eye for it or anything, just like the look of certain things."

"What in particular?"

I ran through the meager furniture database in my head and remembered one of Pappy's prized possessions – a Stickley rocking chair that was likely still in his attic, worth thousands. "We've got a few original Eastlake chairs and a Stickley."

Big smile. "They're absolute staples for us. I sold fifteen Stickley pieces last year. Never go out of style."

Watching him cross, uncross, and recross his legs told me he was either uncomfortable talking to me or uncomfortable with the subject matter. And in an instant I knew why we were here. A tattoo was visible on the top of his left hand when he reached around the chair to grab the water pitcher. Two tridents aimed upward from a diving helmet flanked by sea horses on each side. He was a naval master diver. Jesus.

Diving. *Pearls.* Here we go again.

"But really all I care about is diving. Alena and I have been diving together for years."

"You're not married?" The hound in him reared its head at the mere mention of her.

I calmly shook my head. "Just friends, the best of friends really," I added, making sure my eyes didn't wander from his face.

"Any particular interests?"

It was a great question that kept the conversation one-sided, while he continued sizing me up. "Drift diving in the fjords mainly, though we also dived in warmer climes years ago." I left the conversation there while I paused to sip my drink. Two sips, three, enjoying a silence pregnant with tension, waiting for him to make his move. I knew he knew why we were here and there'd been nothing casual about our encounters, either of them.

"To be honest, I heard you and the woman talking about permits."

"Oh? Please tell me you work for the Canadian government and will grant us an exception." I sighed in feigned frustration, loving the idea that Alena and I had already moved off of the HMS Terror as a possible location. "We've picked out our next dive site but you need a certain type of –"

"I have one." His face changed, eyes wide now, mouth contracted.

"Have—"

"An archaeological dive permit. That's what you need, right?"

"Well, yes. Where are—"

"Come now, Mr. Farin, I think we both know where we're talking about. Unless you were born here, there's only one reason why anyone would ever come up here." He waited. I stared. "I can take you down there using my permit. I can take up to three guests and I've used it before. But this is a short trip for me and so it must be tomorrow."

I rewound the tape on our conversation. Antiques. Great cover story.

"Thank you," I said, rose, and offered my hand. "I don't think we can make it tomorrow. Besides, we've been drinking." So had he. "Are you staying in the hotel?" I redirected.

"Where else?" He grinned now, an engineered pose with the forced stretching of his lips across a rack of perfect teeth. Behind his eyes, though, I saw agitation, maybe even a tinge of fear, perhaps that his attempts to woo or control me weren't working. Right now Alena and I were holding the cards. I just wasn't sure what game we were playing anymore.

I knocked softly on the hotel room door and used my key to get in. She wasn't asleep. I found her poised on the edge of the corner chair staring out the window at the night sky.

"No aurora tonight?"

"Nope," she said without moving.

"Find any empirical answers up there?"

Now she turned away from the window and sat cross legged in the chair, back straight as a pin. Her posture was always flawless. I never knew how she did it, unmoved by stress, indifferent to the primordial pain that crumbles our bones and wears down our years. There she was in front me, still as fresh as she looked first thing this morning.

"Beauty," I said. "It comes so effortlessly to you."

"Hardly. Surprised to see you back so soon."

"Do I really seem the type to be wooed by a guy like Anton Weiss?"

Her brows said yes. "What was the pitch?" she asked.

"Oh…" I waved my hand in the air. "He heard us talking about permits and—"

Her blue eyes rolled upward.

"He apparently has an archaeological permit and can take a guest if he goes with them."

"Like I said, surprised to see you. What'd you say?"

"I'm here, so what do you think?"

"Feels like a setup," she mumbled, turning back toward the window. "Anyway, didn't we already establish that it's not down there?"

I shrugged. "I think it's a possibility that it's not down there."

"Genevieve Lucas was down there," she said, her eyes filled with tears now. "She died down there, Kurt. She was murdered. I don't want the same—"

I sat on the floor, but not in an act of intimacy. I saw a shadow move outside. "Look, if I say no and this guy has nefarious intentions, he's likely to follow us anyway."

She nodded. "You're right. I wish I knew someone who could help us with that."

I smiled. "You don't have friends in low places?" Of course I thought of Victor and his Running From services, which I hadn't taken advantage of before. "I may know someone actually."

"I'm not surprised."

"Besides, I've got a jacket I need to return."

# Chapter 51

At this point, I was considering our situation to be urgent so I texted Victor at 3am to inquire into his extraction services.

*Be with you shortly,* he wrote back. *I'm tracing your GPS coordinates now.*

I took a quick shower while I waited, surprised at the bruising on my skin almost as if this was the first time I'd seen it since the plane crashed. Janus... did that all really happen? I soaped up, shampooed my hair, and felt pangs of the same soul-longing for the silky feel of cold, ocean water.

"I think you got a text," Alena called from the bed, her eyes still closed.

Sure enough, Victor. *Take the first flight tomorrow morning to Calgary. When you land, text the word BADGER to the number 850057 and both of you wait in the restroom behind the Alberta King of Subs next to a Chapters bookstore.*

It sounded like a bad spy film. *Thank you,* I wrote. *Billing?*

*We'll settle up later.*

I booked the Calgary flights and reported the plan to Alena. But I hadn't told Victor I was here with her yet. He'd said *both of you.*

How did he know?

Paranoid wasn't the half of it. My neck was sore from looking behind me every two seconds walking through the airport. We took a 6am flight and arrived in Calgary mid-afternoon. Amazing how easy it was to travel without luggage. I was starving so I bought two sandwiches, chips, and drinks before ducking into our designated sandwich shop restroom.

"Are we, like, eating in here?" Alena asked, nose perceptibly upturned.

I unwrapped my sandwich, watching her eye the spotless fixtures.

Knock-knock. That was Vaughn's signature entry. Nothing would surprise me at this point. I opened the door.

"Weird place to eat lunch but okay," he said, and gave Alena a strange look. Pretty soon I'd just stop asking how and why Vaughn repeatedly showed up on these missions.

I gave my partner a half hug, honestly relieved to see him. We followed him into the dark hallway and down a service elevator. On the bottom level, the exterior door led to a loading area with a white van.

"This way," he said.

"Where are we going?" I asked him, Alena two feet behind me. "Different airport?"

"Same airport, different terminal. WestJet Airlines to Anchorage."

So I surmised that Vaughn, in some capacity now, worked for Victor, though I wasn't certain which of Victor's services were at play here. I asked him after we'd loaded into the van.

"So who's managing the…" I paused to find the right word.

"Victor's got two men on it. Let's say I'm your friendly escort."

The WestJet flight was only half full with mostly balding, suited businessmen with briefcases, probably in sales, probably mostly same-day flights. Alena, Vaughn, and I spent the time discussing logistics. Victor had arranged another one-hour flight from

Anchorage to Kodiak, lodging at a Best Western. The rest of our activities were up to me, he said. And hopefully the services I hadn't yet paid for would ensure our safety from anyone following us. Did that mean Victor's men would be with us on the island when we got there? There were too many questions to worry about. At some point I'd need to just trust – someone, or something.

Alena and Vaughn changed seats so she and I could discuss the dive.

"You do know how far down it is, right?" Vaughn now, snarky as ever, talking across the aisle.

Alena, from the beginning, had learned to sort of summarily ignore Vaughn, offering just enough courtesy to seem neutral, but only barely.

"Five hundred feet," I said, remembering what I'd read of the SS Dix.

"We'll need two tanks each, and a different oxygen mix for that depth," Alena added, then looked directly at me. "Do you feel up to this?"

"I've been so dying to get in the water there are no words."

"Alright, no dying though please."

"Fair enough."

"I'm not clear on how you got from the HMS Terror to the Dix," Vaughn whispered, leaning into us from the other row.

I looked at Alena. "There are two Terror Bays, according to Alena's research, and we think Genevieve used the HMS Terror as a decoy, intending all the while to retrieve the stash from the Dix."

"But why bury recovered shipwrecked treasure on another shipwreck?" he asked.

It was a good question. I shrugged.

"Who would ever look there?" he continued. "Who would think of it and who on earth would be willing to go through the trouble of putting it there?" he asked. "And do you know exactly what you're looking for, meaning type of container or a particular part of the ship?"

"I'll know it when I see it."

So far, Victor's services were working because we were still alive and I'd seen no one pursuing us. And no sign of the illustrious Anton Weiss. Victor booked two rooms at the Best Western in Kodiak. Alena insisted on having her own room and Vaughn and I stayed in an adjoining room, which Victor had insisted on for security.

I liked the rustic hotel room décor. Dated, sure, but the dark blues and browns fit the area, and the climate.

"Disappointed?" Vaughn asked as we shuffled into Room 434.

"What do you mean?"

"You know what I mean."

Alena. "Are you kidding? I can barely shower by myself right now let alone have sex. I don't know if I even remember how."

"Bet she does."

"What does that mean?"

His mouth lifted on one side.

"We haven't been a couple in, God, I don't even know how many years at this point. I'd honestly rather bunk with you. Watching her do yoga was," I shook my head. "A bit much."

Vaughn grinned. "I do yoga. Want me to do yoga for you?"

"Thanks for the visual. Look, I need to ask you something anyway so I'm glad you're here."

"I know you have a lot of questions. I'm sorry that it's not likely I can answer many of them."

"Many? Don't worry about it. I get the feeling you're taking orders from more than just the PD right now, and I don't want to impose myself on whatever other cases you're working on."

Vaughn clasped his hands behind his back.

"I want Jimmy's case file. I've been thinking ab—"

"You have it. Or do you not have access anymore?"

"I don't have access to anything, and I need to understand the bigger picture."

"Of?" he asked.

"Jimmy."

Vaughn lowered his head. "You mean the federal case."

That's what I meant alright. Was this the part of the case I'd never get access to, at least while it was still open? I needed a more compelling pitch. "Back then, we were informed about Jimmy being named in a federal criminal case and he was a co-defendant. Then

Jimmy shot the primary defendant but I never got the exact details of the case and I need that information now because I believe it directly ties to not only the case of Leticia Ames but two other deaths."

"Who?" Now he looked more interested.

"Genevieve Lucas, and her husband, Ben Lucas."

"Why would—were there suspicious circumstances surrounding their deaths?"

I knew this tactic. Turning the conversation from him to me was a way to avoid having to either give or withhold the information I needed to understand the depth of Jimmy's sphere of influence. He'd been our informant years ago, and Jimmy only cared about money. I needed to find out how much. So I pulled out the secret weapon. "I think I've earned access to that file. Don't you think?"

Bam. I saw the impact of my question on his face, eyes and cheeks contracted like he'd been hit with a blunt object. Of course I'd earned that access, regardless of what agency he was working for now. There were a few ways we could do this. He could make a request based on the justification from my head injury, or he could subvert regulations and just give me access on his own. He could also say no.

"Look, you might not be on the payroll right now but you're still my partner, to me anyway." He nodded. I nodded back. "You got a laptop with you?"

"Yes," I said.

"Go to the internal records site and step away. I'll log you in with my credentials long enough to let you see the files, but you can't download anything because that'll be tracked."

"Fair enough."

# Chapter 52

**He left me alone in the room** while he went next door to figure out our food situation.

Looked like Vaughn only had access to three of the official case file documents from the shooting of a bank president named Paolo Rinaldi, President of Cayman National Bank: a police statement and two witness statements. The police statement indicated that Jimmy was observed at the crime scene thirty minutes prior to the shooting of Rinaldi and then fled the scene, thereafter pursued by law enforcement and Interpol officials but, for some reason, not apprehended. There was reference to a related Green Notice Interpol file, specifying notice given to law enforcement agencies in member countries about persons likely to commit offenses in those territories. There were three Witness Statements available, all heavily redacted with names, dates, and descriptions blacked out. That got me nowhere.

I still needed to understand the connection between Jimmy and Paolo Rinaldi, and why Rinaldi was wanted by Interpol in the first place. I opened a browsing tab and looked up the bank, twenty-seven branches, I clicked the company masthead link on the Contact menu and the page wasn't resolving. So I opened a new tab and searched for news articles about Cayman National Bank. New branches opening, now supporting two crypto platforms for personal accounts and investing options. I filtered my search for news within the past year. Next, I tried Paolo Rinaldi Interpol, and oddly nothing came up. How was this possible? Paolo Rinaldi had no Interpol file? The PD had the Interpol notice in the file on Jimmy. I tried James Breslin Interpol, that also revealed nothing.

I got up to get some water from the bathroom and heard raised voices next door. Vaughn had gone to Alena's room. I froze, listening closer to the back wall behind the toilet. Alena was repeating one word, it sounded like *no*. What was going on in there? I wanted to join them but knew the clock was ticking on my file access. I returned to the laptop and saw that the masthead link on the bank's website had finally come up. The Board of Directors on the top row showed President and General Manager, Paolo Rinaldi. Wait. I recognized the clean-shaven face and rugged jawline first, then the lapels on a fucking royal blue suit jacket.

The picture was labeled Paolo Rinaldi.

The image was of Anton Weiss.


I took two steps toward the adjoining door and heard the exterior door to our room open behind me.

"What's going on in there?" I asked.

"I told her I wanted to take her back to San Francisco and that you should take this next leg of the trip alone."

Smart idea, all things considered. "I'm guessing… no?"

"She still says you're not well enough to dive and insists on going with you as your medical consultant."

"That's fine, that's what I'd planned anyway. Do you want to stay with her tonight?"

"Then you'll be alone and you're already a target."

"What a fucking soap opera. I'll go talk to her. Oh," I turned back, pointing to the laptop. "The bank president that Jimmy shot, Rinaldi?" I smiled.

"What about him?"

"The antique dealer I told you about from up north? He's going by the name Anton Weiss now."

"That's Rinaldi? Jesus." Vaughn looked up and examined the ceiling tiles. "You've got the entire underworld tailing you right now. Wasn't that what Victor was supposed to be monitoring?"

"Rinaldi's a bank president, I wouldn't call that underworld."

"I think maybe he's moonlighting."

There was no response to my knock on the inside adjoining door to Alena's room. I scanned the hallway and walked ten steps to her room and listened first. No TV, no hairdryer, no shower. Three knocks, no response. I went back into our room and texted her.

*Hey, what's going on? Are you okay?*

*I'm fine.*

*Are we traveling together or what? Because it doesn't seem like it.*

*Just don't want to talk right now. Our flight's in six hours. I'm going to sleep for a few.*

*Fine.*

*I want to examine you before we get on our next flight.*

*Okay.*

I had no idea what this meant but knew this was all I was getting out of her right now. It had been years, but I still remembered. Travel, it seemed, brought out either the best or worst of the human personality. Alena got easily unraveled by abnormal sleep patterns and even worse when you threw in different time zones. I was surprised this hadn't happened already. Vaughn couldn't be better about travel. Cheerful, flexible, almost like his personality was designed to appease the Alenas of the world. I reported her request to Vaughn, which evoked the same wry smile as when I told him about yoga.

"Examine you. Sounds like fun. Why don't you stay with her tonight? I'll stand guard over here, I'll be fine."

"Not when she's like this. I'd be maimed and killed."

"Alright, what's your dive plan then?" he asked.

"I imagine that's the purpose of the exam, as she put it. She's on my medical team so she could certainly try to prevent me from diving due to medical concerns."

"It's irrelevant. It's not gonna stop you, is it?"

I sat in the cushioned desk chair and examined the rollers, wheeling it around the carpet, stalling while I thought of the best response. Who can I trust? It was the same question nagging me now as before - on Bainbridge, in Nunavut, even in San Francisco before I embarked on this ridiculous quest. No, Alena's hysterics weren't stopping me from following Genevieve's leads because this is what my life was supposed to be right now. I had no way of proving the veracity of this theory, I just felt it. Somewhere on Kodiak Island, maybe on the wreck of the SS Dix or maybe somewhere else, Genevieve left me a clue. Who did I trust right now? Myself, and that was something new.

We ate takeout, Vaughn rotated through the four or five cable channels. I slept off and on, listening to the night, wondering where my life had gone. When did I last wake up in the familiarity of my own bed, shop in a store, go out amongst others in my community, embedded in the world as I'd known it? An even scarier thought was whether I'd ever get to see that world again, or if my medical recovery had irrevocably altered the course of my life's journey. I don't know if I could even picture a life in San Francisco again, unsure if a big city was the right place for me and where I might fit now. My need to hear Brooke's voice was growing every day, it seemed, and the more time between conversations made it ever harder to reach out. I don't know if she even wanted to see me at this point.

Vaughn knocked to let Alena know when our food was here. She didn't answer. I texted her an hour later to check on her, to which she replied, *Sleeping.*

When I knocked the next morning, again there was no answer. Vaughn tried, I tried again, we texted her and this time there was no response to the texts or knocks.

"Are you worried?" Vaughn asked me.

"Call the front desk."

"And tell them what exactly?"

I knew what he meant. If something had happened to her, we needed to get our story straight. A sense of dread filled my chest. Last night I'd pretty much decided to go it alone and ditch the two of them somehow. This wasn't at all what I'd had in mind though.

"The concierge is coming," Vaughn said, hanging up the land line.

"What'd you tell them?"

"That she went to bed early with a migraine and wasn't responding this morning."

Migraine, smart. My dread wasn't that we'd find her dead or ill, but not finding her at all. I tried to remember if I'd heard any sounds in the middle of the night. I was a light sleeper now but remembered nothing other than the feeling of the pillow mashed against my face. The clock radio on the bedside table read 7:35am. It was one of those moments when my brain wanted me to make note of the time. Vaughn stood in the bathroom doorway toweling off his wet hair.

Pop—pop! Two loud explosions bellowed from the rear of the building on the left side. Vaughn slid into tennis shoes and pulled a pistol out of his duffel bag.

"How did you get hold of that?"

"Don't ask. You stay here."

"Wait a minute."

He froze, brows wrinkled. "What?"

"Alena. What if something happened to her and those gunshots were a decoy to divert our attention?"

His shoulders sank. "Right, you're right."

We banged on the door to her room, still no sounds in response, but a chorus of voices echoed from the lobby's tall ceiling. Vaughn took off down the hallway and I trailed him after grabbing our room key off the TV.

"Call the police!" An older woman was crouched down in the lobby by the doors catching her breath, looking back at us.

"Are you alright?" Vaughn asked her.

"Some guy shoved me to the ground and they put a woman in a van."

"Are you hurt?" I asked her. She shook her head. "What did the woman look like?"

"I couldn't see her, I was too late," she said.

Vaughn stared down the street in the direction the van took off, then turned to the woman. "Did you happen to see the license plate?" he asked her.

"I got it," she said and rose. "DL-369."

"That's very helpful," he said, the understatement of the millennia. "Anything about the van?"

"No," she said. "But the men seemed to handle the woman very gently, more than you'd expect. Oh yes, one of them was wearing a nice-looking white shirt."

Hello, Victor.

# Chapter 53

**Anytime any witness came back with a** plate number was miraculous enough. Hail the white dress shirt.

"What the fuck was that?" Vaughn asked, watching my face.

"Victor."

"Did you set that up?"

"No," I blurted. "Well, not specifically. I engaged him to trail us en route to Anchorage, knowing Jimmy's been two steps behind me since I left San Francisco."

His eyes widened. "Behind you?"

"Okay, maybe two steps ahead."

"So if Victor picked up Alena, it must have been because Jimmy was seen on-site. What the fuck would Jimmy want with her now? Is there any connection?"

I sighed. "Yeah there's a connection, her connection to me. She's someone I care about, have a long history with. He must know this. If he's trying to endanger those closest to me, it's to pull me off his trail. He's afraid."

"You're getting close," he said. "Too close."

"Victor was waiting here for Jimmy," I said.

"And the shots fired?"

We stared at each other, listening for additional noises outside. I pressed Victor's number and immediately disconnected, deciding texting would be more discreet.

*Was that you?* I wrote.

*Your nemesis had just picked up your companion on her way back to her room,* Victor typed back. That had to mean Jimmy fired those shots as a warning, knowing he was being pursued.

*I didn't realize she'd left her room. You have her with you now?*

*Yes, she's in satisfactory condition.*

*Appreciate the rescue.*

*Gratitude is no substitute for payment.*

*We'll work that out. Vaughn will contact you to coordinate picking her up.*

*Understood. Do let me know if your future plans require assistance.*

*I will.*

I passed my phone to Vaughn so he could read the exchange while I waited outside on the concrete walkway under a waking sky, sub-zero wind pelting my face. Vaughn was right; I was getting closer. To what, though? To a truth Jimmy desperately needed to protect.

Our operating theory had been about the Margarita pearls based on our historical assumption that all Jimmy cared about was money. What if we were wrong, and that wasn't all he cared about? Or what if we were right but the pearls were only part of the story? I couldn't help thinking about Jimmy's case file. Something in there had caught my eye earlier. I needed to see it again.

"Can I still access that records site? Is your laptop still logged onto that link?"

"Should be," he said. "You go ahead. I'll stay out here a while in case Jimmy comes back. Find out where Victor is now and I'll link up with them and see that Alena gets home safe. You're on your own now."

I looked across the walkway at him a moment too long, the gravity of those words sinking in. "Thank you." I turned, walked to him, and full on shook his hand, unsure if I'd ever see him again.

I ran up to the hotel room to check his laptop connection, but the internal records site had auto-logged me off. Shit. Grabbing my coat, wallet, and backpack, I headed cautiously out front, eyeing every corner of the building inside and out. It was too cold and too dangerous to stand outside. My mind went to the phone booth in Seattle, where I had been picked up by Daniel Farah, the cab driver. Was it worth a try? Of course he wouldn't be in Canada right now. Would he? I texted him a formal ride request. My phone vibrated with an incoming call two seconds later.

"Daniel?"

"Yes, Kurt Farin, the man whose name is so like mine. How are you holding up?"

I loved his jovial voice. It made Jimmy's presence and my solo journey seem a little less bleak. I explained the situation. "Your brother was just here. Or maybe you know this already?"

"Perhaps you noticed when we last met. Victor and I, we're like oil and water. We try to only spend time together when absolutely necessary."

"I noticed, like most brothers I guess. Are you or do you have another driver available for an airport run from my hotel?"

"Calgary? Yes, I can do it," he said.

"How long a wait for a pickup?" I asked.

Then that jolly Santa laugh again. "Zero minutes? I'm out front. Green Subaru this time."

I scanned the hotel grounds before going out, deciding that if Jimmy Breslin wanted me dead, I'd be on my way to the morgue. I opened the rear passenger door to Daniel's car, strapped in and glared at him.

"What are you doing up here?" I asked. "I thought you didn't know Victor was here today."

"No one said I wasn't aware of his schedule. I just said we didn't like each other." More laughing. Love this guy.


Daniel said it would be an hour to the airport. Meantime I worked on booking a commercial flight to Anchorage, where I'd take a ferry to Kodiak Island. My travel weariness was beyond high, so I thought about Kodiak and what might be waiting for me there. I was at a disadvantage knowing nothing about the place. My theory about Genevieve was really nothing more than that. She disappeared from there as a child, was never reported to have been found, and may have possibly buried Ben's stash of pearls on board the SS Dix. Too many theories, not enough facts. And now I was a team of one. I found a flight leaving in three hours, which would be perfect under better, more normal, circumstances. Provided I didn't get shot beforehand, I might even have time to eat actual food before takeoff.

"Solving all the world's problems back there?" Daniel asked me. "Or maybe hacking into the Pentagon?"

"I'm looking for someone," I said, hoping he'd drop the inquiry. Or did he already know?

With no access to the official case file, I could still find out what details were publicly available about bank president Paolo Rinaldi, why Jimmy Breslin had tried, or was still trying, to kill him, and who hired Jimmy for the hit. I'm not saying Jimmy was beyond revenge; just that for him to arrange the logistics and resources needed to pull off something as high profile as offing a bank president, there would have to be sufficient payoff for him. Who hired Jimmy and what would be gained by removing Rinaldi from the business world?

Public details of Rinaldi started with Google and a filtered time-period of the past year.

Tech Republic offered the same details of a boy from a wealthy family leveraging his comeuppance by investing in crypto at exactly the right time. Speculation over how he repeatedly found the right timing for buying or selling spilled into the gray area of computer hacking and insider trading, though crypto was still new and unregulated enough to hover under the radar. My eyes felt strained reading the tiny screen of my iPhone in the dark for so long, no matter how I adjusted the brightness settings.

A Twitter search produced a few posts with the hashtag #cryptoking referencing him by name suggesting antitrust law violations, and one post spawning a 78-comment debate about an anti-crypto witch hunt among conservative financiers. There had to be more.

Reddit's r/conspiracy group brought up the most interesting theory so far. I mentally filtered the results, considering the source to be on par with the National Enquirer. The title CryptoKings caught my eye. I expanded the thread to see if the subject was still Paolo Rinaldi.

I blinked repeatedly to help with my eyestrain, though I was in too deep now to back out. Kome-Kome group member asked if Paolo Rinaldi had an alter-ego, who traded for him. Responses pushed it to Paolo1&2, Paolo's Minime, and the idea that Rinaldi might be funneling his crypto transactions through an intermediary that was actually himself using a pseudonym. Another post, authored by group moderator RyeJackStaten, suggested moving the PaoloPaolo conversation to its own designated subgroup. I clicked the link in that post. Holy shit. The subgroup was started a month ago and already had 600 members. Here the comments turned more rabid, with polarized sides warring over pro- and anti-crypto as well as crypto regulation. The pro-crypto regulation faction referred to him as ShadyShady, the other side sticking to established social media norms like FinancialFreedom.

I returned to Twitter to find more mainstream sentiment. Trending now were how much money Bank President Paolo Rinaldi had, in what form, and where he got it.

# Chapter 54

**I had no experience with this pristine**, majestic landscape other than one story from my twenties. A fellow diver reportedly drowned when the ice froze over him during a fully chaperoned, charted diving expedition. The brain likes to categorize experiences for easy memory-retrieval so, since then, I'd thought of Alaska as a perilous place.

The Raven Air flight from Anchorage to Kodiak was a twenty-seater aircraft. With only three of us on board including the pilot, the updrafts made the ride feel like being in a washing machine, of course reminding me of the trauma of Janus' plane. But the eye-popping views from 20,000 feet distracted me from fear. My mind went to Alena - wondering if Victor had held up his end and put her on a plane home, if Vaughn was escorting her, and feeling guilty for continuing this insane path.

I contacted someone via divealaska.net and had an appointment in the morning to verify that I was certified for PADI Tec Trimix Diving, to show my certification card and arrange for an ocean dive. Contrary to popular opinion, the open ocean waters rarely dipped below forty degrees. I'd be able to rent a 7mm wetsuit, even though I knew I wasn't up to this, physically or otherwise.

I never liked all the prep and gear involved with deep water ocean dives, but the payoff was instantaneous and unmistakable. Floating, I now remember, was the ultimate escape, a silky surrender that could last as long as the air in your tank, unlike swimming that only gave you a single breath of freedom.

I went to Scuba Do and Pacific Diving Services in Terror Bay, Kodiak to get outfitted with gear, including multiple tanks filled with Heliox, oxygen and helium, to prevent the tremors that can result in deep water dives. I had a dive partner with me today, using the story of Alaskan reef exploration as my purpose.

The Terror River flows from Terror Lake to Terror Bay on the north coast of Kodiak and west-southwest of the Kodiak residential community. I remembered that the SS Dix was buried deep in the waters off Alki Point.

It took about fifteen minutes to get to the site, guided by my dive partner who'd been taking divers down here for two decades. I scrutinized his face on the boat, half expecting to see Jimmy.

Ahh, the liquid cool of that deep water. Even through my wetsuit I felt it nourishing my soul, bringing me home. Laying on its starboard side like I'd read about, the Dix was miraculously well intact, despite its violent, five-minute descent. I followed my guide around the length of the hull, marveling at the darkness surrounding us. I missed this and recalled only now my perverse light sensitivity at first. She'd come to me then, Genevieve. *Where are you? You summoned me here, you're still doing it. I've been to your home, your boathouse, talked to your daughter. Where do I go now? Give me a sign.*

Thinking back to the conversation with Jerome and Janus, there was no way to ascertain the "inner bottom" of the SS Dix, not this far down, not with a historical wreck like this and on a supervised dive. So if there was no way for me to do it, the same had to be true for Genevieve. We had only five more minutes before we had to start our slow ascent.

*Sunfish* - the word popped into my head suddenly in a neon flash, just as a school of Alaska pollock flooded past me. Pollock had no resemblance to the huge, bulbous sunfish I'd seen before. Where had this word come from? From her, it had to be. And if I was in this deep, I could certainly go a little deeper.

Okay, sunfish, show yourself. I watched everything around us at every safety stop on the way back up to the surface, reminding myself to never go faster than the smallest bubble. Halibut, cod, but nothing even close to a sunfish. *Sunfish*, she repeated, her voice this time talking to me the same way she had before. Anger welled in my palms, my tight fists, feeling again like a pawn on an invisible chessboard. There were no pearls down here, and not just because I hadn't found them. The SS Dix wrecked near Terror Bay, Kodiak Island. Ben Lucas's pearls were somewhere else. I felt it. Sunfish, what does that mean?

If Genevieve had run away or been abducted as a nine-year old, according to the article, she had to have been rescued and returned to her parents, or else brought up by another family, possibly right here.

The overcast sky was thick with ominous clouds. Back on land, I found a paper version of a telephone book the size of a small paperback novel in a gas station. Sure enough, a *G. Lucas* was listed on Malutin Lane. The dive shop worker called a Kodiak Cab for me. Malutin Lane was off Mill Bay Road with a nice view of Baranof Park. The house belonging to G. Lucas had gray siding, two window boxes out front with dead flowers, hidden from street view with a high fence and tall pines. I paid the driver and shouldered through the branches to the side of the house. An outbuilding hidden in the back made the property's small footprint seem larger. No cars out front, it seemed accessible enough to just pop back there without bothering anyone.

The door was locked, but through the window I saw three hanging wetsuits and two dive tanks leaning against the back wall. Then I saw the unmistakable connection: yellow wood trim, just like on her Bainbridge property, the same exact shade. As usual, it seemed, I had no concrete plan for what I would say if someone came to the door, navigating unlike a detective and, once again, by blind intuition. The grass was midcalf high on the pebbled walkway leading to the front door, also borrowed from the Bainbridge house. I couldn't help but smile, giddy almost that my spiritual detection methods had worked again. I ambled around the vacant property and eventually made my way to the front entrance.

A large, weathered woodcut of a *sunfish* was positioned over the front door. I was in the right place but, as usual, the wrong time.

I rang the bell, knowing no one would answer but that didn't matter. Staring up at that wooden fish over the unadorned steel door concretized a shudder of truth in my bones: I now knew where Genevieve had buried Ben's Margarita pearls.

# Chapter 55

**Disoriented and ears blocked from too many** flights, not to mention a deep water dive, I arrived in Seattle and took an Uber back to Bainbridge. I knew the risks of being followed but didn't bother connecting with Daniel or Victor this time. It was too risky to connect with Alfred, considering his loyalties had been compromised. For the first time in months, my mission finally felt clear. I texted Anabel to let her know I was coming, just so I didn't startle her if she found me hunched over the ground in her backyard. She didn't respond.

The sky had darkened in the last thirty minutes, with only scant daylight left for my critical task.

*I'm in the backyard,* I texted again before heading down her graveled driveway. Was she at work still, on a date, doing research? Stay focused, I told myself, heading past her guest house down the winding walkway in their rambling yard. I saw the crooked edge of the dilapidated boathouse to my right, relieved and comforted by the sight of it jutting past the dead tangle of vines. And on the left side of the path, the koi pond.

Sunfish.

When I stood in front of Genevieve's Terror Bay house on Kodiak Island four days ago, I rang the bell, staring at the woodcut of that hideous fish and suddenly knew what she had done, knew where she'd hidden those fated pearls. I wasn't sure if she left that message for me or maybe for anyone who was clever enough to decode it. She'd left breadcrumbs of clues leading to the HMS Terror in Nunavut, and more clues that they could be buried somewhere on board the SS Dix in Alaska's Terror Bay. But the truth of their whereabouts was in the bloated fish over her front door. Genevieve Lucas hid her husband Ben's stash of priceless Margarita pearls in almost plain sight and in the most ironic and logical location: a treasure chest.

The ground was cold and hard under my knees, my body still racked in soreness with the leftover wounds from the plane crash, now nearly two weeks ago. I peered down into the murky pond water, the eight or ten koi hovering around me, probably thinking I was about to feed them. What did you even feed koi? They looked fat and well fed, so obviously Anabel was caring for them. "No sorry," I said aloud, "no food right now. I've got other things on my mind." But it was impossible to see in there, despite how only one of the underwater lights had come on. Solar lights, sun, sunfish. Genius. Now I just had to find a way to get to it.

I remembered seeing a rusted, aluminum light in the boathouse, but that would still need power, and without several extension cords, I was out of luck. I tried the flashlight on my phone, which looked surprisingly bright in the impending darkness of the backyard. It seemed too easy to end up dropping it, but I had no other options. A scan of the edges of the pond showed only rocks and green plants growing toward the water.

*Closer.* The spoken word came from inside my head, her voice again, the same voice I'd heard while I was sedated. *Is it here? Am I in the right place?* I asked with only my thoughts.

*You know the answer.*

There was only one thing left to do. I climbed down into freezing water for the second time, but now without a wetsuit. Hah! I exhaled as I sank down to my waist, the koi swirling around my hands still thinking I had food. Or maybe they thought I was the food. Careful to keep my phone in one hand high above the water, I moved it toward the surface scanning the edges to gauge the shape and depth. Something metal reflected back. Hammered, silver trim over a weathered wood lid… to a chest.

The bottom was sandy and surprisingly even. I stepped carefully across the width, holding the light close to the water again as I lifted the lid on the chest, heavier than I would have thought. A yellow koi, sunfish, swam into the chest, then quickly skirted out. I couldn't tell its dimensions yet, but the light from my phone reflected against something shiny inside the cavern. I tossed my phone on the grassy bank for fear of dropping it and felt my way in, lifting the cover all the way up with both hands. I touched the inside of the lid, walked my fingers down the edges to the bottom of the box. I slowly dug my hands deep into it, the tips of my fingers right away touching something smooth. Something round. Something large. A single pearl. Jesus. Could it be?

Now immersed up to my chest, I raised that single pearl to the surface and held it in front of my face, but it was too dark. I picked up my phone, wiped my wet hand on my shirt collar, and turned the phone's flashlight to my left hand. A single, white pearl, large, maybe two inches, and not completely round. It was almost tear shaped. I snapped a photo of it because I knew from the weight that this pearl hadn't come from the kind of landscaping stores that outfitted koi ponds. I knew in my core that this came from the Santa Margarita, the Spanish ship that sank in the Florida Keys in the 1600s. I set down the phone again and reached to dig both hands into the chest and felt around. My God, the sensation! Handfuls, what felt like hundreds of pearls down here in all different sizes. I was careful to keep them contained within the confines of the chest and left everything exactly as I found it. The lid had been part way open, so I left it in the same position, leaving all the pearls buried safely inside, and I climbed out of the frigid water hoisting myself up onto the grassy bank again. I sat there shaking for several minutes, shocked by this discovery, thinking. I dried off in the boathouse where I'd wait for Anabel to return, the single pearl hiding low in my pants pocket.

*  -◈- ◈◈- ✛ -◈◈- -◈-  *

I used an old, oil-stained towel to wipe off the outside of my pants. Pointless. I'd parked in front of Anabel's guest house and dragged my backpack through the yard and to the boathouse. I booted up my laptop, fifty-percent charge left, and logged into Anabel's Wi-Fi network, remembering the password she'd written on a page on the kitchen table. My browser window was still on the page where I'd been reading about Paolo Rinaldi on Reddit, an article about how he'd been maintaining more than one identity. Not sure why I hadn't thought of it earlier, but I opened a new browser tab and Googled Paolo Rinaldi, then did an image search to be sure. I squinted to see more clearly when the page came up, showing a tall man with a sculpted jaw, light hair, and one of his double-breasted suit jackets. Paolo Rinaldi, a/k/a Anton Weiss. Made me wonder how many other identities he had, and if he'd followed me here.

I guessed it was about six o'clock. Brooke might be driving home now from the job she hated. She picked up on the first ring.

"You're still alive?" she said. Nice dig.

"Um... I texted you two days ago, so give me a break," I shot back.

"Why are you shivering?"

"Because I'm outside and I'm wet. Where are you? On your way home?"

"Yeah, and then I'm meeting a friend for dinner later."

I knew better than to ask about her love life. I was her dad after all, so that information was need-to-know. "I want to ask you about something."

I heard a long sigh, and the turn signal clicking on her car. "I'm pulling over, one second. Okay, I'm listening. What now?"

"A letter."

She said nothing but I was sure she'd heard me. I walked out to the water's edge and waited, watching the silver moon drip light onto the rippled water on Puget Sound.

"You mean *the* letter?"

"You know about it?" I asked, keeping my voice low. The air was cold but I needed to be outside under the sky right now. I sat on what might be the same flat stone I'd sat on with Alfred Ligetti when I was seven years old. Perhaps the letter had something to do with that day, that memory. "I think it's in Pappy's attic and I really hate to ask you to—"

"I have it," she cut in. "I've had it for a long time."

"What? How?"

"Mom. She knew you'd be wanting it at some point. I think she thought you might sell Pappy's house and never see it. So she gave it to me."

I shook my head, trying to awaken sleeping memories from my marriage. "How did your mother even know about it?"

"Pappy gave it to her after you two got divorced. He told her you'd want it someday but told her not to mention it until you specifically asked for it. I've been dying to know what was in it but she made me promise not to touch it. I didn't."

How did I manage to raise such a classy young woman, despite the divorce, despite the loss of her little brother? Wow. "Thank you for that," was all I could manage. "I feel like I'm ready to read it now. Would you feel comfortable opening it? When you get home I mean."

"I'm just about home, I'll get it now."

"No wait, I don't want to interrupt your dinner plans."

"I was going home to change anyway. Hold on, it's in my room."


I'd texted Vaughn at the airport a few hours ago to make sure he'd gotten Alena home safely. He said he hadn't gone with her but put her on a plane and she should be home by ten tonight. I texted him again from the boathouse, careful not to make noise, knowing I was probably under surveillance this very minute.

*Where are you?* I texted Vaughn while waiting for Brooke to come back on the line.

*Cleveland, how about you?* he wrote back. Very funny.

Just feeding the fish.

There was a chance he'd know what I meant, and I suspected he was here on the Island or at least in Seattle.


"Okay, I've got it here," Brooke said, a little out of breath. "Dad, are you sure about this?"

"I'm sure." I didn't know how to explain to her that things

273

needed to shift for me, somehow, before I felt ready to know what was in that letter. I heard her carefully tear open the envelope, unfolding the crinkled paper.

"Oh my God," she whispered.

"What is it?"

"It's about—"

I sighed. "It's her, isn't it? Genevieve."

"Yeah, um, hold on. My God. I don't know how to..." Her voice trailed off.

I was shaking again but this time not from the cold. "She's my sister, isn't she?" I asked, unprepared for the sound of the words emerging from my mouth.

"How did you know? Have you known all this time?" Brooke asked.

I shook my head, pacing over the polished stones on the beach outside the dreary boathouse, one hundred feet from a cache of stolen Spanish pearls. How much crazier could things really get? "I don't know how, I can't explain it. Maybe for the same reason I've followed that woman's name, her voice, her story, and her life ever since she first contacted me. How would I even explain that to someone who didn't know me? Ever since then, seems like all kinds of unexplainables are now possible."

I heard Brooke breathing heavily, flipping the pages of the letter from my dead father.

"Half-sister, actually. He says he was ashamed of her, ashamed of himself, that he'd never told your mother. He hid Genevieve from her, so he had to hide her from you too, or else your mother would have found out. He says when Genevieve disappeared on Kodiak Island, he came up here with you, disguised as a camping trip. He was frantic."

"I remember him crying on our way home," I said, only recalling that image of him now.

"Her mother, oh my God, I'm so sorry to be reading this to you over the phone, Dad. It's unthinkable."

"What? It's okay, sweetie, keep going, if you're willing."

"Genevieve's mother, when she disappeared, thought she was dead. She killed herself."

We were both crying now, sniffing into the phone, caught up in the web of this intimate, frozen, family moment, our shared history.

"Another family adopted her," she went on after a moment, "and Pappy never saw her again. He said, 'I've had a broken heart ever since, the broken heart I could never share with anyone until writing this letter. This piece of paper is my freedom, my legacy. You and your sister deserve all I was never able to give you. I'm sorry.'"

After a few silent moments of letting the truth float around in the airwaves, Brooke came back to the phone. "There's a little piece of paper in the bottom of the envelope. Looks like an address."

"Malutin Lane, right?"

"You knew that too?"

"I was there today." I couldn't think of words sufficiently adequate to express my gratitude to Brooke, for opening the letter, confirming what I already knew in my heart, and setting those explosive truths free.

"Dad. My God. I don't want to be away from you right now."

"I don't want to be away from you ever again. And yes I'll be home soon. Very soon."

# Chapter 56

**I heard Vaughn's signature whistle fifteen minutes later.**

"Hey," he said, again darkening the boathouse entrance with his silhouette lit up by a dim quarter moon this time. And once again I was sitting in wet pants on the concrete floor.

"Brought you some reading material. Too dark in here I guess."

It looked like a folded newspaper. "What is it?"

"Seems like our friend Marcus Reyes crawled out from under his rock."

"Really."

"He contacted the feds. They brought him in and he's in their custody now. Protected from Jimmy."

I nodded, still reeling from the call with Brooke.

"Where's Anabel?"

"I was just calling her now." I stood. Anabel's phone rang once, twice, no voicemail yet. The ringing stopped, followed by rustling noises.

"Well, hello." It was a man's voice. I put him on speaker. *Jimmy*, I lip-synched to Vaughn with a question. Jesus.

"I'm calling for Anabel Lucas."

"Anabel Lucas?" the man called out. "Are you here? Is Anabel Lucas here?"

I heard muffled screams coming from the other end. Oh my God. What have I done?

"Give me that." Vaughn grabbed the phone from my hand. "Jimmy, this is Vaughn. We know each other, you and me, right?"

Laughing.

"Look. You're a practical guy. There's no reason you need to harm Anabel. Kurt and I are right here. Tell us what you want."

"Kurt knows what I want," he said in his taunting, arrogant thug-voice. "He had it in his bare hands today."

He was watching me. Fuck. So why hadn't he stopped me? Vaughn glared, brows raised in question. I nodded. Yeah, I'd found them. "Where?" he whispered.

As I pointed left, Jimmy spoke again. "We're already here," Jimmy said with a fiendish laugh. "Step out of the boathouse, both of you. Slowly."

Vaughn and I stepped out into the open air, not knowing exactly where he was, too dark to see a thing.

"That's it, I see you. Come out further."

I had my phone on speaker so Vaughn and I could both hear him. "Let me talk to Anabel," I said.

"He-hello." Her voice sounded weak, her nose blocked.

"Come out more, both of you," Jimmy said. "Keep your hands in the air where I can see them. That's it, further now on the walkway. Move away from the boathouse."

"We're coming," Vaughn said.

"Good, far enough," Jimmy said.

A light flicked on down the path. It was a flashlight, Jimmy holding it under his chin. I saw his sick grin and greasy dark hair, Anabel in front of him in a headlock. His other hand gripped a gun angled at her ribcage.

I stood back a few feet to get a better view of things. Vaughn was closer to them. Luckily the pirate's chest was buried about four feet under water with plants covering the top, and no solar lights anywhere near it. It wasn't large, as far as koi ponds go, but in the dark you could be there all night.

"What are you waiting for?" Jimmy asked, angling his head left to see me behind Vaughn.

"Let Anabel go and I'll tell you where they are."

"Nah, I don't think so. You'll –"

While he talked, I turned my back to him and headed toward the boathouse again, a new theory forming in my head.

"Hey! Where do you think you're going? I'll fucking shoot your sweet little tart right here."

"Where are they, Jimmy? You saw me, right? You know where they are, don't you?" I bellowed in a voice louder than I ever remembered speaking, a newfound power. I shrugged. "So go find them yourself."

My theory was that he had no idea where they were hidden, but maybe he'd seen me come back to the house. So in his mind, they could be anywhere on the property. The boathouse seemed as good a place as any to simulate a treasure. If he thought the pearls were hidden there, that could buy us some time to get Anabel away from him.

"Why did you try to kill Paolo Rinaldi?" Vaughn asked him.

I stopped walking and turned. "Jimmy figured out Rinaldi's crypto scam and threatened to expose him if he didn't cut him in on a percentage. Am I right, Jimmy?"

"I'm here for one reason, and it's got nothing to do with that greedy bastard. Now, unless you want to see your little—"

"Cut the crap, Jimmy. Okay? Enough. I've had enough!" My voice didn't crack like it normally would have. Instead it thundered from deep in my core. "If you shoot Anabel, you'll never know where the pearls are hidden. You want the pearls, release her. That's the only way this is gonna go tonight."

I watched Vaughn take two slow steps to his left and I immediately knew what he was doing, putting me in Jimmy's sights so he could sideline him. I needed to keep talking.

"I know about Leticia Ames."

"Yeah, and look where that got you," the sick laugh again. "My bullet stopped you, didn't it?"

"What you didn't know… is that Leticia Ames is still alive. You killed her sister, Jimmy! By mistake."

I saw his back hunch forward like he'd been gut punched.

"And all because of Marcus Reyes, who I heard today is back in the custody of the feds, ready to testify against you. They know you killed Ben and Genevieve Lucas, and now Coretta Ames, Letitia's sister. You can go down for three murders, Jimmy, or you can leave here tonight with a cache of pearls worth millions of dollars." I took another step toward Jimmy and shrugged again. "Up to you."

Jimmy's eyes were frozen on me. I didn't move my head but could see Vaughn had taken one more step left of the path. It was just me and Jimmy now. Two adversaries negotiating the thin line between life and death.

"Find those pearls now!" he screamed, suddenly unglued, loosening his grip on Anabel as he said it, shaking her like a rag doll.

She let out a half-scream that turned to guttural sobs. Jimmy managed to wriggle her back in position, but she wasn't having it this time, now doubled over with emotion. He struggled to hold her arms down and she elbowed her way out, while he grabbed her again reaching forward. Vaughn, like a rabbit, slid out of the darkness and managed to get his gun aimed at Jimmy's head.

"Ready to die, Jimmy?" he asked, calmly.

"Anabel, over here." I snapped my fingers.

She pulled back from Jimmy and darted toward the fence,

hugging the edge of the walkway and over to me. I grabbed her. And held her. My niece. My heart was breaking.

"You okay?" I whispered.

No answer.

"Stand behind me."

"Are the pearls really here?" she asked.

"You're not gonna—" Jimmy started.

Vaughn cracked him in the jaw with his gun, jumped him and I could only hear the sound of fists on skin, moans, legs clamoring over the grass. My eyes started to adjust. Now Jimmy had Vaughn pinned to the ground, his right hand reaching for the pistol a foot away. Two feet from Anabel and me, I let go of her to grab the gun and jammed it against Jimmy's right temple. He toppled left, stayed down for half a second, slowly rose and started toward me. Vaughn wasn't moving.

"Vaughn, you okay?" I shouted.

"Yep," he whispered. Jimmy had been choking him, choking the life out of him. I might have just saved Vaughn's life.

Undaunted by the sight of me holding a gun at him, Jimmy took two steps forward, then another two steps. He reached down toward his foot and pulled a backup firearm out of an ankle holster. He chambered a round back and aimed it at my head.

I fired a shot at his left shoulder, purposely avoiding his heart because I wanted so desperately for justice to be served. He fell back onto the grass, the weight of him landing in a heavy thud. I'd just shot the man who shot me.

"Do you have cuffs on you?" I asked Vaughn.

"Please, allow me."

# Chapter 57

**We decided Vaughn should be the one** to bring Jimmy in. He sat cuffed in the back of Vaughn's car, and I could see his beady eyes working on a way out of this. There wasn't one. Even guys like Jimmy were vulnerable sometimes. He met my eyes in that moment and I liked how it felt, me enjoying a rare moment of power. Ironic though, wasn't it, that getting shot by Jimmy had brought me home, in a way, to my family. Maybe karma, or a weird full circle.

"Did that guy kill my mother?" Anabel asked when I got her settled with a blanket and a brandy in the house. Her wounds, the external ones, were minimal. She said it could have been worse. She had no idea.

"I suspect so. And your father. And a young girl named Coretta Ames, who heroically died to save her sister's life."

"All because of the pearls?"

I nodded.

"Are they really here?"

I motioned for her to come with me into the yard, this time using two flashlights. "See it?"

"I see wood and metal. Is it a box?"

"A chest." I watched her face change from eagerness to bitterness, back and forth, a tangle of excitement, guilt, pain, and sorrow.

"My parents died for these goddamn things. Alright," she said, shaking herself awake. "I guess I need to see them." She had her mother's strength.

I sank into the murky pond water for the second time and pulled out the entire chest this time, surprised that it was as weighty as a normal pirate's chest instead of a garden store plastic replica. It was real wood, the size of a small toaster oven. Vaughn and I carried it into the living room of Genevieve's house and set it on the coffee table, letting pond water drip onto the wood floors. Vaughn kept an eye on Jimmy, locked and cuffed in the back of his car, through the front windows.

"Sit over here to get a good look," I said into Anabel's mascara-stained eyes. "Are you ready?"

She nodded and I opened the box. I held my iPhone flashlight on the contents, finally able to see what my hands had discovered earlier tonight. My breath caught in my throat. Neither of us breathed for a few seconds. They were all different colors and had to be close to five hundred of them, much more than Alfred Ligetti described.

"Gold, silver, gray, white, I didn't know pearls came in all those shades. Can I—"

"Of course. They're yours, after all."

Anabel had reached her hand toward the chest, then pulled it back into her lap. "Mine?"

"These belonged to your father. Whether he had an actual legal claim to them is another story. Maritime law, when it comes to salvaged treasure, is as murky as the water in that pond. But for now, tonight anyway, these were your father's pearls and they're your birthright. What happens to them now... is for you to decide."

While Vaughn transported Jimmy to the police station, I set the chest inside a plastic picnic cooler in a bedroom closet.

Anabel slept. I stayed on the couch in the living room in case we had any other visitors tonight. I didn't mention the letter from Pappy or any of its details. Anabel had been through enough of a shock. We all had. Vaughn reported via text that Jimmy was getting processed in, and that I needed to give a statement in the morning.

I somehow convinced Brooke to take a few days off and fly up to Seattle. We had a lot to talk about, especially now that I'd just learned Anabel was my niece. I got up three times in the middle of the night to check the chest. I made coffee at four then sat up alone drinking the whole pot, my mind churning through too many threads, my body too sore and beat up to rest. I showered, then Anabel showered after me, agreeing to stay here in her mother's house instead of going back to the guest house. I wanted to be within three feet of her right now, for so many reasons. I made a second pot and poured a cup for her with milk and no sugar.

"Did I get it right?" I asked, my voice hopeful.

She smirked. "Not quite. I like a half teaspoon of sugar." She sipped it and took a long look at me. "The way you're sitting…" She pointed at my legs. "My mother used to sit that way too, cross-legged with her back up straight on the couch."

"About that…"

◈ ◈ ◈ ✦ ◈ ◈ ◈

I told Vaughn I'd give him a statement here in Genevieve's house. Under the circumstances, he agreed, but only if I let him look inside the chest.

"What's she gonna do with them?" he asked me.

"I don't think she knows, but honestly I don't think she wants anything to do with them. Why would she, after all? She lost both parents because of them, was kidnapped, nearly shot last night if it wasn't for you. You saved her life."

"Well, you saved mine by shooting Jimmy," he said and held out his hand to me. "I think the feds may want to give you a medal."

I stared out the window, the dark gray yard taking on the first glow of sunrise. I wondered if my owl was out there, watching and waiting.

"I need to know something," I said. "I need to know why you were always three steps ahead of me."

My partner gave me that cockeyed grin and tipped his head. "I think you know the answer. When the department thought you weren't going to recover…" He gave a sheepish shrug.

"You got tapped for another agency? IA?"

"Are you kidding?"

"CIA?"

"One assignment, that's all it was. I was brought in to help apprehend Paolo Rinaldi. It turned into a related assignment for Jimmy because they were really part of the same case."

"The crypto scam?" I asked.

"How do you know about that?" he asked.

"When I was in Nunavut, the other Terror Bay, I met Rinaldi, though he was using the name Anton Weiss and posing as an antiques dealer."

"Very funny. You know what he was doing, right? Stealing billions in cryptocurrency from a decentralized finance blockchain bridge."

I'd read about it. "They called it a wormhole network," I said, remembering the Reddit post.

"Jimmy worked for Rinaldi, found out about the scam, wanted in, Rinaldi refused, Jimmy threatened to expose him and that was the hit Marcus Reyes witnessed."

"So Jimmy tried to kill Rinaldi at the same time Interpol was set to take Rinaldi down for the crypto scam? How, though? Jimmy's no hacker. I read about some regulator's speculation that Jimmy not only found out about Rinaldi's embezzlement but found his way in so he could funnel the earnings back to his own account. Seems too sophisticated for a thug like him."

Vaughn nodded in agreement. "It is but Jimmy didn't need to be a hacker to threaten the whole operation. He found out about it, compiled a dossier of evidence from some recorded phone conversations—"

"Illegally recorded, no doubt and, therefore not admissible in court."

"Probably," he said, "but it would have been enough to destabilize the security and integrity of the operation and make a lot of crypto investors nervous."

I was starting to see the economic impact here. "I would think Rinaldi would have been trying to take Jimmy down himself."

"He was," Vaughn confirmed.

"Jimmy tried to take him out as a survival tactic then. Oh the tangled webs…"

"Yup."

"So then Jimmy was probably trying to get his hands on the pearls so he could cash them in on the black market and continue funding Rinaldi's crypto scam, assuming he'd gotten Rinaldi out of the way?"

"I suspect so."

"What about Alfred? Where is he now?" I asked.

"I don't know but he won't go far. He'll follow the story from his contacts and will stay close to Anabel."

"I was thinking about Jerome and what might have happened to him. I last saw him in Calgary. He's been smack in the middle of everything that's happened."

Vaughn nodded like he'd been expecting this. "Well, that was one thing I was able to uncover in my covert investigation. Jerome's part of the Rinaldi crime family. He's Paolo Rinaldi's son."

# Chapter 58

*June*

**For the next two weeks, while the** legal machinery of maritime salvage churned, Anabel and I stayed in the main house together working through everything that had happened. She left me alone here during the days, while she was at work, to clean out the boathouse and stand on the wobbly stones looking out into the Puget Sound Basin.

It all seemed so obvious, almost ironic now. Jimmy chasing Leticia to ultimately get to Marcus, and then Vaughn and I chasing Jimmy, whose bullet brought me here and ultimately *home*. Funny how the definitions of home changed according to what changes inside you. The idea of my house in San Francisco felt like a tether to a painful past I knew I could now live without. It was time to sell that house. It was time for a lot of things that were never possible before.

I couldn't find the right words, but maybe just standing there every day on the shoreline looking out was enough to thank Genevieve for finding me, for reaching her hand out to me in my most vulnerable moment. Again, so ironic that it had felt like me reaching out to rescue her. You're free now, I told her in my mind. Free from the tangle of sordid agendas, from the guilt I know you still feel about exposing Anabel, and most of all free from the poison of that illicit treasure. It took Ben, it took you, and now it's once again a part of our collective history.

A car horn in the driveway pulled me back to earth, reminding me to get ready. It was Vaughn. I ran out to catch him on his way in.

"Is she here yet?" he asked of Brooke, who'd agreed to come up and meet her new cousin, Anabel.

"Within the hour," I said.

"What are you worried about? It's gonna be fine."

"I can't imagine. I'm actually more accustomed to losing family members. I don't know—"

"There's no instruction book for this type of thing. Brooke's the most important person in your life. Right?"

"Of course."

"Make sure she knows it."

I bear-hugged him for saying that, reminding me of what should have been obvious but somehow, sadly, got caught up in the web of Genevieve. I'd taken Brooke for granted all these months chasing a forgotten part of myself. I owed her more than that. I could, no. I would do better.

"How's Anabel doing?" Vaughn asked.

My palms went up. "Don't ask her about it."

"The pearls? Are they still here?"

I shook my head. "Just don't ask her about them. I think I've exhausted the subject and she's tired of talking about it."

"She's gonna turn them in?"

"I told you, she doesn't want them, here or in her life anymore."

"I can help you guys with the handover when you're ready."

"Good, we'll need it. Just not today."


I didn't bother making Brooke's favorite kind of tea, or any of her favorite foods, because she was too smart. I have a half-sister and now Anabel is my niece. She's now our family member, but it was important for me to make Brooke feel like in my mind she always came first.

I watched my daughter exit her rental car from the large, double casement windows in Genevieve's living room. She'd worn her long, dark hair down, unadorned with any of the little braids, clips, hair ties and other tools she sometimes used. Today Brooke Farin wasn't trying to be anything but her natural self. This felt right to me. They were actually more alike than I'd realized.

Anabel stepped off the back porch to greet Brooke in the driveway, monitoring my expression for guidance.

"Like introducing two cats for the first time," Vaughn mused from the safety of the doorway.

"Don't be a wuss and hide out in the back bedroom," I said to him. "I need you as an ice breaker."

"Damn, busted. Alright fine."

I watched him go to them, one hand on each of their shoulders, probably introducing Brooke to Anabel as his favorite Millennial or surrogate daughter or something. The young women shook hands in a formal show of courtesy. Only time would tell. Back in the house Anabel prepared a tray while Brooke looked around the furnishings.

"Are you by any chance a tea drinker?" Anabel asked, setting the tray on the coffee table, the same table where a chest filled with illicit pearls had dripped nasty pond water all over the hardwood floors. Brooke shot me a glance.

"I didn't tell her anything," I said in defense.

Brooke sat and pulled up the lid on the teapot. "Darjeeling." She looked down at the grooves in the oak. Was she checking in on herself?

"I'm so glad you're here," I said.

"Me too." Brooke poured tea into two of the cups. "I suspect we might have some other things in common. Besides you."

Anabel looked at Brooke. "Pistachio ice cream is—oh my God, I'm so sorry." She put her fingers to her lips.

I nodded. "It's alright."

"You told her?" Brooke asked, gently.

"Ryan's a part of us, he always will be. A part of all of us."

"I'm so sorry for your loss. I can't imagine it," Anabel said.

Vaughn sat in the chair beside her, all of us huddled together in this awkward moment, in the newness of it all.

He and I hung out in the backyard to give the girls some time to feel each other out. It was surprisingly warm, even for early June. Sun high, cloudless sky, water glassy.

"How about you and Alena?" he asked me. "Have you talked since you got back here?"

"No, but I suspect she's mad that I never met her expectations. Of a boyfriend, maybe, but more like of a friend. I'll call her but that's an ice that's not likely to melt anytime soon."

* ─◈─ ◈▩◈ ┿ ◈▩◈ ◈─ *

With Brooke's blessing, I stayed on the island with Anabel for a few weeks to fix up the boathouse after Brooke left. Maybe someday the neighbors might use it for boat or equipment storage. I called to check in on her every night at ten, which was quickly becoming a tradition, sometimes a five-minute call, other times longer.

"You sure you're alright with this?" I asked.

"I'm fine, Dad. I said I was and I meant it. You need time with Anabel right now and, besides, you like it up there. You're happy up there. There's a peace I saw in your face that I haven't seen in a really long time. Maybe ever."

I nodded. She was right.

"Understandable certainly," she said. "Ryan, then Mom. And honestly I need some time alone now too. We don't need to talk every night. I appreciate it but it's not necessary. I'm not a little girl."

"You're my little girl, you always will be. You're a woman now, but in my heart you're still my little peanut."

Jimmy Breslin was in custody pending trial with prosecutors still gathering evidence on three counts of criminal homicide and racketeering charges related to the cybercrime crypto ring run by his boss, Paolo Rinaldi. Rinaldi had his own Interpol Red Notice and was facing extradition by US law enforcement, if they got their hands on him.

After a week of work, I'd emptied the boathouse of all its rusted relics, innertubes, life jackets, stray oars and paddles, flippers, torn wetsuits, rusty nails, and so much sand I could have dammed up the White River. Alfred showed up one random afternoon, clad in coveralls with an array of extension poles for cleaning. He said nothing about where he'd been, but I knew he knew everything. I'd long suspected that Anabel was his daughter, considering his deep love for her and her mother. Maybe someday he'd tell me his hidden truths.

I used three sizes of ladders to scrub down the boathouse walls, even the ceiling, with a combination of mild detergent and bleach, and was amazed to discover that it wasn't just a building I was cleaning out. Tears poured out of me at odd times that week while I purged and cleansed, like exfoliating dead layers of my own skin. I thought about Jimmy, too, the irony of feeling he'd ruined my life and the new truth that he gave it back to me - two new family members I never would have discovered without that bullet. I didn't listen to music either. I wanted the space of time to move slowly, with just the sound of the tide moving in and out and the pristine emptiness of each moment.

And, like after I'd first emerged from my underworld, I took to walking alone at night. All over Bainbridge in all kinds of weather, no coat, just feeling the air, feeling myself in the world. Still deciding what was to come next in my life, the war between doctor and detective pushed on as a constant background program. I loved being a doctor until I couldn't bear it anymore. So I became a detective as an obvious left turn to see with my own eyes the dark underbelly that now lived in my heart, the darkness that came from the hole Ryan left when it was his time. I still felt him with me, especially on those nighttime walks. And that same owl followed me every night. We knew each other now. Maybe it was Ryan protecting me from my grief, or maybe he still needed his father, which I would always be.

# About the Author

Lisa Towles is an award-winning, bestselling crime novelist and a passionate speaker on the topics of fiction writing, creativity, and self-care. Besides writing, one of Lisa's favorite activities is helping other writers, which she does through her blog, speaking engagements, consultation, and 1:1 mentorship. Lisa has eleven crime novels in print with a new title, *Switch* (Book 3 of the E&A Series) forthcoming in 2024. Her novels *Hot House* and *Salt Island* (E&A Investigations Series) were both #1 Amazon bestsellers and each won multiple literary awards. Lisa also writes standalone thrillers, including *Terror Bay, The Ridders, Ninety-Five*, and the forthcoming *Specimen*. Lisa is an active member of Mystery Writers of America, Sisters in Crime, and International Thriller Writers. She has an MBA in IT Management, works full-time in the tech industry, and lives in California with her husband and two cats. Learn more at lisatowles.com and follow her on social media:

Instagram: @authorlisatowles

Twitter: @writertowles

Tiktok: @lisatowleswriter

Facebook: @lisatowleswriter

Contact Lisa Towles at
lisamarietowles@gmail.com

Subscribe to her monthly newsletter here:
https://tinyurl.com/4a3bvdpn

# Acknowledgments

Writing a book is an extraordinary experience. Every book is not only different in storyline but also its execution and process. Each one takes a team of kind souls who collectively keep you on track and sufficiently inspired to reach the last page. Then the real work begins.

To my husband Lee, whose energy, passion, insight and verve are a constant inspiration. Your love and devotion bring me the greatest happiness of my life.

To my inspiring parents – lifelong public school teachers - who continue to surprise me with their talent, wisdom, and endless support. Whatever grit I have in me I got from them.

To my sister, who was with me while I did the research for this book. You were my very first friend in this world and you're still a wonderful companion. Though I'm the older sister, you've always been my role model.

To my precious nieces, Olivia and Cassidy – watching you grow up is an amazing experience. I'm in awe of you.

To my publisher, Lisa Orban, for her extraordinary vision in creating such a supportive community for authors, for her amazing expertise, her patience and compassion, and her tireless marketing and social media energy.

Without my amazing editor, Cindy Davis, this book would not have been publishable in the first place. Thank you for your expertise, support, guidance, and encouragement, and for pushing me to the next level.

And special thanks to the technical advisors whose wisdom, experience, and patience brought accuracy and needed improvements to this story – Lee, John, Jen, Chip, Erica, and Stuart.

Warmest thanks to my kind and tireless beta readers – Gail, Lee, Missy, Dharani, and Ana. Your helpful feedback was so critical to improving this book.

To my graphic designer, Tatiana – you're a genius and incredibly skilled. Thank you for your talent and expertise, and for designing such a beautiful cover.

To my cherished MWA and SinC NorCal writing buddies - thank you for your companionship, advice, wisdom, and inspiration. I am a better writer and a happier person because of you.

To Sara – my wellness touchstone - thank you for your support, wisdom and healing.

To Muhammad, my dear friend and writing partner – I so deeply value our weekly writing practice, as it's the only opportunity I ever give myself to fully let my mind run free.

And to the wonderfully supportive readers of this book and my other books – THANK YOU from the bottom of my heart for your honest reviews, comments, support, and feedback.

You are all a part of my village,
Thank You

# The Ridders
### Political Thriller
### Indies United Publishing House (2022)

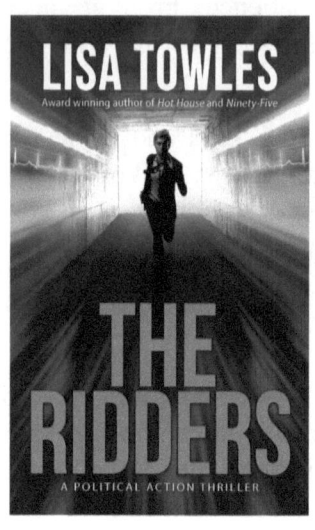

*Young PI, BJ Janoff is randomly approached by a stranger with a proposition he can't refuse – a million dollars to deliver an envelope to a hotel lobby. The pusher forces him to accept the money upfront and threatens to kill him if he doesn't deliver the envelope in three days. BJ's growing obsession leads him down a treacherous path toward the orchestrators of the game, where he discovers a large-scale political controversy, a treasure hunt for a priceless sword, and a global crime ring linked to a WWII-era secret society. When an act of brilliance changes the balance of power, the safety of everyone he loves is in jeopardy. And the more he digs, the closer he comes to truths he can't bear to face – about his missing father and the elusive Bilderberg Group.*

# Chapter One

What would you do if someone offered you a million dollars to bring an envelope to the reception desk of a luxury hotel? That's it. Sure, a no-brainer. A relatively inconsequential risk, easy money, right? Trouble is, anything involving a million dollars might not be what it seems. So many questions. Namely why me, BJ Janoff, should be offered this seemingly innocuous task. There were no answers available, no consultants waiting with details or clarifications. One million dollars in cash to perform this social experiment. Right now. Yes or no?

I know what my older brother Jonas would do. He'd say no because of the multitude of potential hazards his paranoid mind would concoct, keeping him tied to the past, still wearing the same ugly khakis from ten years ago, stuck in the protective bubble of his big house in Ladera Heights and his geriatric Mercedes. So, of course I didn't tell him. Yet.

Then there was Lacy Diaz, the girl-next-door-turned-lawyer, who drives a car flashy enough to get a speeding ticket if she goes over fifty on the freeway.

"Hell, yeah, I'd take it," she said, with about a hundred caveats. What do you expect; she's a lawyer. "Wear rubber gloves," she said. "Ask to see the contents of the envelope first. If it's money, fan it out so you can see the bill denominations. Take photos of the payor."

"Photos of the payor?" I laughed and closed my eyes, a response Lacy inspired by pretty much everything she did. "Excuse me sir, would you mind if—"

"I'm just trying to protect you from potential—"

"Potential. Now you sound like Jonas. His whole world is so much potential there's no room for now."

"He's your brother. You can't choose your family so get

over it."

So be it. A million dollars? Hell yeah, of course I said yes, I'm not stupid. Luckily, the task was intended for not only the most beautiful hotel in LA but the one I went to almost every morning. Sure, the cappuccinos were okay at the Peets counter, but the staff was even more noteworthy.

"Good morning," I said, loping up to the counter.

"Is it?"

"Pretty sure." I didn't let my eyes fall below Raquel's neck, given her choice of a low-cut blouse.

"Usual?"

"Yeah." I watched the Westin Bonaventure Hotel staff moving wordlessly through their tasks today. A keen observer of human behavior, I knew something was going down when Mario the bellhop pushed an empty cart past me and lowered his eyes to the floor. No banter, humming, rapping, high fiving me. No smile. "Hey?" I called after him. "What am I, invisible?" Alena, who managed the daytime housekeeping staff, hurried after him toward the elevators. Her face looked like she'd been crying all morning. No makeup and she was buttoning her uniform top while she walked. Maybe I'm paranoid.

Raquel was moving slowly and clearly not interested in talking. So I took three steps to the left to get a view of the reception desk. The typical chorus line of coiffed, perky concierges today included a confused, twenty-year-old in a wrinkled t-shirt. Something, no doubt related to the FedEx envelope I'd tucked into the back of my pants, was afoot. Out of coffee sleeves, I burned my fingers on Raquel's cappuccino and hunkered low on a lobby sofa watching and sipping. A cadre of men in identical black suits marched to the reception desk. Here we go.

I calculated my distance to be roughly fifty feet from the polished, walnut counter, maybe forty-five. Lucky for me, the acoustics in here rivaled the Guggenheim and I could hear everything. One suited man in front, nine underlings huddled behind awaiting instructions. I heard the word envelope posed as a question. The misplaced pothead behind the counter looked like he might start crying any moment. He gazed through the suits into the cavernous lobby space. Don't look at me, buddy, I don't exist right now. I took three more sips of coffee then back to my morning theater.

My phone buzzed with an incoming call. Jonas, who I suppose qualified as my business partner even though I wasn't paid an equal salary, and there was no legal agreement in place that formalized our working arrangement. "Hey, bro," I whispered.

"Hey, bro?" Repeating was one of his annoying traits. He had so many.

"What?"

"Where the fuck are you?"

"On a job," I lied. "Where are you?" I laughed inside, knowing this would unglue him. He hated the idea of my taking side jobs because he felt I was unqualified to be a private investigator. When our partner Archie Dax was still around, we used to laugh about this. He and I were so similar. He understood me almost better than anyone. I'd only had my investigator's license for less than a year when he died, but he never thought that mattered. Said I had the right head for PI work. Aww, Arch. My world's not the same without you.

"Job? What job?"

Poor Jonas. I still hadn't told him.

"Okay look, we've got the Bergman family coming in at nine tomorrow morning and I need the…" He exhaled long and hard, specifically to relay his frustration and inspire guilt. That ploy never worked with me.

"What, Jonas—WiFi? Maybe you've heard of something called the internet. Yes, I know, and we're good."

"Router, that's it."

Lord. "It's not the router, it's the modem speed and the unit will be upgraded within the hour. We're fine. Just let them in when they arrive."

No response.

"Are you crying?" I asked. "Pacing? Take your pill, Jonas."

"Fuck off. Say hi to Raquel for me."

I hung up and the phone rang again. "Dude, what?"

"And please don't wear your stupid backwards baseball hat. Please? I beg you. The Bergmans have money, a lot of it. We need that right now."

"Okay Jonas, no hat. Happy now?"

"We'll see."

Okay, so about the Bergmans. Jonas had been talking with them, Sten and Estelle, for the past two days about their vanished eighteen-year-old daughter, Anastasia, heir to their multi-billion-dollar estate, and how her net worth made her an especially enticing ransom target to what they described as "the underworld". LA's not utopia but not sure I'd call it an underworld.

Just two more errands today. First, I put a five-dollar bill in Raquel's tip vase even though she didn't see me. She still deserved it for being open at 6 a.m. and for looking so goddamn beautiful first thing in the morning. Then I held a small, black plastic ball in my hands and set it on a side table with a perfect view of the hotel's reception area. The table was on the other side of the seating area so that meant roughly thirty feet from the front desk. The plastic ball, a nanny cam designed to look like an air filter, was partially concealed by the fat leaves on a fake rubber tree plant. Unless someone moved that plant, or the filter for that matter, I'd be able to see the front desk of the Bonaventure Hotel for the next twenty-four hours via an iPhone app, which I suspect would be time enough to see why someone would pay a stranger a million bucks to deliver a stupid envelope.

\*\*\*

"A fast-paced, tense and gripping murder mystery" - *Readers' Choice*

"A captivating tale that engrosses on many levels" - *Midwest Book Review*

"A must-read for fans of suspense thrillers" - *Book Viral Reviews*

Awards: BookFest Award (1st Place), American Fiction Award (1st Place), Millennium Book Award (Longlisted), Literary Titan Award (Gold)

# Ninety-Five
## Techno Thriller
### Indies United Publishing House (2021)

*Troubled University of Chicago student, Zak Skinner, accidentally uncovers evidence of an on-campus, organized crime scam involving drugging students, getting them to commit crimes on camera, and blackmailing them to continue under the threat of expulsion. Digging deeper, Zak discovers that the university scam is just the tip of the iceberg, as it's connected to a broader ring of crimes linked to a dark web underworld. Following clues, Zak is led to a compound within Chicago's abandoned Steelworker Park, only to discover that he's being hunted. While trying to find his way out alive, Zak discovers there's something much more personal he's been running from – his past. And now there's nowhere to hide.*

# Prologue

"Ten dollars… each."

I reached for my wallet. Riley put up his palm. "We're guests of a member."

The bouncer eyerolled. "Who?"

"David Wade," Riley said.

"We're both students here. Asshole." I held out my ID.

"Wade's not here and I'm not going looking for him. Twenty dollars or leave."

I handed the guy two tens, then he stamped both our wrists. The entry doors opened with David Wade on the other side, hair styled like a teen magazine cover. Typical.

"Hope you didn't pay," he laughed. "You're my guests."

"Wade." I had a feeling I'd be doing that a lot this year. We followed him back to a booth by the pool tables.

"I've set up two meetings," Wade explained. "For each of you, and they'll be conducted separately."

"Why? Divide and conquer?" Riley asked.

"I shouldn't even be here," I said eyeing the door. "Riley's way more desirable to a fraternity. He graduated third in our high school class." I was in the top thirty percent, if that.

"Dude, you are not leaving me here alone. This was your idea," Riley reminded me.

"Listen up. Sigma Chi's first, then Phi Gamma Delta." Wade with his frat salesman flair. Fine, I'd give them five minutes.

"What's your finder's fee?" Riley asked the most important question of the night.

A pitcher and three glasses appeared on the table. Funny how I never knew what I was drinking in this place. Just beer. Not IPA, Pilsner, Belgian. We were college students; we'd drink anything, right?

"You mean if you're selected? Less than forty-percent of frat recruits actually make it in." Wade lowered his head. "Even lower for enlistees."

I repeated Riley's valid question. "What do you get out of this? For some of these elitist Republican machines, the dues are like three hundred bucks a month."

"What?" Riley snapped his head toward me. "You're right. What are we doing here?"

"We're socializing, remember?" I said. "We just transferred two months ago. We hardly know anyone." I could barely remember NYU at this point. Chicago's a long way from home.

Wade smiled his smooth, snaky grin, enjoying the logic of my statement. He raised his glass. "Well, here's to new beginnings."

"Choke on it." Riley clocked Wade's glass. He glared at me while he guzzled the entire contents.

Wade refilled Riley's glass and disappeared with the empty pitcher. Now that the pool tables were filled, the noise had doubled, probably because we were getting drunker. Riley hated to drink. In fact, I was surprised he agreed to come in the first place. But it was on campus, just a short walk from Granville West, our home away from home.

"Hey." A new guy shoved into Wade's side of the empty booth. "Sigma Chi, how's it going? Which one of you is Zak?"

Riley and I pointed to each other. The guy had a peach fuzz crew cut. His face looked like it was scrubbed every thirty minutes.

"I can't imagine why you'd be even remotely interested in me," I admitted. "Riley's got a 4.0 GPA and a way better pedigree."

"Yeah, but you have lawyers in your family," Riley shouted in his bar voice. He leaned in and smiled in a way that revealed rising blood alcohol level. "More likely you'd be able to afford the fees."

The frat salesman shifted on the bench, sizing us up. He turned his head back toward the bar, probably looking for Wade, the eternal icebreaker.

"Fees are optional," he said in a bitchy tone.

I peeked one eye at the door, making sure we had a path of egress. Wade was naturally nowhere in sight.

How could Riley bring up my family like that? So crude and indifferent. He never could hold his liquor. I didn't mind paying to get in here, or even sitting through this ridiculous formality. It beat the monotony of hanging out in our dorm waiting for life to happen. But Wade had showed up at the door, vanished, and now I just felt played.

"Oh, I see," Riley broke in. "You only charge them to offset your legal fees resulting from discrimination, rape, and aggravated assault lawsuits? I get it. That must be really expensive. You know, hard to plan when all your Daddy's money's going to—"

"Riley," I clipped. "Shut it. Let's get out of here."

I scanned the interior. Pool tables, dart boards, wood paneled walls; I remembered reading that The Pub in the basement of University of Chicago's Ida Noyes' Hall had been run by descendants of the Medici's. The only thing missing in here was Sherlock Holmes. Raised voices caught my attention from the opposite corner, then the sound of a beer bottle breaking. Ah, the perfect diversion.

I yanked Riley's elbow and we headed for the entrance. Five seconds later, I looked back still plowing through the crowd.

"Where are they?" Riley asked.

I pulled open the door and we slipped out.

Two guys followed. One from Sigma Chi and another I didn't recognize. They were all the same to me.

"Walk faster," I said. "Follow the path, straight ahead." Sure, we needed to get away from these people, but the more important question nagging me was why we would be of interest in the first place. New to campus, barely social, not wealthy. What attributes would be of value to them?

"The Fountain of Time's up ahead," Riley said, speeding up. "Are they behind us?"

As I was about to answer him, two different guys cut

through the evergreens to our left and blocked us.

"Hey guys," one of them said, palms up, toothy grin. "Look, Damen got us off to a bad start. Let's start over. I'm from Sigma Chi."

"And I'm from Phi Gamma," the other said. "Please, come with us so we can talk. That's all we want."

"We're not interested in you frat clowns, the world's fucked up enough already."

Riley drunk always cracked me up.

"We're all here because you think we might have the money to pay your dues so you can maintain your alcohol supply," he added.

The thugs squared off in front of us. Riley stepped back. When he crossed his arms, he lost his balance and fell back on the grass. Nice.

Phi Gamma dragged him off with an arm around his shoulders. Sigma Chi stayed with me, waiting. Watching. He sat on the grass and pulled out a flask. I kept my eyes on Riley, now twenty feet away.

"Liquid courage?" I crouched on the ground across from him, knowing at this point we'd need to listen to the pitch before they let us go. If.

Riley and Phi Gamma were no longer visible. Fine. I'd give this freak five minutes of my life, then I'd go find him. I had no fear of him at this point, just irritation. I watched the guy pour something into two little silver cups—one the lid of the shiny flask, the other from his pocket. What else had been in that pocket?

"Absinthe," the guy said with conspiratorial pride.

I raised an eyebrow. More impressive than Budweiser.

"With or without *thujone*?" I asked of the historical wormwood hallucinogenic constituent.

"You know your poisons," he replied. "Without." He handed me a cup and tapped it, then swigged his down in one gulp.

Where was Riley? What the fuck were we doing out here? I came to this school for a fresh start, as my mother put it, and somehow I didn't think this was what she, or even I, had in mind. Sigma Chi, my salesman, held out the shiny silver cup with a wet smirk on his lips. Was I about to end up in Mexico or as somebody's bitch in Danville Prison?

"Riley, you alright?" I shouted behind me.

No answer. Sigma Chi stared, wiggling the cup. At this point I was more annoyed than afraid. I wasn't happy at this place yet, at this University. Riley wasn't either. But I wasn't ready to throw it all in either. Had anyone ever died from absinthe? I grabbed the cup, swiveled it around a bit, smelled it, then chucked it back in my throat. Like sophisticated licorice. God help me.

***

"A dazzling trip into a dystopian techno-nightmare" – *David Prestidge*

"A riveting thriller" – *San Francisco Book Review*

"Marked by its striking execution and razor-sharp dialogue, this places Towles among the best of the genre" – *Prairies Book Review*

Awards: Readers Favorite Award (Winner), Literary Titan Award (Silver), Clue Award (Finalist), Indies Today Award (Semi-Finalist)

www.ingramcontent.com/pod-product-compliance
Lightning Source LLC
Chambersburg PA
CBHW050136120726
47903CB00002B/383